Salt

AVA DUNN

Salt

AVA DUNN

Ava Dunn is an Australian author of novels *Salt* and *I Lied For You*. Her second novel *Salt* was shortlisted for Allen & Unwin's Faber Academy scholarship. She has a Diploma of Professional Writing and Editing and a Degree in Education. Ava credits driving her way to her favourite surf breaks on the coast of Phillip Island and Kilcunda, where this book is set, for inspiring the work of *Salt*, along with the copious amounts of country music she listens to. She lives on a farm in Victoria with her fiancé and menagerie of animals.

First published by Olive Reads, 2023

This paperback first published in 2023

Cover design © 2023 Elysia Clapin

ISBN: 978-0-6456393-3-9

This book is dedicated to all victims of sexual assault. May you find peace and recovery.

Sanna

January 2011

I huddled into my blankets, sweating in the heat but refusing to part with my cocoon. My first day of Year Nine. The thought of cramming my feet into hot school shoes and wearing a hot, sticky school dress made me yawn. The sunlight hit the surf posters on my wall and I thought of the days over summer I'd spent surfing with my best friend Tamara. My skin still tingled from all the sunburns and my bed rocked like a board on the water.

My phone rang. I answered in a huff, 'What?'

'Eddie said he can take us to school.' It was Tamara. Bright and bubbly, even at six in the morning. She never said hello, never said goodbye – always launched into things, even conversations.

'Tell me it's not true,' I whimpered. 'Tell me the school holidays aren't over today. I don't want to go to school today.'

'Did you even hear me?'

'Um,' I sat up and the blanket fell from my body. 'What?'

'Eddie said…he can…take us…to *school*,' she repeated slowly. 'Eddie. Can take us. In his car.'

'I heard you.'

She snapped, 'Sanna! Eddie, from Boardriders Club!'

'I know who Eddie is.'

'Oh my God; you are so thick sometimes, it hurts. Hang on a second.' There was thumping and a slamming door before she whispered into the phone, 'Eddie's gonna pick us up and we're gonna go surfing instead of going to school, you moron.'

'Not school?'

'Not school.'

My heart lifted with the corners of my mouth.

I clattered across the floorboards of my parents' single-story house, throwing my wetsuit into my school bag with my school lunch, and ran out of the door. The screen door slapped at the doorframe and Mum called out to me, 'Have a go*o*d day!' She was a Swedish export so always exaggerated the oo.

'Thanks Mamma!' I glanced over my shoulder to make sure she couldn't see me grab my 6'8 surfboard from the deck, then I sprinted down the driveway with the gravel crunching under my stiff school shoes and the board thunking at my hip with each stride.

Down at the end of the driveway, Tamara was sitting in the front seat of Eddie Adams's car. I wasn't sure if I liked him much at all. He took us surfing all the time, but never said much. He was a bit of a Neanderthal. Eddie had a shaved head with dark re-growth, and olive skin. Tribal tattoos snaked their way up his right arm. His eyes were a piercing blue that almost seemed silver against his complexion. He was about twenty, so about five years older than we were.

I said hi and he grunted at me, only moving his blue eyes in my direction, keeping a hand on the steering wheel. I hoped we were going to a break where the waves weren't huge, but if I knew Eddie, he was taking us somewhere suicidal.

'Can we go somewhere chill today?' My request was ignored, and we pulled in at Howlin' Powlies. Howlin' Powlies was a hazardous surf spot along a twelve-kilometre stretch of sand beach where the river joined the ocean. High sand dunes overlooked the beach and the water churned with strong currents, facing out into the wilds of the Bass Strait. It was a place only mad keen surfers paddled out, eager to ride the high-energy waves that surged from the ocean to the shore. Tamara had wanted to surf there all summer, but hadn't convinced anyone to take her out. There was a reason for that. Eddie was the only one apathetic enough to let her try it.

Eddie, Tamara and I carried our stuff through the shrubby track and stood on the beach before the water. It was like Bells Beach on steroids; a shore break surrounded with pimply volcanic rock and had thumping overheads that curtained like roller doors around your head.

Eddie looked at us. 'What do youse reckon?'

Tamara was not put-off by the poop-inducing swell. She was too gung-ho to mentally fathom how much skill she might need to surf those waves. My stomach churned at the thought of meeting those waves head-on. My toes twitched in the sand and I had to remind myself to breathe. Self-doubt or self-preservation, I wasn't sure I could do it, and I wasn't sure Tamara could do it, either. She was not as good a surfer as she dreamt of being but she seemed unaffected while I was filled with dread.

Tamara shook her head so her waist-length, wavy brown hair billowed behind her. 'It's the perfect overhead.'

'Yep, it is,' agreed Eddie, beginning to pull on his wetsuit.

'What do you think, Sanna?' Tamara turned to me.

I exhaled. Eddie was getting prepared to go in and Tamara bounced on her toes and wet her lips. If I said how I was really feeling, I'd be stuck here on the beach and miss out. I shrugged, trying to act casual and relaxed. 'Are you game?' I knew she was.

'Yeah.' She paused, then added, 'I am totally game.'

We pulled our wetsuits on as Eddie did shoulder-rolls and lunges along the damp, coarser sand at the water line. Tamara slapped her 5'7 board down and started to paddle out, taking her time in the rip.

Eddie and I stayed on the beach. He didn't answer when I asked, 'Where should we sit?' His eyes stayed on Tamara as she paddled out faster. He followed her, matching her strokes with his eyes fixed on the horizon, moving across the water like a crocodile.

Caution rattled through my nerves as I got to know the water and studied its patterns from the sandy beach – how it behaved with each set that crashed in with effervescent splash back. The rainbows danced like fairies off the spines of the cylinder tubes.

Tamara sat up on her board out the back, past the heaving mountains of water and waved at me. I waved my hand curtly in return; my hand trembled.

Once the lull arrived, I soared through the water and paddled as quickly as I could to avoid taking any of those monsters on the head. The rip moved me faster than I anticipated and I was beside Tamara and Eddie out the back in minutes.

I sat up, the tail of my board sinking in the water. 'What's going on?' I asked. 'Why haven't you guys gone for one yet?'

Tamara scrunched her nose back into her face like a pig. 'They're a lot bigger once you're out here.'

A wave rolled by beneath us and it was like seeing a building fall when you're standing on the balcony. The big swell made my head spin with vertigo as the water disappeared from below us. My hands and feet trembled and I even felt a little sick.

Tamara was right. The waves were heaps bigger than I thought. I couldn't even see the beach past the water as it rolled through beneath us before it fell away with a deafening crash. The mist was thick and sprayed us like rain. All I could see was water. Beyond that, the rolling green hills of the countryside were in the distance. I took a deep breath in and looked down at the stringer of my board. In that small glimpse down, I was surprised to feel all right. I had paddled out with a hammering heart and the feeling like I needed to poop in my wetsuit, but now that I was out there amongst giants, my toes itched and my heart raced, making me sweat and breathe harder. I wanted to give it a go.

I said, 'Well, we're out here now.'

Eddie shrugged. 'Only one way back in.'

A set rumbled in. Eddie paddled. Missed. Scowled. Lined himself up for the next raising wall but missed that one, too.

'Well, if Eddie's not getting any – we'll never get any!' Tamara whined.

'So?'

'He's a better surfer than we are.'

'Bull shit,' I spat even though it was true. Eddie had been surfing for at least twice as long as Tamara, so at least a lifetime longer than I had. He surfed at this break all the time and I reckoned it was a major reason Tamara wished she could surf there. She wanted to show him up or even get his respect by nailing one of those barrels. He was always trashing us girls; he dropped in on us "just coz". He was the classic dingus-head who we really should have hated, but Tamara followed him around like a groupie. She insisted he was the best surfer this side of the state. He was sponsored. He won competitions. He travelled to Indo and Hawaii. Everything Tamara wanted to do with a surfboard, Eddie had done. She didn't just want to be a surfer – she wanted to be *the* surfer. The next Steph Gilmore. She even reckoned she could be it…the surfer that breaks down the gender gap and got to surf (and win) in a unisex World Surfing League competition. She wouldn't be able to do any of that if she was unnerved by Howlin' Powlies though, so I set my teeth and readjusted myself on the board, ready to go.

'Hey – it's just the same as the waves we always surf. Let's show Eddie what we can do.' I swivelled my board and looked over my shoulder at the dark turquoise ramp raising behind me. I paddled. My board dropped from under me and I jumped to my feet. I couldn't suppress a girlish scream as I became airborne, soaring down the face of the wave. My heart in my throat was momentary – a wobble, and a quick readjustment and there I was: in the perfect position, dancing along the face of the wave like a pinball. It was amazing! I did a bottom turn and attempted a cutback, but I'd left it too late, enjoying the downhill ski too much. White water slammed the rail of my board and sent me flailing into the wash.

Underneath, it was both loud and muffled. The sand churned up from the bottom and the water rolled through its cycle, yanking me and pushing me in different directions. Once it was still, I surfaced with a laugh and flung myself back onto my board, paddling like crazy across to the rip to avoid being pummelled by the incoming waves. Eddie was on a wave, and sent me a shaka as I rose above on the shoulder. I couldn't wipe the huge smile off my face.

'Did you see that?' I exclaimed to Tamara. My heart pounded and the salt made me tear up, but I was frothing.

'Did you get hurt?' she asked.

'No! It was awesome!' I laughed, thinking of the speed alone.

'Good.' She chewed her lip and watched the waves rolling past us. Her shoulders slumped.

I rolled my eyes. 'Tee, you're being stupid. Just go for one!'

'Shut up.'

'No.'

'Shut up!'

'No! You're being a baby.'

'Ah, frigging hell, Sanna. Get off my back!'

'Fine. Then I'll catch this next one, shall I,' I retorted.

'Good then.'

'Fine.'

'Fine!'

I lined up for the wave, keeping her in the corner of my vision. I expected her to go, but she didn't. I didn't charge hard enough and hesitated on the take-off. I nosedived, and was held under. My lungs screamed. My brain panicked and I fought to stay relaxed. I let go and surfaced, gasping for air, a little rattled. I vowed to never hesitate again in fear of eating shit like that.

Despite my vow, I hesitated on the next wave and chickened out, turning off it. It was too big and steep. Tamara laughed at me.

'Now who needs to catch one?'

Eddie laughed, too. Tamara laughing at me was one thing – but Eddie laughing at me was high-pitched and it boomed across the surface of the water. The two of them laughing made me feel like a failure, an outsider and my mouth puckered as I glared behind me. 'Come on,' I muttered. The next one reared up and I dug in hard with my palms. Three deep paddles and I was being shunted off into space. I jumped up to my feet and nailed a cutback, the world almost upside down. The top of the wave reached above my head. I could get a barrel, I thought excitedly. I never thought I'd get one. I did what I saw all the surfing legends do and crouched. I skated through just as it closed into a tunnel. The wall flung me through the barrel of blue and I dived over the outside lip with both my middle fingers stuck up at Tamara. I'd done it. Suck on that, moll!

We weren't fighting. It was just how we surfed under pressure: like rabid dogs. Or so I thought. I didn't realise she was panicking and resenting the fact that I was riding the waves and she wasn't. I was not supposed to be braver or better than she was. I was not supposed to supersede her as the stellar surfer. I was not the surfer. She was the surfer.

She was frustrated so I left her alone. Eddie and I snaked waves from one another and Tamara let wave after wave go rolling by her, hissing spray back in her face but at least giving her a rainbow to gaze at in her moments of bitter hesitation. She eventually cracked it with herself and went for one. Too late. Too steep. Too much weight on her back foot. She was gone over the falls in less than two seconds.

Eddie shook his head at me and shouted, 'She's mentally unstable.'

I couldn't say anything. Sure, I agreed, but she was my best friend. She stormed out of the break and threw her board on the sand. I dutifully followed her in. Eddie kept surfing. Our morning of awesome surfing was over. Tamara's temper had ruined it.

Tears streamed down her puffy, freckled cheeks with no shame. 'I can't do it!'

I put my arm around her and tried to be supportive, but my eyes kept drifting to the peaks. I'd swallowed a lot of water – I could feel it burning in my chest, but those waves were it.

Tamara cried, 'Sorry, Sanna, for being a kook.'

I shook my head. 'Don't be sorry.'

'They're really big.'

Big, they were…and it. I could taste it. It trickled down the back of my neck and made me shiver.

I couldn't sleep that night. My bed rolled and lulled beneath my sore and stiff body. *Go to sleep,* I willed. *Go to sleep. You have school tomorrow.* I closed my eyes. Barrels and sea spray flashed on my eyelids. I opened my eyes again. Those waves. They were it. Everything. School? Screw school. I wanted to feel that speed again as soon as I could.

This time when my alarm went off at six, it was me who called Tamara, pleading her to come surfing with me.

'We don't have a ride,' she said.

'We'll hitchhike. I don't care if it takes us all day – we have to get back out there.' I almost added *you have to get out there* but bit my tongue. I waited for her to give in.

'Okay. Let's do it.'

Wobbling along the highway carrying our boards while we steered our bicycles, Tamara and I giggled at how silly we must have looked. Our bikes veered and then leaned as we struggled to pedal and steer with our cumbersome boards clunking into our knees. Cars honked at us and the school bus whizzed past, sending us into fits of anxious laughter at the thought of being caught wagging. Realising we were getting nowhere fast, we decided to walk instead, resting our boards between the handlebars of our bikes and on the seats.

Our thongs slapped along the bitumen in a chorus and the road seemed to sizzle. The road above us wavered in the heat. Sweat dripped down my back and gave me the uncomfortable sensation that I'd wet myself.

After a while, a white ute pulled up on the other side of the road. A guy, around Eddie's age, wound down his window and shouted across at us. 'Going to the beach?'

He had an American accent and Tamara and I glanced at each other, wowed by the twang in his voice.

'Yeah,' Tamara called back. 'Going surfing.'

He beckoned us over with a tanned, muscular arm. 'Come on. I'll give you a ride.'

We crossed the road as he got out of the car. The American tipped his hat at us and made us blush. He wore jeans despite the heat. He lifted our bikes like they were nothing and put them in the tray. Tamara and I carefully placed our surfboards on the back too. The guy reached a hand for me to shake. As I shook it, he smiled down at me with green eyes. 'I'm Jake Ryan.'

'Sanna Smith.'

'Tamara Jenkins.' Tamara swayed and flashed her braces up at him. 'Thanks for the ride.'

'Not a problem. It's too hot for you to walk all the way. Jump in.'

SALT

Tamara sat in the front next to him and I sat in the backseat, moving aside another hat and a pair of chaps. They were heavier than I expected and I hid my exertion with a measured breath out, keeping my hands in my lap.

'Which beach?' Jake asked.

Tamara told him where to go and gushed how nice he was for driving us there.

'No school today?' he grinned.

'Nah, we're wagging.' She giggled. 'We're waggers.'

'Yeah, me too,' he said.

I leant forward to the middle. 'Wait – you're in school?'

'Year Twelve.'

'You're a wagger, too,' Tamara grinned and winked at him. His Adam's apple bobbed as he looked away with a swallow. She pulled down the visor and caught a polaroid of a girl in her lap. 'Oops.' She pinched it between her fingernails, painted white, and flapped it gently. 'Who's this? Your sister?'

'My girlfriend. Her name's Tessa.'

Tamara looked out the window and murmured, 'She's pretty.'

She was boy crazy, so I ignored her disappointment and watched the paddocks whoosh by outside. Tamara and I had managed to walk from our homes to the main road on the island where we lived. The island was mostly undulating farmland, cows, sheep and horses freckled the landscape before it met the sea. It was a coastal community, as well as a farming one. There were plenty of towns, enough not to know everyone, but a centralised identity of being an islander ran through our blood. It took twenty minutes to drive from one end to the island to the other, dodging cyclists, kangaroos, wallabies, koalas and large grey Cape Baron geese who walked around like they owned the place. In a way, they definitely did.

Tourists came to our island to visit year-round. Tour buses were shuttled in on the daily. Our island's main attraction was a nightly parade of the Little Penguins, coming in from the ocean where they battled with seals, orcas and Great White

10

Sharks, to the beaches where they waddled for kilometres, often up sheer cliff faces to their nests. I loved living on our island.

Jake drove us to a beach off our island, close to Howlin' Powlies, but closer to the island. Tamara gave him the directions. I'd wanted to go back to Howlin' Powlies but Tamara had refused. Jake said this beach worked for him because he lived up the road on a dairy farm. He chatted good-naturedly about living on the farm with his parents and I assumed he would drop us off and leave.

When we arrived at the beach, Jake parked and got out. He handed us our surfboards and we thanked him, expecting him to leave but he followed us down the sandy track in his brown, leather boots.

'You're a bit out of place here, country boy,' Tamara teased. She pulled off her shirt and Jake looked away, up at the pinnacle in the distance where waves pounded and rebounded. Tamara and I got changed into our wetsuits as Jake went and sat up on the hill that was freckled with marram grass, pulling his hat down over his eyes as he reclined, crossing one ankle upon the other.

'Is he really going to just watch us?' I whispered to Tamara, glancing at him as we turned to walk down to the rip.

She shrugged. 'Who cares if he watches us? He's hot. Pity he has a girlfriend.'

'He's older.'

'Exactly,' she smirked then laughed.

I rolled my eyes and we paddled out side-by-side.

The waves that day weren't it. They were big enough to rocket along like I was shot from a cannon but the power wasn't as behemoth as Howlin Powlies. The waves shouted, more than roared. The wind was also coming in from the west a bit, so the tops of the waves were lumpy and pockets and divots formed on the faces as I steered around the scum of the whitewash. At least we had the beach to ourselves – well, except for Jake. My eyes went to him as a landmark to make sure I wasn't drifting too far left or right. He sat still on the beach, sometimes watching, sometimes looking down. I wondered while I tread water. What was he thinking about? What made him stop to pick us up and then waste his day while we partied out there with the marine life?

'Will you stop watching him and watch what you're doing?' Tamara jerked me back to the line-up. She moved her board closer to mine. 'He's allowed to watch.'

'I know that,' I scoffed. I looked past her at the horizon and called the next one. It was a bit weak and I had to pump my board with my driving foot as if it was running out of gas. My tail sank and so did my heart. These waves were not it. I growled as I paddled back out. 'I just want a good one!'

'These are fun; they're fine.'

'That's because you didn't catch any of those big ones yesterday.'

She clucked her tongue and lay on her board, ready to catch the next wave. It was a steep one. It flew up like a startled pigeon and scooped Tamara up, throwing her down its face where she stood and hollered in exhilaration. I raised my hands and cheered for her, but my board rolled under me and I was pitched into the green water. I clambered back on top just as the second one in the set walled up. I held my breath and paddled as hard as I could, thinking *don't get caught up on the lip, don't get caught*. It grabbed me and we danced in the rolling flow.

Once the ride was done, I glanced again to Jake, wondering if he saw me. He stared out at the water as if he couldn't see anything. I went to call out to him to get his attention but hesitated. He was a stranger. Why would he care if I caught a good one or not? I got back onto my board and paddled back out.

Tamara eyed me and went for one, but pulled back, scooping her hands up in the water. If I went for one, she barked at me to get off – it was her turn. I waited for the next few to pass her by, before I snapped, 'I'm going for this one! You're piking out all the time!'

'No, Sanna! I have priority! For God's sake! It's the rules.'

'THEN GO FOR ONE!'

Three more went past and I paddled sideways away from her and jumped in on the shoulder, but she followed me and took off on the peak, wiping out spectacularly. The waves were getting bigger and meaner closer to low-tide. They were spitting us off if we weren't in the perfect position.

'You dogged me!' I yelled.

'Get over it!'

To get her back, I dropped in on her on the next one. Misjudged the steepness. Fell backwards, my board careening upwards along the line. Tamara looked around at me as I fell, and the board went on, seeming to be in slow motion.

There was a thwack as the nose of my board collided with Tamara's forehead. The sickening crunch and thud went through my board, to my feet, up my legs to my heart.

We fell into the water that swirled red under the booming wave we'd crashed on. I surfaced and grabbed for her, screaming her name and saying sorry over and over. I grabbed at her board but she was gone. The foaming water surged around me and I ceased thinking. I yanked off my leg rope and threw my board aside, running for Jake, yelling. He jumped up and met me at the water's edge where he grabbed my board as it floated towards us in the knee-deep water. I glanced at the nose of the board and saw the ding and a red smear. I gasped for air and pointed at the water.

'I dropped in on her! I-I-I hit her! I can't find her. She's just gone! She hasn't come up yet!'

Jake's eyes went out to the water where Tamara's board was being washed around in the breakers. He pointed and said, 'There!' He splashed into the waist-deep water and grabbed her board. A wave hit him in the face, tilting the board in his direction. He looked down in surprise to see Tamara wasn't attached. The leg rope dangled, unattached to an ankle.

I scanned the water for any sign of Tamara and began to pant. I couldn't turn away. She was there in the water.

Somewhere. Jake's knuckles were bright white from his grip on Tamara's surfboard. My blood went icy and I couldn't tell if I was breathing or not anymore. My eyes swept over the water again and again until I saw her floating face down, being turned over and over by the incoming white walls of surging water. I leapt for her. She was cold.

'Tamara!' I shouted in her face but there was no response. Her forehead was split open and was pulsating with blood. I dry-reached and grabbed her by the neck of her wetsuit and pulled her towards the shore. A wave hit me in the back and her body got away from me, rolling over a couple of times while I cried and grappled at her. Jake was beside me in a second, helping me pull her to the safety of the beach. Once we got her on the damp sand, we let her go. Jake sprinted to his car to get his mobile phone to call 000. I knelt by Tamara's side and choked myself on tears and gasps. I couldn't tell if she was breathing. Surely, she wasn't dead. The water lapped at her toes, in and out and I crumpled beside her, sobbing into her neck.

'Please be okay. Please, Tee, be okay.'

Jake returned, panting as he ran and shouted into the phone, 'I think she's alive! Is she breathing? Sanna, is she breathing? SANNA!'

I was crying too hard to answer or hear a breath.

Whomp whomp whomp whomp whomp. The air ambulance hovered before it soared off with a loud rush of engines and blades, taking Tamara to the hospital. I sat on the bitumen of the carpark, knees crushing my chest.

'Sanna.' An ambo tucked my hair behind my ear as she knelt beside me to get my attention. Everything was aching. There was blood on my legs and my cuticles were tinged with red. My arms threatened to pop out of place from dragging Tamara to the sand with Jake. I couldn't feel the tips of my fingers or my toes. I should have just gone to school like I was supposed to.

I replayed the phone call I'd made that morning and it made me want to slither out of my body and hide. The paramedic led me to the back of the ambulance and took my blood pressure, reporting that it was too low – as if I cared.

I studied my fingers. They were pale; my skin shrivelled. My fingers hadn't shriveled up like that in a long time, not since I had started surfing with Tamara. Surfing was my whole life. At least, I thought it was my whole life. Right then, sitting in the back of the ambulance, I wasn't so sure if surfing was all it was cracked up to be. I'd been addicted to it ever since Tamara took me out on her younger brother's "foamie", a long and wide red board made for beginners. I had stood up on my first attempt and Tamara had called me a natural. It's what we ended up doing most days. What a waste of time, I thought, looking back.

'We're going to take you to the hospital,' the paramedic said. She was a young woman, who honestly looked too young to be a qualified ambo. She had short blonde hair and dimples and her skin was littered with freckles.

'But I'm not hurt.' I wrapped my spongey fingers around my Puka shell bracelet and looked over at Jake. He'd tried saving Tamara's life, and she was alive, thank heavens. Yet I still felt as though I'd killed her. Her body had been limp when the paramedics had loaded her into the helicopter in the carpark. They had shut her inside before I could say goodbye. What if she died on the way to the hospital? A crowd had gathered when the first ambulance had arrived. Locals gathering in the carpark near Jake's ute and were whispering about what had happened. When the paramedics stretchered Tamara up from the beach, Jake carrying her board, the word "shark" began to get louder amongst the whispers. Luckily the helicopter rotors roared and cut their voices off before I heard the words I dreaded hearing. The truth.

Jake leant now against his truck and spoke to a police officer. He gesticulated every now and again and I wondered what he was saying. The young ambo patted me on the shoulder and said, 'It's best to get checked out. I'll call your mum and dad on the way.'

I went to the hospital to be looked over. Mum ran in with her hair coming out of her bun and the strap on her shirt trailing down her arm. Her mouth was gaping and her eyeliner smudged. She saw me sitting there and breathed a sigh of relief before joining me and holding my hand. She didn't need to worry. I was fine. I had a grazed arm, grazed back and a little bit of water in my lungs. The doctors weren't too concerned but they peered at me and told me I may have PTSD. PTSD was an acronym for Post-Traumatic Stress Disorder. It might manifest itself in a variety of ways and I might not even feel it coming on. It might affect me, or it might not. It might affect me tomorrow, or five years later.

My forehead was tight and began to pound, and I rubbed at it with my fingers. The wound on Tamara's forehead from my surfboard, from *me*, flashed before my eyes and I dropped my hand and swallowed. Whatever pain I was feeling, I had no right to complain. I tried to listen to the doctor explain that I may not want to leave the house one morning, or I could do something reckless. I shook my head and told them I would be fine.

'You've been through quite a shock, Sanna,' the doctor told me. 'We'll get you a referral for some counselling.'

'Whatever. Can I have my shoes back now, please?' I swung my bare legs off the bed and the nurse handed me my thongs. I gathered up my shredded wetsuit that they'd cut off me in case I'd hurt my neck and hadn't known it. They had taken it off as soon as the X-ray came back clear.

I shoved my wetsuit into the paper bag the nurse gave me and headed for the exit. I had no idea why I was even taking the wetsuit since it was rubbish but I gripped the bag in my hand and refused to let go.

'Sanna, that was rude,' Mum scolded.

16

I stumbled on my thong and she caught me by the elbow, making me wince. We both gazed down at my thong – it had snapped. Mum told me she would bring the car around and told me to wait. She left me on a bench near the ambulance bay and jogged off.

I waited. A woman in a hospital gown hung around me, continuously looking at me. I tried not to stare at her straggly blonde hair and her missing teeth.

She leant closer to me. 'You got a smoke?' She had a slack lower jaw and she tilted her head at me.

I shook my head.

'Oh.' She looked around then sat next to me on the stiff bench. 'I don't suppose you got a couple of bucks I could borrow either.'

'No.'

'Oh.'

I looked down at my feet.

She pointed at my bracelet. 'I like that. That's real pretty. Where'd you get it?'

I chewed the inside of my lip and mumbled, 'I don't remember.' I did remember. Tamara and I had bought matching ones last Easter weekend on our trip to Bells Beach for the Rip Curl Pro. We'd sat on the beach for three days watching the world's best rip it up. We'd even got a glimpse at Taj Burrow in a café.

Tamara had poked me. 'Go say hi.'

'No way!'

'Go on. You'll regret if it you don't,' she had said.

I had sunk down further into my seat and squeaked, 'You go.' So, she had. She'd gone up to him and tapped him on the shoulder. I could see them talking but I couldn't hear what they were saying. He had eventually signed her tee-shirt and she had come trotting back over to me with flushed cheeks. 'I'm going to marry him some day!' We had celebrated by buying ourselves the bracelets.

The woman asked, 'What are you in for? Visiting?'

17

'No,' I replied, wishing my mum would hurry up. 'I was just getting checked out.' I wondered how Tamara was. She'd been taken to a different hospital.

'Oh.'

'Yeah. How about you?'

'I just had a baby.' She didn't smile. In fact, she glowered.

'That's good?'

'I don't want it,' she sighed.

'What are you going to do?' I asked. I couldn't imagine having a baby and then giving it away. But from the looks of that woman, I might have made an exception for the baby's sake. No baby deserved to be unwanted.

She shrugged. 'I'll move in with me parents and they'll probably look after it.' She held out her hand and I squirmed at the thought of taking it, but I did. She was nice, after all. She got up and left me sitting there alone. How was I going to get through school, not to mention life, without my best friend if she didn't survive?

'Sanna, I put your surfboard in the shed.' Dad came into my bedroom, wiping his hands on a tea towel. I didn't lift my head from my pillow. 'Sanna?'

I muttered, 'Okay, Dad.'

'I didn't want to throw it away…I thought you might like to keep it, despite the, um…' The ding and the blood stains? It made more sense to throw it away than to keep it, but I couldn't. Tamara had helped me pick out that $800 board. Looking back, I was surprised Dad had spent that much money on it. He was a stickler for a budget.

He took a deep breath. 'Well, it's in the shed if you're looking for it.'

'Thanks.' I waited until he left before I sat up and contemplated going out into the shed. I never meant to hurt Tamara. We were just mucking around. I'd called her a bitch for snaking me on the wave before and we'd joked about it.

18

Then I'd dropped in – not expecting her to be so close to the lip that I'd collide with her. God, what had I done?

Later in the day, I stood at the door of the shed and decided against going in. I'd always been afraid of the shed with its dark corners and spider webs. I really should have gone to the beach where a vigil for Tamara was underway. Girls she hated were probably standing on the beach, throwing flowers into the water, crying and hugging, praying for the girl they liked to call freckle-face, surfers'-slut and wharf-rat.

When I walked back inside and sat at the kitchen bench to watch my mother cook dinner, she asked in her Swedish accent, 'Would you like to go to the beach, Sanna?'

I hesitated before I nodded. I would probably regret it if I didn't go.

Mum pulled up alongside the carpark and I got out with trembling legs. She told me she would come back in an hour because had to go to the shops to buy almonds for the dessert she was making just for me. Mum drove off with a puff of black smoke spewing from the dilapidated Nissan Patrol. I considered sitting by the road and waiting for her to come back. The carpark was full and I dreaded walking down the steps and having so many people stare at me and whisper, 'That's her best friend. She was the one who did it.'

I made my way down the steps to the beach and a few people did stop and stare at me. I stood apart from the mass of my peers. I scanned the crowd for a familiar face. I wondered if he'd be there. The American. Jake. But he was nowhere to be seen.

There were some surfers out on the flat water, past the rocks, sitting on their boards as though in shock.

I kicked at the sand for a few minutes, listening to girls nearby, sobbing, and a boy I knew from school named Michael playing an acoustic guitar. I sat on the sand and watched a sea

19

bird circle ahead, its eyes checking on us. I heard someone say, 'She doesn't even care that her best friend is hurt.'

I sat, staring at the waves with contemplation. I could just paddle out like I always did, but the thought of getting back into the water made me nauseous.

As the crowd began to clear, the waves picked up and the surfers began to play. Michael strode over to me, holding his guitar by its neck. He also carried a boogie board under his arm.

'Hi, Michael,' I said, shielding my eyes from the late afternoon sun with my hand.

He sat next to me and glanced out at the water as he said, 'It looks like it's getting pretty neat out there.'

I nodded. 'Yeah.'

'I get it, you know,' he said.

'Get what?'

'Why you're sitting here on the beach instead of going out in the water.' He gave me a big, goofy smile and revealed the braces on his teeth. 'I hit a rock one time. Almost drowned. Scared the absolute shit out of me.'

'Where did that happen?'

'Bali.'

I scratched my nose and gazed at his almond-coloured eyes that looked off into the distance as though he was remembering the day.

'It was tough getting back in the water, man,' he glanced at me and corrected himself, 'man*ette*.'

I snorted and scratched at my bare arms. The sun was beginning to lower over the water, and the midgies and mosquitos were coming out to bite. Excluded from the crowd that had gathered to hope and wish well my best friend, my eyes were watered and my skin itched.

'Why are you talking to me, Michael? Nobody else is.'

He replied, 'I know how you're feeling.'

'You ever hurt somebody, Michael?'

He shook his head no, making his brown dreadlocks rattle against his head.

'I made a stupid call to go when I shouldn't have.'

He squinted at me.

'So, you don't know how I'm feeling, Michael.'

'Ever hit a rock at thirty kays an hour, been held under by a squally set, lost consciousness and woken up two months later in the hospital from a coma and been told that you might not walk again?' he asked in a level voice.

I stared at him and he stared back.

'...no...'

He twisted around, lifting his shirt to reveal a lumpy, pink patch of skin on his back that extended across and then up to his neck. It stood out on his even dark complexion. He pulled his shirt down again and explained, 'I had coral imbedded in my skin and I needed a skin graft.'

Wow. I swallowed hard and imagined Tamara in the hospital with a bandage on her head. Maybe she would need a skin graft too. Michael stood up, casting a shadow over me but he lightened my mood. If he was talking to me and saying he understood, then maybe Tamara would understand too. It was an accident, after all.

He sat back down and the scent of woodchips and deodorant, neoprene and vanilla hit me. I slowly leant into him and whispered, 'Sorry that happened to you.'

He put his arm around my shoulders and said, 'She won't blame you, you know. It was an accident.'

The watering in my eyes splashed out and coursed down my face. He smiled and brushed the tears off my chin. 'Don't think that you're the only one that has ever been afraid of the water. Afraid of yourself.'

'Sorry,' I said.

We looked out at the water for a while before we looked at each other and laughed. I wiped my tears away and said again, 'Sorry,' while biting my lip. He smiled and squeezed me tightly.

21

That night, the news reported that a teenage girl had been air lifted to the Alfred Hospital with head injuries after a surfing accident. A picture of Tamara was shown. A photo of her on the beach in a peach-coloured singlet, looking sideways at the camera, mouth open in an about-to-burst-out laughing expression, with wide blue eyes and messy brown hair. Her body was constantly in motion, and the photo showed that perfectly – the outlines were blurred and she was about to run towards the camera. Her body in the water came to my mind. Her eyes rolling back into her skull, her breath gone and her lips blue. I shuddered and fought the urge to vomit.

Mum turned the TV off as she caught my expression and the way I was clawing at the sofa. Dad teared up and coughed to hide it, praying to Jesus.

I snapped, 'She's not dead, Dad.' Prayer wasn't going help.

He sipped at his beer and I got up and went to my room.

On Sunday morning, we went to a church service to pray for Tamara. They'd advertised it on the television and everything. Halfway through, I walked out, feeling people's eyes on my back as I pushed the door open. I couldn't sit there and pray for her when my mind was racing and my gut was so heavy I felt sick. I stepped into the bright sunlight and squinted, waiting for my eyes to adjust.

Outside the church, there was a ute parked, and a guy leant against its side. Him. The guy who had saved Tamara. Jake Ryan. He was holding a freesia flower. He spotted me and gave me an unsure little smile.

I walked up to him and stopped inches from his dirty boots. I said, 'You came.'

He nodded.

'Why didn't you come in?'

He scuffed his boots on the ground and looked up at the church behind me. 'I don't do churches.'

'Oh.'

He scratched at his chin. 'I wanted to come meet Tamara's parents and show my support.'

I was glad he said her name. He wasn't such a stranger if he said her name like a friend. I breathed in and told him, 'They'll be a while. It's not over.'

'But you're out here.'

I frowned. 'I couldn't hack it.'

He asked, 'Do you want to get out of here for a while?' Before I could even answer, he handed me the flower. 'Let's go.'

Jake and I went to the nearest beach and sat down together in the deep sand. I tucked my skirt around myself, brushing sand away from my legs.

'I dreamt I saved her the other night...' he told me. 'You were there.'

'You did save her.'

'No, I mean, like...She was awake and okay.'

I chewed on my bottom lip until the skin peeled back and made me wince. A wave barrelled in on the sandbar. The sound made my heart beat quicken, and not in the good, fun, exhilarating way that it used to when I paddled hard and rode one. I watched every bit of kelp, every rock that seemed to move with the tide and put myself on edge. The water drawing out and rushing in pressed my nerves and made me want to flap my hands and run away.

Jake cleared his throat and seemed to study the water with the same tentativeness.

'You sat there and watched us surf.'

He looked at me with wide eyes as though I was accusing him.

'Why weren't you going to school?'

'Why weren't you?' he asked.

'Surfing was more fun,' I replied with a shrug.

Jake gritted his teeth before replying, 'I don't go to school much.'

The beach pounded along and we stayed quiet, although my mind was abuzz with questions I wanted to ask him. Where did he come from? How long had he been in Australia? Why didn't he go to school much? Why didn't he "do" churches? Why did he pick us up that day? Why did he stay at the beach watching us?

I blurted out, 'I think you're a little strange.'

He grinned at me but still managed to wear a sombre expression. '*I'm* strange?'

I snapped, 'Shut up. You don't know me.'

He scoffed, 'Well, you don't know me, either.'

'We're complete strangers!' I threw my hands up in the air and then crossed them with a pout.

'We would be strangers if we lived in a perfect world. But we don't,' he said. 'I know you better than you think, and better than your friends do.'

I rolled my eyes. 'How could you possibly know me better than my friends do?'

He leant in towards me and said, 'Because I was there.'

I gaped at him. I wish I could read him the way he could read me.

He said, 'Did you hope I'd come today?' He took the flower from my hand and twirled it around.

I admitted, 'I did.'

We sat in silence for a moment, a seagull squawked overhead. I said, 'I couldn't stay, though. She's my best friend and I couldn't even stay to pray for her. I don't deserve to be there.'

'You are her friend; of course you have a place there.'

'They keep expecting me to cry,' I mumbled and studied my fingernails. 'I don't want to.'

He shrugged. 'You're in shock.'

'What?' I croaked.

'Oh, come on!' he cried. 'You were there when your best friend nearly died. Do you think they expect you to cry and everything will be fine?'

'No,' I said.

'Well, good, because it doesn't work that way.' He picked unceremoniously at his teeth and I watched every wiggle of his finger.

'Are you this nice to your girlfriend?' I asked.

Jake looked thoughtful and a little sad as he answered, 'I treat her so good it hurts her.'

I stared into his green eyes. They were always moving from item to item, so it took a while to really notice the colour. He had an oval-shaped face and thick brown hair that was laced with sweat under his hat. The collar on his flannel shirt was high, primp. His fingers were stained from the dirt. He was only in Year Twelve, yet he looked like he was in his twenties. Sun-tanned and mature.

He added, 'She's the most gorgeous girl on this planet. She just doesn't know it. I tell her all the time but she calls me a liar.' He laughed, amused with his adorable girlfriend.

I asked, 'Does she know what happened to Tamara? Does she know about me?'

He bit his lip and shook his head. 'No. No, she doesn't.'

'Why not?'

His Adam's apple bobbed in his throat. 'Because I don't want her to worry about me.'

He stood up and dusted off his jeans. I stayed on the sand. He held out his hand and I hesitated before I took it, allowing him to help me up. The day was warming up but the sand remained cool.

'Are you going to go see her in hospital?' Jake asked as we walked to the car.

I would have to go. She was there because of me. I would have to go see her and face what I'd done to her. As if Jake could read my thoughts, he gave me the flower back and said, 'Don't worry about it, Sanna; it wasn't your fault.'

Everyone kept telling me it wasn't my fault but it was. 'How much longer will it hurt like this, Jake?' I didn't mean to ask him that. It slipped out.

He forced a smile. 'One day.' He placed a hand on my shoulder; his facial expression was soft and kind, his eyes mirrored my own sadness. 'I know what it's like to lose your best friend and be completely lost.'

I gaped at him in wonder. I had even more questions about him now that I wanted him to answer. Who had he lost? How? He didn't elaborate. He only opened the door to his ute and said, 'I'll take you home; just tell me where to go.'

The town where I lived was one of the smaller ones on the island. It was a charming village, surrounded by the landscape of inlets and estuaries leading into a muddy bay. It was on the northern edge of the island, sheltered from the wind of the oceanic southern side. Wetlands and farmland, Rhyll was a peaceful place to live. I shared the house on fifteen acres with my parents, sheep, gum trees, dams and cockatoos that shredded things apart.

After we arrived at the entrance to my driveway, his eyes remained on mine as he nodded at me. 'You're going to be fine, Sanna.'

'You're not a good example,' I said. 'You're not fine.'

'I will be...one day.'

I said quietly, 'Thanks for coming today. It means a lot.'

He smiled.

'Keep in touch, Jake.'

'Absolutely.'

I got out of the ute but leant against the open window, longing to ask him all those questions just so I could know the kind of person he was. I got the sense he was good and I wanted to get to know him better, but didn't know how to. He filled my silence with, 'Have a nice life, Sanna.'

He drove off and left me standing at the gate. I lugged my beaten soul and body down the long, dusty driveway, kicking at the little stones in the dirt. The few sheep we kept looked up at me and glared from behind their pig mesh fences, their small mouths working hard on the grass. Ingrid, Elin and Astrid all stared at me as though I was a common enemy and maybe I was. I did eat lamb, after all. We kept the sheep for their wool rather than their meat but I believed they weren't as stupid as people said.

As I neared the house, the front door flew open and I was met by my hysterical mother. She cursed and cried in Swedish at me until she was not only blue, but a slight shade of purple in the face. She huffed at me and waited for an answer. As if I could understand her in the first place. Dad came out from behind her and ushered her inside. He stood on the porch and crossed his arms over his chest.

'Are you all right, Sanna?' He made sure to get his priorities in order before punishing me. 'We thought you'd just left for some air, but couldn't find you. We were about to call the police.'

I didn't answer. I trudged up the wobbly, wooden steps and collapsed into his arms. He was the world's best hugger. His hugs were neither too loose nor too tight. While I buried my head into his chest, he asked, 'Where did you go?'

'I went to the beach with a friend.' I always told my dad everything.

'We were so worried about you,' he said, taking a deep breath, his chest rising against my cheek. 'Are you sure you're okay?'

I smiled and recited what Jake had said, 'I will be…one day.'

Jake

I sped down the dirt road towards home. Home. If that's what it was. It was a house on 278 acres of green hills and dairy cows. The town I lived was smaller than where I'd lived in Texas. My new town bordered a bustling old mining town, but only had a post office, a pub, and a church. There were more cows than people.

The road was dusty and I accelerated more, creating a dust cloud so thick I couldn't see what was being laid to rest behind me in the rearview mirror. I imagined the truck hitting a tree, mangling the metal into shredded ribbons of steel flesh, just as like my brother's car. The day the wreck came home, my dad had sent dust plumes into the air around him as he threw his hat down, stomping on it, jumping on it, kicking the dirt as he pounded his fists on the crushed car before he eventually fell to his knees and wept.

Now, tears poured down my cheeks from some bottomless pit inside me, willing my dad to please, please, please forgive him. Forgive my twin brother Alex for driving into a tree. Forgive me for not fixing the seatbelt that could have saved his life.

I pulled the truck over at the side of the road and panted as though I had run all the way from Texas, where my brother had died. I watched the dust settle behind me, and once it had, I wiped my eyes and got back on the road. I was full of it when I had told Sanna she would be okay one day. It had been two years since Alex had died and here I was, willing to go the way he was – by slamming the car into a tree.

We'd moved to Australia the year he died. We left him on the golden plains of the Texas Panhandle, swapping beef cattle for dairy cows and the rolling hills of Gippsland. I had looked over the rounded hills, round as mushroom caps, speckled with green trees that swayed gently in the afternoon breeze. The grass had been yellowing that mid-summer and the bitumen was sticky. My voice had caught in my throat having to start at a new school without my twin. Bloody rough, as the Australians would say. Alone in the southern wilds, adrift on land that was not mine.

I had started speaking to myself in the mirror. Quietly, as though I was praying to God. Quietly, as though I was shattered inside, but being the tough guy I was, I'd never admit it to anyone, but it was never me I was speaking to. My family left my brother's body in Texas, but there he was in the mirror staring back at me in my face.

I'd completed Year Eleven at my new school, a Christian co-ed school in that old mining town, but I was struggling to go back again after having six weeks off for the summer break. I was now in my final year of school, already eighteen and older than my classmates. I was already isolated from them. I was the weird, smart American kid. A Bible basher. Oh, the Australian humor. Lately, not even Tess's quirky personality could tempt me to go to school. God, she was beautiful. Her shoulder-length curly blonde hair bounced around her ears, and her jade eyes sparkled as she smiled at me with her straight, white teeth. Her skin was tanned and her arms had white hairs that shimmered as she brushed her hair behind her ears.

'Hey, Cowboy,' she'd tease. It wasn't long before my name at school evolved from New Kid, to Americano, to Bible Basher then to Cowboy – as if those kids weren't from farming families too – like they weren't running out into herds, jumping on cows and being flung into dung when the cows all bucked them off with startled calls. Joke was on them, really, calling me Bible Basher and Cowboy. I was neither. Not anymore.

I got home and turned off the truck with a sigh. I stared at the white weatherboard home with its collapsing porch that made you feel like you were walking on water. My mom sat on the step with her Bible and raised a hand to shield her eyes from the sun as she looked up at me. I trudged up to the house and her eyes returned to the book and she didn't say anything as I passed her. I kicked off my boots and went inside, found my dad lying on the couch, snoring. Rolled my eyes, walked back out past my mother and out to the machinery shed.

I started the four-wheeler and it burbled to life inside the shed, echoing off the steel rafters. I drove it to the pasture, shaking my head and muttering under my breath. I'd have to milk the girls again because Dad was passed out drunk. As usual. The farm would fall apart if I didn't carry it.

All the girls were crowding at the gate of their field, bellowing at me.

'I know, I know. I'm late.'

I heaved open the rusted, rickety gate and got out of the cows' way to the milking shed. I puttered along on the four-wheeler and made my way past them before parking it and getting everything set up. On my own.

I stayed there until the sun went down and the last cow was done. The girls all walked out to their field and I shut the gate behind them, dodging all the cowpats as I walked back. I sat out in the yard of the farm and pulled off my hat to scratch my sweaty head. A glance up at the house revealed my mother had gone in and my father was still inside. My stomach rumbled, but instead of going in to get something to eat, I walked over to the old barn and reclined on a pile of dirty old horse blankets. The musky dust billowed around me like a curtain. I messaged Tessa. *Come over. Bring food.*

The chirping of birds and the warbling of magpies at dawn the next morning woke me. I stole a glance at Tessa's breasts beside me before she sat up and pulled on a shirt, covering herself.

'That was a lot of fun,' I said.

She smiled as she climbed unsteadily to her feet. She looked at her watch and groaned, 'We slept too long. My dad is going to notice I'm gone if I don't hurry up and get home.'

'Do you want me to drive you?'

She shook her head and started getting dressed. I sat up. As Tessa grabbed her boots, she flashed her eyes at me and batted her eyelashes. 'I think I love you.'

My mouth opened but I couldn't say the words so my mouth merely gobbed uselessly. My cheeks burned and I looked at her, helpless. She bent down and pulled on her boots, not even noticing me squirm.

Tessa turned to me and grinned, 'I'll see you when I see you.' She jogged out of the barn, departing into the bright morning sun. Tessa knew I probably wouldn't make it to school again. I'd have to do the cows first. God knew my dad wouldn't.

I lay back on the dirty blankets with a grunt. It was going to be a good day. If there were no issues with the cows, I'd be able to slip to the beach. But my dad shuffled into the barn and stared down at me in amusement. I stared back, refusing to move.

His skin was dusted with dirt, because he rarely made it into the shower these days. He wore his stained, worn-out Wrangler blue jeans. His plain blue shirt was comfortably wrinkled, his boots scuffed and his Seratelli beaver-felt hat was dented from too many tramplings. His dark eyes narrowed at me.

I flinched under his glare and put my shirt back on, putting my back to him to slide my jeans on.

He asked, 'Yer got a girl in here?'

I didn't reply, just held my breath.

'Well, do yer?'

I breathed. 'No, Dad.'

'Why yer sleeping out here?'

'It's cooler than the house.' I wasn't lying. I took another I-don't-give-a-damn breath and added, 'I've got to get going. I slept too long. Cows have got to be milked.'

My dad picked up a horse headcollar and said, 'I want yer to go to school today. I'll do 'em.' I lingered in the aisle of the barn and he blinked a couple of times as if confused why I wasn't moving. He added, 'Yer need to go to school and make somethin' of yerself, son. Stop lyin' and screwin' 'round and get yer butt to school.'

Dumbfounded that my dad had even noticed I hadn't been to school yet for the new year, I walked out of the barn and squinted at the searing circle of light in the blue sky. Making something of yourself was a lot easier when you didn't feel like you killed your brother, and you were disappointed in your parents.

The heat was already in the air with a purple haze over the fields. Dad got onto the four-wheeler and made his way to the cows to bring them in. I stood by my horse Rio's yard and he snorted over my hands. Dad had saved him from the meat market when we'd moved to Australia. Rio was the oldest horse I'd ever known. He was around thirty years old according to his teeth, but was as lively and bright-eyed as any young horse could be.

I often hung my arms around his neck and breathed in his scent to self-medicate. My dad self-medicated with booze to the point of stupor, but I loved the smell of horses. Their sweet smell reminded me of home. My real home. The home before everything went to crap. The way they chewed on their hay calmed my nerves. Rio couldn't chew hay. His food was a sloppy soup of beet pulp and coagulated pellets that he slurped and lapped, spilling and staining everywhere. There was not much comfort that came from being covered in wet horse slobber. Yet, I stood there anyway, watching his food being flung in a small pile. The liquid food covered his red nose. He was still saving me from tripping into a dark place, the same dark place my parents had stumbled into. Moving to Australia was meant to help things, but it hadn't.

After saying goodbye to Rio, I climbed into my truck and drove to the beach. I bumped over a fallen ti-tree branch and I almost lost the back end of the truck. I righted her and breathed a large sigh of relief. The adrenaline was, however, satisfying.

I came out onto the highway and admired the greenery of the countryside's rolling hills. I could see the deep blue of the ocean on my left and I couldn't wait to get to it. I'd been obsessed with the ocean since I was a little kid, when I had seen the Gulf of Mexico for the first time. Alex and I had gone to stay with my uncle Jimmy in Houston one summer break. He took us to Galveston Beach to see the sea. It was incredible. The scent of seaweed clogged our nostrils and the salt lined our lips, making our faces pucker whenever we licked at them. There were sea birds flying everywhere, squawking. Choppy little waves pounded the yellow sand and I stared at them, both transfixed and terrified. Alex had run straight into the water without hesitation and ended up catching a bad chill from sitting in his cold wet clothes for the rest of the day. I had just stood back and observed it, admired, and adored its beauty. It was Heaven to my eyes. Maybe it was. Maybe that's why Alex had run in. Maybe it had been a sign that he would go too soon.

When my parents and I arrived in Australia and I first saw the ocean that we were now living so close to, the hairs on my body tingled with excitement. The ocean had been almost a twelve-hour drive away from home in Hartley. Getting to the beach within five minutes was too good to resist. When I first went to that nearby beach, I had stood there, staring at the beautiful Bass Strait. I loved it at first sight. The sand was clean, soft and deep, and the water was blue and bright. The waves astounded me. Maybe I had the soul of a surfer in me because I stared at the barreling waves as if they were beautiful women. The water both terrified and captivated me.

Going to the beach had been an almost daily sojourn. Seeing the girls walking that day with their cumbersome surfboards, I'd stopped and taken them along with me. Sitting on the beach, watching the way the surfers moved their athletic bodies like dolphins, with intrigue.

The day the accident happened, the two girls had cut across the waves. I had laid back on the sand and closed my eyes, and was just dozing off when I heard her screaming. Sanna. Pulling her friend Tamara to the beach haunted me. As I sat down now, the waves barrelled into the shore and I stared at the place where Sanna and I had pulled Tamara in.

Sanna had been panicking and I couldn't think of a single word to say to console her. In moments like that, words didn't matter anyway. Sitting there now, a tear fell down my cheek and I wiped it away, smearing sand over my face and getting it into my eye so it watered even more.

In the afternoon, my parents went to church and I went to Tessa's. She lived on her grandfather's farm, in a house that sat at the top of the steepest hill I'd seen in my life.

I sat glumly on her porch swing, beheading buttercups that littered the fields with yellow.

Tessa asked, 'Did you hear the news – about the girl who was attacked by a shark or something?'

I glanced at her before I admitted, not bothering to correct her, 'Yeah. I did.'

'She used to be in my dance class.' She shook her head. 'It's really sad.'

I threw the stems of the buttercups away and sighed.

Tessa tilted her head and said, 'It's getting to you, isn't it?'

'I have a lot on my mind right now.'

'Such as...'

'Tamara Jenkins nearly died. I lost my brother. It's thrown me a bit, okay?'

She crooned, 'Oh, baby – I didn't realize – I should have. I'm so sorry...' She stood up and hugged me tightly while I kind of hung in there like a limp fish. I peeled myself out of her embrace, stood up and fidgeted.

'I don't want sympathy, Tessa. After all, I didn't even know that girl,' I lied. I didn't understand why I didn't want to admit that I knew Tamara Jenkins. Or that I'd met her. I didn't know her, much. But I'd saved her. Kind of. She was the kind of girl who made you feel like you knew her even if you didn't.

She nodded and said, 'That's okay, you know. Girls in my dance class who met her once are acting as if they just lost their best friend. As if she's already dead or something.' She waited for me to laugh, or even smile, but I didn't. I thought about Tamara's best friend Sanna instead.

Tessa patted me gently on the back and said, 'Don't worry about it, Jake. This time tomorrow, you'll have forgotten all about it. I'll see you later, okay.'

She turned around and walked into the house. I couldn't believe a girl could so kindly kick me out. I grumbled, 'Yeah, see ya then.'

I pulled the keys for my truck out of my pocket and strode to where I had parked it crookedly, across the driveway instead of driving up the steep hill. The door hinge creaked as I pulled open the door. I stared out of the windscreen for what felt like hours, thinking about Tamara, the girl I didn't know yet was so invested in.

I was startled when somebody walked up to my drivers' side window and asked, 'You got a problem with your wheels, mate?'

I looked into the crisp blue eyes of a man in his 60s. He was very red in the face, presumably hot in his jacket. He was wearing a beige R.M Williams stockman's hat, shading his leathery face from the sun.

I replied, 'No, I just stopped here to answer a phone call.'

He smiled and said, 'You're parked over my driveway, is all.'

'Oh!' I said, twisting in my seat to see that I was indeed stopped over his driveway. I realized this was Tessa's grandfather. I'd never met anyone from her family before. I gave him an awkward smile and said, 'No problem; I'll just move.' I started the truck and tried to move it forwards. The wheels spun and the engine squealed as I tried to drive out of the ditch. Why on earth had I parked it so badly? My face burned as I looked him in the eye and admitted, 'I seem to be stuck in a rut.'

He shrugged and said, 'No worries. Put it in neutral and I'll pull you out, eh.' This was the mannerism that I loved most about Australians. Most of the time, they took everything in their stride and never hesitated to call you a "mate" and treat you like one too.

He extended his hand for me to shake, which I did. He introduced himself as Coop. I introduced myself too. He nodded with recognition of my surname, and probably my accent too. 'I talk to your dad down at the feed store sometimes. Nice enough fella.' He didn't mention anything about my dad always being at least a little bit drunk, but a look passed between us that reminded me nobody ever had to bring it up. He waited for me to reply, but I said nothing. He got to business then, 'Okay then.'

Coop attached the pull rope to our cars, got back into his old ute and pulled the truck until it bounced and detangled from the grassy ditch.

We got out of our cars and I leaned against the side of the truck and rubbed at my face. 'Thanks for that,' I said.

Coop looped up his pull rope and hung it over his shoulder before leaning against the car beside me. 'No worries, mate. I'm glad I met you. Your old man has said a lot about you.'

People do this a lot: they mention that somebody has said a lot about you to break the ice, feeding you a compliment by telling you somebody thought you were decent enough to talk about. I doubted my dad had said anything about me to some random farmer. I doubted my dad told himself anything about me, let alone a stranger.

Before I could ask what my father had said about me, Coop continued with a sad sigh, 'Yeah, he told me about what happened to your brother – said it hit you really hard. He's worried about you.' Coop peered at me before adding, 'You're his pride and joy, Jake.'

There had once been a time when I was my dad's pride and joy. He'd take me fishing in the lake on our farm and we'd pull up bass, bluegill, and even some rainbow trout. Alex had been the football crazy kid and Mom's favorite. He'd never been into fishing. He'd made his own games by dangling thick twigs in the lake when he got bored and he'd dare to do some ridiculously dangerous things – like taunting the feral cat hidden up a tree.

Since Alex had died, I was nobody's pride and joy. I was just Jake. The left-over.

'Goin' fishin' with your old man next Saturday at Powlett River. You should come along with your old man. I reckon it'd be good for both of you, eh.'

'Sure. I will see you there.'

Later that night, I stood in front of my bedroom's dusty mirror. Alex and I had been identical our entire lives, until now. My features were changing. It was almost like letting him go completely and I wasn't ready to. Every day I changed a little, departing from my brother more and more.

I dreamed that night. The day Tamara had disappeared in the surf recurred in my mind, but the moment that I had grabbed her board, she was there, gasping for air and clinging to me for dear life. Carrying her onto the beach, I knew something was wrong. Sanna was gone. I called for her over and over again, but it was as though she didn't exist. There weren't even footprints in the sand.

The sound of a screeching corella outside my window woke me up at dawn. The dang bird screeched some more and then, satisfied it had woken me up, flew off to be with his buddies in the nearest gum tree.

I rubbed my eyes and yawned. I headed out of my room to milk the cows, but Dad stopped me at the door. 'I've got them, son. Go to school today.'

I nodded and swallowed. I supposed if he was finally pulling his weight on the farm, it was only fair that I did what he wanted me to. I went to school.

My first day of Year Twelve took place an entire week after it should have, but I made it. At the end of the day, I knocked on the office door of Ms. Hollinday. She was my teacher for most subjects. She looked up at me from her desk with her gentle brown eyes. She had smooth, creamy skin and mousy coloured hair that hung in waves around her face. She was skinny and walked awkwardly in the lowest of heels. Sometimes when she looked at me, one eye turned in a little. She was a soft-spoken woman and a great listener.

'You wanted to see me?' I readjusted the heavy backpack on my back. If I wasn't busting my hump on the farm, I was busting it carrying books.

'Yes, come in.' Ms. Hollinday put her pen down and pushed aside a pile of paper. I sat in the chair opposite her. 'Jake, I asked you to come see me because we have a problem.'

Uh-oh. 'We have a problem…or I have a problem?'

She smiled. 'I'd like to say we, Jake, because you've been absent all week. That's quite a reflection on me, too, you know.'

I balled my fists and stared at my feet.

'You're a bright, young man, Jake – one of the smartest in my classes, but I can't let you throw away your final year of school.' She gestured at the pile of work. 'You're already behind on your weekly homework because you missed every day last week and there is no reason supplied to me why you weren't here all week.'

My shoulders slumped and my jaw clenched. 'I get it. You're telling me to get my act together.'

She nodded and handed me a slip of paper. 'Your parents need to sign this so they can acknowledge that you've already failed to bring in your first week's homework.'

I rolled my eyes and took it from her but she held it so I could look her in the, albeit crooked, eyes. 'Don't miss any more classes, Jake. I mean it.'

I swallowed and nodded. I really would have to get my act together after all. Failure wasn't an option.

The Saturday morning fishing trip came up faster than I expected. I had been to school for four days that week and my mind and body were shattered, but I forced myself to get into the passenger seat beside my dad. He hadn't had a single sip of alcohol the night before so he could drive. He had dark circles under his eyes and he moved stiffly, exhausted. Ironic that if a sober person drank too much, they woke up with a hangover. If an alcoholic didn't drink enough, they had an even worse hangover. I couldn't remember the exact moment my father's addiction became a problem. He knew he had a problem and was only now making an effort to stop. The alcohol had numbed the urge to scream with grief and that awful lost feeling we all felt – death in the family was too hard for it just to be labelled a "curveball". Just enough time had passed now. We had to face our pain.

My father swerved the old truck and I glanced at him, holding onto the seatbelt across my lap. 'You okay, Dad?'

He squinted with concentration but gave a curt nod. The early morning without booze in his system sent his deprived body reeling. When we had first moved here, he had risen every day before dawn but as he slid further down into his burn, fueled by alcohol, he had risen later and later until he hadn't risen anymore. The last week, he'd been getting up to take over the cows for me. I had resented him, even hating him in my exhaustion. But he was trying.

He croaked, 'It's real nice to feel the mornings again, thank our Lord.'

'Amen,' I murmured, feeling my skin crawl. Fuck our Lord. He didn't save Alex. He didn't help my mother talk to me. Sure, didn't help Dad in his darkest days.

At the river bank, Dad parked the truck beside Coop's and we piled out, collecting our new, unused fishing gear. We had bought it all when we moved. Dad had planned to go fishing more often with his boy, me, but the drink had taken hold and Jim and Jack were his favorite sons. I was happy to be out there with the morning sun beaming onto my face. It felt good. I was excited about the fishing. Sand dunes towered on either side of the meandering stream cutting through.

'Hey, Cowboy.'

I stopped in my tracks and dropped my fishing rod. Tessa was sitting on a camp chair, sporting a sundress, wraparound shades and a bandanna. She was a spunk. Her sandals were off and I could see her bright blue painted toenails burying into the grass beside the river. She was smiling up at me.

'What are you doing here?' I asked.

'Who's this?' Dad asked.

40

She stood up and offered her hand for him to shake. 'I'm Coop's granddaughter. My name is Tessa.' She looked at me and gave a suggestive blink with her chin lowered.

'Yeah,' I said. 'We go to school together.'

My dad nodded and put his tackle box down beside her. He looked around and asked, 'Where's Coop?'

She replied, 'Oh, he and my dad just went for a walk to check out the beach.'

Beyond the massive sand dunes that made the mouth of Powlett River so beautiful, a humongous swell was pounding against the rocks.

'Is that the beach where that girl nearly died?' asked my dad. Tessa explained where Tamara had been surfing. I could barely hear them over the waves in my head. They sounded monstrous and I had the odd fear that they would be big enough to engulf us, swallowing the sand dunes and crashing upon our little bodies. I used to love waves; they would make me smile and draw my eye, numbing everything, but now...I looked at them and I teared up. What was wrong with me? I sat down in her chair and the canvas sagged under my weight. I stared at the river and tried to block out the sound of Tessa chatting gaily with my dad.

'So, a pretty girl like you must have a boyfriend.' *Smooth, Dad, real smooth.*

Tessa replied with a pointed look at me, 'No, I don't.' I hadn't introduced her as my girlfriend. I didn't really understand why I refused to do it, besides the awkwardness that it would create. *Hey everybody, this is the girl I've been sleeping with. Let's all celebrate how I've been hiding her for months!*

My dad seemed to sober up out of his non-alcohol hangover as he stood around, chatting. Maybe it was the sunshine but maybe it was Tessa's small smile that told everybody that she was shy, but it shone for the world whenever the clouds parted.

After twenty-minutes, Coop and his son, Tessa's father, Frank, came back and I was glad. I had been growing increasingly more and more uncomfortable with how well Tessa and my dad were getting along. Luckily, Coop hadn't told anything to daddy-dearest Frank about Tessa and me so I didn't have to impress the oldies nor let it slip to my dad that we were an item.

Coop and Frank set up their chairs and offered them to Dad and me, which we politely declined. I kicked myself for not thinking to bring chairs as I got up out of Tessa's and sat on the damp grass of the river bank after casting our lines out.

Two hours passed and none of us had caught a single organism, let alone a fish.

Coop sighed, 'Years back we caught a ton of fish right here in this very spot.'

Frank replied, 'Things change, Pa.'

'Yeah, it's that bloody De-Sal plant, I tell you what.' Coop glared in the direction of the desalination plant under construction beyond the bluff.

My dad put in, 'Maybe y'all should try surf fishin'. I hear that's fun but I've never tried it.'

Coop and Frank both nodded and conceded that they would like to try that too one day.

The guys cheated at noon. They had expected to catch a fish and fry it up on Frank's fancy camping stove but with none having been caught, they went into town for a take-away run. I stayed with Tessa, still waiting for a fish to bite. I wasn't looking at her but I could see her in the corner of my eye, watching me and shredding a blade of grass.

She said, 'I don't know what you're talking about all the time, Jake. Your dad seems really nice.'

I turned to her and replied, 'I never said he wasn't nice.'

'Then what did you say?'

'He has a drinking problem.'

She mumbled, 'Oh…okay.' She paused then asked, 'What happened to you this morning? You acted like you didn't know me.'

I hoped a fish would bite so we could stop talking, but the fish must have wanted me to simmer in awkward humiliation.

Tessa asked, 'Are we…all right?'

'We're fine.'

She moved closer to me and held my hand. I didn't say anything. Hand in hand, we stood and gazed over the rippling river. In the distance, a large wave crashed onto the sand and the rocks, making me flinch and pull away.

Sanna

February 2011

My dad drove me past the beach every morning on the way to school. 'Looks good out there,' he'd say.

'Yeah…it does,' I agreed but did not even look out the window. He'd take a deep breath and take us both home, no doubt wondering what he was supposed to do with this sullen version of me that had crept in and stolen my identity for the last three weeks.

'Do you think it'd be a good idea to go to the counselling sessions, Sanna? That the hospital gave you?'

I glared at him in disbelief. Betrayed, I couldn't believe he thought I needed to see a counsellor. Of course, I felt bad. I was supposed to! I'd done something ridiculously stupid and almost killed my best friend. She was in the hospital with a "significant head injury", her parents had said. Counselling wouldn't help. I was a terrible friend and a terrible person for what I had done. How on earth did he think that counselling would help?

Nevertheless, the next day I ended up sitting in a counsellor's office – a dodgy adapted garage of a local island woman who had turned to offering counselling because she'd been so good at it when she'd been a teacher.

I stared around the room. There were toys and ornaments scattered higgledy-piggledy all over the place and a scented candle that made my eyes water. There were books about family, raising the confident child, social contexts, and sex. A box of tissues sat atop the arm of the armchair I was sinking deeper into despite being perched on the edge. On the wall behind me, there was a photo of a wave with the caption: OPPORTUNITY.

Eyeing the glassy face of the wave in the picture, I felt the sickening thwack of my board meeting Tamara's forehead and I winced.

The counsellor-nee-teacher watched me, pen poised above her notepad.

'Why don't you go visit Tamara in the hospital, Sanna? It may help.'

I shook my head. 'No. It won't.'

What was I scared of? I kept asking myself. She was probably sitting upright, eating ice cream, and enjoying the attention she was getting. Would she be wondering when I would come? Probably. I imagined her sitting there, resting, a white bandage wrapped around her head.

'Tamara, honey,' her mum and dad would croon. 'Time to get some rest. Put the surf magazines away and rest.'

She'd pull a face and put them aside, counting down the minutes 'til they left so she could keep reading about how to do an aerial and dream she was in the water instead of in a stinky hospital.

In the converted garage, the counsellor cocked her head at me. Waited for me to say something. I picked up the tissue box, crushed it in my hands and threw it to the floor.

45

She met with my mother as I sat in the car with my arms crossed. No doubt telling her I was an awful little brat and she refused to treat me. When Mum got back into the car, I was surprised when she said, 'I'm glad you found that helpful.'

'I what?' I snorted derisively.

'You're hurting, Sanna. You're stuck in the moment you hurt Tamara.'

'It was an accident.' My voice cracked and I looked away before she could see that I was beginning to tear up. This was all just shit. Why couldn't they just leave me alone?

Mum said, 'You need to go see her. Don't take too long to go, honey.'

I stomped my foot on the floor well of the car. I'd had it. Everyone at school was whispering behind my back. I was sick of Dad taking me by the beach and forcing me into counselling. The counsellor and her stupid face. Mum NAGGING me to go visit Tamara. Why didn't anyone understand that I WOULD BE FINE ONE DAY and I didn't need to go get screamed at by Tamara for dropping in on her? I was over the teachers being SO CONCERNED ABOUT ME and trying to help. They were always asking me how Tamara was doing – not me – Tamara. I'd lie to them of course. 'Oh, she's doing really well. She says hi to everyone.' They'd always give me a funny look, nod and smile and the conversation would cease, however they'd glance back at me as they walked away, as if they were worried I would implode with guilt. Truth was, I already had.

Mum said, 'We'll go on Saturday morning. I'll let Mr. and Mrs. Jenkins know that you're coming.'

I simmered in the car all the way home, and I simmered all the way to the hospital on Saturday morning.

The Alfred Hospital was located close by the city and was close by a lake, lined with palm trees that were out of place in the cold climate. Close to water, even when she was injured in a hospital in a metropolis – lucky Tamara. As Mum and I walked inside, I clutched her hand and walked to the elevator.

Mum knew exactly where she was going because Tamara's parents had given her explicit instructions.

As I stepped off the elevator with Mum, I noticed we were in ICU. 'Why is she still in ICU, Mum?' I asked. 'Shouldn't she just be in a ward by now?'

Mum patted my hand and swallowed hard.

'Mum,' I said pointedly.

She gently pulled me off to the side and put her arm around me. 'Now, Sanna…we haven't told you exactly everything. We wanted you to come and see her for yourself, first. Then we'll answer any questions you have, okay.'

'Okay,' I said slowly, allowing her to lead me to Tamara, now feeling as though I'd been horrendously naïve. I walked despite my legs feeling like they weren't connected to me. I spotted Tarryn and Murray, Tamara's parents, standing next to a bed. They turned to us.

'Sanna,' they said, and both said something along the lines of how glad they were I'd come. Tamara would be happy.

'Where is she?' I croaked.

They glanced at my mum and then stepped aside to reveal Tamara, except…it wasn't her. This girl had a halo of metal around her head, puffy cheeks, wore an oxygen mask and her eyes were taped closed. Taped. Closed. A heart rate monitor steadily beeped and the oxygen sucked and huffed. Tamara's arms lay limply at her side, connected to an IV and pricked and bruised from God knows how many injections.

She looked like she was dead. Her skin was grey and she was motionless. The nurse at the desk had said how happy Tamara would have been that I'd come. The counsellor said visiting her would help me heal. No wonder the teachers gave me funny looks when I said she was doing well and she said hi to everyone. She was not doing well. She was almost dead.

I took a sharp intake of breath and spun on my heel and marched away.

'Sanna!' Mum called.

'No.'

47

'Sanna, come back!'

'LEAVE ME ALONE!' I screamed and ran back to the elevator.

I punched at the buttons until the door opened and I fell inside. As the doors closed and I started to descend, I let out a wail I'd never heard anybody make before. How was this supposed to help me?

I refused to speak to the counsellor again. I stopped speaking at school. I attended each class and got my work done. That was it. Yes, I was technically "withdrawn" according to the teachers. Those concerned glances back were looks from people who knew Tamara had been in a coma, on life support, so badly brain damaged nobody knew if she'd make it.

They knew I had no idea. They knew I was already imploding after all.

'Sanna, I'm sorry, I wanted you to find out on your own terms. I had no idea you thought she was fine…' my mother would say anytime I got really quiet. I'd just get up and walk away. I couldn't do it anymore.

Friday night, I made my way to the beach and sat watching the water come in and go back out as if trying to hypnotise me.

Michael walked over to me.

'Hey, Sanna.'

I looked up and mumbled a hello. He stood there awkwardly, lingering. He gestured behind him towards the car park. 'I've got a six pack of beer…'

I chortled and said, 'Good for you.'

'Want to hang out?'

I needed something for a distraction, so I said yes.

We sat on the beach and smoked marijuana, and drank the beer Michael had pilfered from his older brother's minifridge. We lay beside each other, giggling and freezing our arses off.

'Sanna,' he wheezed between hits. 'You're like…the bestest chick around.'

I cracked up laughing and the universe above us seemed to twirl around. The sand moved beneath and the wind howled over us and flattened the marram grass.

He leant over me. 'I'm serious, you know.'

'Mm-hm. You're serious.' I clapped my hand against his cheek. 'You're serious, and you're very, very handsome.' We kissed. My first kiss! I let him nuzzle into my neck and grind up beside me.

'Sanna,' he said.

'Yeah?'

'I reckon we should do it.'

I laughed. 'No way.'

'Well…I like you, and you're my friend. We could practice on each other.'

'I'm only fifteen,' I said, shaking my head. I closed my eyes to keep the dizziness away. I swallowed the urge to vomit. 'And I don't love you.'

He lay back beside me and sighed.

We lay in silence in the sand but he put his hand in mine and tickled my shoulder with the other. I kept my eyes closed yet wanted to gaze into his, but I was afraid if I did, I would give in and I'd let my parents down. Michael's warm body beside mine made me lie still and at peace for a change. Tamara wasn't on my mind. It was just he and I lying on the beach, with the sound of the ocean.

We fell asleep on the beach together well into the night. A hot bright flame from a torch burnt my retinas and woke me. I shot up with a gasp.

'Sanna!' my father yelled. He'd come looking for me. 'We've been looking everywhere for you! I was about to call the police!' His voice was high-pitched and cracking in parts as if he was going to cry, but a vein on his forehead bulged with fury.

'Daddy,' I croaked. 'I fell asleep.'

'Get to the car – now!'

'Why are you so mad?' I asked. I got to my feet, straightening up and feeling my back pinch. My toes were numb. Sleeping on the beach was not as idyllic as movies made it out to be. Michael sat up, still half-asleep. Oh, *that* was why Dad was so mad.

He sniffed. 'You've been smoking.' His eyes went to the empty cans of beer beside Michael and me. 'And drinking! This is not very Christian behaviour.'

Seeing the anger and disappointment on my dad's face made my eyes burn with tears. Michael stood beside me. He gave his head a little flick and his dreadlocks moved like a windchime.

Dad sneered, 'Who's this?'

'Dad, Michael. Michael, this is my dad.' I lowered my eyes to the imprints of where we'd been lying in the sand – I couldn't bear seeing the way they shook hands. Michael cleared his throat and said, 'Well, I suppose I better head home.'

'Get in the car, Michael. I'll drive you home as well.'

Michael and I glanced at each other. In the back seat of the Nissan Patrol, he jiggled his leg. The dark ti-trees flew by as we headed to Michael's place. I was curious to see his house. He lived with his older brother Billy, whom Michael didn't like talking about.

'I'm looking forward to meeting your parents and telling them what their son has been up to with my daughter,' Dad said with a thin mouth.

'Dad!' I leant forward in my seat. 'Nothing happened.'

'I'd like to believe that Sanna, but the truth is that you stink of marijuana and beer – and I think Michael's parents would like to know about this.' He made a fist and pounded his knee. 'His parents deserve to know what their son is doing on a beach at night with a vulnerable teenage girl.'

'Dad,' I groaned. 'I'm not vulnerable!'

He glared at me but didn't add anything.

'Sir,' said Michael. 'Nothing happened, I swear.'

'Dad, we're not like that.'

He frowned. 'You just stayed out 'til two am drinking and smoking?'

'Yes,' we both whined.

He pulled up in Michael's driveway and looked towards the dark house, and saw a ratty old car in the driveway, parked crookedly with a trail of beer bottles that led to the front door. Dad switched the high beams on and we all saw Michael's brother Billy, lying unconscious on the porch.

'Oh, heavens, who's that?' asked my dad, peering with concern.

'Some town drunk, I s'pose,' said Michael, his shoulders deflating and his chin ducking towards his chest.

'Uh...' my dad turned to me and Michael and his eyes flicked from each of us to the other. 'Michael?'

'Yes?'

'How would you like to just sleep at our house tonight? My brother's a copper down at Inverloch. I'll give him a call and get him to get rid of that...uh...town drunk for you.'

I reached forward and hugged him. 'Thanks, Dad.'

'Yeah, yeah,' he mumbled and doused Michael's house back into darkness.

Michael stayed the night on the couch and I could barely sleep knowing he was so close. The last person who had stayed over had been Tamara, and she had slept in my bed with me. I peeked out in the middle of the night and observed Michael's shape on the couch. He was sprawled on his belly with a puddle of drool flooding upon the couch cushion. My mother's favourite blanket was draped over him, making him look like a little kid. I smiled affectionately, closed the door and went back to bed.

In the morning, Michael was already at the breakfast table, chatting easily with my mum when I sat down.

'How did you sleep?' he asked.

'Great.'

He helped himself to the bowl of scrambled eggs that my mum had made. He shared the eggs over three pieces of toast. Mum stood nearby, watching us quietly, sipping from her coffee mug with the gold handle and paisley flower design I had given her last year for Mother's Day.

'I slept awesomely,' Michael said, biting into the toast and dropping bits of egg into his lap. 'That couch is amazing.' He spoke with his mouth full and I could see my mother's disapproval written all over her taut Scandinavian face.

'Where's Dad?' I asked.

'He went to see his brother,' said Mum. I glanced at Michael. 'He will be back soon.'

Michael stopped chewing.

I twisted in my seat and gave my mother an interrogative shrug and glare. She crossed her arms over her chest. 'Seems that he wanted somebody arrested and your uncle had to have a discussion with him about it.'

Michael coughed. 'That's probably about my brother.'

'Why did you lie to us, Michael?' asked Mum.

He grimaced. 'My brother was lying there, out cold, drunk. I was trying to prove to your husband that I wasn't that bad of a kid.' He forced a smile. 'I'm really not like him.'

'Where are your parents?' She sat at the table with us. Michael shrugged and replied it wasn't a big deal and he got by because when things went bad, he just went boogie boarding.

'You are welcome to come and stay here, any time you need to, all right, Michael.'

'Yes. Thanks, Mrs. Smith.'

I breathed a sigh of relief. Whoever said parents didn't understand was unlucky. Good parents listened and at least tried to get it. My parents did. All the time. My heart was full of love because my parents always listened and tried. Even though I'd been an awful headcase lately, they were still trying to hear me and listen to what I wanted. I was very lucky to have them.

March 2011

Michael's brother Billy went on living the way he did, but his parents stopped leaving for days at a time. It was much calmer around their house. One Friday night, I was chilling out in Michael's bedroom with him.

'I never got the chance to thank your dad for all his help,' Michael said as we tilted our heads off the bed, letting our hair flow over. His hair stuck out at strange angles and he resembled a porcupine.

'He wanted to help. You don't need to thank him.'

'Yeah, but still...It was pretty amazing what he did, don't you think? He could have just flicked me off the face of your planet like a gnat but he took an interest and tried to help. He did help.' He swallowed – a tricky feat when you're hanging upside down off the edge of a bed.

'I guess your parents had a guilty conscious, leaving you alone with Billy all the time.' I slid a little farther to the floor. I slid and slid until I landed on my neck. Michael stretched out his arm and poked my belly. He smiled. 'I guess they did...'

I laughed as he came down on top of me and I wrestled him over so I was straddling him. He reached up and started to unbutton my pants. I placed my hand on his, making him stop.

'Are we...' I laughed awkwardly. 'Are we together?'

'What do you mean?'

My hair fell in front of my face as I mumbled, 'I only want to do this if we're...together.' I took a deep breath.

He pulled his hand away and said, 'We're mates. Do you want something more?'

I gestured at my buttons and said, 'Obviously you do.'

He smiled but didn't reply.

I tried to explain how I was feeling. I wanted to be with him, but we could only go further if we were together. An item. It was old-fashioned but my family's Christian values were important to me. To have sex, we needed to not be just friends. It needed to mean something.

I said, 'I guess if we have sex, it would be crossing a line...if we're just friends.'

He frowned. 'Is that a bad thing?'

'Well...' I looked around him, trying to find the words that explained how I felt without scaring him completely away, then spotted a foil square with a ridged edge. A condom wrapper. Torn open and empty. Michael followed my line of sight and said, 'Oh. I meant to tell you about that.'

'You were with somebody else?' I swallowed hard and tried to understand why it hurt my feelings so much to know that he had been with someone else. We weren't together, but it was beginning to feel like we could be.

He sighed. 'I don't think you'd understand. It's complicated.'

'No, I get it.' I climbed off his crotch and stood to the side of him, clearing my throat. 'I understand. I do.'

'Yeah? I was worried that you might get upset.'

I shrugged with faux-calmness. 'Why would I get upset?'

'I would have, with you...down the track...but I didn't want to wait.' I think my heart just about broke right then and there. He didn't want to wait. Waiting was worthless. Waiting was pointless. Waiting was what boys didn't like to do. Waiting was what boys *couldn't* do.

I swallowed hard. 'Are you dating her?'

Michael shrugged. 'I don't think so. We were drunk when it happened so...' He caught my eye and said, 'It didn't mean anything. It wasn't even good. I probably won't call her or anything. It didn't mean anything, Sanna. I promise.'

I nodded. 'Okay.'

His bedroom now seemed dirty, clothes strewn all over and the musky smell that came with boys – it was like he hadn't showered and I could smell the sex on him. I wiped my eyes when he wasn't looking and I tried to smile when he cracked jokes but my hands were shaking. I tried to act like I didn't care but all I could think about was the fact he had rushed into something he claimed didn't even matter to him.

At a party the following Friday night, Michael asked me, 'Where have you been, Sanna? You haven't been here, not really.'

I shrugged and dug around in the ice-filled esky for a flavoured vodka. 'I don't know what you're talking about.'

He stared blankly at me. 'Is something bothering you?'

I shook my head as I took a sip of the drink. He tilted his head at me and said, 'I don't believe you. You haven't been the same since I hooked up with Celestial.'

Celestial; She had a weird name, weird like mine. I took another sip to prevent my tongue spitting her name all over the ground and stamping on it. I hated her even though I'd never met her. She stole my friend and she stole my opportunity. I vowed to never wait. If a guy asked me if I wanted to, I knew it would be social suicide to say no.

'She's coming later, by the way.' Michael took my drink from me and gulped it down. His eyes stayed on me the whole time.

I looked down at the ground and leaned against the veranda pillar. I tried to smile. 'Great, then I can meet her.'

He laughed as he handed my drink back to me. 'I don't know. Actually, I'm kind of nervous about it.'

'Why?'

'Sanna, I had sex with this girl!' He scoffed. 'It's complicated. You have no idea how weird it is. I haven't spoken to her since it happened.'

So, he was still thinking of her in the same way I thought of him. I wondered how it felt to share that much of yourself with somebody but then feel ashamed and anxious about it. When I eventually had sex, I would be excited to see the person again. I'd want to be with that person all the time. It was odd to me

55

that Michael hadn't reached out to her to at least say "hey" or ask "how are you?"

'How'd you know she's coming tonight, then?' I asked curiously.

'This is her friend's party and her friend told me.' He pointed out Celestial's friend and even though I didn't care, I looked at her. I didn't know her. She went to a different school than Michael and me.

'How did you meet her anyway?' I asked.

'Who?'

'Your date.'

'You're my date, Sanna,' Michael smirked. He snatched my drink back and swallowed the rest of it. He put his hand on my shoulder and said, 'I still think we should, even though you were right and I didn't wait.'

'Whatever, Michael,' I snapped. I avoided him for the rest of the night, which turned out to be surprisingly easy once Celestial showed up. I didn't meet her; I fled from her. I ended up drinking so much I passed out on the front lawn and some P-plater had to drive me home, where I skulked into my bedroom and accidentally missed my bed when I tried to lie on it, causing a loud thud. I waited for my parents to burst in but exhaustion took over and I fell asleep on the cold floor. I woke up with a headache and blissfully carefree about Michael and his ho.

April 2011

The Surf Shack was the best local surf shop on the island. The owner was a hip 35-year-old woman with sun-stained hair and orange, burnt skin. She looked at me from the other side of the plastic table in the staff room at the back of the shop and asked, 'What are you hoping to gain from working here?'

I replied, just as my dad had taught me, 'Business skills and work experience.'

Ms. Kelly then asked me the critical question, 'Do you surf?'

I faltered. Would it be lying if I said yes? I hadn't surfed in two months. Should I tell her about the last time I surfed and get some pity? No, that would be cheating. Should I be half honest and say "Not a lot" or should I be completely honest and tell her that I didn't think I'd be brave enough to surf again?

I smiled and answered, 'Not as much as I'd like to.'

I got the job and worked on Friday nights, Saturday mornings and all day on Sundays. I needed the distraction outside of school because if I wasn't in school, all I could think about was Tamara lying there in the hospital. I loved the job. Even though I was doubtful I would be surfing again anytime soon, I still felt like I belonged in the surf culture. Seeing surfers whom I both knew and didn't coming in and out; and the odd parent on the search for a birthday present now and then, I was happy. But I was happiest after closing time when I could sit alone in the dark, nestled on the floor among the stacks of surfboards, both short and long. I ran my hands down the rails of each board and felt comforted by the smooth fibreglass reminding me of freedom and the smell of salinity. I did, however, have a slight hiccup one Saturday morning. Ms. Kelly came in and announced, 'Sanna, we're closing. Surf's amazing!'

I froze. 'Oh, okay...I'll just call my dad to come and pick me up.'

I picked up the receiver of the store phone but Ms. Kelly took it from me and laughed, 'Don't be silly. We'll go out together. An old friend of mine is in town. I think you'll like him.' She winked and added, 'We'll just go have a good time for a couple of hours. The whole surfing population is out at Woolamai anyway. Nobody's gonna come into the shop.'

My heart hammered in my ribcage. 'I don't have a board.' I didn't particularly want to admit that my surfboard had a damaged nose and still had blood stains on it from me committing the epitome of surf crimes.

Ms. Kelly grabbed a six-footer Tim Carroll import off the rack – one of my favourite surfboard designs. Ms. Kelly gestured for me to follow. 'Come on, hurry up. Last one in the car is a rotten egg.'

I followed her slowly, my legs stiff in my denim shorts. What was I supposed to wear? What was I going to do? I sat in the backseat of the crappy minivan with Ms. Kelly and her friend. Our eyes met, and all the heartache came back. It was Eddie. I stared at him and he looked at me with ever-increasing narrow eyes. He didn't say anything from the front seat when she introduced me to him. I said, 'We know each other.'

He cleared his throat and looked out the window, away from me. I sat in the back and twiddled my thumbs while Ms. Kelly drove the five kilometres to the beach. I leant away from the surfboards, stacked in beside me. They rattled against each other with the vibrations of the bad suspension and the bumpy road to the beach.

The car park was jammed to the hilt when we arrived. Ms. Kelly laughed maniacally, parking in the path of an Audi four-wheel drive that had stickers for Melbourne City all over it. 'City dweller kooks,' she muttered as if that justified blocking them into their spot. 'Make way for the locals,' she added to the car as she stripped off and started pulling on her steamer. We needed wetsuits even in the warm months. I stared down at the tattoos on Ms. Kelly's feet and mumbled, 'I don't have anything to wear.'

'You got underwear on, don't ya?' grinned Eddie. He yanked off his shirt and I had to hold on to the doorframe of the car to stop myself getting back into it and hiding. But he winked at me and puffed his chest out, and I noticed. I had never noticed what Tamara had seen, but as he looked at me with soft eyes for a change, it was clear. His muscles drew my eyes in and I took off my shorts and shirt, thanking God I wasn't wearing daggy underwear. My skin was the palest it had been since I had started surfing.

My thighs seemed fatter and my middle seemed softer. *Oh Sanna*, I told myself, *you have to surf again, you just have to, simple as that, girl.* Girl...that was something that Tamara would always say. Girl, you're a natural. Girl, I hate you. Girl, I love you. You're going to be my girl forever, girl.

Ms. Kelly handed me the Tim Carroll board and warned me, 'Don't ding it. I'm selling it as second-hand, not damaged goods.'

I shook my head and clutched it closer to my body. The fibreglass was cool on my skin. I was going to freeze out in that Bass Strait water.

I followed Eddie and Ms. Kelly down to the beach and stood silently while they discussed where they should go. They pointed out at breaks and talked about them before some other surfer would claim it and own it. I chewed on my lip, holding the board tighter and tighter with each passing second. I dropped it in the sand. Ms. Kelly glared at me and I fumbled with it as I picked it back up. 'Sorry, sorry, I'm so sorry...'

Eddie pointed out at a humongous break past the crowd of surfers. 'Look at those lines!'

She shrugged. 'Okay, then. Hope you've had your Weet-Bix.'

He laughed and sprinted into the water. Ms. Kelly glanced at me. My heart was hammering harder now – my chest even hurt. 'Are you coming?'

'Yeah, of course,' I retorted, my eyes on Eddie as he paddled against the foam, disappearing with a pointed toe as he duck-dived.

'Okay, see you out there.' She glanced at me again before she strode into the water. I took one step and felt out of breath. The water surged towards me and I backed up. I broke into a sweat.

I want to go in the water, I thought, gritting my teeth. Surely positive thinking would trick my body and brain into believing me. I want to go in the water. I will go in the water. I want to surf. I want to do this. This is fun. This is fun. You want to do this. You can't do this, Sanna. Shut up, Sanna. Do this. This is fun. You can do this.

I took a few wobbly steps to the waterline and the cold water enveloped my ankles. The sand washed away from beneath me and I forced my legs to keep moving. The water covered my knees. I started to shiver and my jaw went tight. I paused a moment to slap the Tim Carroll down on the rippled surface of the water. It didn't feel right. It was shorter than my board yet felt like I was holding onto a tree trunk. It was alien in my hands.

I looked up and considered backing up and sitting on the beach to just watch Ms. Kelly and Eddie surf. Maybe I needed to take this slower. I had been in an accident, after all. It was going to be a long run to recovering my confidence. Then I thought about that girl in Hawaii who had an arm bitten off by a shark. She was back in the water and surfing big league in no time. Me, I was just a sook. I didn't need that much time.

Would I come face to face with doom on my first day back in the surf? Probable? No. Possible? Yes. It was that possibility that froze me in the water, clutching onto the board.

A grom paddled past me, no older than nine, and gave me the stink-eye. I was a kook. I bit my lip too hard and tasted blood. I took a few raggedy breaths and then got onto the board, on my belly. The current moved the board beneath me as I clutched the rails. The grom caught a wave and then paddled back. He caught three more while I lay there, frozen in the shallows. I could see Ms. Kelly and Eddie surging down the walls of massive waves. I couldn't do this. I laboured to turn the board around and my world suddenly swam when I noticed how far I had come with the current. The rip, of course. *Don't panic. Do not panic.* I sat up on the board and looked around for a landmark. I wasn't that far out. The water beneath me wasn't even deep – only about five-feet down there were rocks looming.

I scratched at my bare thigh and noticed the goose bumps covering my skin. I was so consumed with my brain that I had forgotten how cold I was.

I looked up at the horizon. It was beautiful, really. The big open blue sky mirrored the big open blue ocean with white caps in the distance. Picturesque. If only I had a camera. I'd missed that view. I jumped with fright when Eddie paddled over and sat up on his board beside me.

'Hey Sanna,' he said, panting a bit. 'You catching one?'

I scratched at the board's surface before I shook my head.

'Well, you're in the water. That's progress.'

'Excuse me?'

'You're in the water...after what happened. That's progress.'

'You know what happened?' I sputtered.

Eddie blew his nose into his hand and washed it in the water. He squinted at me. 'Of course, I know.'

'Does Ms. Kelly know?'

He shrugged. 'I dunno,' he said, looking over at her ripping it up. 'I don't think so.'

I nodded. 'Okay.'

'Are *you* okay?' he asked.

I hesitated and then shook my head. 'I can't do it.'

'That's okay, Sanna, it really is.' He leant over and pulled my board closer to his. They clunked together in the water. Our knees touched and I blushed. He gripped my thigh suddenly to balance himself and he quickly let go and said, 'Sorry.' I giggled. We stared at each other. He was stunning. He was amazing. He was gorgeous. He was perfect.

Eddie leant forward a little more and I followed suit. Our lips touched and we kissed, careful at first. Then we kissed again with our mouths apart. His tongue met mine and I pulled away, wanting to laugh suddenly. I gazed at the water and noticed it was getting deeper and our boards knocked together so I pulled away. A set came roaring towards us. We were going to be caught inside. I back-paddled to get the board away from his.

'What's wrong?' he asked, glancing at the wall of water behind him.

'I have to get to the beach.' I paddled like crazy and I puffed and panted until I reached the shallows. I dragged the board to the sand and sat down, breathing hard with adrenaline. It felt as though I had ridden the gnarliest wave of my life, but I hadn't even been close to that wave. I lay on the sand and felt the cold seep into my bones.

It was over. I had failed. I rolled my head until I could see Eddie and Ms. Kelly. I had expected Eddie to follow me but he was out there on the water, paddling for the next wave in the set, like I was nothing to him.

Once we got back to the shop and I offered to strip the wax off the Tim Carroll to clean it up. Ms. Kelly replied that it would be great if I could because she was heading home. Eddie stayed behind while I scraped off the old wax in the work shop.

'Haven't seen you out for ages,' he murmured.

I shrugged. 'Didn't feel up to it.'

'So…you're not okay, then.'

'No…I guess not.'

He stood behind me, watching my progress. My wet underwear was soaking through my denim shorts and was chafing me, but I didn't mind. Eddie watched me scrape the wax off and I found myself wanting to impress him, to matter to him.

His hand went to my lower back and he leant in beside my ear and whispered, 'You're doing well.' I smiled.

After the board was done, Eddie helped himself to a beer and gave me one. We sat on the floor against the tin wall, beside each other. He took a sip from the longneck bottle and watched me as I gulped mine down. I hadn't realised how parched I was.

Once I finished one, he gave me another, watching me with his piercing eyes.

'How long are you in town for?' I asked.

'In town?'

'You obviously left for a while after Tamara.'

He nodded. 'Indo.'

'And you're going again soon?'

He nodded again.

'Cool,' I said and finished my beer. 'So, I've always wondered…. How long have you been surfing?'

Eddie smiled and handed me another bottle of beer. 'I don't even know. I just picked up a board and went for it. I think I was just a little tacker...maybe six or seven.'

'Why aren't you competing these days? You're really good.'

He shrugged. 'I don't give a shit about competing anymore. I like surfing. I don't like competing. Those dickheads that compete are just narcissists and poofters.'

I almost choked on the beer as I cracked up laughing and nodded. 'Fair enough.' I'd never really connected with him before or liked him, but as the beers went down, I found him charming and I liked his honesty.

'Cool,' I said and finished my third beer. Eddie took my bottle, and gave me a fourth.

He asked, 'How old are you now?' As if it had been years since we had last seen each other. In some ways, it felt like forever had passed, but it had only been two months.

'Fifteen.'

'Cool.'

'Yeah.'

'Remember how I'd pick you and Tamara up and take ya both surfing?'

I nodded, revelling in the fuzziness the beer gave me. With it, I could think of Tamara without drowning.

'Yeah, I still got me ute – it's parked outside.' I glanced out the window. It was dusk. His ute was the lone car in the car park. I took another couple of gulps of the beer and felt my head swim.

He put his beer down on the floor and tucked his knees up to his chest. 'I taught her how to surf, you know.'

'Wow,' I mumbled.

He wet his lips with his tongue and asked, 'Do you want to kiss again?'

My stomach dropped and I needed the toilet. My forehead burst into a sweat. Then I felt normal again, just a little buzzed. 'Um...' I smiled. 'Okay.' So, we kissed again. I could get used to this.

Eddie said quietly, 'Want to go for a drive?'

'Okay.'

We walked outside and I locked up the shop. My legs wobbled under me and I knew I'd drank more than I should have. It had all gone down too easy in that cozy back room of the store, surrounded by the scent of epoxy and fibreglass. Now Eddie needed to place a hand on my lower back to guide me and walk towards his ute. He said, 'Get in. I'll take you for a drive and we can talk some more.'

It was a new car and I liked the slight aroma of salt water mixed with wetsuit neoprene. The car also smelled a little like marijuana and I didn't even think how many beers Eddie might have already had. It never entered my mind until we were doing 180 in a 100 zone.

I squeaked, 'Could you please not speed?' My chest was so tight with fear I could barely breathe.

'What?' asked Eddie, turning down his stereo that was pumping out Metallica.

'Please slow down!' I cried, watching the cats' eyes on the road lines zip past in a blurry line. My uncle was a cop. I had heard enough horror road crash stories to know I didn't want to be in one.

Eddie shrugged off my request and said, 'It's fine – there's nobody around.'

'Please.'

'Lighten up and just relax. Enjoy the ride.' He smirked and sped up to 195 and wobbled the wheel with a giggle.

I snapped, 'Stop the car! Let me out now!'

He shouted, 'It's my car so I'll drive it however I want!' The road came to a bend and he slammed on his brakes to avoid going off the road. I grabbed the door handle and gritted my teeth at the sensation of the G-force as we sped sideways around the bend. I waited for a crashing impact and certain death but we made it through. The surprise turn seemed to put Eddie back in his place and he slowed down. He glanced at me and laughed. 'You're white as a sheet, Sanna. Are you okay?'

'I want to go home,' I mumbled, fiddling with my seatbelt. I was so glad I was wearing it.

He replied, 'Actually, I'm taking you somewhere else. It's real nice and I think you'll like it.' He gave me a smooth smile and I disliked that, too.

'What are we going to do?' I asked, my voice trembling.

He grinned. 'You'll have to wait and see.'

As if I had a choice in his speed capsule, rocketing towards unknown territory. I replied shakily, 'I'd rather know.'

'That's natural.' He smirked at me. 'You'll love it. Never known a girl to not like being with me.'

'Maybe,' I lied. 'But I don't think it's a good idea. You've been drinking. I think maybe I should just go home.'

He replied, 'No, no, just wait and see. You'll love it.'

It was beautiful. I'll give him that. We drove up bumpy roads that hadn't been roads for decades. The hill had once been a housing community but penguins had taken back the landscape. An entire town, flattened, gone and nothing left but lumpy ground and penguin holes.

The wind fiercely slapped in from the south-west making the car buffet as Eddie negotiated the dirt road. We parked by the cliff edge and stood out above the water and what seemed like the end of the earth. The sun set and Eddie handed me his jacket. I sat and crossed my legs at the edge of the cliff. Eddie stood, looking over the water, listening to the boom of the waves as they rolled in. He mumbled, 'It's perfect here, don't you think.'

'It's nice,' I agreed.

He came and sat beside me, leaning in towards me. I leant away. 'Are you comfortable, Sanna?' He brushed my hair back behind my ear and kissed my neck.

I leant further from him, but his weight kept coming towards me. I laughed but it came out hollow. Was he joking? He knew how old I was. His hand went to my breast and I pushed it away.

'I don't want to have sex, Eddie. I've never had sex because I want to wait until the right one. I mean, I don't think I've ever been in love so of course I've never had sex but I don't know...I don't know if I can.'

He laughed through his nose with a blank expression. 'You say that but you're up here with me.'

Wait – what?

'Um...' My mind was racing and rambling. It must have been the alcohol he had given me. It had stopped me thinking clearly. Was he right? Had I already said yes? I tried to replay the conversations we'd had leading up to sitting there with him but I couldn't recall them exactly.

His mouth sought mine out and I flinched as his tongue invaded me. I was fine with a kiss but his tongue was so aggressive and wet that it made me recoil away from him, but he leant harder and harder into me. As hard as I tried, I couldn't stay upright. My core muscles, which I had once prided on being so strong, burned with the effort.

Eddie pushed me down and put his hand up my shirt and into my bra, pulling it down so the wire jabbed into my rib. His hands, one hand under my bra and one hand on my wrist, were freezing and I shivered, resigning myself to look up at the stars. *Let him do what he wants and maybe it will be fine.*

'It's okay,' he whispered between his kisses. I shuddered as he moved the hand from my breast down my stomach and into my underwear. My heart pounded and gave me enough adrenaline to spring up into a sitting position, but not quite enough. Eddie pushed me back down, kissing my neck. 'Ssh, you'll love it.'

'I can't, Eddie, I can't – please, I can't!' I squeezed my thighs together to try to block his hand but he was so strong. I sobbed.

The vein in his forehead bulged and he spat on me. 'Just fucking stop crying! You wanted this!'

I shivered uncontrollably. I could hear penguins rustling in the undergrowth and birds nesting, seals splashing over by the rocks and the distant bell of a trawler. The world went on around me as Eddie pulled down my shorts and wrenched my legs apart. The violence of it made me vomit. All over him. All over myself. He reeled backwards with a growl.

I got up off the ground, sobbing and dizzy, grateful to have gotten out from under him before he could unzip his pants and penetrate me. His eyes met mine and terror reverberated through my body and made me move. I ran. I sprinted down the lonely dirt road in the dark.

The dirt and the sand and the grass gave way to the real road and I ran. He came after me. My vision blurred for a moment – or was it my mind? Glimpses haunted my memory. His footsteps crunching as he caught up. I was out of my body in fear.

His hands on my neck, then on the back of my head. Breathing in dirt. In my teeth. His calloused hands over my mouth as I gasped for air. Leaves in my hair. My face skidding along the side of the dirt road, his weight slamming against my back and into me. My hair being snatched and my head yanked up.

When he was done, he threw me down and stalked back to where he had parked his car, zipping up his pants. I got up and kept running as if I hadn't just been slammed into the ground, but the road never seemed to change. It was like I was running on a treadmill. Ahead, headlights came around the bend. Was it him?

I couldn't breathe, but I screamed as I ran towards it. *Please don't be him. Please.*

The car stopped and I stopped. I put my hands on my knees and I put my head down, gasping for air but the in part of breathing didn't want to work for me. It was staccato, stuttered. My head swam.

'Sanna?'

I looked up and squinted into the white light. Jake Ryan got out of the car. A pretty blonde girl got out on the other side. We locked eyes and she covered her mouth and her eyes watered.

'Hey! Are you okay?' Jake asked. He hurried to my side and I fell into him.

I cried and I screamed. I fell to my knees and he and the girl lifted me. I gazed up at him and his lips twitched and his eyes were wide. I hugged him tightly wondering how the heck I had found myself on the side of the road with my shorts gone, and blood running down my leg.

Jake

April 2011

Her eyes were white, when they had once been blue. It shattered me to see her the way she wasn't focusing. It was as if everything was blurry. She sat between Tessa and me in my truck, silent, with her body clamped closed. Her shirt and her knees bloody, a trail of blood meandering down the inside of her leg down to her foot. There were leaves in her hair.

As we neared the main road, Sanna clutched at Tessa's hand and inhaled as if she could breathe again. Tessa and I shared a tense look and she held Sanna's hand just as tightly back. I pulled up at the police station and killed the engine. The blue and white light shone onto Sanna's white face, but she still did not blink.

'Sanna, we're here,' I said.

She shook her head and said, 'I can't.'

Tessa cleared her throat. I rested my elbow on the door rest and ran my forefinger over the steering wheel, unsure of what to say.

'Maybe the hospital?' Tessa suggested.

'No!' Sanna shouted. 'Home. Take me home.'

'Sanna...' Tessa began but Sanna threw her hand away and crossed her arms. I shrugged and drove her home. I didn't want to talk about the blood or the leaves in her hair. Something awful had happened to her but her silence made me mute. I didn't know what I could say. Her icy stare twisted my insides and I would have given anything to never see that stare again.

When I stopped at her driveway, Sanna got out of my truck and said, 'Thank you.' I felt as though I'd arrived on a murder scene. The throat had been slashed and all I could do was sit there and watch the victim bleed out. The blood evaporated in my veins and was replaced with helplessness.

Sanna began walking to the house, now wearing my jacket around her waist. 'Sanna!' I called. She looked up at me, finally blinking. I said, 'Call me.'

She nodded. Tessa and I watched her walk to the door where the porch light was left on.

Tessa mumbled, 'We're too young to deal with this, Jake.' I stood there with no reply. 'Please tell me we're going back to the police right now.'

I took a deep breath and said, 'No. We don't know what happened.'

Her eye twitched. 'Jake, it's pretty obvious what happened to that girl out there. We have to do something!'

'We don't know for sure.'

'Jake!' she shrieked. 'I can't believe you right now!'

'What do you want me to do?' I asked, holding my hands out.

'Tell the police!'

I gestured to Sanna's house. 'You just heard her. She didn't want to.'

'Are you really just going to stay quiet?'

70

'It's what she wanted.'

'Oh my God. Are you an idiot?'

I didn't reply. Maybe I was. It wasn't as if I didn't guess what had happened. I chewed the inside of my mouth. Tessa was right – we were too young. I had no idea how to help Sanna other than to let her call the shots on what to do.

Tessa burst into tears and said, 'Take me home.'

The next morning, I woke with a start. I'd dreamt of the blood sliding down Sanna's naked leg. The night before, Tessa had stormed out of my truck insisting we should have done something. She was right, but Sanna needed time. She would make the right decision. She needed to process. That was it.

I had a twinge in my gut as I thought about her. I couldn't let her go. I got myself organized and drove back to her house. She answered the door, dressed in an oversized tee-shirt. Her blonde hair hung like a curtain over her eyes. She gaped at me and pushed her hair back.

'Jake, what do you want? I'm about to go to work.'

'You work?'

'Yeah.'

'Where?'

'At a surf shop near Cape Woolamai,' she replied.

I cleared my throat. 'Are you okay?'

She said quietly, 'You said I'd be okay one day.'

I looked down at her bare feet. Her toenails were painted yellow. I murmured, 'I did say that, didn't I.'

'I don't think I'm going to be okay, Jake.'

I sighed. 'Yeah...I don't think so, either.' I hesitated before I asked, 'What happened last night?'

She gripped the door and moved it, almost swinging it towards me as if to close the door but she swallowed and said, 'I don't know. I thought I knew the guy...I thought...' She sighed. 'I got it wrong, that's all. He turned out to be a jerk.'

I pictured what must have happened to Sanna to make her knees bleed, her face graze, her hair fill with leaves, and for blood to run down her leg. She thought she got it wrong, but no jerk makes a girl run for her life. I rubbed at my nose to stop it running and asked, 'Did he do something to you?'

'He...' She cleared her throat. 'No.'

'Sanna.'

'What?' Her eyes hid behind her hair again as she looked down.

'What did he do? He did something.'

'Jake, drop it.'

'Sanna, you can tell me.'

'He just – I don't know – I don't think I'm remembering it right.'

I closed my eyes to curb my frustration and balled my hands into fists before opening my eyes up to look at her with sympathy. 'You were on the side of the road, with no pants on. I don't think you are remembering right. Something happened to you out there!'

She said in one-breath and a gasping sob, 'I-don't-remember-anything-else-please-Jake-just-shut-up.'

I crossed my arms.

'I know...' She took a deep breath. 'It was a mistake going out there with him, that's all. I'm grateful you were there and could drive me home.'

'Sanna!' A man's voice came from behind her. 'Are you getting ready for work? Who's at the door?'

'Nobody!' she called back. She pushed me in the chest and said, 'Leave, Jake. I don't want my parents to know.'

'Why?'

'I just don't!' she hissed. She wrung her hands together and said, 'I've got to go. Goodbye.' She shut the door and left me on the porch of her house, scratching at my head. Tessa had wanted me to do something. I had done something. Surely this was enough. Sanna's denial about what had happened to her perplexed me. I could go to the police and report it, but I

72

hadn't seen it. Jerks don't make girls run for their lives. Monsters do.

Every day, I walked past my reflection in the mirror and couldn't see Alex anymore. I had become my own person. That day, returning from Sanna's, I was startled when I looked at myself. I stopped mid-stride at the mirror in the bathroom and squinted. I was not the same as Alex anymore. I started to think about the lines and angles of his face and gasped when I couldn't recall exactly how he had looked.

I turned the house upside down searching for a single photograph of him but there were none. I sat on my bedroom floor and cried like a baby. Afterwards, I stared into my reflection and at the boiling anger of my tears. For a moment, it was not me I saw, but my father. I longed to see Alex again, but he was completely gone from my face. I was no longer the walking corpse of my brother – I was now the shadow of a drunk's son with angry eyes.

School started uneventfully on Monday morning.

'It's good to see you again, Jake,' Ms. Hollinday said brightly on the first day back as I took a seat in her maths class. I couldn't bring myself to tell her that I didn't feel the same way.

At the end of the school day, Tessa met me by my truck.

She asked, 'Are we going to the police?'

I recoiled. We were going to be having this argument for what felt like forever.

'No,' I breathed.

'Jake! That girl was raped.'

'She doesn't remember.'

Tessa slapped the hood of the truck and shouted, 'Jake Ryan, do not be a coward!'

The people around the school carpark looked over at us and I pushed Tessa into the truck and started driving, shaking my head. 'I spoke to her yesterday. She doesn't remember.'

Tessa crossed her arms and stared out the window, refusing to make eye contact with me but I didn't mind. I could focus on the road instead. 'She needs help.'

I agreed, 'You're right. She needs help. She needs us to do what she wants.'

'But the guy is obviously a predator,' she snapped. 'He needs to be caught and locked away.'

'I don't disagree.'

'Who is she anyway?' she asked.

I glanced at her.

'You obviously knew her and she knew you.'

I chewed on the inside of my mouth and replied, 'We've met before.'

She looked me up and down and I could see her mind going to the worst -case scenario. 'Mm-hm.' She asked, 'Do you think she's pretty?'

I pulled up outside Coop's farm and said, 'I don't want to talk about this anymore. Can we move on?'

She got out of the truck and muttered, 'Yeah, right. Move on.'

As I drove home, I tried to place where I'd seen such pain that was in Sanna's face and Tessa's, too. It was in my father's face on the morning Alex's mangled car had been brought back home on the back of a tow truck. The flashing lights and reversing beep had alerted me before Dad could shoo me inside. The twisted mess of steel had been my brother's crypt for over six hours in the dead of night.

Dad had stared at the car's bent skeleton and its shattered windscreen with his hands up on the back of his head before he turned away from it, his face contorted in a way that made his mouth seem bigger than his entire head. His legs had wobbled beneath him before falling to his knees to sob. He had leapt up and smashed the car with his fists and bellowed through his tears. We had been a family. Alex and I had been everything to each other, then...he was gone and it was only me, and my parents alone on their respective islands. The pain in the girls' faces was the same as I had seen on my father's face, my mother's face...but mostly my own.

It was a strange week of weakly existing. Every morning, I was late for school, but I made it there. Categorizing and compartmentalizing all the classes and getting through each one, writing down the tasks in a notebook with colored keys. Every afternoon, I dropped Tessa at home – our conversations became shorter and shorter – then I'd go to the beach.

I parked at the edge of the cliff and looked down at the black specs in the water, ducking through the walls of surging white foam and occasionally skiing down the face and up to the lip. There was so much patience needed in surfing. They had to wait for upwards of ten minutes for a ride that could last mere seconds.

I watched for Sanna, always expecting her to be out there, but she never was. But I could be patient too. The water was flat when school finished for the term on the Friday but I still sat there, watching the water move from the horizon to the sand. I sat there with myself and the spirit of Sanna. I imagined her in my passenger seat, watching the waves with me. Tamara was still alive, as far as I knew, but it was as though Sanna had died.

Who had she really been before that day when I met her? I had no way of ever finding out, but I did know that that girl was gone.

That Saturday night, I took Tessa to the river as a date, to try to reconnect with her. We'd had a rough week, hardly talking and when we were talking, we'd argue flat-out about telling the police about what had happened to Sanna.

We sat beside each other, staring into the crackling flames of the campfire we had lit. Tessa's skin glowed in the orange light.

'Jake,' she said. 'I have to tell you something.'

'What?'

'I'm quitting school.'

I did a double-take and shifted my weight. She wasn't even halfway through Year Twelve. She had no qualifications. She was barely eighteen. Quitting school would be a mistake for someone like her. Sure, she wasn't the best academically, but she would be screwed for life.

'My music teacher wants to take me to Tamworth next week.' Her music teacher was an older guy named Walter who she saw on weekends and after school for lessons.

My heart plummeted but I smiled. 'That's great. I'm happy for you.' She had always wanted to be a country music performer. She took music lessons four days a week and was always scribbling down (terribly corny) song lyrics.

She smiled and explained, 'It's just to record a couple of songs so I can, you know, hand around demos and stuff.'

I asked, 'How long for? Why quit school altogether? Just take a couple of weeks off.'

She swallowed hard and replied, 'No…I'm…moving to Tamworth. To increase my chances.'

I tilted my head and asked curiously, 'How are you going to afford all this?' I expected her to tell me that Coop was digging into his life savings for her because that's what he always did, but instead, she looked to the dark ground and she whispered, 'Walter.'

Walter was a balding, fat man in his mid-forties and recently divorced because his wife had found out he had a hot side piece. A young side-piece…with blonde hair. The realization was like zooming through a bright tunnel with wind squealing past and making my eyes water. Tessa was the side-piece.

'How long has it been going on?' I asked, trying to disguise the disgust in my voice.

'How long has what been going on?' she asked with a sticky swallow.

My voice trembled. 'How long have you been sleeping with him?'

'I can explain everything.' Her eyes were red and wet.

I yanked my hand away from hers and snapped, 'Can you really?' I stood up to get distance between us because she was making my skin red, hot and clammy. 'It sounds like you've been cheating on me and using him!'

She jumped up to face me and shouted, 'He's going to get me a singing career, Jake! At least I have an idea what I'm going to do and I'm going somewhere! You have no idea. You can't make a decision to save your life!'

I reeled away from her.

She sniffed. 'I cheated on you because we were never going to last.'

I backed away and stumbled into the darkness. She cried out, 'So this is it? You're just going to leave me here, Jake?'

I walked faster. 'Watch me!' I got into my truck and sobbed, letting the tears and snot soak my face. My vision smeared and the dark blended with shapes through the tears. I cried more for the points she had made than for the loss of the relationship. I was about to turn the key in my truck but the bench seat made me think of Sanna, sitting between us with that stare and leaves in her hair. I couldn't leave Tessa out there in the dark, so I swore quietly under my breath and traipsed back out to the campfire, which she was throwing dirt on with a resolved, solemn expression on her face.

She jumped when I stepped on a twig and it snapped. She squinted at me in the dark.

'Come on. I'll take you home.'

She followed behind me with her head down.

'Well done, Jake – another A+,' said Ms. Hollinday as she handed me back my science test.

I scoffed. 'Another?' My face went hot and I couldn't keep a smile from painting my face scarlet. Looking back over all the ticks, I knew I had done well and the feeling filled me when I had been so nearly empty.

Ms. Hollinday asked, 'Do you have any idea what you want to study towards a career, Jake?' A career: success: a way out.

I shrugged and replied, 'I've never really thought about it.' When I had been young, I'd just wanted to be a rancher like my dad and my granddad, and his dad and so on. Now we didn't have the ranch in Texas anymore, I supposed I could do dairy but it was cold, wet, soggy and didn't inspire joy.

'Would you like to study music, Jake?'

A buzz went over my skin and I flinched. 'What makes you say that?'

'I've seen Tessa play at the pub. She's a very gifted young musician, and she's told me that she's leaving. I was curious if you would go with her.'

'No,' I said. 'That's Tessa's thing, not mine.' I sighed. 'Besides, we're over.'

'Oh…I'm sorry to hear that.'

I nodded.

She smiled. 'More time to focus on your school work because you could do really big things if you keep this work up, Jake. I'm proud of you.'

'Thanks,' I said with a smile.

'I'm serious – if you do the VCE exam like this and get these sorts of scores…you could pick any career you want.'

I shifted my weight. 'What – are you saying I could even be a neurosurgeon or somethin' flash like that?' My heart beat faster.

'Mm-hm, sure. If you keep up this work, you could even cure cancer!'

78

That night as Dad and I stacked hay in the barn, I told him about all my good marks and put my career options to him.

'What would you say if I wanted to be a doctor or a scientist, or something like that?'

He sniggered. 'I'd say you'd need a brain transplant with some rich, smarty pants kid.'

'Do you ever pay attention, Dad?'

He squinted at me, realising that he'd hurt my feelings.

I explained, 'Because I just finished telling you I've aced every subject so far. I've tried really hard.'

'Well, that's an improvement.' *Well, duh.* He added, 'I'm impressed.'

'Thanks.'

'So, what is it you want to be?'

'What?'

'A doctor...or a scientist?' He glanced at me as we lifted the last bale into the loft.

I dusted my hands off on my jeans and shrugged. 'I don't know yet.'

'Well,' he said. 'It's about nearing the time you'll have to start thinkin' about the next step in your life, son.' His eyes drifted to the left and he smiled. 'Now, your brother...he knew what was next for him as long as he was able to throw a football.'

I stared at him.

He scratched his stubbly beard, clapped a hand on my shoulder and said, 'I'm sure you'll make us proud, Jake. I believe in you.'

'You believe in me because I'm all you have left,' I muttered. I didn't think he would hear me, but he did.

He said, 'You're not all I have left because your brother's gone. You're all I have left because you're my son.'

Easter came around quickly near the end of April. There was a party held at the most popular kid's house – obviously not my place. All the kids who went to my school pulled up at an old farm house and staked the land as our own. We filled truck beds with ice and loaded them with beer, which may or may not have been purchased illegally. Music blared from every car and echoed through the paddocks and thumped in my veins.

The air was getting cooler and a fog separated the pink sky and the black green grass of autumn. A boisterous guy named Clint strode up and said, 'Hey Billy Ray Cyrus.' I glared at him and waited for the next insult, but he shook my hand and said, 'It's about time you came out and partied instead of studying all weekend like a noob.'

'I didn't know I'd been invited to any parties.'

He replied, 'They're open-house parties, mate; anyone can come.'

Anyone did come. I was on my eighth beer and pretty much stumbling over my own feet, laughing at thin air, utterly wasted. Most of the night, I gravitated towards the only guy at school I actually liked – Johann Kuijpers, a fellow import to Australia from another land. I slapped him on the back and guffawed like a classic hillbilly. I happened to look up and Sanna was standing on the porch, watching me with cynicism.

In my drunken state, I slurred, 'Santa?' She looked at me with such dislike that I sobered up immediately, at least for a moment.

Johann giggled, 'Ho, ho, ho.'

I shoved him away. 'Get out of here, man; give us some space.' The word space seemed to shiver as it dove off my tongue like it was a high board, and drawled out in slow motion: spaaaaaaaace. Sometimes my accent echoed back even to me – a drawl amongst the mumbled shortened words of the Aussie accent.

Sanna retorted, 'No, that's okay – I'll leave you two boys alone.'

'Well, that's what you want but what about what I want?' I was drunk – I didn't have to make sense, right?

Sanna disguised a laugh and repeated, 'I'll leave you alone.' She turned to walk up the steps of the porch but stumbled, landing on the ground at my feet.

I pulled her up by the crook of her elbow. 'Are you okay?'

She winced and nodded. 'Yeah.' She waved her hand over her nose and cried, 'Pee yew. How many drinks have you had, Alco-breath?' She obviously couldn't smell her own. It was so drenched with whiskey that I was sure her mouth could have burst into flames.

I said, 'I'm eighteen so I can drink until I pass out. You're fifteen. What's your excuse?'

Sanna shoved me away, leaving my chest to ache. It occurred to me that drinking wasn't new to her. I stepped back with my hand at my chest, and I stared at her, and I really noticed her. Her eyes were weary and old. She had lost far too much weight in three weeks for it to be healthy. She looked like she was in agony somewhere on her body that I couldn't quite pinpoint.

I straightened my back, sobered up as best I could and said, 'We need to talk. Let's go.'

Sanna followed me inside the house and into a quiet little bedroom upstairs, away from everybody else and their wolf whistles. She looked around the room, picking things up and scouring the CD collection before she opened the window. She lit a joint and I couldn't help dropping my jaw. She glanced at me as she smoked and snorted, 'What?'

'What's happened to you?' I wished she was a stranger because then it wouldn't hurt so much to see her looking this way.

Sanna smoked in silence but shot me one hell of an angry glare.

I asked, 'Do you want to talk about it?'

'Talk about what, Jakey?'

I cringed at the nickname but answered, 'I want to talk about the fact that you're smoking and drinking, even though you're only fifteen.'

'Yeah, well, I don't feel only fifteen, *Dad*,' she snapped.

'It's not funny.'

She nodded and said, 'I know. You think I have a problem, but let me tell you: underage smoking and drinking is normal.'

'Well, it's not cool,' I mumbled as I sat on the bed.

'I'm not trying to be cool,' Sanna whispered as she sat down beside me. She sighed and lay flat on her back. I gingerly took the joint from her, surprised she allowed me to take it and put it out. She mumbled, closing her eyes, 'You just put me out.'

'You're not a joint.' I studied her condition. Her hip bones stuck out like wings.

She opened her eyes and explained, 'I burn like one.' She smiled and propped herself up on her elbows. 'How is Tessa?'

I looked down at my boots and said, 'Yeah, she left. Cheated on me.'

Sanna snorted and laughed loudly. 'I can't believe that girl.'

'Neither can I,' I mumbled, the betrayal hitting me harder in my drunken state. It felt too wrong to even be talking about her.

Sanna asked, 'What are you going to do?'

I swallowed hard. I'd been thinking about it a lot since Tessa said I had no idea. I did have ideas. At least, I was beginning to, thanks to Ms. Hollinday. Those ideas were coming.

'I want to go to university and become somebody.' I thought about a future without Alex and my face felt numb. Being abandoned by my closest friend on top of everything else felt too much, so I thought about my future at university, settling in and making myself into a new person, someone completely removed from the kid who lost his identical twin brother. I needed to find something to do other than being too tired. Find something worthwhile to do.

Sanna broke up my blurry drunk thoughts. 'That's good, Jake. That's really good.'

'Do you wanna talk to me about what you're feeling?' I asked, as I lay beside her.

She sighed. 'I don't feel anything, Jake.'

'Isn't that the problem?'

'No.' She chewed on her lip and I watched the way her teeth dug into the pale red lipstick, making it smear onto the white enamel of her teeth. She asked, 'Have you got another girlfriend yet?'

I shook my head. 'No.'

'You know I'm available, right.'

I looked at her with a frown.

She sighed. 'I'm not a little girl anymore...I'm all grown up.' She groaned and ran her fingers through her hair. 'Even though I hate it. I hate it. I don't want to grow up.'

I sighed. 'Growing up can't come quick enough. I hate being young. I just want to get on with my life and get out of here.'

Sanna's eyes darted all over my face. We were so different but I lay beside her with my head almost at her shoulder and I held her hand.

'It's not that bad here,' she murmured.

I snorted.

She continued, 'Older you get the more complicated things get and nothing is as complicated as how things are these days. I can't bear things getting any worse, Jake.'

'Well...I guess not.'

'Do you wanna know something about me, Jake?' she whispered.

'I want to know a lot of things about you, Sanna,' I replied quietly, touching her face.

'I only got into your car the day we met because I thought you were hot.'

I cracked up into manic laughter. I laughed so much that I ran out of air and had to cough and wheeze air back into my lungs. 'Thanks!' I gasped.

'I'm being truthful,' she said. 'I've always wanted to kiss you.'

I picked at the blanket beneath us. I said finally, 'You should, then. While we're young.'

Sanna leaned in and we kissed. It felt strange at first but she was so into it that I relaxed. It just felt good to forget about Tessa for a night.

I sighed and Sanna tucked her head onto my chest and fell asleep. I wrapped my arms around her and held her until the morning.

Sanna

April 2011

Jake was right. I shouldn't have been drinking. Each sip of my dad's whiskey helped the pain disappear, but mostly it made the pain worse because it reminded me why I was drinking in the first place. Whenever I drank, my head swam and for a moment my heart would lurch and I'd gasp for air. The disorientation reminded me of the way my vision had blurred that night and my body had shot up with Eddie's hands on me.

I clutched at my chest, convinced I was having a heart attack. I paced the room and watered down my dad's whiskey after a second sip. The second sip always quietened the panic. Dad would come inside and I'd have my backpack on my back and I'd be standing at the door, biting my lip.

'Ready to go to school?'

A nod, and I'd follow him out to the car. I had come to hate school. I had never really *liked* it, but sitting alone in science and having to have the teacher buddy me up with someone because I had no friends hurt more than I liked to admit.

This second term, I had homeroom with Michael, though. We had homeroom with our school house groups rather than year levels.

I sat in homeroom with him and he wittered on and on about how much fun he had camping with Celestial. The two of them were getting pretty serious. I didn't even know it could get much more serious than sleeping with each other before they'd even exchanged numbers, but I guess I couldn't understand. I didn't have Eddie's number either.

I thought of Eddie and I gasped. Vomit lurched up from my stomach. I made an ungraceful dive for a nearby sink – luckily our home room was the home economics classroom. My peers watched me with disgusted expressions and surprise. Michael held my hair back for me, reminding me of how we used to lay on the beach together. I wanted to cry.

'Are you okay?' he asked, looking a little green himself as he glanced at my chunky vomit in the sink. It burned bad because of the whiskey.

I wiped my mouth and turned on the tap to wash the vomit down the drain. The smell didn't disappear in a circle with it, though. I nodded and replied shakily, 'Thanks; I'm fine.'

Later during second period and a lecture on the reproductive system of the human female, the urge to vomit returned. My mouth tingled and watered so I sprinted down the steps and flew out into the corridor, vomiting spattering in my hands. There was no nausea. It just came soaring up from my gut and I couldn't hold it back. The teacher insisted I sit in the sick bay for a while until I felt better and let a girl named Karina sit with me.

'What do you think is wrong?' Karina asked.

'I'm just under the weather, I guess,' I insisted.

'Uh huh,' she mumbled. She leant closer to me and whispered, 'You're not pregnant, are you?'

I automatically replied, 'No.' I was still a virgin. Flawed, I know. I was getting used to wiping the night with Eddie from my memory, despite flashes continuously haunting me. Our encounter was getting clearer and clearer with time. My face, on the road, his power…I shuddered.

Karina noticed my expression and she giggled. 'Uh-oh…looks like you're remembering something.'

I shifted in my seat and waggled my finger at her. 'No. No. No. No uh-oh – I'm not pregnant – I can't be – I haven't even had sex, well, not *really*…'

'I saw you go upstairs with that American guy from the mainland, Sanna. Are you trying to tell me nothing happened with him? You were both drunk! Come on.' She snorted. 'No guy could hold back like that.'

I wanted to correct her and tell her that Jake wasn't like other guys. He was protective, good, brotherly, a dedicated friend and he hadn't taken advantage of me. But I thought again of Eddie and my heart beat at stilted pace for a moment and it made me dizzy. My shoulders slumped and Karina gave me a sympathetic smile.

'Hey…maybe you're right…maybe it's just the flu.'

'I don't think it's the flu,' I mumbled with numb lips.

'Mum,' I murmured, pressing my forehead against the cool glass of the Nissan Patrol as she drove me home from school. My voice was hoarse from vomiting and the glass cooled my face. 'How did you and Daddy meet?'

She smiled with the memory and replied, 'I came to Australia on a church group tour and he was a volunteer.'

I picked at a peeling spot on the interior door and asked, 'You never went home again?'

'Well, yes. I had to acquire my Visa and say goodbye to family and friends, but no, after that…I never went home again.'

'Why didn't you, though?' I pulled myself upright and imagined living away from my family and not being able to see Tamara or Michael again. I scowled with the realisation that I was already halfway there. Tamara was in the hospital, brain dead, thanks to me, and Michael was off with his girlfriend and probably wouldn't be my friend forever. Even Jake came to my mind and I pinched at the bridge of my nose, overcome with a sudden headache. I sighed. 'Your entire life was in Sweden – why did you uproot it just for a boy?'

'When you fall in love, Sanna, you will understand.'

'Well, didn't you ever want to go back?'

'I want to go back every day! I miss everything about Sweden – the lakes, the deer, the wildflowers, the snow and the people, and oh the language…'

'Then why haven't you ever gone back?' Roots and groundings seemed very important to me, which was a puzzling development. I couldn't imagine myself living in a different country, with a different climate and a different language. I thought of everything I was familiar with being removed from me and I couldn't breathe.

Mum thought for a moment before she replied carefully, 'Because once you leave a place, it's never home again.'

We pulled into our driveway and I said quickly, 'I have something to tell you but you have to promise not to tell Daddy.'

She looked at me sharply and asked, 'Tell him what?'

'Promise.'

We bounced in a pot hole before the Nissan Patrol rolled to a stop under the carport, shrouding us in grey shade. Mamma turned the car off and turned to me. 'I promise.'

I think I was raped. No, I was raped. I know I was raped. I was definitely raped. A boy held me down. No. A man held me down. I lost my pants. I ate dirt and he destroyed me. He raped me.

My throat made a squeaking sound and my mouth went dry and ached. *I can't admit this,* I thought..

I swallowed and whispered, 'I miss Tamara. I think I want to go see her again.' Familiarity. Grounding. Keep me ashore and stop me drowning.

Maybe it would be different if I saw Tamara again. Maybe she'd finally woken up and I could talk to her. It had been a while, after all.

As I followed the nurse and my mother through the hospital corridors, I was surprised we didn't go to the same place. I began to feel hopeful that I hadn't been completely wrong. We weren't going into the Intensive Care Unit anymore. Wasn't that a good thing?

Tamara was in a completely different wing of the hospital. She was in an acquired brain injury rehabilitation wing. Tamara's parents had told my mum that she was technically out of the coma, but she was still recovering, so still slept a lot.

It was quieter there than in the ICU. Dimmer lights and nurses spoke in slow, soft voices and looked up with hooded eyelids. My stomach fluttered as I placed one foot down at a time as though I was walking through mud. The corridors felt hollow and as if they were narrowing in me with their acrid scent of Dettol.

Tamara was in a room by herself, beside a window with drawn curtains. Beside the curtains there was a sofa and beside the bed was an armchair, making the room seem goadingly homely. Mum opened the curtains to allow the afternoon light to wash over Tamara, tucked up in the bed. Her freckles were paler.

'Can you leave us alone, Mum?' I asked. She looked as though she was going to argue so I said, 'Please.' She nodded and left the room, closing the door with a click.

I sank into the armchair, having to readjust my weight so I perched on its edge. My eyes went over the room. It was so different to the ICU. It was painted light blue and had photos on the wall. Huge photos. There was one of a pier and another of a pelican.

I reached out with a trembling hand to touch hers, expecting her to pull her hand away but she didn't move. I tucked my fingers around hers and held her hand like we were children skipping down the street. Her hand felt like a rubber glove and I wasted no time letting go of it again with a shudder. It was as though she was dead. I'd hoped there'd be something, a twitch, a squeeze...something that showed me that she knew I was there.

I took a deep breath. 'So...I'm finally here, Tee.'

About time, huh. I'm really sorry I ruined everything. I'm really, really sorry. I could say sorry a thousand times a day for the rest of my life and I'll still never forgive myself. I'm screwing up. I'm pushing people away and they just want to help. I'm so confused. I just wish I had you to talk to.

The words died in the back of my throat and I couldn't utter a thing.

I focused on my heart thumping and closed my eyes. I took her limp hand again and willed my heart to beat life through my hand into hers.

'I don't know how to tell my parents this...maybe you could help me.' I opened my eyes again and leant in to whisper in her ear. 'I was raped....and I think I'm going to have his baby.'

I sat back in the chair and put my hands to my mouth. I'd said it. I'd actually admitted it. Tamara lay, motionless in the bed. Supposedly out of her coma but in a deep sleep now. Had she heard me? Wasn't it a thing that coma patients could hear what you said? I shouldn't have said anything, I immediately thought. Tears sprung to my eyes and I wasn't sure if I was crying because of what I'd done to Tamara or for what had been done to me. I cursed to myself and left the room.

My heart raced, setting my pulse at a gallop as Mum drove us home from the hospital in silence. I knew I'd have to tell her. It wasn't like I could hide it. But the thought of Mum knowing what happened to me paralysed my tongue and sent my heart rate on its way to a personal best for highest ever.

It took me forty minutes to work up the courage to speak. I had to start at the beginning – the day everything had started to go wrong for me: the day I cut school to go surfing with Tamara and Eddie. I should have been safe at school. My parents obviously knew I hadn't been at school the day of the accident, and I loved them for never bringing it up and guilt-tripping me about my bad choices. Maybe they should have. Maybe I wouldn't have gone with Eddie that night. They didn't know I'd been pinned down, my mouth filling with dirt and gum leaves, twigs tangling in my hair as I attempted to roll over, clutching at my shorts but finding them gone. How that day had started out with my attempt to get back in the water, back to myself and who I was, but had ended in disaster.

My voice cracked as I admitted from the silence, 'I haven't surfed since the day Tamara almost died.'

My mum's eyebrows went up and her chin tilted. She whispered, 'But you go to the beach...you work in a surf shop.'

'I haven't surfed since that day.'

'That happened three months ago, Sanna.' I nodded as she said, 'You should have told us you were having trouble.' She pulled the car over on the side of the road and turned to look at me.

I blinked furiously and swallowed hard to stop myself from crying. I was shocked that it wasn't the fact this seemed to hurt my mother. I had been hurting for so long without telling her or Dad about it. I croaked, 'I feel dead, Mamma.' I couldn't hold back the tears anymore; they just burst out of me.

She reached over and we hugged.

I whispered into her shoulder, 'There's something I need you to do for me.'

'Anything, *älskling*,' crooned my mother, using the Swedish word for loved one, or darling.

'I need you to promise you'll still love me.' She looked at me with curiosity but I stared at my lap. I said quickly, 'I had sex.'

My mother looked like I had punched her in the stomach. I studied her and she stared out of the window.

'Michael?' she asked.

I shook my head and admitted, 'No.'

She nodded slowly. 'Talk to me. A promise is a promise.'

'I think...'

I stopped. Her eyes widened at me. I felt myself leaning away from her into the door.

'*Herregud*, you're pregnant.' Her hand flew to her mouth and the words made me gag.

Mum fluttered her hands and started to drive again, pushing too hard on the accelerator, making our heads jerk back. She shook her head. 'Sanna, I am so disappointed in you. Disgusting. I can't believe you would make such bad choices. You're still a child. You're FIFTEEN.'

Exactly. I was fifteen. I stayed silent on the way home. What could I say? If I admitted to her that I was raped, I'd make her feel bad for judging me. So, I stayed quiet, fiddling with my jacket zipper.

'We need you to take a test.' She drove to the pharmacy and bought one. We took it home where Dad was waiting. Mum ushered me into the hallway, and opened the bathroom door. She demanded, 'Now.' My face burned with humiliation. Dad looked at both of us with confusion. I went into the bathroom and Mum followed. She shut the door in his face.

'What's going on?' he called.

'We'll be out in a minute,' she replied, unwrapping the packaging on the home pregnancy test. She held it out for me to take, which I did with trembling hands. It was an alien object, light plastic and small but it felt huge in my hands. I stared at it for a long minute and my mother turned her back to me.

'Are you serious? You're going to be in here while I do it?' I asked.

'Just get it over with.'

I could have died with embarrassment. I heaved a nervous sigh as I buttoned my jeans back up, holding the stick in the one hand and my buttons in the other. My mother snatched it from me so roughly that I hoped it would snap. After two minutes, she stared down at the result and then looked at me with a ghastly, horrified expression. 'Oh, Sanna…'

I stared at the little lines and my eyes filled with tears. 'No, no, no, no, no. It's wrong – it has to be wrong.'

'We'll have to take you to the doctor – he'll do a pelvic exam and a blood test.'

'What's going on?' called my dad from outside the door, his voice full of concern.

I rushed to the door and flung it open. I pushed past him and ran outside and into our paddocks. I reached the windmill in the back paddock before I stopped running. I stared up at it, gasping for air. Then I bawled my eyes out. I screamed. I stamped my feet but no tantrum that I could throw at God would undo what had been done.

Dad followed me, his shoulders up around his ears and his face as red as a fire hydrant.

'How could you do this? You've sinned beyond belief!' he bellowed and I sobbed into my hands. He threw his hat down. 'I can't believe you've been so stupid, Sanna!'

'I'll get an abortion!' I wailed.

He slapped me across the face so hard I fell back onto my butt and gaped up at him in disbelief. He'd never hit me in his life. His lip disappeared behind his teeth and his eyes watered as he clenched his fists. His voice cracked as he cried, 'You've already let me down; don't you dare murder that baby.'

I sniffed and looked at my shaking hands. Dad started crying and turned away and it felt like I'd been dropped from a tall building.

'Daddy, I...'

I held up a hand. 'Don't. Sanna, I can't...I can't even listen to you right now. Just go. Go stay with Michael tonight or something. I can't talk to you. I can't even look at you.' He walked away, leaving me in the paddock under the creaking and whining windmill.

Jake

April 30 2011

She called me six times. Tessa never called me but Sanna called six times in the span of five minutes. I was taking Rio for a chilled-out style of ride through the paddocks. When I finished and hung up my boots, I checked my phone. I had missed every single call from Sanna. I called her back as I stretched out on top of my bed, crumpling my English notes: welcome to the final year of high school Jake Ryan.

She didn't even say "hi". 'Jake, I've been trying to call you!'

I tugged my notes out from under me and said, 'I'm very well, thanks. How are you?'

'I don't have time for this, Jake. I need to see you,' she said quickly.

I blew out a sigh. How could I let her down? I knew lying on the bed with her that night at the party would be a mistake but we'd both needed it at the time. 'I don't think that's a good idea, Sanna.'

'You don't understand, Jake,' she replied with frustration, 'I need to see you.'

I sighed and gave in. 'Okay, okay. When?'

'Now.'

It was getting a little strange. 'Do you want me to come and pick you up?'

'Yes,' she answered. 'Now.' She hung up abruptly. I stared at the wall for a minute and then I stared at my notes – maybe I could rewrite them and procrastinate. I guess I couldn't really use that as a valid excuse though: sorry I was late; I had to rewrite my already really, really neat notes.

My mother met me at the door as I was about to leave. 'Where are you going, Jake? I'm about to serve up dinner.'

I pulled my boots back on, wishing I could just stay home. I replied, 'A friend of mine called and they sounded pretty weird so I'm going to go find out what's up – but then I'll be back, Mom.'

She smiled and said fondly, 'You're such a good friend, Jake.' She gave me a peck on the cheek and added, 'You're a good boy.' This kind of attention – affection – coming from my mother was still new to me and still made me uncomfortable. I loved her for trying but I could still feel the hollow pit in my stomach from all the times she had looked right through me as though I wasn't alive. She'd been trying lately since she knew I was trying to do well at school.

I muttered, 'Thanks, Mom,' and made a beeline for the exit.

I pulled into Sanna's driveway and had to brake hard because she was standing in the driveway, toting a backpack and a suitcase. She threw the suitcase into the bed and climbed into the passenger seat, removing the backpack as she did so. I stared at her and asked, 'And where are you taking a trip to? I didn't realize I was your chauffeur service.'

'I'm running away, Jake.' She sniffed. 'My dad doesn't want me living here anymore.' Her lip trembled and she moaned, 'I don't think he loves me anymore.'

I put the truck into park and turned off the engine. 'Wanna talk about it?'

'Not here,' she said. 'Take me somewhere else.'

I nodded. 'Okay, let's go.'

I drove her further down the straight stretch of narrow road to the waterfront part of Rhyll. I parked outside the boat yard, near the Yacht Club, and we sat inside the truck looking out over the calm stretch of water of Westernport Bay. It looked more like a lake – it was so still. Fishing boats out on the water were harangued by pelicans and seagulls. Sanna didn't say a word but I could see her mind running over with thoughts.

'Are you doing all right?' I asked, just to get her talking.

She snorted and exclaimed, 'Of course I'm not doing all right, Jake! God!'

'Sorry,' I muttered and added, 'I meant: are you in some sort of trouble?'

'I'm in a lot of trouble, Jake,' she answered. I was thinking that most likely her dad had found out about her drinking and they'd had an argument, leading him to suggest maybe visiting a shrink or something. I'd wanted to say all those things to my father. *Get out of our house and go to a doctor to get help; you're giving us more trouble than we need and you need to leave; Get out, we hate your drinking habit.*

The mid-fall sky was clouding up with cobalt and the air outside seemed to steam. It looked like it was going to be the last fine day before winter grey and winter rain set in. The window fogged up and blocked my view. I wound down my window to get it to de-fog. I was feeling claustrophobic not being able to see the world outside.

I waited for Sanna to explain what was going on, but she only squirmed in her seat. I burst out laughing.

'Why are you laughing, Jake?' she asked quietly.

'I don't know,' I replied with tears in my eyes and a burning belly. 'I don't understand you sometimes, kid.'

'I'm not a kid.'

'You're a kid,' I sighed.

Her eyes brimmed with tears and she choked out, 'Not anymore.'

It started to rain. I could hear the stormy heavy rain droplets thudding all around us and slowly I understood. I stared outside at the storm and felt like the storm of my life was beginning along with it.

'What are you talking about, Sanna?' I asked but my voice cracked.

She covered her face with her hands and moaned, 'The one time I had sex – and I didn't even want to – this happens to me. Now I'm stuck with it.'

I looked at her with narrowed eyes. 'Are you...' I tried be relaxed by clutching the bar above the window, and taking a few wheezy breaths. 'Are you...'

Sanna glared at me between her fingers and I swallowed a hard lump of dread. She dropped her hands and sighed, somehow finding a composure that was still hidden to me while I tried not to have a panic attack on her behalf. She said, 'I have to go to the doctor...then I can know for sure.'

I nodded and murmured, 'Okay.'

'I'm sorry I called you, Jake...but you're the only one that knows about what happened to me.'

'It's okay, Sanna. Don't apologize...I've got you.'

We sat there watching the storm for a while before we drove to the nearest medical centre. Sanna had all these undesirable connotations thrust upon her by her family and the guy that had done it? Free as a bird and living his best life and it made my teeth hurt.

Walking into the medical centre with Sanna through the sheeting rain of the fall storm, I felt like I had gone forward a few leaps into adulthood that I hadn't expected to. It was like I was looking back over my shoulder calling out *wait, I shouldn't be exposed to this much yet, I think I missed a few turns and now I'm a bit lost and stunned in a completely unexpected, strange town...*

The morning after Alex died was strong in my memory. Knowing that life would never be the same.

After I took Sanna to the doctor where they confirmed she was pregnant, I took her to the pub near my place. I bought her everything she wanted, including a succulent side dish of ice cream, nuts, banana, strawberries, brownies and fudge. She ate it with silent tears rolling down her cheeks.

'I'm sorry, Sanna,' I mumbled, fiddling with the straw to my cola. I craved root beer but places here in Australia never had it.

'You're sorry?' Sanna echoed; her voice hollow and miserable.

'About all this,' I explained. 'I'll do whatever I can for you.'

She crossed her arms and uncrossed them. She crossed her legs and uncrossed them. A sound escaped her lips but she didn't say anything for a while. I waited. Man, this really sucked. Finally, she whispered, 'You don't have to be sorry. You saved my life. Who knows what would have happened if you hadn't been there?'

I shivered and felt the lights of the pub hitting me in the eyes. I squinted at the light that was suddenly too bright. *Jake Ryan, the guy who saves people just a bit too late.*

Sanna came back with me to my place to stay the night. I set her up in the barn on the horse blankets on the floor, just as I used to do for Tessa. I laughed a little as I sat down with her, taking off my boots.

'What is it?' she smiled.

'I used to stay here with Tessa. Trying to keep her a secret...It felt so dirty and fun...' I looked around at the rafters and sighed. 'Funny how things change.'

She paused and then said, 'You're still hoping she'll come back to you, aren't you.'

'She's not coming back.' I sighed. A part of me was really hoping that she would come back and another part of me was literally waiting for her to come back. I wasn't used to people leaving. If they didn't die, they could always come back. I felt guilty for wanting Tessa's dreams to die, so long as she would come back to be with me.

'It's okay to hope that she still loves you,' said Sanna.

'She never loved me,' I said. 'If she had, there'd be no way she could have left me.'

'Loving and leaving aren't on completely different ends of the scale, Jake,' she said, with a slow blink. 'I just left my parents – it doesn't mean that I don't love them...even though they don't love me.'

'They still love you.' I held her hand. Her face crumpled and she cried. Seeing her mourn for her life this way and thinking about how she'd ended up in this position make my head throb and my neck stiffen up. She shouldn't have felt ashamed. She shouldn't have felt like she had made a mistake. Her parents needed to support her. If they weren't going to, I would.

I swallowed hard and took a deep breath. 'Tell them it was me.'

Sanna stopped crying and gaped at me. 'What?'

'Your mom and dad...if you don't want to tell them the truth about what happened...It's okay if you...tell them it was me – that I'm the father. I'll look after you.'

She was silent until she murmured, 'You're the father...' into the dark. She mumbled it again as though trying to convince herself. I squeezed her hand and I shut my eyes firmly.

May 2011

April disappeared overnight. In the morning, the dew on the grass crunched under my feet. I gripped Sanna's hand as I led her from the barn, where we had slept, to the house. I hoped she'd think through the offer I'd made the night before. If she told her parents I'd look after her, she wouldn't be kicked out of home and she could hide the fact that she had been raped. Until she was ready.

As we walked inside my house, a sense of hope filled my soul. Maybe it would all be all right. Laughter came from the kitchen.

I gripped Sanna's hand and said, 'Come on; let's do this.' My folks were sitting at the kitchen table, picking at bacon, eggs and sausages, laughing at each other as they ate. They looked up as Sanna went very pale, gagged, and dived for the sink. She vomited with her back heaving. Fantastic.

My mother rushed to her side to nurse her better but Dad remained sitting at the table, his eyes on my mother's hands as they made small, smoothing circles on Sanna's convulsing back.

After a glass of water, Sanna seemed better but my mother forced her to sit down at the table beside my dad who eyed her warily in case she threw up again. My mother looked to me – I was still standing shell-shocked in the doorway. She snapped, 'Jake, don't just stand there. Go get me a damp wash cloth from the bathroom.' I nodded and turned. My mother added, 'Also, grab one of my shirts for your friend.'

I did as I was told. I went to my parents' bedroom and opened my mother's bottom drawer to grab one of her blouses. Inside I found a photograph of a baby – one of those tacky professional ones that you get done for $9.99 at the mall. My brain recognized the juvenile and my stomach lurched with the realization that I soon would be pushing a stroller through a mass of people in a mall, my life's purpose to get my baby's photo taken on a lamb's wool blanket for $9.99.

I squinted at the photograph and wondered if it was me or Alex. We had looked so much alike in our younger days that even we couldn't tell each other apart when we had looked at our old baby photos. I decided I would ask Mom so I took the photo with me into the kitchen along with the blouse and the damp wash cloth.

Sanna smiled at me as I handed her the blouse and the wash cloth, seeking support, but I ignored her and looked only at my mother. She was rinsing the sink.

'I found this.' I held up the photograph.

My dad looked at it and turned away with his shoulders hunched. He hissed, 'You told me that you threw them all away.'

My mother's mouth open and closed before she said, 'I couldn't; I needed to keep it.'

I peered into the baby's big blue eyes, ignoring the tension between my parents. I asked, 'Is it me or Alex?'

'It's Derek, Jake,' Dad replied.

I frowned. 'Who's Derek?'

'He was our first born...He died before you and Alex were born,' Dad explained. I looked at Mom and noticed the dullness of her skin, the wrinkles around her eyes. There had been a baby before me and Alex. If there were any more revelations that week, I was pretty sure I would need a stint in a mental asylum.

I gripped the photograph tighter, its edges crushing beneath my fingers. 'How'd he die?'

'He had a brain tumor...didn't even make it to his first birthday,' Mom said weakly.

I stared at Dad and asked, 'Why would you make her to throw all the pictures away – Alex's pictures, too?'

He casually sipped at his coffee and replied, 'Because they're gone – I don't want to see their faces anymore.'

'You don't want to remember them.' Sadness washed over me like a cold bucket of water.

'We all grieve in different ways, Jake,' my mother mumbled. I knew she was right. I knew everybody dealt with loss, success, happiness, joy, depression, addiction and parenthood all differently. I remembered Sanna was in the room. I had planned on announcing the pregnancy, but now didn't seem like the right time. The words formed in my brain "we're going to have a baby"; I opened my mouth but my eyes fell onto the baby face again: we had been babies. We had been babies so recently that it felt impossible that I would become a parent so soon.

I handed the photograph to my mother and wiped my sweaty hands down the front of my jeans. 'I, um…I need to take a shower,' I announced instead.

My mother said, 'Oh, Jake, consider your poor friend here.'

Sanna said, 'Oh, thank you, I'm fine, really. The sickness just hits me but it passes quickly. Besides, Jake and I are only acquaintances.'

I rolled my eyes and corrected her, 'We're dating.'

My parents looked confused and Dad asked, 'What happened to Tessa?'

'Another time, Dad,' I said through gritted teeth, refusing to look at the shocked look on Sanna's face. No, I hadn't told my parents that Tessa had dumped me.

My mother, realising my father's rudeness, chirped to Sanna, 'We're very happy to meet you, sweetheart.'

Sanna smiled graciously. My dad grinned. 'Well, you've caught yourself a big fish here, girl. Our Jakey is going to university to become a doctor or something flash like that.'

'Dad,' I warned.

'What's your name, honey?' asked my mother.

'Her name is Sanna,' I mumbled, leaning against the bench. I wrinkled my nose as the odor of vomit finally reached my nostrils.

'Suzanna?' asked my mother.

'No, Sanna,' corrected Sanna. 'But you can call me Suzanna if you find it easier to say.'

'I'll call you Suzie, is that all right?' Sanna nodded and they immediately became the best of buddies. It was awkward seeing them bond so quickly. My mother latched on to Sanna, which was a good thing, yet as I watched her speaking easily with my mother when I couldn't get many words from her, my throat narrowed. I couldn't share such affection with either of my parents since Alex had died.

My dad finished his coffee with a long gulp and said, 'Well, anyway, I've got to run into town to the feed store before church. Would anybody like to join me?' He looked at me pointedly.

'Jake, go with your father and help him carry the bags. Suzie can stay here and have a shower. We'll keep one another company until you get back.' My mother was already eager to have a girl-to-girl-chat with Sanna.

I looked at Sanna for confirmation and she said, 'I like that idea,' so I shrugged and said to my dad, 'Okay, let's go.'

We took my truck but Dad drove. As we turned out onto the dirt road, he said without even looking at me, 'She's pregnant, ain't she?'

I stared at him but he merely glanced at me. So that was why he had reminded Sanna of my "bright future."

I asked with a little bit of a surprised scoff, 'How the hell did you know?'

'Son, I saw your mother through two pregnancies – I can read the symptoms.'

'Oh,' I muttered.

'Is it yours?' he asked just for "good measure" and probably a bit of hope. I nodded. 'Are you sure?' he pushed.

'Pretty sure,' I mumbled, not sure if I should be taking the out while I still had it or going along with it.

My dad shook his head and muttered, 'You're a gosh darn idjit, boy, a gosh darn idjit.'

Sanna

May 2011

I liked Jake's mum. She was very nice to me. She started to clear the table of the breakfast dishes and put the photograph of Jake's brother on the table in front of me. I gazed at the baby boy. I wondered what my baby would look like. Would it have that flat nose that Eddie had and would it be evil like him? I tried to picture a baby that Jake would father and what it would look like. Brown hair, green eyes. A small mouth and a narrow jaw. It would look like this baby in the photo, I decided. I said, 'He's so cute. Tell me about him.'

Jake's mum grimaced but replied, 'His name was Derek William. He was only a couple of months old when this picture was taken...Not long after that,' she sighed, 'I thought he was acting a little funny. I couldn't describe it to Will or even to a doctor. They all thought I had that post-natal depression.' She smiled grimly. 'A mother just knows, Suzie. One day he couldn't sit up. I took him to the doctor...and they agreed to do some tests.' She cleared her throat. 'The doctor was "very, very sorry".' She looked me in the eye and I thought I could see a layer of tears that refused to fall. 'He was ten months old when he died. We were very sad about that.' She sat down opposite me with a handful of tissues. 'I don't think my husband believes that I ever got over him, even when Jake and Alex were born.'

My throat was closing and I started crying. I sniffed and wiped my running nose on a tissue Jake's mum handed me. 'I'm so sorry,' I said. My eyes felt like they had been sandpapered. I'd never cried so much over a stranger before.

'Did you know that Jake used to have a twin brother?' she asked.

I nodded. 'I know he died before you all moved here to Australia. I'm so sorry.'

'Alexander James. He was Jake's twin brother; three minutes older.' She smiled as she said, 'They were identical but they were nothing alike; not really, not to me.'

'Losing two sons must be so hard,' I whispered, thinking of the fetus growing in my womb. An alien in a strange land, unwelcome right now.

Jake's mum's eyes narrowed at me and she took hold of my clammy hand and said, 'I never had a daughter. I am so happy that Jake has brought you here for me to meet. I didn't get to meet the last girl he dated.'

'Jake and I aren't really dating,' I admitted. 'I think he only said that so you wouldn't hate me.'

'Why would I hate you, honey?' she asked, withdrawing her hand from mine.

I bit my lip as I bit the bullet with a deep breath. 'I'm pregnant – we're pregnant.'

'Jake is going to be a father?' She gasped when I nodded. 'You have to get married.'

I sputtered and croaked, 'I don't think Jake has that in mind.'

'You can't live in sin!'

Why the hell did I always have to be "in sin"? I couldn't stop my eyes welling up with tears of self-pity. Jake's mum wrapped me in an axe-swinging strength hug. 'Jake would love to marry you, Suzie. Now, let's get you cleaned up.'

She ushered me off to have a shower in Jake's slimy ensuite. I stood there in the shower, completely naked and stared down at the part of my stomach that was already swollen. The mark of the devil. Maybe I was imagining it. I ran my hands along the ill-kept grouting and watched the black bits of mold spiral around my toes before diving down the plughole. I stared at my toes and started to zone out.

I readjusted the bracelet that I had gotten with Tamara at Bells Beach as the water went cold. I stayed in the shower a little longer. The cold water reminded me of surfing. I used to surf until I was shivering through my steamer. How could I have loved doing something so much and then not do it anymore? Oh yeah...the accident...and that awful cold fear that rested in my chest whenever I went to the beach, unless I was with Michael. I wondered what he was doing so I turned the water off and got out of the shower.

I sat on the closed lid of the toilet, naked and letting the water drip all over the floor as I put my mobile phone to my ear as to call Michael. We weren't even speaking but I wanted him to know. It rang out and went to the message bank so I left him a message.

'Hey, Michael, it's me...Sanna...um...I'm in a bit of trouble.' The tears were coming again and I knew I sounded shaky as I said, 'I'm pregnant. I, um...my dad kicked me out...well, no, not really...I couldn't take him yelling at me anymore so I just left. Ha,' I coughed out a barking kind of laugh and said, 'Anyway, I'm staying with the guy I um...I guess he's kind of my boyfriend...but I don't know...we don't know each other too well so that's why I feel so crap about it.

Anyway, I guess I'll talk to you at school...and if you tell anybody about this, I will not hesitate to kick you in the face!

Okay, um...gotta go...see ya...' I hung up and looked at the background photo of me and Michael posing together like stoners and I burst into tears.

Jake's mum sat me down in the hot living room with a glass of homemade lemonade. It tasted dreadful but she insisted that it would help with my morning sickness. She gave me a sideways look as she asked casually, 'How old are you, Suzie?' It sounded casual but I knew what she was thinking. I was jail-bait.

'I'm fifteen,' I replied, sweat beads popping up on my forehead despite the cool morning.

'Do you have a job?' she asked.

I swallowed the lemonade with a forceful gulp, disguised a grimace and said, 'I have a part-time job at a surf shop, over on Phillip Island.'

'Will they allow you to work there when you begin to show?' she asked with a critical tone in her voice and a raised eyebrow.

I hesitated. Surfing had a particular image. Right now, I suited that image fine, but in a few months, when my belly expanded and my hands and feet would swell up, would I still be accepted into the world of six-pack-abs and suntans? 'I don't know,' I admitted. 'But if they fire me, that's unfair dismissal and I could sue them.'

'They'd find a different reason to fire you, Suzie,' she told me gently. 'Trust me; I tried to work at a refrigerator store when I was pregnant with my first boy, Derek. It doesn't work.' There was heavy lifting involved in a refrigerator store job but I kept my mouth shut. I was relieved that she had given me the benefit of the doubt after I revealed The Big Sin and admitted to being a Hell-deserving-cretin.

Jake and his dad, Will, came back about an hour later. Will cleared his throat and announced, 'Isabel, I'd like to go for a walk with you outside.' Jake's mum's name was Isabel. I felt ridiculously rude for not even asking when she had asked me so many questions. She stood up and allowed her husband to take her outside.

Jake replaced his mother's position in the creaky armchair that desperately needed restoring. He leaned forward, placing his elbows on his legs, which were set wide apart. He asked, 'How are you coping?'

I nodded and replied, 'Just fine.'

Jake raised his eyebrows and said with surprise, 'Wow, just fine.' He grinned and we both giggled. 'So, you told her?'

'I told her,' I admitted.

Jake said, 'My dad knows, too. I think he knew as soon you puked.' He sighed. 'He might be a drunk but he's really switched on; sometimes it scares me.'

I said quietly, 'I didn't know your dad was an alcoholic.'

'You didn't know that? I thought I told you that.'

'You don't tell me anything, remember?'

He removed his baseball cap and wrung it in his hands. He said, 'I'm taking a dive here but I don't usually take my father's advice, but he is a smart man. I don't like it but I believe that I want the best for you.'

I smiled, my cheeks blushing then burning.

Jake carried on. 'Of course, you are too young for what my father suggested we do…' he paused before he added 'but if there's a promise, we can wait and we'll be fine…your parents won't disown you.'

'What is this plan?'

He skidded down onto his knees before me and took my hand. 'We get engaged.'

'What?' He was out of his mind.

'This will work,' he insisted. 'We're friends, right? What's better than to be engaged to your friend?'

'How about marrying your soul mate?' I snapped.

'Maybe I'm not your soul mate, but I am all that you have,' he replied quietly. 'And you're all I have.'

Oh dear, Jesus. What else could I do but try to believe him? My lip trembled. 'Okay.'

Jake nodded. 'Good.' He leaned upwards and kissed my sweaty forehead.

I mumbled, 'We have to go tell my parents.'

He stood up and paced the room again. He was close to breaking his baseball hat with his ferocious wringing. He muttered, 'Well, this should be interesting.'

We headed out there later in the morning, just before lunch. Mum made us all sweet tea, served with *Kardemummabullar* (Swedish cardamom and cinnamon buns). Jake tasted one tentatively but then he ended up eating six of them, licking his fingers after each one to get all the pearl sugar off. Dad glowered at us from the other side of the living room. He refused to switch the football off.

'Um,' I said with hesitation. 'Jake is the dad...and we are engaged.'

'A shotgun wedding, perfect,' snapped Dad. 'You think that makes it all right for spitting in the face of our Lord?' He rubbed so hard at the flesh on his face that it looked like he just wanted to peel it off.

Jake cleared his throat but stayed quiet.

Mum held Dad's hand and I saw her squeeze it pointedly. He looked at both of us before he said, 'Well, I s'pose it's better than nothing.' I couldn't once look him in the eye while we sat in the living room together.

'Can I come back home, Daddy?'

He nodded and got up to leave. I breathed a sigh of relief but I trembled all over.

Mum got up and handed me a glass of water. She smiled. 'It's okay, Sanna. We forgive you.'

We forgive you? I wanted so much to smash the glass of water on the coffee table and scream until I ran out of air and collapsed on the floor. Why did I need their forgiveness? What did I have to be forgiven for? Something had happened to me – it wasn't me that needed forgiving. I breathed sharply in through my nose and clutched the couch arm so tightly that my nails snapped. It had happened to me. It was MY TRAUMA. My mother sitting there and telling me that she and my father had forgiven me for being a rape victim made me shudder. I raised the glass and drank the entire glass of water to stay silent. I burped and earned a reproachful glare from my mother. Jake placed his hand on top of mine and grimaced. At least I could live at home, right?

I went to school the next day and somehow everybody had got the news. It has spread through church and then it reached school. The rumour was that Sanna Smith had been knocked up and my parents were seriously considering sending her to a nunnery – too bad I was Christian and not Catholic.

People seemed to give me a wider berth than usual, as if I was sick. My favourite teacher pursed her lips and wouldn't look me in the eye when she handed my French project back: C-, the lowest score I'd received all year. The teachers had all been giving me "soft" grades because of what had happened to Tamara. I'd stopped studying, but now we were in a completely new term, their sympathy seemed to have worn off. I stared at the C- with disappointment. I hoped it wasn't because I was pregnant, but deep down I knew it was because I'd slacked off.

Friday afternoon, I arrived at work and found Ms. Kelly manning the store and telling me, 'Sanna, I don't need you in today.'

'Why not?' I asked, my hand still on the store door.

Her nose wrinkled as if she could smell something bad as she told me, 'I thought you would have morning sickness or something.' She narrowed her eyes at me as she said, 'You can go home. Come back when you feel better.'

'But I feel fine.'

Ms. Kelly didn't budge and neither did I for almost a minute. Until my face screwed up and my eyes leaked. I liked my job and the boss showing up and banning me hurt more than I liked to admit. I turned on my heel and left quickly before she could see that she had made the emotional, hormonal, pregnant teenager cry.

Outside, I sat on the gutter and sobbed, feeling sorry for myself. My dad had dropped me off – he was slowly returning back to his affectionate old self but I didn't want to cross him. He was already gone and I didn't want to annoy him by calling him and asking him to come straight back. So, I pulled out my phone and called Jake. He was my fiancé after all; surely, he would come get me. But he couldn't. He had an appointment with the careers officer at his school, but he did promise to call somebody to come and get me.

Half an hour later, Will pulled up in Isabel's beaten-up old Corolla. He got out of the car and offered me a hand before I even recognised him. He looked shy and uncomfortable, and I related. I took his dirty, calloused hand and allowed him to pull me up. He was the perfect gentleman, opening the car door and helping me with the stiff, unrelenting seatbelt. The car was so old that the seat creaked beneath me, the springs dreaming of their former youth and elasticity. Will sat in the driver's seat and asked, 'Do you want to talk about it?'

I started to cry all over again until I rolled my shoulders and said, 'I hate this.'

He nodded. 'That's okay. You're allowed to. It's a big deal.'

I sighed and knew that it was silly to be so upset. I hadn't been fired or something like that. Ms. Kelly had literally just covered my shift for me. That wasn't so bad, but it felt like I'd been shoved aside. I said, 'Thanks for getting me.'

'Will you be all right?'

'Oh, I'll be fine.'

He raised the corner of his mouth into a crooked smile that only hid half of his chipped teeth. 'So, you feel up to comin' to Jake's party tonight, then?'

I asked, 'What party?'

'Tonight, at our house. He said it was his turn to host for all his friends.' Will changed gears, causing the car to growl and vibrate under my feet as we picked up speed along Phillip Island Road. 'I can wait while you get changed, you know, doll yerself up and get yer hair all pretty and whatnot.'

'Whatnot?' I couldn't help giggling.

He laughed too. 'Sorry. I don't know what girls do.'

I smiled and replied 'That's okay. I'd love to come to the party. I'm sure Jake just forgot to tell me. That's all.'

Will glanced at me as if he didn't want me to notice. I directed him to my house and went home to "doll" myself up and hoped Jake wouldn't mind me gate crashing his party.

Jake

May 2011

I wiped my muddy boots on the doormat, juggling two twenty-four packs of cola and a case of beer. I bumped into Mom as I walked into the cramped kitchen. 'Sorry, Mom.'

She opened the lid on our mega-sized cooler, or *esky*. She had packed it full of ice. As I filled it with the drinks, I asked, 'Where did you get all this ice?'

'Your dad picked it up from a gas station in San Remo,' she answered. The strap on her dress was coming loose and kept falling off her shoulder. She continuously had to swipe at it to correct it. 'On his way back from getting Suzie.' She looked me up and down. 'Whom you forgot to invite.'

My stomach tightened a little and I leaned back against the doorframe. I hadn't invited Sanna. I knew it was a jerk move, but part of me knew that I didn't want her around the guys from school. We were in two separate worlds. What I'd offered to do for her felt so far away from the guys and trying to study to get out of here. I busied myself with fixing the drinks in the esky, but my hands were heavy with responsibility, and I let them sink into the ice.

'I'm not off to a very good start with Sanna, am I?' My knuckles ached from the cold but I deserved each throb. I was already regretting doing what I had done. It wasn't supposed to be the end of my life. It was only meant to help Sanna get back to her parents and feel okay enough to keep going.

'I can see that.' Mom turned her back on me and scrubbed the bench top. She threw the sponge down and walked away, mumbling, 'I've raised a jerk.'

It hadn't been my idea to get engaged. It wasn't supposed to be that permanent. I was supposed to be the absent teenage boyfriend that still had the freedom to go on with his life. Dad had talked me into it at the feed store. Said I had to be responsible. A good man. As if I could let her be a single mom at fifteen. I had hoped it would just ease the tension between Sanna and her parents. Then she would come to her senses and adopt the baby out or something. Having to actually step up and be there in the marital sense made my neck cramp. I just wanted to live my life. Too late now.

I winced as I pulled my hands out of the ice, turning them over and studying my red knuckles.

In the quiet house, I heard Sanna laugh from the patio out the back. I followed the sound to the window. She was standing there, with my father, chatting easily.

'I don't know what I want to do when I finish school, but I know I definitely wasn't expecting to have a baby.' She laughed, but it was too high-pitched and short-lived to be genuine. Forced.

My dad asked, 'Where are your folks from originally? Your name's a bit different from all the names around here.'

'My dad's from right here.'

'Right,' said Dad.

'But my mum moved here from Sweden when she met Dad on some church tour,' she explained.

'Whereabouts in Sweden?'

'Dalarna. It's kind of in the middle, but I think it borders on Norway, too.'

'Your folks are pretty Christian, eh?' said Dad. Sanna didn't answer but I imagined her nodding. Dad asked, 'How did you and Jake meet?'

'Didn't Jake tell you?' she asked with unchecked sadness.

Don't tell him how we met. Keep that between us. Special. Keep that day special.

'Jake likes to keep things inside his head. Doctors told us that it was normal for somebody who has lost somebody so close to them. He doesn't mean to shut everyone out – he can't help it. He comes around eventually and spills his guts.' It felt as if I was floating sideways. There was my alcoholic father telling Sanna about my problems. It should have made me mad, I guess, but I just wanted to hear her response.

'I can't help but take it personally.'

'Some things you can take personally, Suzie,' said Dad. 'Believe me. Just because my son has the communication skills of a sloth doesn't mean that you can let him go leavin' you out of things.'

'Like this party?' she said.

'Like this party that he didn't tell you squat about,' he concurred. The subject shifted back. 'So, tell me about how you and ol' Jakey-Cakes met.'

Sanna replied, 'On a beach…he was wearing a baseball cap.'

My dad laughed. 'Details are important.'

She laughed too, hiding pain again. I waited for her to tell him all the real details, but she didn't.

'Do you love him?'

'…I would if he'd let me.'

The guys soon came around but nothing much happened. It went from party to get-together pretty quickly. The football was on the TV and the guys all sat glued to it, as I sat nearby, wishing we could just hang out properly instead of watching meatheads wrestle each other and kicking an oblong-ball between tall poles. Sanna introduced herself but didn't mention the pregnancy, or even the relationship.

Johann poked me in the ribs. 'She's cute.'

I shoved him. 'Shut up.'

He had a point. Sanna was cute. She was a pretty girl underneath that low self-esteem. Sunkissed, blonde, big blue eyes, small mouth, round face. After she introduced herself to the guys and they asked her zero questions – oh, the conversation skills of my friends – she moved into the kitchen to hang out with my mom instead. I found myself straining to hear their conversation. I wanted to hear her talk about her life and who she was. I only ever seemed to see her at her worst moments. I wanted to know her when she wasn't almost being running for her life or accidentally giving her best friend a head injury. Who was Sanna without all that salt making her skin rough to touch?

She hated school, but was eager to learn. She loved animals, but feared them. She liked to fit in, but didn't want to be like everyone else. She was trying to love me but she didn't know me…I wouldn't let her.

Letting her in was difficult. Knowing that we were unofficially engaged made it harder. There was this immense pressure that I had to be in love with her, and the more I tried to fall for her, the further I recoiled at the thought. Every time she looked at me, I wanted to tell her 'I love you' but I discovered that if I thought it was hard to say those three little words – it was even harder to say the four: I *don't* love you.

Once everyone left the party, Sanna lingered by the front door. I scratched at the back of my neck, then tucked my hands behind me, squeezing them between myself and the wall.

Sanna nodded and pursed her lips. 'Good time?'

I scoffed. 'Not really.'

'You didn't invite me, Jake.'

'I'm sorry.'

We stood there in silence for a moment before Dad walked in from outside. 'You taking Sanna home?'

I nodded.

Sanna grabbed his hand and he stopped mid-step and blinked at her. She said, 'Thanks, Will. I really appreciate you bringing me.'

He pulled her into a hug and his eyes hit mine before I looked down. I had to do better. I led Sanna out to my truck and we drove back over to the island.

I asked, 'Do you want to go straight home or are you up to hanging out a bit?'

She smiled. 'I thought you'd never ask.'

We parked along the main street of Cowes, the biggest town on the island. The main road along the island drew people to the jetty. Sanna and I walked along it in the dark, lit by the line of lights every few metres. Down the hill from the esplanade, we were hidden by the world. We sat on the edge where it turned in an L shape to the right.

'Why didn't you invite me by the way?' she asked, narrowing her eyes.

I shrugged. 'I screwed up.'

She chewed on her lips as if biting away the temptation to say something else. 'I'm glad your dad could bring me.'

'Yeah, me too,' I lied.

'Your friends seem nice.'

'Meatheads,' I scoffed.

'You don't like them? They're your friends.'

I shook my head. 'They're not really my friends,' I admitted. 'They're just guys from school. Johann is okay.'

'There's no point trying to be friends with people that you don't want to be with,' she said quietly.

I cleared my throat. She was right, but it wasn't as simple as that. We needed people. We had to be with people. For their welfare as well as ours. I changed the subject. 'Have you heard anything about Tamara?'

'She's out of the coma. I went to see her last week, but she was still...out.' She flicked her hair back. 'Sometimes I want to talk to her but sometimes I think it'd be easier if she died.'

I thought that was an odd thing for her say. I asked with a raised eyebrow, 'What do you mean?'

'I don't think I could go on if she blamed me.'

'She wouldn't blame you.'

'I did this to her.'

I shrugged. 'It was an accident.'

She laughed in that same high-pitched, short-lived way that she'd laughed with my father. 'You didn't know her the way I did.'

I raised an eyebrow at her use of the past-tense, like Tamara was gone. I said, 'No...I don't.'

Sanna let out a stream of air and shivered. My face went hot and I nodded, unable to think of what to say. She studied my face before she leaned in. I turned my head and faked a cough. She folded her body and looked down at the black water that lapped against the pillars beneath our feet.

I started driving from school to Sanna's each day. My school finished at 3:00 but hers finished at 3:15. She was flustered, and teary. Nobody was speaking to her and she wasn't understanding the maths. Her teachers were mean. Her only friend had a lover and she wanted to avoid them because it made her uncomfortable. It was good to drive her home or to her part-time job each day to get to know her better, but she mostly used that short drive in the afternoon as a vent session, and it wore me down.

On Friday, a week after the party, I picked her up and her face was streaked with tears. I was meant to take her straight to work, but her boss had texted her to say don't bother coming in. Just work Saturdays.

'One shift a week?' Sanna wailed. 'How am I going to afford anything on one shift a week?'

'You're fifteen – you don't have to pay for anything,'

I was only trying to make her feel better but she scoffed and retorted, 'I won't be able to work much with a kid, Jake. I have to try to save up money while I can. I don't want to be on the dole.' The dole was the Australian welfare payment system. Sanna's pride was stressing her out more than it should have. Who cared if she needed financial help? Nobody would judge her. She was going to be a teenage mother. It would be unusual for her to not need support.

However, I didn't say anything, and took her back to her house. Her dad booked her in for more counseling sessions and said she could withdraw from school. She never bothered asking me to come along to counseling.

It was agreed between my parents and hers that Sanna would quit school and come stay at my house on the weekends, so she and I could adapt to living together. Sanna agreed because her mother was driving her crazy, harping on about European child rearing. My mother wanted her to live with us full-time once the baby came and whined about the fact that Sanna's mother had taken offence to that. I rolled my eyes and snapped, 'Mom, seriously – it's her daughter, not yours.' I imagined myself telling her that it wasn't even her grandchild. I could almost feel the slap she would land across the side of my head in stereo. Instead, I left it at that and she gave me a sideways glare and didn't talk to me for the rest of the day because she drove Sanna to a shopping mall to buy baby clothes and the littlest sized shoes I had ever seen in my life.

Seeing those shoes made me smile. Little feet would go in them. It made me excited to meet Sanna's baby. The little shoes would one day be too small for even that child. Life would go on. Life would become a new venture for an entirely new person. Humbling.

I was even excited about going with her, during my lunch break at school, to the first ultrasound. The only draw-back was that both our mothers also tagged along.

I asked eagerly, 'Is it a boy or a girl?'

The technician smiled and replied patiently, 'We'll be able to tell hopefully with the next ultrasound – it's a bit too early at the moment to give you a definite answer.' But she smiled and added, 'What are you hoping for?'

Sanna said, 'I want a boy.'

'And what does Daddy want?'

Who knows what the father wanted? I blinked. Oh, that was meant to be me. Right. 'Uh…I don't mind.'

The women all giggled and I sat there in my school uniform feeling like a Martian.

'Oh, will you look at that!' exclaimed the technician, turning up the volume on the machine that detected the heartbeat. Suddenly I wasn't the only Martian in the room – the heart beat sounded like an alien transmission from another planet.

'Is it supposed to be that fast?' asked Sanna.

'Yes, but…' said the technician with a frown. 'There are two heart beats.'

'Our baby has two hearts?' I cried, my heart galloping in the same rhythm as the baby's.

We all craned our necks to see the screen better. The technician tapped a flashing section on the screen and said, 'You've got some twins in there.'

We were all silent. The technician turned down the volume of the heart and made a note into the keyboard. She asked nervously, 'Are there twins in either family? They're usually genetic.'

Well, that was too convenient. 'Me. I'm a twin,' I said with a nervous swallow. I stuttered, 'Well, I was – I was…' I cleared my throat. 'I was a twin.'

The technician smiled. 'Well…congratulations.' She zoomed in and squinted at the screen for what felt like forever, while tapping keys on the keyboard to pinpoint certain things.

Sanna asked nervously, 'Will I need to do anything special to…make sure they're okay?'

The machine beeped and the technician turned the screen off. She looked to Sanna. 'There's the risk that your twins are sharing the placenta, which could be harmful, even fatal. I'd like to book you in to see a specialist as soon as possible so we can know as soon as we can.'

Sanna blinked and asked again, 'Do I need to do something?'

My mother answered, her Texan accent thicker in the small dark room, 'Oh, darlin, you'll just need to put your feet up some more and relax. You and our little snow-peas will be just fine.'

I surprised myself when I hoped she was right.

Sanna kept me company in the evenings while I checked on all the cows and fed Rio. She walked slowly, burdened with a stiff back and sore feet. She carried a flashlight while I carried Rio's bucket of slop. We walked in silence, following the bouncing beam of light.

'Jake.' I stopped to look at Sanna. She asked, 'Are you hoping they won't survive?'

'No,' I said.

Sanna's eyes brimmed with tears and her lip trembled. 'Because I'm worried that I am.'

'No, you're not. You're just scared.'

'Then why do I feel like I'm just expecting them to die?' she wailed.

'Because you didn't want them.' It slipped out but at least I was talking to her. I shrugged. 'I mean, it's pretty normal, given how they got here.'

Her eyes widened and her face paled.

I added, 'It wasn't what anybody wanted.'

She whispered, 'What do you want?'

I sighed as I replied, 'I told you. I want to graduate and become somebody.'

Sanna narrowed her eyes and furrowed her brow as she studied my face. 'I want that for you, too.' She smiled and we continued walking slowly through Rio's paddock.

I said, 'I hate to admit it but I ain't gonna lie: I'm gonna be a crappy father.'

'But are you going to *try* to be a good dad?'

'Of course,' I replied.

She smiled and leaned into me until I tentatively placed my free hand around her. She pushed a few strands of oily hair off her face and said, 'Then that means you'll be a fantastic dad.'

I laughed. 'Yeah, positive thinking will do it.'

'Yep…it will.'

Sanna

May 2011

Jake sat beside me in the specialist's office in Melbourne, and we linked our pinkie fingers together between our two separate seats. This was what I had always wanted from a boyfriend. Well, not quite. I didn't want to weigh five kilos more than I had. I cried every day. Now doctors were telling me that there was a complication and I'd need more scans, more tests and ongoing *surveillance*.

'Well, it seems like there is a monochorionic placenta here,' said the specialist. What did that news mean to me? Nothing. It scared the crap out of me that it meant absolutely nothing to me.

The specialist explained that if the babies were each receiving equal nutrition and blood flow, they would be fine. However, if it began to appear that one was receiving less, that baby would have to be terminated to save the other.

Jake and I both drew in air with a shudder. Avoiding abortion at all costs, until the doctors may have to use it anyway. One murdered baby or two dead babies – take your pick. At the current time – I was around seven or eight weeks, or fifty-five days if I counted the days since Eddie held me down – the babies were both okay.

The termination of one baby, called a selective reduction, wasn't likely but we needed to be aware it may need to happen if the situation became severe enough.

Jake and I nodded our heads in a daze. All I could think about was getting back to our hotel opposite the Flagstaff Gardens and lying down on the big king-sized luxurious bed. I was exhausted. Our night away in Melbourne was paid for, courtesy of my mother. Anything we wanted on room-service, cable television and whatever Jake wanted from the mini-bar. She called it her gift to Jake for how much she appreciated him staying with me. Like he had a choice when they thought he was the father.

We took a taxi back to the hotel but we didn't go inside. We crossed the street and we went and sat on the swings in Flagstaff Gardens, overlooking the bowling club. I started swinging furiously, gritting my teeth and trying to get as high as I possibly could and enjoyed the rush of soaring upwards and then falling downwards as though I was being shot out by a cannon. Jake swung gently beside me.

'They'll be okay, Sanna,' he said.

'Shut up, Jake.'

'I'm just sayin'...they'll be fine.'

'I told you to shut up.' I took a risk and flew off the swing and landed neatly on both feet. It hurt. It felt like I'd been electrocuted and I bit my tongue to keep myself from swearing. 'Sanna!' he cried and rushed to my side. He let me lean into him. 'Are you crazy? You could have fallen over and hurt yourself, and the babies.'

'It doesn't matter if I do, does it?' My lip trembled hopelessly. 'One of them is probably gonna die anyway.'

He wrapped an arm around my shoulder. 'I know it sucks.'

I wiped my eyes as tears sprang out. 'I feel so bad. It's not the baby's fault, you know.'

'I know.'

'We wouldn't have a choice, though, would we?' I sniffed. 'If it came to that. It's either kill one to save one or lose them both.'

Jake shrugged. 'It doesn't seem like there's a choice. They wouldn't do it if it wouldn't save the other one.'

We started walking around the park and I just talked about anything that popped into my head. I closed my eyes, imagining he was Michael. I could open up to him if he was Michael. I talked about how I wished I hadn't gone to the beach that day, and how I'd almost been a really ripper surfer but now I was too scared. Being in the water freaked me out. I was worried I had nothing to look forward to in life now.

Jake nodded and said in a quiet voice that he was worried about not being a success, too. When he spoke, I found his drawl comforting. It made me slow down, and stopped me from panicking so much. His voice was so slow and crafted, it made me feel safer. It wasn't anything he said, but how he said it that softened me. I would never let him know that I wasn't listening though.

I sighed. 'It's not fair.'

'Tell me about it,' he agreed. 'I don't even like the idea of abortion but it seems like medicine is just stamping me down – stamping you down, too, of course.'

'Didn't you want to be a doctor? Study medicine?' I asked.

'Yeah, maybe. But I don't ever want to tell a woman what she has to do with her own body.'

I paused. 'Is that what you think?'

'I couldn't take away someone's choice.'

He looked away and I grabbed his hand and leant into his body. A choice was all I had ever wanted, and I hadn't even known it.

I sighed. 'Kill a baby to live...don't kill the baby and it will die anyway...' I kicked at a fallen leaf. It was getting later in the autumn and the big oak trees were almost bare – their gold and brown leaves had flooded the pathways and were now getting soft and soggy.

Jake squeezed my shoulder. 'I don't know what I can say...but I bet my mom will say a few things that will make you feel better.'

I smiled. 'I kind of already do feel better, Jake...better as can be, anyway.' It was like carrying around a cold block of ice. I kept my hand on my belly and tried to imagine that my babies could feel my hand upon them. 'Do you want to come with me to see Tamara while we're in the city?'

Jake stiffened against me. 'I don't know.'

'Come on,' I urged. 'I'll be mostly on bed rest for a while until we get the all-clear. I might not get the chance to see her again for a while.'

He nodded. 'Okay.'

Tamara was perched up in the bed when I walked in with Jake. I peered at her with my pulse quickening. She stared blankly ahead. The nurse came in and stood by with a polite smile.

Jake cleared his throat but Tamara didn't respond. Her mouth was parted slightly and the nurse went in and wiped some drool away.

'Hey,' I croaked. 'Tee, it's me. Sanna.'

Tamara blinked a couple of times but still did not look at me.

I swallowed and asked the nurse, 'Is she...brain damaged?'

The nurse busied herself with checking Tamara's heart rate monitor and medication. 'She's getting better every day. We won't know for sure until she stops improving so rapidly.' She smiled.

'What do you mean by that?' Jake asked.

'Coma patients improve rapidly so it's difficult to say for sure what the damage is until their improvement slows down. The brain kind of runs fast to repair itself, until it gets to the point it can't. That's where we're at with Tamara.'

I wanted to touch Tamara's hand again, but the way she was conscious but vacant had me rooted to the spot away from her. Jake stood behind me, silent. I turned and walked away. He didn't follow me at first, but then came jogging after me. I stood at the elevator and shook my hands after pushing the button, waiting for it come collect me.

'You okay?' Jake asked as he caught up.

'I don't...' My voice stopped working so I held up a hand and then shook my head. Everything was unfair. Why was I up, walking and talking, when I had been the shithead that had dropped in? I guess I'd got my come-uppance in the end with Eddie and now this pregnancy. The monochorionic embryos were God's punishment upon me. Maybe they would both die, and everything would go back to normal, but then looking at Tamara that way made it so very clear that nothing was normal anymore, and it would never be like how it was.

June 2011

Staying in bed at first sounded like something relaxing, but as I lay there, staring at the wall, I wished I could get out and do something – even the thought of going back to school was appealing. My stomach cramped on and off and no matter what I ate, the mere scent of it on the plate made me sick.

Mum played the television too loud and vacuumed whenever I managed to doze off and I wanted to scream and pitch a fit, but I was too busy bolting out of bed to the toilet. The only time I felt fine was first thing in the morning. I could walk around the house and function almost as if nothing was wrong, but the second I ate breakfast…it was all over, which was apparently the opposite to how my mother had felt during morning sickness with me.

I started reading books from my school book list. I wasn't getting to study *Night* by Elie Wiesel or *Looking for Alibrandi* by Melina Marchetta at school, but at least I could read them. I bawled my eyes out while reading both books.

While reading a book that Mum had given me, a voice said, 'Hello?' from the doorway of my bedroom.

I looked up to see Michael. My skin pulled a little as I smiled. I hadn't moisturized enough – at all – since getting pregnant and the hormones made my skin even drier than it could be after surfing in cold, salt water.

'Michael,' I said. 'Where have you been?'

He came in and leant against the door of my wardrobe. It was on rails and swayed with the pressure. He shrugged. 'I've been at school. Where have you been?'

'Here,' I laughed. 'Stuck in bed.'

'Because you're pregnant? I didn't realise that meant you couldn't walk anywhere anymore.'

Blood pulsed to my face and my head rocked back as if he'd hit me. I put the bookmark into the book with trembling hands and put it on my bedside table slowly, wondering how I could respond to that. He didn't care. He didn't get it. I'd hung on to the good of Michael when I was with Jake, but now that Michael was here, I longed for Jake's understanding. I sighed. How could he understand? He didn't know what had happened to me. He had no clue.

I said while looking at him with my sternest expression, 'There's something wrong with the babies.'

His eyes widened. 'Babies? You're having twins?' he asked.

I nodded. 'I just have to rest up until the doctors give me the all clear in five weeks, after another scan.' There was no point telling him that they may not be twins forever if they weren't growing properly. All he cared about was what I used to care about: going to the beach to hang out.

I said, 'After that, I'll be able to get out of this bed. We can go to the beach and hang out.'

He shook his head to get a dreadlock out of his eyes. 'I don't think that would be appropriate. What would your boyfriend think?'

I stared at him but he only looked straight at the floor. 'What's your problem, Michael?' I asked.

He sat down on the edge of my bed and hissed, 'My problem is that you let yourself get knocked up by some guy. You said to me on the phone that you barely even knew him! "I don't know him that well". So, you obviously couldn't have loved him, could you?'

'I,' I began but he cut me off. 'No, I'm not done yet, Sanna! How could you live with yourself? Look at what you've done to your life!'

'Excuse me?' My heart thumped and my stomach cramped, but the main thing I focused on was the way his words made the back of my throat feel – as though I'd swallowed acid.

'Did I say I was done?' he shouted.

'No, but since when do I do what you want me to?' I would have done anything for this boy a month ago. Now I wanted to kick him in the face.

He nodded and said bitterly, 'That is so true, Sanna. Since when. Since when have you given a damn how I feel.'

My mouth had been gaping, but it shut when his voice cracked. I clutched at the doona so hard that my fingers were beginning to hurt. If I let go, my fist would fly at his mouth. He had no right to say anything. He was the one who went and slept with someone else. He might have thought this was the same thing, but it was, most definitely, not the same thing.

He murmured, 'You always said we couldn't be together because you didn't love me that way. You said "I don't love you" so we couldn't be together – remember?'

I felt as though he'd just shoved me off the bed and forced me to lie inside a mirror, looking at myself from all the awkward, unflattering angles. He was right. I released my blanket – and all the anger went with it.

'Michael...' My voice shook too much to continue.

My mum popped her head in the doorway. 'Everything okay? I heard yelling.' Michael and I nodded in silence so she left again, leaving us to stare at each other with shame and embarrassment, and mostly nostalgic longing.

He said, 'Sorry. Look, I'm just...sorry. I didn't come here to go all Gestapo on you. I came here to hang out with you.'

'Gestapo?'

'Sorry – studying Nazis at the moment at school.'

'Oh...' I thought about all the things I was missing out on, not just Nazis. I asked quietly, 'Does anybody ever ask about me?'

'Who would they ask?' he said quietly, biting a hangnail from his thumbnail.

'I dunno,' I admitted and then added, 'You.'

He shrugged. 'I guess when you got knocked up, people thought it was me. Nobody really talks to me now because they think I'm a dog because I keep saying the kid isn't mine.'

My heart sank. 'I'm so sorry.'

He shrugged. 'It's all right. It's your life – you can choose what to do with it.'

I wished I could have more choice. I longed for the nights when we had sat on the beach or gone to parties. I'd give everything up to have my life back to how it was before. I hadn't even thought that people would assume he was really the father. I never would have thought he'd cop the same amount of crap and judgement that I had. Of course, people would have thought the kid was his. He was a dropkick boogie boarder from a dropkick family. But I knew the real Michael – he was honest, caring and smart. A survivor, just like me. I wished for a moment that he really was the father.

'I'm sorry,' I croaked. I hugged my teddy bear.

Michael came in close and got under the covers with me, resting his head on my swollen breasts. 'Mmm,' he teased. 'I like these better this way.'

I walloped him with my teddy bear and we laughed.

We lay together all afternoon and chatted about our lives. I told him all I knew about my monochorionic twins and he told me how much he liked studying history at school. He liked creative writing too.

'Have you written anything I could read?' I asked. I gestured at the pile of books that I had to read. 'Because I am in constant need of new material.'

His lips twitched and he forced a smile. 'I don't know. I don't have anything good.'

'Oh, come on. It's you. Everything you write would be awesome.' He agreed that he would give me a story he had written, with plenty of warnings that it was really bad, that it was unpolished, it was only a draft, he didn't think the plot was very strong, the character arc seemed a little weak but he *was* happy with his opening line.

'You can tell me what you think. Be honest,' he told me as he pulled on his jacket to leave.

I nodded but knew that I would have to swear on my life that I liked it, no matter how bad it was. 'You'll come visit me soon?' I asked.

He gave my forehead a little peck. 'Absolutely. I'll try again next weekend.'

I grinned with glee and waved him out the door. 'Bye.'

'See ya, Sanna.'

He closed the door and I was left completely alone and bored and lonely once again, reflecting on our relationship and what could have been if I had just made a different choice, or at least been given the chance to have one in the first place.

Jake

June 2011

I sat in the edge of Sanna's bed and handed her another book. It was one in a series of books, something about vampires, a bit about werewolves; some hocus pocus garbage about angels. She took the book and read the back. I'd gotten it for her from the library. She'd read six in the series since she'd been ordered to bed rest. I dropped in on her before and after school. I was exhausted but I looked better than Sanna. She had puffy limbs and features, sallow skin, and dark rings around her eyes.

'Do you need anything else before I go to school?'

'Could you get me out of this?' she joked.

I squeezed her hand and got up to leave. Before I left, I took my token morning Swedish bun from Sanna's mom. I drove all the way to school, to my advanced chemistry class. I'd moved up this term after Ms. Hollinday put in the transfer. No more pleb science for me.

SALT

As Ms. Hollinday introduced potassium chloride and its solubility, my mind wandered to the selective reduction. Potassium chloride. That was what the specialist had explained would stop the baby's heart. As Ms. Hollinday continued lecturing us and gesturing to the diagrams she had scrawled on the board, I slowly raised my hand.

She looked to me and paused. 'Jake?'

'I have a question about potassium chloride and how it's used to stop the hearts of fetuses in monochorionic or multiple births, Miss.'

The rest of the class swivelled in their seats to stare at me as Ms. Hollinday blinked at me in disbelief. I dropped my hand upon the desk and waited. She replied simply, 'I don't know what you want me to say, Jake. I don't know what you mean.'

'It's called a selective reduction…and I was kind of hoping to go to medical school, and this has come to my attention.'

'What even is it?' Clint asked.

'I can look it up and we can talk about it next week, all right, Jake,' said Ms. Hollinday. She turned her back on me with a slight shake of the head as though she'd just had ice water poured down the back of her neck. 'Copy these notes down, class.'

I wrote down the notes with a heavy hand and a flick, fuming that she couldn't answer my question, and explain to the entire class why the medical profession might possibly be a bad choice for me and the other hopefuls.

As the bell rang to signal recess, Ms. Hollinday stopped me by placing her hand on my forearm. 'Jake, a moment.'

'What is it?' I sat on the first table in the row of tables and let my backpack drop to the floor.

She fiddled with the whiteboard markers and said, 'Jake, I am aware of what you were asking me. Is this something you'd like to talk about?' I shrugged so she explained, 'I don't think it would be appropriate for me to discuss that procedure with a class full of Christian students.'

'Oh, yeah, religion…' I said, looking down at my shoes.

'I could lose my job.' She crossed her arms. 'But you clearly have questions about it, so ask.'

I hesitated. 'Do you think it's the right thing to do?'

'Right?' She laughed a little and squeezed her arms before she sat down on a table beside me and sighed. 'I asked myself the same question when I first heard about it. Medicine may be a challenging field for you if you have concerns like this, Jake.'

I bit the inside of my lip and admitted, 'Doctors told Sanna she might have to get one.'

'Sanna?'

I peered at her with surprise. 'You don't know about Sanna?'

'No.'

I laughed gently. 'Wow. I thought everybody knew about that scandal.'

'Jake, you will have to fill me in. How could you not let me in on a scandal?' she teased. 'I thought I was your favorite teacher.'

'You are. I guess I was in denial. I haven't even told Johann.'

'That must be difficult…to keep something so big a secret.'

I nodded.

'So, a friend of yours might need this procedure, and you're upset about it?'

'She's supposed to be my fiancée actually.' She widened her eyes at me and I nodded again with a smile. 'Yeah, you heard right.'

'What about university?'

'It'll work out.'

She tilted her head and studied my face. The fluorescent lights above hummed in the quiet lab as if our conversation was an ongoing ellipsis. I wished I could pinpoint the way I felt about Sanna's pregnancy. One minute I was happy, excited, elated, then other times I was resentful, dreading and miserable about how I'd sacrificed everything just to avoid seeing a look on her face. I was all over the place.

Ms. Hollinday finally said, 'You obviously have some unresolved emotions and thoughts, as well as questions, Jake. Why don't you have a chat to somebody about it, somebody who knows all about it?' she said. Ms. Hollinday placed a hand gently on my shoulder and said, 'Jake, you've got a bright future ahead of you. I don't want to see you throwing that away. Medicine is so difficult to get into.'

'I know – I can't throw it away,' I swallowed the heavy lump in my throat and squeezed it down to my gut. 'What makes you think I'm throwing it away?'

Her lips formed a reedy line. 'I think you should go have a chat to the school counselor. They'll be able to help you out with a lot of the issues that you have right now.'

As Ms. Hollinday suggested, I went to see the school counselor at recess. What could it hurt, really? Maybe I'd be less all over the place if I could talk about this stuff. One second I was keen to help Sanna and the other I felt like I had ruined my life, but then I felt guilty that I had any goals in my life given what happened to her, but didn't I owe it to my brother to live a good life and be a good person? Yeah, I was all over the place, all right.

I went to knock but had a second thought. Why should I talk about how I was feeling? What was the point? They didn't understand what it was like. They hadn't been there the night Sanna was raped.

I crumpled up the slip and made me way to the library to search for more books I could borrow for Sanna. One that caught my eye was one with a surfer on the cover. I read the back. Apparently, it was a best-seller and the edition I was holding was about the eleventh edition – it was just that popular. I'd never heard of it. It wasn't about vampires or werewolves, but it seemed to have something to do with surfing so I took it out in my name and decided to read a little bit of it before class was over.

'You've been checking out a lot of books, Jake,' said Johann later at lunch as he eyed off my book bag. 'How do you have time to read all of them?'

'They're not for me. They're for Sanna,' I said, not taking my eyes off the words on the page. The story had hooked me in. It was about a guy growing up on the coast, and feeling alone and let down by his mentor, a reckless guy who did crazy stunts that got people hurt. I could see why it had been so popular.

'Pretty girl from your party, yeah?' he said.

I looked up at him, surprised that he remembered her this time, since he hadn't remembered her from Clint's party. 'Yeah.'

'She likes books *and* she's cute.'

'Yeah.'

'Why do you borrow them for her?' he asked, peeling the sticker off his apple. 'Why doesn't she just borrow them from her school?'

'I don't know,' I lied. 'She's my friend and she asked me to, so I do.'

'You see her a lot, then?'

'Yeah.'

'How many times a week?'

'Every day, Johann,' I said as I rolled my eyes. 'Just say what you wanna say, will you?'

He leaned forward and took a bite from his apple. 'Are you in love?'

'No.' Whoa, that came out a little too fast. I think I loved what was in her womb more than I loved her. How was that even possible? Why couldn't I even lie and say yes?

'I'm curious,' Johann admitted. 'Why do you care so much about her to see her every day, then?'

I rolled my eyes again and just shut the book. I'd ask Sanna how it ended. I glared at Johann as he stared at me, eating his apple.

'Is she a relative?' he asked.

'No.'

'Is she a friend?'

'Yes.'

'Is she your girlfriend?'

'No, Johann,' I groaned and then decided that I might as well come clean about the whole thing. 'Look,' I sighed. 'She's really my fiancée, okay?'

His eyes widened and he coughed. 'But...'

'I know, I know.' I leaned in a little closer so I could speak quieter. 'She's pregnant.'

Johann choked.

I could keep this secret, unlike Sanna. I was grateful for being a guy, free of the burden of pregnancy on the physical body and all the judgment that came with it. Especially being so young. As I leaned in closer to Johann, I thought of the way I'd gone upstairs at Clint's party with Sanna and decided it was the perfect opportunity as to the timing of our fake courtship. I whispered, 'You remember Clint's party – how drunk I was?'

Johann nodded. 'She was drunk too.' He smirked. 'I get it.'

I nodded. 'So can you shut up about it now, please – and don't tell anybody.'

'When is she due?'

I shrugged. 'That hasn't really been discussed very much. There's a complication. It's complicated.'

'Tell me about it – you're not even dating and you're not even friends.'

'We are friends.'

'Would you be friends if this hadn't have happened?' he quipped.

I hesitated. Yes, no. Probably not. We had been complicated even just as friends, but Johann didn't need that story. I lied, 'Of course. We were friends before and we'll be friends after.'

'No. Correction: you'll be husband and wife.' He sniggered. I kicked his ankle under the table and he only laughed harder.

AVA DUNN

In the afternoon, I walked into Sanna's bedroom and she smiled at me, her eyes half-closed as if she'd just been sleeping. She sat up as I sat down on the edge of her bed. With a yawn, she asked, 'How was school today? Let me live vicariously through you.'

'I asked my teacher about the procedure,' I admitted and shook my head. Her eyes widened. 'It didn't go over very well.'

She pushed her messy hair back over her face and grunted. 'Can't see why it would.'

I suppressed a laugh at myself. 'I cornered her and tried getting the answer in class.' Looking back, I'd just been frustrated at how I couldn't control anything. It had been silly to hold the dang teacher accountable when all she wanted to do was teach me about how potassium chloride behaved with water. Jeez, I was a jerk.

'Oh,' said Sanna.

'Yeah.' I stretched out and lay across her bed, looking up the dust gathering in the corner of her ceiling.

'So, you didn't get any kind of answer at all?'

I groaned and sat up again. 'Well, she actually pulled me aside and told me that she knew about the procedure and how inappropriate it would be of her tell the whole class about it.' I looked down at my hands. 'She thinks I have a bright future...' It was difficult to see any brightness in the dank bedroom. 'As a doctor...so if I have a problem with this procedure...I might have some problems with my career.' I sighed and turned to Sanna, waiting for her to say *She's right; you have a bright future; you should just go and do this, Jake...Don't worry about me. I'll come clean and admit I was raped even though I can barely admit it to myself. These babies are my responsibility – not yours. You are absolved. Thanks for the offer; you're so kind...* but she didn't. I knew she wouldn't, but it didn't stop me hoping.

All Sanna did was nod and say, 'I see.'

I admitted, 'I told Johann about the babies and us, too.'

'Wow, you've had a busy day.'

I laughed. 'Yeah, I guess I have.' Remembering the book I borrowed for her, I reached for my backpack. 'I got you another book from the library.' I handed it to her. 'I read a bit of it, and it's really good – you'll have to tell me how it ends.'

She flicked through its pages and smiled weakly. 'Thanks, but I think I can tell you how it ends.'

'Have you read it before?'

She shook her head and sniffed, avoiding my eyes. 'Jake, there's something really wrong with me.'

'What?'

She chewed her lip as if chewing through her words. 'I really, really, really loved to surf. Surfing was my whole life. I used to get up at crazy hours – like four o'clock – so I could go surfing before school. Even on the weekends, I'd be up early and down the beach. I used to be in the water so much that being on land felt wrong and sticky to move through – like glue!'

'Okay,' I said, perplexed.

She shook her head. 'I haven't surfed since the day Tamara got hurt. I mean, I've tried. I've gone out on the water once but I freaked out and came straight back into shore. That day was the day…Now I'm worried I can't do it at all.'

'You don't really talk about what happened.'

She shrugged. 'I'm alive, aren't I? What actually happened doesn't mean anything.'

'It does.' I considered telling her about how Alex use to go off swimming or hiking or riding with his friends, how I was always left behind. His days had always been more exciting to talk about around the dinner table because he did this, he did that, he saw this, he saw that. I'd be quiet and my family would talk around me. I'd always been the quiet one. I wasn't sure if I had gotten quieter when he died, but the silence became more noticeable. It would have been a bit easier for my family to continue on if it had been me that had died, and for some reason I felt guilt that it wasn't. I considered telling Sanna all this – that being quiet about things that happened is not always

140

the best way to deal with things, but I would have been the biggest hypocrite this side of the Earth, so I shut my mouth and we were both quiet until I got up to leave.

'Wait, Jake.' She wiped her eyes and said, 'Why don't you stay here for a little while? It's so boring sitting here all the time.'

'I've got a lot of homework.'

'Well, I have a desk over there that you can use. I can read so it's quiet for you to do your homework.'

I looked at her desk, crowded and cluttered with books and piles of clothes.

She said, 'Just dump all that on the floor.'

'Okay.' I did as I was told. As long as we could be quiet, it was all right. I could tune out the page turning and the sound of her breathing or moving nearby. It wasn't as though I was any more comfortable at home.

While taking a break, I looked up at the hutch shelf on her desk. There was a red and white painted wooden horse. It had stiff little legs and a thick neck, with a floral design on its back like a saddle. It was awesome. I picked it up and showed it to Sanna. 'What is this?'

'It's called a Dalahäst. It's a traditional Swedish symbol of strength, and courage.'

I swallowed as I turned the horse over and studied it.

Sanna shrugged. 'You can have it if you want.'

'Seriously?'

She nodded.

I said, 'Thanks. It's really cool.'

'Yep.'

'I love horses.'

'I love them, too.' We went quiet and stared at each other awkwardly for at least a minute. It was the perfect time to say those three words, perfect...yet I couldn't do it and by the squeamish look on her face, Sanna couldn't say them either.

The twelve-week scan took place in the second last week of term two…right before mid-year exams. I was under so much stress that my gut flipped and rolled as though I'd drank two gallons of coffee on an empty stomach. The scan was going to tell us whether we needed to have the procedure or not, and we would know for sure whether one or both twins would survive. It felt as though I couldn't concentrate on my studies until I knew. I had to know.

Mom picked me up from school early on the Friday and drove Sanna, me and Sanna's mum to the radiology clinic. I sat with my mother in a café a block away while Sanna and her mum went into the clinic. Sanna hadn't wanted me in the room.

Mom stirred her cappuccino but never took a sip. I sat there nursing a double-shot espresso that didn't help my nerves at all.

'This is going to kill her if one needs to die,' I murmured.

Mom nodded and said, 'It is not a nice thing for a young mother to have to do.'

'It must be a twin thing. Only one can survive,' I muttered under my breath.

'Don't be silly, Jake,' my mom replied, stirring until the chocolate and the coffee and the crème all melded into one. 'Plenty of twins live.'

'I miss Alex,' I sighed.

'Don't bring him up.'

'Why not?'

'Because it hurts too much,' was the simple answer. I hid a tear by pretending to yawn and wiping my eyes. My mother should have understood that it hurt me more to not talk about him. She wasn't allowed to talk about Alex, or Derek, with Dad because he just couldn't cope with the pain. She should've talked about Alex with me because I wanted to hear about him. When I remembered him, it was like I could see his face and hear his voice again, smell his scent and feel his elbow digging into me when I said something I shouldn't have. If I brought

Alex up at such a difficult time for Sanna, I would look selfish, seem careless. She could be losing a child today. The loss of a brother still seemed prominent and hurtful.

That thought soon changed, though, when we went to pick Sanna up and I saw the beaming smile on her face, with cheeks wet from tears. I almost laughed with relief seeing her smiling as she embraced the nurse and the receptionist, then my mother. All of them laughing and smiling, shoulders finally dropping from around their ears as tension left their bodies. It was all going to be okay. The babies were fine.

I folded my arms around her and let my own tears bleed into her messy blonde hair. That little extra baby would survive. It didn't need to be sacrificed. Nobody would ever know I cried with relief for that child and its survival. Nobody.

July 2011

After my last exam of the week – maths – I sprawled out in the common room and stared up the ceiling. My brain was too exhausted to function. The relief of the exams and the ultrasound being over made me feel as though I was a puddle that needed to ooze across the furniture.

Ms. Hollinday came over and leaned over me. 'Are you all right, Jake?'

I stared up at her for a moment before I asked, 'What?'

'Are you all right?'

I looked around. The common room was empty. The bell for the end of the day had rung and I hadn't even heard it. School was out for the winter. I sat up. 'Oh, man. I completely zoned out.'

Ms. Hollinday chortled. 'Is zoned out a new hip way of saying you fell asleep?'

I rubbed my eyes and laughed. 'I guess so.'

'How did it all go?'

'Good, I think.' I yawned. 'No, I'm really sure it went great, actually.' I grinned. 'Thanks for all your help.'

'That's what I get paid for.' She winked.

I nodded and stood up, picking up my notes. 'Anyway, better get going.'

'Jake, before you go, I wanted to ask…I didn't want to ask before in case…'

I gave her a quizzical look.

She explained, 'Your mother called in last week and told us a very important scan was happening last Friday, and that you might need a bit of support if it didn't go well.'

'Oh.'

'So…how did it go?'

I smiled. 'Everything is fine.'

To my surprise, she didn't look relieved. She didn't smile. 'That's good.'

'Yeah.'

Ms. Hollinday nodded, still not smiling. She bit her lip and began walking away. I knew she was desperate to salvage a chance of a scholarship and I was determined to not let her down.

I drove over to Sanna's. I knocked on the door and walked right on it, calling out hello.

Sanna's mother was in the living room, typing at her laptop. She looked up when I walked in and dropped my notes on the coffee table. 'Jake – just the person I want to see.'

I tilted my head. 'Everything okay?'

'I took Sanna to the beach earlier today – she was having a bit of a down day.' I nodded, listening. She wore a grim expression so by a down day, it must have been a terrible day.

'I've got a bit caught up with work, so would you mind driving over to Cape Woolamai and picking her up?'

144

I had a heavy sensation in my gut as I drove over to Cape Woolamai. What was wrong now? I hoped nothing bad had happened.

I found her sitting on the sand, slightly off the walkway from the second carpark.

'Sanna!' I called out and she looked over at me.

She rolled her eyes. 'My mother sent you, didn't she?'

I walked through the sand and sat down next to her, knowing that my mom was going to whine that I'd gotten sand all over my school pants.

'I just wanna sit here alone for a while, okay, Jake?' she snapped.

'That's okay. So, I'll go.'

I bent my knees, ready to stand but she said, 'No, that's okay. You can stay.'

I smiled. 'You know, I had this crazy thought that you'd be out on your board.'

'I wish I was.' A flock of gulls came flying past above us, squawking and squabbling. We watched them land nearby and dip their little paddle-like feet into the shallow water as it lapped at the shore.

'Why don't you?'

'Why don't I what?' she asked.

'Go in the water. Surf.'

'Onshore wind – the water's all choppy – the waves aren't forming properly.'

'I didn't mean now,' I said.

She scoffed and moved her hands like she was going to shove me but placed them firmly onto the sand. 'It's not that easy.'

'Why not?'

'Because!' she exclaimed as if that was a satisfactory answer. She got up and paced before me, back and forth. Surprisingly agile for a girl that had just spent about a month lying in bed. 'You and my mum – you're exactly the same. Just when I think you understand, you don't!'

145

'Why?'

'Because it's complicated okay!' She threw her hands down and howled at me. 'I'm afraid, all right!'

I pulled my jacket tighter around me. The wind was whistling over the bluff and flattening the grass, blowing straight from the water and into my eyes, making them burn. My throat ached from the cold as I asked, 'Did you tell your mom about what happened to you yet?'

She shook her head and hugged herself. 'She tried telling me to give up the babies for adoption...and not sacrifice my future and yours.'

I tucked my chin to my chest as if the words were ice themselves, and waited.

Sanna sniffled and said, 'I told her she has no idea what I've been through and to butt out.' She collapsed beside me and huddled into my side. 'I couldn't go through all of this just to...say goodbye to them.'

I put my arm around her and understood but wished Sanna would consider it. Her mom had a point. I was giving up more than I reckoned for.

'Why don't you...tell your mom about what happened?' I asked after she stopped crying.

'I don't know...I just can't.'

There seemed to be a lot of things that Sanna thought she couldn't do. This was a girl that I'd met on the day she'd made the biggest mistake of her life. I really had no idea what she could and couldn't do, but she had run for her life and survived. Got up the next morning and said 'let's get on with it'. She would surf one day. I knew it. She couldn't give it up. One day she would reconnect with the salt water in her veins, and she'd heal. Until that day, I'd be there. Making sure she didn't sink into the swash.

As I drove her home, she rifled in her canvas beach bag and pulled out the book I had borrowed for her. She flicked through to the end. 'Want me to read you the end?'

'Yeah,' I said eagerly. I drove to the waterfront of Rhyll and parked while Sanna read me the last couple of chapters. Sometimes she misread a line by skipping to the next and was momentarily confused before she flushed red and then read back over what she had already read out to me to find her place. I just smiled and let her continue making a mess of the excellent work of the author. She finished it and grinned at me with pride. I clapped. She said, 'It was really good, huh.'

I nodded and she flipped through the novel, a cold rush of breeze coming off the pages.

She said, 'My friend wants to be a writer. He's going to give me some of his stories to read.'

I said, 'That's cool,' flinching at her use of he and his. Sanna was not Tessa. I didn't need to worry about her cheating on me, but for some reason, it made me anxious. To hide my reaction, I gestured to the coffee shop opposite us. 'Want to get a coffee to warm up?'

She smiled. 'Okay, then. Your shout.'

We walked into the coffee shop and parted a small group of elderly women. They all looked at the at the little belly bump Sanna had and I saw her excitement and confidence shatter. I handed her my parka and said, 'Cold?'

She took it and put it on with a small, grateful smile. We sat at one of the tables outside and shared a delicious sticky date pudding. With her mouth full and lips lined with icing sugar, Sanna asked, 'What are we gonna do about names?'

I shrugged and spooned another heap of pudding for myself. 'I don't know.'

'I asked if they were boys or girls.'

I raised an eyebrow.

'They said it was too early to tell yet. But I think I have a name for one.'

I waited with anticipation but felt a bowling punch in the gut when she said, 'We should name one Alex.'

'I don't think that's a good idea.' I looked down at my lap and pushed the pudding away.

'Why?'

I shrugged. 'I just don't.' I slammed my foot down to stop it bouncing under the table.

Sanna flopped back into the chair back and picked at her nails. 'Okay, fine. We won't name one Alex.' We finished our coffees in silence.

Sanna

July 2011

Michael and I sat at our usual spot at Cape Woolamai beach. There were a few surfers out there on the water. I'd been alarmed when I first saw them, worried that it was somebody who might recognise me and notice my burgeoning belly that I constantly tried to hide. The swelling wasn't just limited to my belly. My shoes didn't fit anymore so I needed to wear sandals everywhere, even though it was winter. My face was round and my jaw was swollen from vomiting all the time.

They must have been from out of town because I'd never even seen them come into work and every surfer on the Bass Coast came into The Surf Shack. I was miserable about losing my job at The Surf Shack. Ms. Kelly had let me go when I needed time off for the bed rest. It almost made me want to scream with anger.

Michael asked, 'Do you like it?'

I had read his short story twice. It had been about an eighteen-year-old boy with a mental health issue. He ended up homeless before walking into a kindergarten to beg his mother to forgive him for accidentally killing his younger brother in a car accident. It ended with a single hug. I had wiped tears from my eyes and read it again immediately. It was beautifully written.

'It's really good,' I said.

'Good means bad, doesn't it?' said Michael, picking at a piece of marram grass.

I shook my head. 'No. It means it's good.'

'Awesome.'

'Yeah,' I said, handing the notebook back to him.

He tucked it into the back pocket of his jeans. 'I reckon you must be happy to be allowed out of bed.'

'Gee, let me think,' I joked. 'Of course.'

'It's good news about the baby, eh?' I nodded. He lit a joint and turned away from me so I didn't inhale any second-hand smoke. It was pointless because the wind blew it back towards me anyway. 'So, what time does Jake come round to your place?'

'About four. Sometimes he stays for dinner.'

'Coolies.'

'I'm gonna move in with him in a couple of weeks,' I said. Michael peered at me curiously. 'He's doing Year Twelve and doesn't have time to keep driving back and forth to visit me every day. And when the babies come, he can actually help out and stuff.'

'Whose idea was that?' he asked.

'Jake's mum.'

'She nice?'

'Yeah, I really like her.' I stretched out and studied the mound that was my belly.

Michael lay beside me and laughed. 'This brings back memories...'

'Ha.' I said, 'I wonder if this would have happened if I had let you.'

Michael swallowed and looked at the sky. 'I think it's gonna rain. We should probably call your mum to come pick us up.'

'I don't wanna go just yet, Michael,' I whined. 'Can't we just lie here for a while like we used to?'

'We can – but we're gonna get wet.'

'It's us. I don't know about you, but I've heard that surfers and boogie boarders are wet more than they're dry.'

'Smart arse,' he said. 'But you, my dear, are not a surfer anymore.'

'Yes, I am,' I snapped. 'I'm just not surfing at the moment.'

'But you will, eh?' he said.

'I will,' I said with determination.

'Just I watch, eh?'

'Yes.'

'Tomorrow. Bring your board,' he challenged.

I gestured to my belly. 'I can't surf until these things come out, you doofus! I'm still high-risk.'

He looked a little let down. 'Oh yeah. I forgot for a second.'

I smiled. 'Yeah. Me too.' I sighed. 'I have to get an ultrasound every two weeks to make sure everything is okay. We won't be completely safe for another two months.'

'Shit eh.' He rolled the joint around in his fingers and the smoke made me cough. I forced my lungs to constrict so I wouldn't breathe in so much. 'It's good that things haven't really changed between us.'

'Yeah,' I agreed, though I longed for him to touch me.

'When am I going to meet this guy anyway?'

'The babies? They're due in January, but the doctors want them out in December.'

Michael blew the smoke away from us but looked me in the eye with those almond eyes. 'No. Jake. Your future husband.'

I forced a smile and it made my cheeks split. 'Soon.' I guess I was having a good time acting like how I had with Michael before I was pregnant. Time with him made me indulge in the freedom of forgetting about everything – the imminent end of my life as I knew it.

Growing up and moving in with Jake terrified me. I was only fifteen, and wouldn't be turning sixteen until January. I was having to leave my nest, and I was still just a baby bird myself.

Jake visited each day that week and took some of my belongings each time. Summer clothes, my dented surfboard, books, shoes, my lamp, and my bedside table. All I had left by the weekend was maternity clothes, my teddy bear, my bedding and my bed. Only a few of my photos remained in the room and I stood in the empty room having to slow my breathing to stop myself from panicking. Life was moving too fast.

I hugged my mum as I packed the last of my things. 'I don't want to do this. I don't want to go.'

She played with my hair. 'We will still see each other every day. I will visit so much you'll be sick of me.'

I hugged my dad and he patted me on the shoulder blade. His hugs had never been the same since Eddie.

Will and Isabel opened their front door for us and greeted us with hugs. Isabel could not keep her hands from my face as she told me how welcome I was. Their house was bigger so it made more sense to move us in. Will and Jake got started setting up my bed in the corner of their spare bedroom.

The room smelled like dust and mildew. The window was narrow and had no curtain so Isabel hung up, lopsided, one of my beach towels. My mum bought me two cribs from IKEA, and she and Dad scowled and snapped at each other as they assembled them beside my bed.

I crossed my arms and leant against the doorframe watching them get more and more frustrated. I waited for the frustration to be levelled at me, but they instead lashed out at one another.

'The little peg goes here, not there, you idiot!' my mother shouted. She cursed at him in Swedish and I had to stifle a laugh. My mother was a little woman, barely over five feet tall. She had a petite, pretty face and blonde hair that was always neat – until right now, yelling at my father. Her hair was frizzy and was falling out of her plaited bun.

'Will you just shut up and let me do it?' snapped Dad.

'*Håll käft,*' spat my mother.

'No, *you* shut up,' snickered my dad, earning himself a little victory as my mother stared at him in astonishment. He'd never indicated that he ever understood any Swedish before.

Will shuffled over, sipping at a steaming mug of black coffee. 'Do y'all need anything…or help?' He winked at me and I giggled.

'I don't know about my husband, but I would love one of those coffees,' replied my mum with a smile.

Will nodded. 'No problem.' He headed to the kitchen and I followed him. He was startled when he noticed me following him down the narrow hallway. 'Suzie.'

I said, 'Will, thank you for letting me move in.'

'How could we say no?' he asked as he switched the kettle back on. I sat down at the table as he went about the kitchen making the coffees. He paused and asked, 'I don't know how your folks have their coffee.'

'White with two for both,' I answered, remembering the simple days of how I used to have their coffee ready at sunrise on the weekends so they could get up and drive me to the beach so I could go surfing. Sometimes we'd pick Tamara up, too and I'd have a thermos full of the pre-packaged, sachet of just-add-boiling-water cappuccino.

'They're taking this well,' said Will, leaning against the sink as the kettle limped to the boil.

I scratched my nose and said, 'They are.'

'You've got another ultrasound tomorrow, don't you?'

'I do. My mum's gonna take me,' I said. I dreaded going into the small, dark rooms every two weeks. The nervousness of something being wrong each time was exhausting.

'Fourteen weeks?'

153

'Yep.'

'More than half way to safe, kiddo.'

'I feel done,' I said with a sigh, slumping so my bit of a belly protruded from under my boobs which had gone from an A cup to a C cup, seemingly overnight. 'Hard to imagine that I'll get huge.'

'When can you find out the sex?'

'Next month.'

'You goin' to?' asked Will as the kettle clicked off. He poured the water and stirred it with the milk, coffee and sugar. I kicked my ankle accidentally and winced. Will misread it as a grimace. 'Just thought I'd ask.'

'My mum said she had a dream that they were girls and I named one Poppy,' I said.

'You and Jake discussed names?' asked Will.

I shook my head and avoided his eyes as I said, 'Not really...I wanted to name one but Jake said no so we left it at that.'

Will had to put down the mug that he had just lifted. He sighed and said, 'Oh? What was the name?'

'Alex,' I replied.

His hand shook so he wiped it on the front of his shirt as he swallowed and looked away. He paused then said, 'It's good you're respecting his decision...let the child be...its own person.'

I didn't understand why Jake had not wanted the name – wasn't it a nice thing to do? I was hoping Will would be on my side, but he started to tidy up the kitchen bench as if we were done. I'd have to leave the name argument for now, again. I pursed my lips and nodded. We'd find new names, together, but I still believed it was a nice way to respect Jake and his family for everything they had done for me. In honour, and all that.

Will said, 'Want to take these to your folks for me?'

I nodded and carried both coffees to my parents who were still bickering over how to assemble the cribs. They thanked me for the coffees that Will made and drank them with furtive glances at each other. I lowered myself to the floor and pulled my hands up into the sleeves of my oversized white jumper. I asked, 'Mum, Dad...do you think it's wrong for me to name a baby after Jake's brother, Alex? He died.'

'Oh, that's nice,' said my mother.

My dad shook his head. 'I disagree.'

'Oh, of course, you must,' said my mother with a roll of her eyes. 'Well, I think it's a nice gesture to name a child after a loved one who has passed away.'

Dad snapped, 'I wasn't going to let you name her after my mother. No child deserves the name Thelma Louise Smith!'

'*You* chose my name?' I coughed at my father, surprised that it hadn't been my Swedish mother who had chosen the Swedish name.

'I liked the name,' he said with a shrug. 'Believe it or not, ladies, the father does have right in naming the child.'

'Less of a right,' muttered my mother.

'A right nonetheless. Besides, I really liked the name because it means truth – and truth is important.'

I swallowed hard and looked down. My name meant truth in Swedish and I was living a lie.

'Don't name them something Jake won't be happy with,' he added with a nod.

I stretched out my legs and felt them ache. 'I thought it would be a nice thing to do, but Jake and his dad don't like the idea. Said I should let the child be its own person, or something.' I shrugged. 'I get it, but I still like the name.'

My parents looked at each other and their expressions towards one another softened considerably. They were best friends again in one second – one glance. It was amazing. I knew Jake and I would never have that lightning-fast forgiveness of one another. It was crazy to even hope we would.

The fourteen-week ultrasound went well. Everything was fine, still on track. I breathed a sigh of relief. The following week, Jake resumed school after the winter break, and I went to the doctor for a check-up.

'So…you're fifteen-weeks pregnant now…On your way to halfway…' said the GP. 'How are you feeling?'

'Tired,' I paused before adding, 'Miserable…like this is the worst hangover in the history of the world.'

'Have you been going to school?' he asked, peering at me from over the top of his straight-edged glasses.

'School isn't really for me.' I squirmed in my seat. That morning, I'd gone back through my school notebooks and tried to convert my English book into a journal. I'd written out how I was feeling. In the end, I'd begun writing about what had happened to me. About Eddie. About that night. Two words gleamed off the page at me because I'd pressed the pen so hard on the page. *It hurt*. Was hurt the right word? It had been terrifying more than anything. I had stared at it for half an hour before I scribbled it out and all I was left with was *it*. Regarding the disgruntled reactions to one of the baby's names, I felt the same way; left with nothing but it. It was my child. I had more of a right over its name than Jake and his family did, all things considered. But considering what Jake had done for me? Allowed me to keep the rape a secret, a thing to be more ashamed of than the babies? What had we been thinking?

I had too much to process, too much on my mind. How was I meant to go to school?

The doctor pursed his lips and stared at me.

'I pulled out. People were saying some pretty mean stuff about my situation. People are so judgemental, like just because I'm young, I shouldn't be doing this but it's not like I had a choice.'

He crossed his arms and said, 'You have a choice, Ms. Smith. You are fifteen years old. Your future is still important. You have always had a choice.'

My cheeks got hot and tingled.

He scribbled on a notepad then tore off the page. 'I'm recommending that you attend this group that meets every Thursday in Wonthaggi. You can study with this group and still get a high school certificate.'

'A group?'

He handed me the note and said, 'Yes, group. It's a tight-knit, supportive group of teenagers that have had an interruption to their education. Some of the students have even managed to get back into mainstream education for their VCE.'

'Cool,' I said. I wasn't going. No way. Or so I thought. Turns out I didn't get a choice in my education either.

Mum dropped me off at the educational group in Wonthaggi three days later.

The group met every Thursday for an intensive "day program" in an old classroom of a derelict building, converted into community centre. The classrooms may have been freshly painted, but the floor still creaked underfoot and the foundation tilted slightly in a way that made me nauseous as I walked into the room.

The program was made up of three girls: Amanda, Lauren and Jessica; and three boys: Adam, David and Josh. I was the only pregnant one. Most of them were kids from further inland, like Churchill and Leongatha.

They were welcoming and friendly but their eyes all went straight to my belly. I was used to eyes going to my abs – not my small bump that helped people assume why I was there. They could assume, but they definitely did not have the entire picture.

157

SALT

I sat at the back of the class room and listened to the six of them argue over the meaning of "melancholy". The teacher was a hippy-ish young woman with crazy blonde ringlets. Her name was Lolita and I didn't believe it for a second. Surely, she was really a Jane or a Mary.

'Sanna here is fifteen and is from Phillip Island,' Lolita/Jane/Mary said. 'She's four months pregnant so she's come to join our group so she can keep up with her schoolwork.' I wanted to run out of the room, screaming in horror that everyone knew my business.

She asked, 'What do you like to do, Sanna?'

I shrugged and all the boys sniggered. Adam, a bizarre boy with some kind of mental inhibition whispered to the boys that I liked sex. I ran my tongue over my gums and then bit my lip so hard that it bled to prevent myself from screaming. Lolita/Jane/Mary hushed them. They shut up and looked at me.

My hands dove into my pockets and shrugged again, my shoulders seeming to creep further and further up into my ears. 'I used to surf. I liked that a lot.'

'Did you ever think about sharks?' asked one of the girls.

I used to tell people when they asked that question "not at all" but honestly, I kind of did. It's every surfer's nightmare – they just won't admit it because that would be against the theory that they're at one with the ocean. How could it be possible that a shark would mistake them for a seal? Now I thought more about Eddie than sharks. It wasn't sharks that were keeping me out of the water.

'I didn't think about sharks, no,' I answered.

She gushed, 'You're so brave.'

At lunch break, I sat with her in the courtyard on a bench, surrounded by eucalyptus saplings.

'My sister has a baby,' she told me as she unwrapped the plastic that encased her sandwich. I picked at my chicken salad and said, 'Yeah?'

158

'Yeah; she had him when she was sixteen.' She took a big bite of her sandwich, wolfing it down as though she'd never eaten in her life. 'Do you regret having sex?' she asked.

'That's kind of a weird question,' I said, a little put-out. I didn't even remember her name but she made me cringe.

She shrugged. 'Sorry. We're all used to "talking about our problems" here. I forget my manners sometimes.'

'That's okay,' I lied.

'So, when can you surf again?' she asked.

'I guess as soon as I can,' I replied, gesturing awkwardly to my little belly. It was already bigger than what single baby pregnancies were, and I hated it. 'But I don't know if I will.'

'Why not?'

I felt and saw the nose of my board colliding with Tamara's forehead with a sickening crunch and thud, falling into the water and swirling around under the booming wave we'd crashed on. I lied, 'Because now I do think about sharks.'

She stared at me for a while before she finished her sandwich. I ate my salad. We never spoke again for the rest of lunch. She glanced at me a few times during the next session – the whine-about-life-session – as if she expected me to say something woeful about my life. I was fifteen, and four-months pregnant; I didn't need to talk about my problems – the whole world could see them, and it would only be more obvious as time went on.

When Mum picked me up in the Patrol, she asked, 'How was it?'

'Why can't I just be home-schooled?' I asked. 'All those kids have issues.'

'You have a few issues yourself, my charming daughter,' she muttered at me as I did up my seatbelt.

'What did you say to me?' I cried.

'Nothing,' she smirked.

'Mum!'

She laughed. 'Nothing, nothing, I said nothing!'

I groaned but couldn't help smiling. 'Mum, you're such a weirdo.' I'd missed this. Mum had always joked around with her dry humour that could make me laugh even when I was sad. We were always kidding around and making fun of each other before the accident. Most kids had to deal with their father telling dad jokes, but for me, it was the mum jokes. It almost felt like before when she made fun of me. It was great to have her joking around with me again.

August 2011

The weeks continued to go by. I discovered an aversion to the smell of chocolate and eggs. They both made me bolt to the toilet and made me spend most of my time hugging the lid for dear life. Mum came to pick me up to go to the course, but found me puking into the toilet.

'I'm not going, Mum. I can't. I feel like crap!'

She crossed her arms in the hallway and frowned. 'So, you're giving up this as well as school.'

I rolled my eyes and groaned into the toilet bowl. 'Mum…'

'Your education is important, Sanna! It's only been three weeks of the course.'

'Not now.'

She shook her head. 'You will regret this, *älskling*.'

My lip trembled as I spat into the bowl. She was right. I knew it at that time but I just couldn't do it that day. Why did me missing one class mean that I couldn't go the next week? Why couldn't I just get on with it next week? I was nineteen weeks. Pretty much halfway to my due date at 37-38 weeks. The doctors said I would have to go at 37-38 weeks because of it being a twin pregnancy. Surely that meant I could take it easy. I was exhausted. The last three weeks, my bump had bulged into what definitely looked like a pregnant belly. It was beginning to get in the way. It was past my boobs already.

I flushed the toilet and got to my feet. Mum helped me up. I explained, 'I don't *want* to quit...but I think I have to, Mum.'

She chewed on her lip for a moment before hugging me. Isabel came into the hallway. 'Are you all right, darlin'?'

I squeezed my mum harder and she replied, 'Yes...she is all right, thank you.'

Once I was feeling a bit better, Mum took me to the local supermarket just to get me out of the house. Sadly, it had become a habit that I only ventured out on Thursdays to go to the education group or every fortnight to the doctor and to have my ultrasound.

When we arrived at the supermarket, Mum shifted her weight in the seat and looked at me directly. 'Would you like to come in or stay in the car?'

'I'll come in,' I said. 'I want to get some Shapes anyway.' Shapes were an Australian staple: a cracker cut into a shape that was designated to the flavour they were. I'd never really liked them in the past but in the last couple of weeks, I'd eaten about twenty of them every day and even polished off an entire box of the cheese flavour.

Mum smirked. 'My grandchildren must have a savoury tooth.'

We went into the supermarket and hunted down the Shapes, as well as the fennel tea that Mum was looking for.

'Sanna, it's up there,' said my mum, pointing to the fennel tea at the very top display shelf.

I groaned. 'That's handy.'

'You'll have to reach it for me. You are taller than me,' said Mum.

I reached up my arm and my boobs touch the rows of tea. I shuffled a little closer to get more height but my Mount Vesuvius of a belly smacked into the products. I moved too far to the left and managed to swipe the entire shelf's contents off. The tea packets fell onto the aisle like a tidal wave. Mum and I stared at the chamomile and green varieties on the floor in horror at first but then we looked at each other and cracked up laughing. I laughed so hard that my sides hurt.

'Suck it in, Sanna!' Mum teased. I had to double over and gasp for air, crossing my legs, praying I didn't pee my pants.

A pimply, lanky boy a bit older than me came over. He was wearing a handwritten company name tag that said SPAWN. He asked, 'Do you need any assistance, ladies?'

Mum and I straightened up. She cleared her throat and pointed to the fennel tea. 'I would like to have a packet of the fennel tea, please.'

He reached up and grabbed a packet of it with no straining, no tippy-toes and certainly no avalanche of tea packets. 'In future, call for assistance.'

We left the supermarket with our tea and Shapes, still giggling.

September 2011

Mount Vesuvius became active nine days later, officially at twenty weeks. I was watching TV beside Jake on the couch, resting the remote control on my belly when a baby gave a violent kick and sent the remote clattering to the floor. Jake stared at me in horror. I felt like I was bruised, or bleeding internally. It had to be a future soccer player or AFL player to have a kick like that.

'Was that the babies?' Jake exclaimed.

I nodded. He picked up the remote and put it back on my belly and watched it to see if the baby would kick it off again. I felt a baby move but it didn't kick again. Jake sat down next to me and grinned.

'That sure was somethin',' he said.

I was always bored, sitting at home when Jake was at school, Will out working and Isabel was always busy doing something like cleaning, gardening, shopping or doing something with her church. I stared at the static on the television, too lazy to get up and fix the rabbit-ear antenna. I decided that I couldn't take being shut in the house any longer. Jake had a solid night of sleep and then went to school. Mount Vesuvius kept me awake because I couldn't get comfortable and then I couldn't sleep during the day either.

The regret of quitting the education program begun setting in as I paced the empty house. At least I could have gotten out of the house.

I stood at the window to see if I could see Will working in the milking shed. I kept away from the milking process. It kind of creeped me out, especially now that I had huge swollen breasts. My nipples were sensitive so it hurt to wear a bra, but I couldn't not wear one because my boobs were so heavy. Some days I tried not wearing a bra, but it only made my back, neck, chest and breasts ache.

I was struck down with a cold and spent my days sniffing, coughing, and crying. I didn't brush my hair every day like I should have.

I wanted to go to the beach, preferably by myself but I needed a lift. Will was busy and Isabel was at the farmers' market. Her friend from church had picked her up and they'd gone off like giggling teenagers, excited about picking up pie and fresh flowers. She always liked to have fresh flowers about the house.

As my nose ran and I wiped it for the hundredth time with a tissue that scraped against my skin, I growled and thought "stuff it". I needed to get out of the house. I was going to the beach. I packed some potato chips and a few cans of cola into an esky and then loaded that into Isabel's beaten old Corolla and drove to the nearest beach. I didn't even have my learners permit for driving, but I knew how to drive. Dad taught me how when I was twelve, bumping along the uneven, bald paddocks of our farm.

At the nearest beach to Jake's house, I waddled down the sandy track and sat down on the sand and indulged myself in the sensation of sand between my toes and listened to the sound of the rough surf pounding on the rocks nearby.

This beach, Kilcunda East Beach, was the closest beach to the farm but it was also the beach where Tamara had almost died. I didn't even think about that until I looked out at the seagulls hovering above the water searching for fish. My breath was cut short. 'Oh!' I hadn't thought about this beach in so long. Somehow the beach itself had faded into nothing behind the memory of my board hitting Tamara's head. I sat there and thought of Tamara and had a pain in my chest. Tears came to my eyes and I decided to speak to the sea as if it was her, and as if she could somehow hear me.

'Since you've been gone, I've been lost. I've smoked weed, and I've gotten drunk a lot. I've been trapped into a life I never expected. I'm engaged to a man who gave up his own reputation and life to save mine. We're engaged but we don't touch — we don't hold hands. We don't kiss. We don't love each other. I got knocked up. I've had to grow up, move out of home, quit school; I lost my job. I barely see my only good friend. I don't surf anymore. I've tried. I'll try again when I'm okay and I have the babies. I'm scared.'

I put both my hands on Mount Vesuvius and grappled with how I felt. Terrified but excited, resentful but some warmth to these babies. Sometimes the fear of becoming a mother made me as scared as I was on the day of the accident, maybe even as scared as I was when I had run away from Eddie. I spent so much time running away from everything, especially the truth. I'd learnt some hard lessons in the last few months, especially about sacrifice.

Sometimes it felt as though it would have been easier if Tamara had died that day. I wondered if I would have been all right. Somehow the way she was hovering, here but not the same, made it worse.

I murmured, 'Are you in pain? I hope not. If it all that never happened, I never would have met Jake and who knows…Eddie would have left me alone. I would still be surfing…My babies…wouldn't exist…ever, and that would have been better.'

That sounded mean so I stopped and tried to feel happy, content with the bursts of early spring sunshine breaking through the sky, with the sound of the water but all I could think about was Tamara and how much I missed her. She made the beach the best place in the world. Without her presence, it was just…sand and water, seaweed, and the scent of salt in the air.

'I wish you were here so you could be with me,' I whispered into the air.

I stood up and walked to the rocky edge of the water exactly where Jake had pulled her out of the water. I pulled up my pants and let the water swell over my ankles, making me gasp with the cold. The water came in, and it flowed out. After a few laps, my skin adjusted to the temperature and I waded slowly further in, allowing my pants to get wet. Just as the sand sloped down and away, I stopped and gasped for air. I had stopped breathing. The water came rushed into Mount Vesuvius. I could easily go further in and float, weightless and free in the current, but the cold stopped me. I smiled and laughed. Water. In my veins, in their veins. I'd go out again one day. One day, I'd be okay.

I wiped a tear away from my face but trailed sand all over my cheek. With both hands on my belly, I yelled. Happy. Angry. Scared. All combined. I stumbled free of the water and lay on the sand and sobbed, letting the tears roll from my eyes and into my ears. I probably looked insane, but it was what I needed. I needed to be one with the beach where my life had fallen apart.

Jake

September 2011

On a Saturday morning, Dad and I had breakfast with Sanna while Mom went to a local market to sell some of the crafts she'd made at church with her church friends. Dad had a newspaper open and he mumbled, 'Well, will you look at that. There's a country music concert in town tonight.' He looked up at me. 'That'd be good for you and Sanna to get out of the house.'

I looked at Sanna and shrugged. She said, 'Yes!'

I'd never heard of any of the acts and Sanna didn't even like country music but we went. I wore my best jeans, my boots and a beige suede jacket with wool inside. I placed my black Stetson on my head and glared at my reflection. Cowboy. Here I was again, being the cowboy. I rubbed my hands together and forced myself to walk out the door with Sanna.

We arrived at the venue late, amid a downpour. I tried to chivalrously give Sanna my jacket but she didn't even notice. She was too occupied walking and fussing over her sandal that still refused to fit her because of the pregnancy. She then had to jog to the ladies' room almost straight away and I stood there in the crowd wondering how to look less-American Cowboy, more Aussie-Battler style. Flannel seemed popular, and high-vis shirts. We were almost the same. Aussie cowboys were less rustic, more stained. Worlds apart, yet connected over the love of the land and a can-do attitude.

The band got under way and Sanna was still not back. I looked around, still eager to blend with the crowd but glanced at the back-up singers on the stage and saw her: Tessa. She was the shortest of the harmony singers and the youngest by about ten years. Her hair had new highlights and was glammed up with elegant waves. Her big, bright red lips seemed to make out with the microphone as she sang, swaying her hips along with the music. The Wrangler shirt she was wearing was too short and her belly peeked through, her naval twinkled with a belly-piercing. That was new. I liked it. As far as I knew, she hadn't seen me but I stood there, rooted to the spot, drooling over her newly discovered sex appeal. She had made it as a singer after all, and I couldn't keep my eyes off her.

After three songs, Sanna found her way back to me. Her mascara had smudged and her cheeks were red. I casually stepped in front of her to block her view of the stage. 'I want to go home,' she said. 'My stomach is upset.

My eyes went to Tessa. Leaving would mean I wouldn't see her anymore. Sanna's hand burrowed into mine and I had to force my hand to close around hers. Yes, I was with Sanna. I wasn't with that sexy girl on stage anymore. I backed away, getting a last look at Tessa before finally dragging my vision to Sanna.

I nodded and said, 'Okay.'

I drove us home in silence and went straight to the shower where I could be alone with the vision of Tessa in my mind. I leaned against the cold tile wall of the shower when I was done, trembling with post-coital pleasure and guilt.

When I emerged, Sanna asked, 'What took you so long?'

'Nothing,' I said with a lump in my throat.

'Are you going to pretend that you didn't see her?' she asked quietly.

I started to pour myself a glass of water but stopped and blinked at her. 'Is that why you wanted to go early?'

She stayed silent but stared at me.

I shook my head. 'I don't want to talk about her.'

'What if I want to?'

'I said no!' I snapped and stormed into my bedroom, slamming the door like a nine-year-old girl throwing a tantrum.

The next morning, Sanna lied to my parents about the reason we came home so early. She said she simply was too tired. My mother hugged her and they spoke about how exhausting pregnancy is. I yawned.

Later, my dad met me in the barn and asked, 'What'd you do?'

'I didn't do anything.'

'That girl is lying.'

If he only knew.

I shrugged and said, 'Whatever.'

He snapped, 'Don't turn yer back on me, son. You had the chance to prove to her that you can be a good man for her and you brought her home after an hour. Yer a coward.'

I snapped, 'You can talk!'

Dad grabbed a leather headstall and pelted it at me. I dodged it but caught the furious glare he levelled at me.

I shouted, 'I didn't realize last night was some sort of test! Not to mention that none of this is any of your business!'

He screwed up his face with anger and asked, 'Can you really just not stand to be close to anybody?'

I could count them on my hand: Tessa; I had been close to Tessa. I had been close to Alex and my friend Johnny back in Texas who I had to leave behind. My old dog that we left behind when we moved to Australia; My mother and I had been close, even though all closeness had gone now. My relationship with God was also on the extinction list. I didn't feel close to many people anymore. Rio. Maybe Johann. Certainly not my parents. Not even Sanna with how much responsibility I had now as a result of being close with her.

I didn't say any of that, however. I left it bottled up inside and walked away.

The third term ended sooner than I anticipated. Doing nothing but studying and arguing with my father, preparing for the imminent end of year exams. The morning of our last chemistry class of the term, Clint ushered me over to him in the small corner where he smoked cigarettes and did things with girls that nobody should do in public.

'I hear you're doin' really good, Ryan,' he said as he lit a cigarette.

'I've worked hard, Clint,' I said tersely. I thought I knew exactly what he was going to say. He probably wanted me to give him some help over the spring break so he could actually pass his exams next term.

'My folks have got a place in Blairgowrie – right near the beach. A couple of guys and me are gonna go down and party next weekend. You up for that?'

I would have said yes if I didn't have a fiancée and imminent fatherhood to children who were not even mine. I shook my head, disappointed. 'I would have really loved to, but yeah nah, I can't.'

'Yeah nah,' he imitated my try-hard Australian vernacular. He laughed and patted me on the shoulder. 'No worries, mate. Thought I'd invite you because your buddy's coming.'

'Johann's going?' I said with utter shock. Johann hated Clint and his buddies. They teased my accent but they ridiculed Johann's. Clint nodded and breathed in deeply on his cigarette.

Maybe it would be okay if I went for a night. Maybe even two if Sanna could go, too. I asked, 'Are girls allowed?'

Clint winked. 'Girlfriends are welcome.'

'I might come for a night or two.'

'Sure, sure. Let me know!'

I went home to find Sanna hanging a picture of a horse in her bedroom. 'Hey!' she said.

Her blonde hair was tied back in a ponytail and it accentuated the angle of her cheekbones. Her cheeks were puffy but you could still tell that she had the face of an active girl under that mask of hormones. I took a deep breath. It was harder than I thought it would be. How hard was it to ask your fiancée something? The answer was: easy. How hard was it to ask your fiancée something when you were only engaged because she was expecting? The answer was: not easy.

She rubbed her bare arms. The winter was hanging on into early spring. Winters in Gippsland were rainy, windy and icy. The sky rarely ever cleared of clouds. The sun came in bursts, or usually at sunset, like a tease. The clouds parted only for rain. It had been the wettest winter in fifty years. It rained a lot back in Texas, but nothing compared to the mud and the constant bitter ache of the cold seeping into your bones. The temperature was always above freezing, but it felt about twenty below. How Sanna could walk around in just a tee-shirt in winter was beyond me.

'I have a question to ask you,' I said.

'Oh?'

'A couple of guys from school, including Johann, are gonna go down to Blair...' I forgot the name of the town. That was terrific! Not.

'Blairgowrie?' said Sanna after a minute of me searching my brain.

'Yeah, Blairgowrie,' I said. 'You know, on the holidays as a one-last big party before we sit our exams.'

'You want to know if you can go with all your mates and leave me here.'

'No, no! I want to know if you want to come to Blairgowrie with all my mates.'

She gave me a blank look and the put her hand on her belly. 'I'm like…twenty-five weeks pregnant with twins right now, Jake. That's the size of what most women are when they're full-term.'

'Yeah, I know,' I admitted, scratching the back of my head.

'I don't know if we can risk it. The doctor said I have every chance of going early…and if I go now, they'll be way too little to survive.'

Here we go. Doctor said this so we can't do that. Doctor tells me to do this so you have to do that. Doctor said doctor said doctor said. I groaned. 'Just for a night. Please. It'll be fun.'

'What the heck do you have in mind that we do down there in Blairgowrie? Go surfing at Flinders, snorkel with the seals of Portsea? Go bushwalking up and down Arthur's Seat?'

I had no idea what she was talking about. I shrugged. 'I don't know. Just relax. Watch movies, play video games, sit on the beach…'

'We can do all that here,' she whined. 'I'm really tired all the time, Jake. What happens if the babies come early?'

'That won't happen.'

'You can't say that,' she said.

'You can't say that it will.'

She huffed at me and we stared at each other like two outlaws with their hands at their hips, where guns were lying in waiting. Sanna said quietly, 'If I wasn't pregnant, I'd really like to go.'

'Funny that's what I told Clint,' I muttered. 'I figured you'd want to come with me.'

She looked at me incredulously and exclaimed, 'You're going to go with or without me, aren't you?'

'Yeah,' I said nastily. *Oh, Jake what are you doing?* I took a deep breath and tried to be calm. 'I deserve this. I deserve to have fun.' *Don't forget what I'm doing for you.*

'And I don't?' Her lip wobbled. *Please don't cry*, I thought.

'Yes, you do! That's why you should come. Just for one night. What harm could it do?'

She sat on her bed and covered her face with her hands. I leaned on the architrave and waited quietly for her to make a decision. She muttered, 'I'll go but only if Michael can come so I have somebody to talk to.'

'What?' I asked, not sure if I heard her correctly through her hands. She uncovered her face and repeated herself. 'Who's Michael?' I asked.

'He's my best friend.'

'The writer guy?' I said suspiciously.

She nodded. 'Take it or leave it, Jake.'

What kind of couple would we be perceived as if I rocked up at Clint's holiday home with my fiancée who insisted on bringing another guy? If Sanna was so keen on this guy, what would happen if the guys started questioning if the kids were even mine? I really wanted to go hang out at the holiday house and get away from the farm for a few days. Getting away from the mud, the cows, the smell of manure and raw milk was the most appealing thing to me in the world at that moment. Who cares about some guy and if others started to doubt Sanna?

I nodded and said, 'Okay.'

October 2011

I met Michael for the first time the morning we left for the party. I was surprised to see he had dreadlocks. I hadn't expected him to look the way he did. A sideways grin, sleepy eyes but friendly and genuine. He had a manner with Sanna that I envied – they knew each other. Not in the way I knew her. Closer.

I shook his hand and we began driving, me as the third wheel as they talked and joked, leaning into each other, and giggling at jokes I didn't get. Sanna was in the passenger seat and Michael sat in the middle, all our stuff taking up the space in the backseat. Michael was lanky in frame; his legs almost seemed to have to curl up under the dashboard of the truck. I put on my baseball cap and a pair of sunglasses and drove down the Bass Coast Highway out of town while Michael and Sanna chatted about people I'd never heard Sanna mention before. Maybe he would be a better father than I would be. I had only thought a week in advance when I had made the offer to Sanna. For someone that was so obsessed with his future, I sure hadn't thought it through with her.

We stopped at a roadside attraction. A wooden tower twisted itself upwards and overlooked the swampy marshland of the flat area of land. There was a food van, and we ordered hot dogs. Michael bought us Gatorades. I hated Gatorade but I drank it anyway. The faster I drank it, the better. Michael made small talk while we waited for the hot dogs to cook.

'So, Jake,' said Michael. 'Heard you're from Texas.'

'You heard correctly,' I replied, glancing off the marshland at him. He grinned at me. He looked so much like a stoner with a crooked grin like that. Hanging around with Sanna, he probably was.

'Is it cool being from Texas?' he asked.

'I don't know,' I said with a snort. 'How would I know? I don't know any differently.'

'Did you like Texas?'

'Stop saying Texas,' I grumbled.

'Why don't you like me saying Texas?' he asked with a frown. Sanna shook her head and looked up at the tower.

'Seriously,' I said.

'Why'd you move here to Australia?' he asked.

'I just did, okay,' I said. 'My parents moved here so I kind of had to follow them, you know.'

'I'm just making conversation, man,' he said. 'I'm not being intrusive or anything.'

'Yeah,' I said. 'That's fine.'

'I'm curious, that's all.'

I sighed. 'Uh-huh.'

'So, you gonna tell me or what?' he laughed.

'Michael,' said Sanna sharply. 'Shut up.'

He rolled his eyes and went to the tower, stepping up with his gangly legs.

'He's seriously a pain in the ass,' I said to Sanna. She laughed. 'This is going to be a long weekend.' We took the hot dogs from the person at the food van and thanked them.

'He's being really weird,' Sanna admitted. She slopped a bit of tomato sauce on her pants and she groaned. 'Damn, that sucks.'

'I'm the king of the world!' shouted Michael from the top-level of the observation tower with his arms stretched out like an idiot.

'I feel very inclined to leave him up there,' I said, wiping at Sanna's pants, glancing up at Michael.

'He's not usually like this,' she said with a mouth full of processed meat and bread. 'I'm going to have to talk to him.'

'How far until we get to Blairgowrie?' I asked, standing up straight and leaning against the bed of the truck. 'I can't take much longer of being crammed in like a sardine.'

Sanna laughed. 'I'll talk to him.' She walked to the steps of the observation tower, encumbered by her belly and stiff hips. 'Michael!' she shouted. 'Get your butt down here!'

The way she shouted made me cringe then laugh. With her belly poking out, her flip-flops on and her hand on her hip, shouting at the top of her lungs – she looked like trailer trash and it was adorable. All she needed was the bare feet.

Blairgowrie was another hour drive, but Michael was subdued for the rest of the ride. He looked at me in the corner of his eye and I looked at him with the corner of mine. I left him and Sanna to chat while I navigated the signs that pointed us in the right direction.

We arrived at Clint's house around lunch time and Johann met us in the driveway. 'Jake, hey,' he said.

'Hey.'

Sanna and Michael followed me.

'Sanna,' said Johann, saying her name spot-on correctly. 'Good to see you again.' They shook hands. Michael stepped forward and introduced himself. He got along well with Johann. There was no weirdness radiating from him the way it did when he spoke to me. He went inside with Sanna, carrying her bag for her.

I stood beside Johann who said, 'He likes her, you know.'

I shrugged. 'So?'

'So, I'd watch out.'

'I don't even care anymore. Where's the party?'

I spent the night drinking with Johann and the guys from school. Clint gave me money to go down to the drive-thru bottle shop to pick up more alcohol. I hit the gutter and rode up on the nature strip a couple of times. I was lucky that I didn't have an accident. Sanna spent the night with Michael. He smoked about two packets of cigarettes and Sanna sat nearby, talking, always talking. She didn't seem to care about the smoke hurting the babies but at least she didn't smoke.

'So, who's that guy with your girlfriend, Texas?' asked Clint, lighting the woodfire with drunken caution.

'They're friends,' I said, glancing at them. They were sitting in the corner of the dark living room, still talking. 'School mates,' I added.

'I'd be a bit pissed if my girlfriend brought another dude here,' he said, sinking down into a well-worn bean bag. I expected the bag to disintegrate and the beans to all flow out on to the floor, but it stayed intact and supported Clint's muscular frame.

He said, 'I mean, how are you gonna have sex with her tonight if you've got this other guy in the way?'

I shook my head. 'Subtle, Clint, real subtle.'

'They're not going to have sex, doofus,' said one of his friends. 'She's already knocked up. Hell, I'd be putting a god damn cage on my dick for at least a year if I knocked a chick up.' This made the entire group of boys to roar with laughter. Even Johann had a giggle. The boys all argued whether or not Clint's friend could indeed either a) sleep with a girl in the first place to knock her up or b) literally put a cage on his genitals. I stood and said, 'I'm getting another beer.'

'You've had nine,' said Johann sharply. 'Don't you think that's enough?'

I glanced at Michael and Sanna talking animatedly in the corner and said, 'No, I don't think that's enough, Johann.'

I woke up the next morning outside on the patio. I woke up in a puddle of drool and my body covered in goose bumps. It was freezing. I wrinkled my nose in disgust and got up. Johann was asleep on a deck chair beside me. I shoved him awake. 'Hey, where's Sanna?'

'I don't know,' he said and went back to sleep. I walked into the house. All the guys and their girlfriends, or dates, were asleep, strewn around the living room. Sanna and Michael weren't among them. I went into each bedroom, not even waking the naked couples that occupied the rooms.

I found them asleep in the bed of my truck under a wool blanket and a few jackets. I opened the tailgate and Michael sat up. 'Morning,' I said with tight lips.

'Hey, Jake,' he said sheepishly. I shook Sanna's foot. She curled into the fetal position and grunted.

Michael grinned. 'She snores.'

'She's six-months pregnant, Michael,' I snapped. My head was killing me. I didn't care about any little thing about Sanna that he was charmed by. I narrowed my eyes at him. 'She's *my* fiancée.'

He paused before he said, with a lack of expression, 'She's not yours, Jake. She never was.'

I blinked and let go of Sanna's foot. With that, she opened her eyes and stretched out. She wiped her eyes and opened them slowly. She saw me and she saw Michael. 'What's going on?' she asked.

Michael shoved his skate shoes on. 'Nothing,' he said without looking at her as she sat up beside him. 'Jake and I were just discussing boys' business.'

'Boys' business?' she asked curiously, looking in my direction.

I ran my hand over my lips and replied, 'Sports and beer and...sex.'

Michael glared at me. Sanna scoffed. 'Yeah, right.'

'Go grab your things,' I said.

Michael snapped at me, 'Hey, Jake – who was that girl you were sleeping with before? I saw you.' He was smug with his lie.

I stared at him and Sanna stared at me. 'What?' she asked.

'I didn't sleep with anyone,' I spat.

'Looked that way to me. All the other guys said you two were pretty hot for each other.'

I looked to Sanna whose eyes were tearing up. 'He's full of crap, Sanna. I wasn't with any girl.'

'Brunette. Kinda Iranian looking,' said Michael.

'Shut up,' I snapped. 'Nothing happened,' I added to Sanna. She stood up and jumped out of the tailgate. She stumbled as she landed and cried out. 'Sanna!' I cried but she staggered to her feet and jumped into the driver's seat of my truck. I met her at the window. 'What are you doing?'

'Why would you cheat on me?'

'I didn't!' I shrieked. 'He's lying!'

'Michael would never lie to me. You're the liar, Jake Ryan! By the way, we're over. Deal's off. I'll do this alone.' She grabbed the key that I left in the visor and started my truck. She planted her bare foot on the gas. The tires squealed loudly before the truck lurched into gear and bumped down the driveway at sixty kilometres an hour, at least, all with Michael hanging tightly onto the rails of the bed as she drove.

'Damn it!' I screamed. A couple of people came to the front porch to see what the disturbance was about. Johann stood beside me. 'Shit!' I said, balling my fists in anger.

'What do we do?' he asked, biting his nails.

'I don't know,' I said. I ran my hands through my hair and resisted the urge to cry. I loved that truck.

'Call her mum,' said Johann.

'No way; she'll blame me.'

'Call the police then.'

I hesitated and then nodded. 'Okay.'

Sanna

October 2011

The road was narrow and lined with ti-trees and paperbark trees. The powerlines dipped so low they nestled in the foliage the way my foot dug deep into the accelerator. I'd never driven so fast before. I sobbed and wiped my eyes clear.

I passed cars, cyclists that had to swerve onto the dirt shoulder and an elderly couple walking a dog. I had no idea where I was going, except to the main road and the beach. When things went wrong, I always went to the beach, like a compass finding north.

I couldn't believe Jake had done what he had done when he'd tried so hard to be nice to me. He was such a liar! That scumbag! I screamed but it made my hands shake too much and I jerked the wheel.

It was as though I was destined to be a screw-up. First I nearly killed my best friend, then I got knocked up by a sociopath and now even the good guy ended up being bad because he'd laid eyes on Tessa at that concert and then couldn't help himself and cheated on me with some other girl. I would never be anyone's favourite person. Heck, even my parents had practically kicked me out when they found out I was pregnant. I was always everyone's last choice. Jake even liked his ute more than he liked me.

'This stupid car!' I yelled. 'Your precious ute!' I had a wild idea of driving it off a pier. It seemed like a great idea until I reached a pier and I chickened out.

I parked it in the carpark and cried some more.

'Sanna!' somebody called from outside. I yelped and sat bolt upright. It was Michael. His hair was dishevelled and his tee-shirt was almost coming off one shoulder. He opened the door and I fell into his arms. He hugged me and I clutched at him like he was Jesus Christ come to save me.

'This can't be my life!' I shouted into his neck.

'I know,' he said, resting a hand on the back of my head. 'I know.'

'How could I mess up my life like this?' I wailed.

'Sanna,' he said and hushed me like he was soothing a baby. I pulled out of his embrace and wiped my face with the back of my hand. 'Oh my God,' I whined. 'Why did I let this happen to me? I shouldn't have let him talk me into coming. I shouldn't have kept this pregnancy.' A deeper, more powerful anger rose up inside me as I thought of what Eddie had done to me and it turned to the babies. 'These stupid babies!' I exclaimed with hate. I didn't need the constant reminder of being raped. That was what they were. Nothing but hurt and misery. 'I hate them! I'm giving them up!'

'No,' said Michael. 'You don't hate them.'

'They've ruined everything!' I wailed.

'No, they haven't. It's gonna be okay,' he said. He pulled me back into a hug and I let him hold me for a while. My throat was sore from screaming and my face felt like the Hindenburg blimp. After a while, Michael said, 'Let's go for a swim.'

I looked at him. 'What did you say?'

'Let's go for a swim,' he said, pointing down the pier. 'It'll make it all better.'

I let him take my hand and lead me down the pier. We stood at the very end – where the tide buffeted the wooden construction around beneath our feet. I curled my toes over the edge and took a deep, miserable breath. 'A year ago, I would have jumped off here in a flash.'

'We're gonna jump now,' said Michael with a smile.

'What? No way,' but I looked down at the emerald water. 'It'll be freezing.'

'Come in the water with me, Sanna,' he said. 'It'll be like a fresh start...or a new beginning. A do-over, you know.'

I put my hand on Mount Vesuvius. There were no do-overs. I knew that at least, but I stepped closer the edge. 'I'm ready.'

Michael took my hand and counted to three. We screamed and jumped into the water from the end of the pier. Hitting the water took all my breath away and I inwardly gasped and allowed the water to hold me, weightless and free.

As we surfaced, Michael and I laughed. We shivered in the water, staying close. I held onto his shoulders and watched his face grimace with the cold. His mouth was open, lips chattering. The water beaded off his cheeks. I allowed him to scoop me up in a bridal carry and closed my eyes, feeling my back and abs constrict with the cold. I could feel the morning sun on my eyelids but it gave no warmth. I could sleep like this. This. Here. In the water, with Michael.

'Sanna,' he whispered. 'I love you.'

'I love you, too.' I opened my eyes. He bent to kiss me but a sudden warm gush under the water made me bolt upright. 'Oh no.'

'What's wrong?'

My mind raced as I felt with my hands. Yes, the warm gush had come from me. Was that my water breaking?

Michael's eyes widened at me as I gasped, 'I think I'm having the babies.' My brain did the maths. Twenty-six weeks.

I was still way too early. Don't make me go through I've been through, God, just to make them come early and probably die. I couldn't swallow. My body stopped being able to do anything except panic.

'I'll get you to the hospital!' Michael rushed me out of the water and up to the truck. On the sand, I fell to my knees as a cramp set in. Michael pulled me up and bundled me into the passenger seat. He jumped into the driver's side and drove Jake's ute down the road. As we drove, he took a deep breath. 'Sanna, I've got to tell you.'

'What?' I gripped the door handle.

'I lied to you.'

'What?'

'About Jake...there was no girl.' He looked across at me with a frown. 'I don't know why. I didn't want to hurt you.'

'I lied to you, too...' I mumbled.

'About what?'

'Jake's not the father.'

He braked at an orange light and did a double-take at me, but a contraction started and I wailed in pain, causing him to floor it through the light after it had changed to red.

'I'll get you to the hospital, Sanna. Just hang on!'

A police siren rang out behind us and its red and blue lights illuminated the car. Michael groaned and pulled over, burying his head. 'Crap.'

The police officer strolled over and said, 'How's it goin'?'

'She's going into labour! I didn't mean to run the red light – I'm so sorry – I just need to get her to the hospital!'

The police officer took off their sunglasses and peered in at me. I waved awkwardly. The police officer gulped and nodded. 'Right. Jump in my car. I'll take you to the hospital.'

By the time I arrived at the hospital, the contractions had stopped. I waited for the contractions to come, and I held Michael's hand. The police officer wished me luck and left to

182

go tell Jake that his car and his fiancée had been found, and that he should probably get the hospital because she was in labour with his children.

Michael squeezed my hand but then let go, to put both his hands on top of his head and curse quietly to himself. 'Not the father…shit.'

I looked down at my swollen feet and continued to wait for the next contraction. One still hadn't happened since being in the car with Michael, and I was beginning to think something was wrong. A nurse, or midwife – I couldn't tell – came over and asked if I could walk. I nodded and I followed her into the dark ultrasound room.

She stuck me with heart rate monitors and started scanning my bump.

'Is everything okay?' I cried as she pushed against Mount Vesuvius.

'All looks completely fine.' She wiped the tool off with a towel, then my belly. I gaped at her, waiting for an explanation. She said nonchalantly, 'Sounds like you had Braxton Hicks, my dear.' She smiled. 'Completely normal.'

'But, no…there was…my water broke.'

She smiled at me with pity. 'You might have accidentally peed.'

'What?' I scoffed.

'That's normal, too. You're only little. It's a lot for your body to handle. It's completely normal to have some incontinence during pregnancy. We'll get you back home with some pads…'

'I have to wear a nappy?' I cried incredulously. I started to cry. 'This…this is…I can't believe this.'

She touched my arm and said, 'Like I said…completely normal. You and the babies are fine. The Braxton Hicks are false contractions. Your babies are still baking away, and your body is just getting ready to give birth. It'll be okay.'

I walked out of the room, stunned and dazed, shuffling along and my thongs slapped and squealed from getting wet. I sat back down in a huff on the edge of the waiting room chair and Michael put his arm around me.

'What did they say?'

I opened my mouth to tell him about the incontinence but shut it again. He didn't need to know that. It wasn't his baby. I murmured, 'False labour. I'm okay. They're okay.'

A nurse came by to drop by a packet of incontinence pads and a discharge letter for my GP. Michael looked at the pads and gave me a quizzical look. I burned with embarrassment and eased myself to my feet to walk out.

I had at least two months left. If I had the babies now, their chance of survival would be critically low. I kept one hand on Mount Vesuvius as if I could stop them falling out too early. Stay in there, babies. Don't be hasty. No more jumping off the pier for me!

Jake picked us up. He got out of the ute and pulled me into a tight hug. I wept into his neck, not even knowing why I was crying. I was overwhelmed by everything that had happened. Absolutely everything – all the way back to Tamara's accident.

Michael remained quiet until Jake dropped him at his home. Rubbish was scattered in the front yard. He squeezed my hand and said, 'Here if you need me.'

Jake and I watched him go inside and shut the door before I said, 'I know he lied. I'm sorry I overreacted.'

He deflated like a balloon and said, 'I'm so sorry for dragging you along to this party. I was selfish. I never would have forgiven myself if I made you lose the babies.'

'It was me!' I cried. 'I jumped off the pier. I shouldn't have done that.'

Jake laughed. 'Nah, maybe not…but these Braxton Hicks…they're normal, so don't beat yourself up.'

I leant over to him and awkwardly hugged him. He laughed and said, 'Let's go home.'

Jake came with me to see Tamara almost two weeks later. He didn't come in. He stayed in the car, wanting to read through his notes and text books. He'd gone back to school that week for the final term, and was studying like a maniac. We were both counting down for things – me for the babies to be born and him for his exams to come and go. Both were as terrifying to us as the other.

It was a warm day, 25 degrees, and I was boiling. I waddled my way into the rehab clinic and the cool air of the air conditioner hit my face and I could have melted on the spot. I said hello to the nurses as I waddled down the corridor to Tamara's room. My heart hammered as I knocked on the door.

I opened the door and peered into the room, but it was empty. I stepped back out of the room and made my way back to the front desk where the receptionist was sitting. I asked with a waver in my voice, 'Where's Tamara Jenkins?'

'She's with the occupational therapist right now doing some therapy. I can find out how long she'll be?'

I shook my head and hurried away with tightness in my hips stopping me from being able to stride out. I got back into Jake's ute with some difficulty and he asked, 'What's wrong?'

I wiped the sweat from my face – I'd never sweat so much in my life – and shook my head. 'She's busy.'

He chewed on his lip before he asked, 'Doing what exactly?'

'She's with a therapist. I didn't want to wait.'

'Why not?'

My face flushed again and I swallowed, the acid reflux making me want to vomit or drool everywhere. 'I don't know.' I shook my head and added, 'It's like I want to see her…but then I don't. I get scared.'

'It's okay to be scared,' Jake murmured. 'Do you want me to come with you?'

'No. I…I think I'll just visit her another time.'

Jake looked at me as though he didn't believe me. He said, 'I don't think I'll be able to take you again this side of my exams…Are you sure you don't want to just go up and wait?'

I hesitated. He was right. In two weeks, he'd be in the midst of his exams, and I'd be 30 weeks pregnant – with twins…which is the equivalent of being pregnant with what would probably feel like a dinosaur in my uterus. It was getting harder and harder for me to get around. Two weeks ago, I could jump off the pier – with consequences, though – and now even walking was painful. The next time I'd probably see Tamara was after the babies were born. That thought made my heart palpate and I made my mind up.

I kicked off my thongs and said, 'It's okay. It's not like she's going anywhere, right?'

'It's your call.'

'I'll go see her when the babies are born. Then she can meet them, and they can meet her.'

'Sounds like a plan,' he said with a smile. I cranked up the air conditioner to high and sighed as the air fanned on my face.

The next week, Jake was at school and Isabel was out shopping. Will was outside, fixing the tractor and I was sitting around with my feet up, almost dozing. The level of tiredness was off the charts. Next level exhaustion. Even just getting up in the morning knackered me.

Will startled me awake by sprinting into the house and running his hand under the tap, muttering to himself. I heaved myself off the couch and asked him what had happened.

'I burned myself on the exhaust.' He held out his hand to show me. It was bright red. 'Son of a doohickey.'

'Ouch…Can I help?'

'You could bandage it for me?'

'Sure.'

He told me where to find the bandages and he kept his hand under the water until he couldn't stand the cold anymore. It was still red but it wasn't blistering or bleeding.

I wrapped his hand in the bandage and he smiled. 'Thanks Suzie. You're a good girl.'

'I aim to please. Does it hurt?'

'Like crazy.' He grinned. 'But I'll live.'

'That's the important thing,' I said with a smile. One of the babies kicked and I winced. It actually quite hurt when they moved or kicked now. I was getting close to getting over everything.

'They kickin'?'

'Yeah – they're violent little sods.'

Will laughed and touched Mount Vesuvius gently and his eyes faded. 'My boys used to kick like crazy.'

He put his hat back on and sniffed. 'Still can't believe Alex is gone.'

I eased myself down into the chair so I could get off my feet. 'Jake doesn't talk about him much.'

Will nodded with a grim smile. 'I guess that's my doin'. I refused to talk about him because it hurt too much. Nothin' prepares yer to lose a child and heck…he was the second one.' He winced and nursed his bandaged hand. 'Feels like God is against me half the time. It's why I started drinkin'.'

I could understand that. The way I used to drink after Tamara's accident was testament to that. I asked, 'Do you think Jake knows how much you miss Alex?'

Will shook his head. 'Nah…But I do know he was there the day the car was brought home on the back of a truck.' He sniffed again. 'He saw the mess of the car and must have felt the same way I did.'

'How?'

'Like how violent his death must have been…and angry that it had gone that way.'

I hadn't even known it was a car accident. I'd always been nervous to ask how Alex had died.

'It was his own fault,' Will said, his lip trembling and tears springing to his eyes. 'I was so mad at him that he had been such a fool and done something so stupid.'

'You think Jake feels exactly the same way?' I asked.

Will nodded. He wiped his face with his good hand and said, 'Ah, listen to me blab on. Sorry, Suzie. Thanks for listening.' He stood up and went back outside. I sat at the table for a moment, thinking through what he had told me.

He needed to connect more with Jake. Instead, they avoided each other and even argued. Jake was so quiet and reserved, and he stuffed everything inside, just like his dad. He would end up being like him in every way if he didn't express himself somehow.

When Jake returned home from school that day, I cornered him in the driveway before he could even get into the house.

'What's going on?' he asked.

'I want you and your dad to spend some time together.'

He scoffed. 'Okay then.'

'No, I'm serious. You guys have a lot to talk about.'

He shook his head. 'No, we really don't.'

'About Alex. Yes, you do.'

He walked away but turned his head to say, 'No, Sanna. He doesn't want to talk about him.'

'What kind of father do you want to be, Jake? One like him? Or one that lets their child talk about how they're feeling?'

His eyes went to the ground but he didn't say anything. I shifted my weight from one foot to the other, and found no comfort in either position. I waddled to the patio swing and lowered myself, leaning my head back with a sigh. His face softened and he sat next to me, his hands tightly together between his knees.

'Your dad had a drinking problem, Jake,' I sighed. 'He struggled so bad when Alex died.'

'I know he did,' he whispered. 'We all did.'

'Can't you help each other?' I asked.

'I needed help then...I don't need it now.'

'He does.'

He looked me in the eye and I stared back at him. His green eyes searched my face for extra details but I gave him none. He finally said, 'I'll see if he wants to go fishing this weekend.'

I smiled and hugged him. 'Good.'

Jake

February 2009

Last year, Dad said we were moving. My mother stayed quiet, sitting at the table with her shoulders straight, her hair curled and her fingernails, un-painted, digging into her palms. Her lipstick was smudged at the corners of her mouth from having her mouth so downturned. I watched her take a breath slowly in and breathe it out three, two, one, but she stayed quiet.

My father was animated. He spoke about a place his uncle had left for him upon passing. A farm down-under. Australia. It wasn't so different to what we had in Hartley, Texas. We had cattle. Australia had cattle. How difficult could it be?

Looking back, I know he was running away. Running away from the road where Alex had died, running away from the house with all the memories of his sons. He could run away from the place, but his memories would come with him.

We moved on Christmas Day 2008. My mother wouldn't look me in the eye without a slight wince. I'd screwed up and Alex might have lived if it hadn't been for me. I went mute.

In Australia, I had become more isolated from Texas and my family. I'd cracked the window open to cool the room down. It was stifling. The day had reached over 100 degrees. Coming from quite a cool Texas winter, my body shocked and revolted against heat that I would ordinarily snort at.

My mother fanned her face and my father wiped his brow before sinking into his armchair the moment he could to kick off his boots and even his pants. I wandered around the new house, with its stained timber walls and green carpet. Ugly. It was ugly.

My dad started drinking at the pub to fit in with the Aussies and he cried with them when fires ripped through parts of the state. Our area had been lucky, but all the Aussie farmers were shellshocked after knowing people that had died or been burned, or lost their livelihoods and farms. The fires killed 173 people. 173 Alexes. My voice had caught in my throat and I couldn't say anything. The locals at the pub drank to appease their loss, and my father sank right on down with them.

October 2011

I'd started to forget what it had been like moving to a new country and setting up a new life with a fractured family. I'd started focusing on getting into university so I could get away and become somebody that I had never imagined becoming. I'd started to forget that some fathers sacrifice themselves for their children. I knew Sanna was right. I had to spend time with my father and let him be the father he used to be, before our lives were redirected.

The night Sanna accosted me, I noticed my father tidying around the barn, so I walked out there to give him a hand.

'How's the studying going?'

'Maths is doing my head in,' I replied. It was my weakest subject. The class, maths methods, was not even the most advanced maths you could take, but it would be enough to get me into a science degree to then get into medical science. I decided to add, 'It's got me worried.'

My dad took off his hat and wiped down his brown hair. It was getting thin on top. 'I'm sure you'll do well. You're working really hard.'

It was awkward to receive praise from him so I picked up a spanner and tapped it in my hand. 'What are you doing?'

'Just tidying up around here.' He gestured out to the hills. 'Never can be too prepared for a bushfire.'

I nodded. Moving to Australia just before the deadliest fire in their history roared through had made him extra-diligent. He pulled out the fire hose and inspected it. It was only late October, but he was going to be ready.

'I was thinking…well, Sanna was thinking…'

He looked up at me as he wound the hose back in. 'Uh-oh. The missus has put you up to something.'

I laughed. 'Yeah…Want to go fishing this weekend?'

'What about your studying?'

'Could be a nice break.'

He smiled. 'Could be.' He nodded. 'Sure. Let's go fishin'.'

Saturday morning, Dad and I sat on the edge of Powlett River and I thought for something to say, but kept going blank. He stayed quiet as well. We didn't catch anything and we walked back to the car with a heavy mood. As we were packing our toolboxes, Dad said, 'Maybe we'll have better luck next time.'

'I hope so, because that was bad,' I laughed.

He leaned against the back of the truck and crossed his arms. 'So why did Sanna think it would be a good idea for us to come fishing?'

'The fishing was my idea.'

'Why?'

I shrugged. 'We used to go fishing a lot before Alex died. I miss it.'

He wet his lips with his tongue and nodded slowly. 'Right.'

I narrowed my eyes. 'Don't you?'

'Don't I what?'

'Miss fishing.'

'We're not really talkin' about fishin' though, are we?'

My cheeks burnt and my jaw tensed. 'What else would I miss?' He gave me a pointed look from under his hat and I rolled my eyes and shoved my fishing rod into the bed of the truck. 'I shouldn't have bothered.'

'Son, I –'

'No.' I pointed my finger at him. 'You don't get to make a big deal out of me wanting to spend time with you. You're my dad. Either act like it or shut up. I could be studying right now, but no.'

'I miss it too, for crying out loud. Is that what you want to hear? I miss fishing. I miss fishing with you. I miss Alex. Okay!'

I took a step back, stunned that he'd verbalized it.

He shrugged. 'There. I said it. Now can you?'

I swallowed and gritted my teeth. Maybe the problem wasn't that my father didn't speak; it was that I didn't. What kind of father did I want to be? I wanted to be the way my father used to be, before Alex. But people change in big moments. Things happen and we're never the same. I choked on my words for a moment before tears came to my eyes. I wiped them quickly away before Dad could see, but he stepped towards me and pulled me into a hug, slapping my back in a way that made me breathless.

'It'll be okay, son. It'll be okay.'

November 2011

The exams came fast. English came first. A three-hour grueling session of essay responses from nine in the morning until noon. I walked out in a daze, utterly exhausted. One exam down, six to go. Biology was the next day – one of my best subjects. That exam was just under two hours and the number of multiple-choice questions made me soar through it with ease. I approached the weekend with the sense that everything was going to be all right.

The morning of the first part of my maths exam, I woke with a start at 4:00 am. It was still dark and I hadn't meant to get up for another hour. I wanted to go to the school library to study in silence. My stomach somersaulted and sent blood rushing to my head. I gasped for breath through tight chest muscles. I had to do well. I had to nail it.

I got up and started studying in the kitchen. An extra hour of maths and an hour less of sleep – it would be okay. The tin roof creaked as it expanded as the morning sun warmed the beams. The magpies began warbling. Sanna's heavy footsteps approached. She came into the kitchen, yawning and saying she had heard me get up. She could barely sleep these days with her gigantic belly and nightmares. I chewed my toast and said I was sorry for waking her.

I grabbed my bag and headed out the door, 'Got to go, see ya.'

'Where are you going?'

'My exam.'

'It's barely past five in the morning.'

I lingered in the doorway. She stared at me. She didn't understand. I had to tell her. I sighed. 'I can't study here, with you. I've got to go.'

Sanna's face looked as though I'd hit her.

'It's nothin' personal! I just…need quiet.' Quiet and to not be around her because it was a constant reminder that I may just be suffering these exam nerves for them to not even matter. It was only half a lie.

She nodded. 'Okay. Good luck, Jake. You'll do great.'

I smiled weakly, feeling my toes trembling in my boots and I went to go start the truck. I turned the ignition key and it whinnied at me like an old hoarse horse before whining and going dead. Shit. I sat in the driver's seat, hands on the wheel as though expecting it to just suddenly go.

Sanna stood at the door, wrapping a robe around herself. 'Jake?'

I sat there; brow furrowed.

She walked over and asked through the window. 'Why are you still here?'

I closed my eyes. 'The truck won't start,' I mumbled. I got out and lifted the hood. 'Damn it.'

Sanna smiled. 'Guess you're stuck here with me for now.'

Yeah. I guess I was.

I had to wait for my dad to get up and drive me in the Corolla to school. There was not much time to study. Just an hour. My heart was racing and the hive mind that was Year Twelve made my heart beat out of rhythm with the buzz of nervous chatter. I stood with Johann outside the performance room where we'd be sitting our exam. He rubbed his arms and made small-talk about how cold it was and what he was going to do after the exam. His dad was going to take him to look at cars for his eighteenth birthday at the end of the year. When the door opened to let him in, I recoiled. This was it. My hardest exam. Part one.

Filing inside, finding my name on my singular table, forcing myself to breathe in for four, hold for four, out for four. This was how my life was going to change…if I could nail it.

The maths methods exam took place over two days. While I sat at the individual desk and sweated my way through algebra, calculus and functions of graphs, my dad stayed at home and fixed my truck. At the end of the week, it was running and I could drive myself to the environmental science exam. I hit the weekend running, with only one exam to go: chemistry.

Ms. Hollinday stalked the school corridors and popped in us in the study room to see how we were going. Our heads never came out of our books aside from occasions we would lift our heads to laugh in frenetic fits of nerves at things that weren't even funny – like a poster sliding down the wall, having lost its stickiness in the rising warmth of the spring.

Sanna hit thirty-two weeks and became unbearably miserable. I found myself longing for the exams to go longer because it would keep me out of the house longer and I wouldn't have to help her get this, get that – pack these diapers in that box, move the rocker over there. She'd taken the weekend of my final exam as the chance to prepare the nursery.

'Can't you just wait until Tuesday when I'm done with all my exams?' I had snapped.

She had thrown a baby's jumpsuit at me and cried in the bathroom, earning me a reproachful look from my mother.

The chemistry exam took place at 9:00 am, and I followed my usual routine of getting to school ridiculously early. Ms. Hollinday arrived at seven, and handed me and Clint a croissant and cup of hot chocolate each. She pumped her fists. 'You can do this, boys. Make me proud.'

We both entered the exam room uncomfortably full but eager to get it done. Two hours later, it was done. My exams were done.

I walked out and the sunlight hit my face and made me wince more than squint. My neck cracked as I pulled my shoulder blades back and staggered towards my truck. Clint jogged up beside me and jumped against me, hollering that it was done. Johann's last exam had been the last Friday – horticulture and agriculture, so it had just been Clint and I left out of our friendship group.

'We're done, Texas!'

196

'I can't believe it.' I had to shake my head.

'Where to now, eh?' His eyes glittered at me and his cheeks went red.

'Hopefully Bachelor of Science then…Doctor of Medicine,' I murmured. 'What about you?' It had never occurred to me why Clint was even taking chemistry.

'I want to do forensics. Be a top-shit detective like in the movies. Maybe a blood-spatter analyst like *Dexter*.' He grinned and I laughed.

He wrapped me in a bear hug and said, 'We're at the start of our lives, Texas.'

I rolled my eyes and shoved him with a similar jest about what state we were from, 'Yes, *Victoria*…we are.' He laughed and poked me in the ribs, almost folding me in half.

School life was over. All that could be done now was to wait for the results and university offers…and wait for the babies to be born.

I worked hard and silently, beside my father in the weeks that followed the exams. We fixed fence after fence out in the pasture, and fixed the troughs that were jammed or leaking. Every now and then Dad would sip on his beer, staring at me as he swallowed. He couldn't give it up completely. He still needed to have that beer every day. Dad didn't know that I could see him looking at me. We didn't speak unless we had to. Ever since we'd gone fishing, we'd been trying to talk to each other and to listen, but mostly it was the same old silence.

I went to the feed store every Thursday afternoon for supplies. I bought flowers from the farmers' market every week for Sanna and my mother while they went to church with my dad. I groomed Rio every day and slowly noticed that his shine vanished a little more with each day.

On the morning of the 27th of November, I found him way down in the back paddock. He would never shine again.

I collected a shovel and ropes and set myself the back breaking job of burying his body myself. It took me twelve and a half hours. Two days after that, a mail contractor came by the house and gave me a special registered letter that I had to sign for.

Sanna was eating a bowl of ice cream when I read my letter of "available scholarships". 'What's that?' she asked.

I sat down at the kitchen table with her. I passed her my letter and she quickly read it. She looked up at me sadly and said, 'Oh, Jake, I'm sorry.'

Wait a second. 'Why are you sorry? This is good news.'

Sanna was pensive as she handed the letter back. It was at least a whole minute before she said, 'You do realize that you can't go.' She saw my horrified face and added urgently, 'You can't go next year…at least until the babies are old enough for school and I can either get a job or go back to school.'

I said, 'My parents will look after them for us.'

'You can't keep using your parents like that, Jake. Your dad is already paying for diesel for your car and all our food. How do you think it makes me feel, being a guest and not paying for anything?' *Ouch, good point.* She added, 'Besides, I feel bad enough as it is. They do so much for us.'

'Your parents could…' I didn't finish. Her eyes turned icy and I didn't dare continue. She looked down at the dirty tablecloth and I knew that she was right. I had just turned nineteen-years old and I had a fiancée with two babies on the way that weren't even mine. I thought about telling her the deal was off. I needed to live my life, but the damage that would be done… My dreams were dashed. It was all beginning to look over before it even started.

That night, I made a bonfire and invited Johann over to celebrate his scholarship opportunities – he wanted to study veterinary science over in South Australia. We drank two beers and then I stood up and walked to the bonfire, close enough to feel the heat blistering my skin. I took my scholarship letter out of my jeans pocket and unfolded it. I read it again. I had this huge opportunity presented to me, yet it wasn't possible. I tore the letter in half and caught Johann's confused expression. I threw the letter into the fire and stuck my hands into my pockets to prevent myself from desperately grabbing the pieces back out of the fire and sticking them back together.

'What are you doing Jake? You worked hard for that,' said Johann stiffly. 'I thought you wanted to get out of here. Come with me to Adelaide.'

I glanced at the house and then back to the fire. 'I can't, Johann. I've got to work hard at something else now, mate.' We each cracked open another can of beer and drank in silence.

Sanna

December 2011

The first day of summer was a let-down. I wanted it to be sunny and clear, but it was overcast and it showered on and off. The rest of December was mostly the same. On the 17th, I shuffled around the house and watched out the window, hoping for the sun to break through. It was Michael's seventeenth birthday. I'd got him a card and braided him a rope bracelet. He was being dropped off to visit by his brother – I just needed to wait for him to arrive.

Isabel came up beside me and asked, 'Why are you so nervous, Sanna?'

I jumped and pinched my fingers together repeatedly. 'No, no, not nervous. Just…' I laughed. 'I don't know.'

'Your friend is going to love her gift.' She turned and walked away and I stood there, wondering what to say. She thought my friend was a girl. What would she think when she realised they weren't? Would I suddenly not be allowed to have this friend over because he may be a threat to her son? It might look improper.

Eventually Billy's car swung into the courtyard and parked beside the Corolla. Michael and Billy got out. I waddled to the door to meet them, hoping we could just get into the car before Isabel noticed I was leaving with two males.

'Sanna, what's going on?' Michael said.

'Go, go, let's just go.'

I got into the back seat as Isabel came out of the house. 'Suzie?'

Michael looked to me then looked to Isabel. Billy stepped up to Isabel and offered his hand. Damn.

'How ya garn; I'm Billy. Michael's brother.'

'Michael,' said Michael, clearing his throat and shaking Isabel's hand. 'You must be Jake's mum.'

'Yes I am. Nice to meet you, boys.' She peered in at me. 'Suzie, where are you going?'

I sighed and rolled down the windows, working up a sweat in the process. Billy's car didn't have electric windows. 'I'm going to the beach for Michael's birthday.' I looked across to Michael and Billy. 'Come on.'

'This is your friend?' Isabel's lips narrowed to a thin line.

I nodded.

'Nice to meet you, Jake's mum,' Michael muttered with his head down. Billy waved and got into the driver's seat.

I waved to Isabel as we drove away. Michael turned in his seat to look at me. 'Why are we going out? I thought we could hang out at yours for a bit.'

'I got a weird vibe. She thought you were a girl.'

'She's right,' Billy sneered and slapped the steering wheel.

'Shut up, Billy,' I snapped. 'Just take us to the beach.'

Once we arrived at beach under the rail bridge, Billy stayed in car to smoke a cone. Michael and I walked slowly down to the sand. I was as cumbersome as a whale on dry land. I sat against the sandbank and stretched out my legs. The sea was unusually flat against the basalt cliffs.

Michael slipped his new bracelet on and tousled my hair, glancing back at Billy in the car before he squatted beside me and kissed me.

I leant away and he pulled back, licking his lips and looking down.

'Sorry…I shouldn't have done that.'

'I'm engaged.' The words bounced around in the air as if they were echoing.

'I know. I'm sorry.' He groaned as he lay beside me, on his side. His hand went to my belly. 'You're getting huge now.'

'I get induced on Tuesday.'

His eyes widened. 'So that means…that's it. They're done. They're cooked.'

I laughed. 'Yeah, pretty much.'

'I can't believe it.'

'Me either.'

We traced shapes and patterns in the sand until our fingers interlaced and we eventually held hands, squeezing our palms together. I frowned. It was so easy with him. I could melt into him and give him everything. I could barely hold Jake's hand. It wasn't fair.

He said, 'So you told me something back when you…had that thing…'

'Right…?'

'That Jake wasn't the father.'

I dropped his hand and it fell upon the grains of salty sand. 'Who is?'

I shook my head and stared out at the sea. There was nothing but a horizon and a shade of turquoise to see.

'Don't I deserve to know who else had your heart long enough for you to have sex with them? Does Jake even know?'

I closed my eyes as if I could block out his words. Block out the truth. I eventually said, 'It was Jake's idea to be the dad. He helped me out.'

'What do you mean he helped you out?' Michael snorted in derision.

'We said it was him who knocked me up so I wouldn't have to tell my parents, okay.' I opened my eyes and locked eyes with him. Just understand. Just understand without making me say it.

'Tell your parents what?'

I stared at him.

He stared back for what felt like the longest time. My eyes began to water.

Michael looked down and murmured, 'Something happened to you?'

I nodded and he looked back at me, stricken. 'Something bad.' I nodded again.

'Did some arsehole rape you?'

I nodded and burst into tears. Michael sat up and hugged me.

As we were driving back to Jake's place, I couldn't get comfortable in the backseat. I readjusted the seatbelt and tried putting one foot up across the seat to relieve the pressure in my lower back. I arched my back and tried to pinpoint where it was hurting before it scooped around to the front.

My stomach lurched and I gripped my hand to Mount Vesuvius as I realised what was happening. 'Uh...guys...'

'Yeah?' said Michael and Billy.

'I think I'm going into labour. For real this time.'

'WHAT?' They screeched.

Billy turned to look at me and I pointed and screamed, 'Look out!'

He spun his head back in time but didn't brake in enough time. He ran into the back-end of a Ford Fiesta with an impact that sent my senses reeling. As we came to a sudden stop and the engine hissed, Michael and Billy moaned, nursing their heads. The airbags had deployed. A cramp ripped into me and lasted for a good thirty seconds. I cried out in pain and disbelief.

The driver of the other vehicle got out of the car. 'You idiot!'

Michael helped me get out but I struggled to straighten up. My knees locked at a bent angle and each step ricocheted up my back. Billy got out and started explaining and apologising to the driver, but their eyes went to me.

'Shit. We need an ambulance, now.'

'Don't call the cops, mate,' Billy pleaded. 'Just take me details, mate.'

I staggered with Michael's help to the side of the road and he helped me perch on my knees. I straightened as the contraction passed and I spat out the hair that had got in my mouth.

'Are you sure it's not the same thing as before?' he asked.

I nodded. 'Definitely not Braxton Hicks.'

The Ford Fiesta driver jogged over to me. 'I'm calling an ambulance for you. What's your name?'

'Sanna Smith.'

'Jeez, can't believe this,' Billy groaned with his hands flinging into the air.

'Billy, stop making a scene!' Michael yelled.

'Fuck this! I'm out of here.'

'You can't leave!' The driver of the Ford Fiesta shouted. 'You caused an accident.'

A new ripple of pain began to set in and I grit my teeth and held my breath through it. Michael rubbed my back and said, 'Don't hold your breath, Sanna. Aren't you supposed to breathe?'

'It hurts to breathe!' I sobbed.

The pressure in my pelvis was intensifying. How was this going so fast? I thought it would start out as a little pain that got worse. No, this was just intense pain that came and went, getting closer together in waves.

Michael said to the Ford driver, 'He's my brother. I'll make sure he goes to the police. Can you just call that ambulance now?'

When we arrived at the hospital, I made sure to tell the staff that I was scheduled to have a caesarean on Tuesday. I was meant to have the caesarean because my twins shared a placenta. They reassured me that it would still be happening. The obstetrician that I saw was luckily available and came to see me.

'Ms. Smith, your babies are excited to join the world, it would seem.'

I gripped the handles of the bed. Michael sat beside me, leaning over his knees, no doubt wishing he could run away but was not being able to leave me out of pity. A nurse stuck a needle into my hand for the IV and apologised for the prick that felt like a tickle in comparison to the cramps shredding me in half.

'We've got to get you up to the anaesthetist for the epidural, Sanna,' she explains. 'Would you like your partner to come with you?'

Michael's head shot up. 'I'm not the father.'

Glances by all.

'Call Jake,' I told him. He nodded. I told the nurse, 'No, I'm here alone.'

I was wheeled away to the anaesthetist with my heart pounding. I was about to meet my children. I was about to become a mother. My head swam and I nearly passed out.

Jake

December 2011

I was at the feed store when my phone rang. Sanna's number.

'Hey, you.'

'Hey, Jake. It's Michael.'

I frowned. 'Why are you calling from Sanna's phone?'

'We just had a little car accident.'

I tasted vomit as I pictured what Alex's car had looked like on the back of the tow truck. The crushed nose, the shattered windscreen, the bent tyres…the blood on the dashboard. I pictured Sanna there, dead in the car, too.

'Oh, please, God…' I gasped, hunching over, clutching at my stomach.

'Jake, you there?'

'Is she – is she all right?'

'Well, yeah, but she's in labor.'

'What?'

'She's having the babies now. Come to the hospital.'

I made it there and raced to the reception. 'I…my fiancée, she's having babies…uh…I don't know my way,' I gasped.

The receptionist smiled at me. 'I'll take you to the birthing unit.'

'I'm the father.' Those three words sounded alien coming from me. They rushed off my tongue because they tasted foul and stale. Rehearsed, cliché – I wasn't sure. I didn't like the sounds the sentence made.

I followed the receptionist down the reflective, buffed, pine-scented corridor to the maternity ward. I wondered if I should have called my parents first. These were their grandchildren, after all. My mother was so excited about becoming a grandmother. She'd even abused somebody from the church because they called Sanna and me sinners and said we shouldn't even be having sex, let alone having babies. They had reasoned that we'd be horrible parents. She'd hurled abuse at them. The reverend had agreed with her every word and hadn't kicked her out of the church. She'd knitted booties. She'd woven woollen bonnets. She'd worked out a feeding schedule in the middle of the night to help Sanna out. I would make sure to call her as soon as I could.

I arrived in a small private room where Sanna was asleep, connected to a heart rate monitoring machine with an IV in her arm. She was completely alone, her face bare and her hair loose around her chest.

I lingered in the doorway until a nurse came in. She must have noticed that I looked concerned so she reassured me by saying, 'She's all right.' I swallowed a big lump in my throat. She put a needle into the IV. The needle was so huge that it looked like a machine gun and just as lethal. 'She is just exhausted.'

'The babies?'

'They're all right, too,' the nurse added with a smile. 'Just getting warm in an incubator while their mummy has a rest.'

I sat down in the chair beside Sanna's bed. 'Do you think I could go give my parents a call? They'd like to know.'

'Sure, go ahead. The midwife will be here in about fifteen minutes with the babies to feed.'

I glanced at Sanna and her eyes blinked slightly, filling me with relief. 'I'll be back, okay,' I said and the nurse nodded.

I hurried through the corridors back to the waiting room and almost took three wrong turns; my sneakers skidded and squealed on the sanitized floors. 'Jake!' somebody yelled out. I skidded to a stop and noticed Michael walking towards me.

'Michael!'

He stepped up beside me. 'How is she?'

I paused and took special note of the genuine worry and concern on Michael's face before I said, 'She's out of it at the moment so at least she's not in so much pain.' I pointed back over my shoulder. 'I got to go. I'll, um,' I said, 'I'll come out and tell you...keep you updated and, um...' I smiled. 'Thanks for calling, Michael. Thanks for...calling me...and being here.'

He shrugged. 'She's my girl, too, you know.'

After calling my parents, I walked back to Sanna slowly. Michael was right. She was his more than mine.

I gently squeezed onto the bed next to her and held her hand. When her eyes finally opened, she asked groggily, 'Where – where are they? Is it done? Have you seen them?'

'Not yet,' I whispered. 'Have you?'

Rolling wheels echoed through the hallway and we looked over to the door as two nurses rolled two Isolettes into the room. I lost my breath for a moment as I processed that the babies were now out of Sanna and out in the world. It was as if someone had punched me in the ribs and knocked all the air out of me.

Sanna sat up abruptly and gasped in pain, and I had to grab hold of the back of the chair to stop myself falling off. I stood up and peered in and saw babies swaddled in pink blankets.

One of the nurses lifted the smallest baby up and laid her across Sanna's open arms. Sanna took care to support the neck and head, and gently brushed a fleck of fluff off her cheek, just like a good mother would do. Age meant nothing; experience was nonessential. She was a mother.

I held the bigger one and felt like I was going to fall through the floor. They were both small, ugly and squishy. They were the first newborn babies I had ever actually held or looked at closely. Their little faces were covered in a light fluff that the nurses said would disappear soon. I was transfixed by their little mouths. I couldn't help laughing when I stroked her little hand, the tiny fingers curled as if to hold me then yawned widely, her entire body trembling.

She was huge compared to her sister. She was a healthy seven pounds but the other one was barely four point five.

'Have you decided on names?' asked a nurse.

Sanna shook her head. 'Not yet.'

The nurses showed Sanna how to breast feed and even tandem feed, but I left and made my way to the waiting room, and stood with Michael, my mouth refusing to quit smiling.

'They're...perfect.'

Michael grinned. 'Cool. Can't wait to meet them.' He cleared his throat. 'Um...Sanna told me...that it was your idea to say you're the father.'

I gave him a sharp look, stunned that Sanna had finally opened up about what had happened to her.

Michael continued, 'You're a good guy, Jake.' He swallowed and held out his hand for me to shake which I did. 'Not sure many men would do what you're doing.'

I sighed. 'Yeah...I guess not.'

'I'm...happy to help you guys out.' He shrugged. 'I'm not good with kids or anything, but I'm...here if you need me.'

Sanna chose their names later that day. She chose Audrey Isla for the strong twin and Bellare Olive for the little one that had survived like a little warrior.

Sanna

December 2011

They cried. They screamed. They screamed and gasped their way through demands they couldn't even understand.

We had stayed in the hospital until three days before Christmas. I was almost paralysed with the pain in my stomach from the caesarean, but my mum and dad drove us home where Jake and his parents were waiting eagerly at the door to greet us. I didn't have to lift anything. I fell into bed and slept for an hour before my mum woke me up with a gentle kiss on my forehead saying that she had to head off – and it was time to feed the babies. I said goodbye to my parents and found Jake carrying Audrey around, bouncing her as she cried in fitful squeals. Bellare remained quiet in the carrier, content to listen to the sounds her sister made.

Will dangled a Christmas decoration in front of Bellare but there was no real interaction. Her eyes went all over the place.

I took Audrey from Jake and went to my bedroom to feed her. As soon as she was burped and content, there were screams coming from the living room where Bellare had suddenly given up her silence with a vengeance.

All they seemed to do was drink, vomit, burp, fart and poo. They slept sporadically, separately. Audrey would wake up every two hours at least, and scream as loudly as she could. Bellare would just doze off and then Audrey would give her the jump scare of her life by screaming the house down.

On Christmas morning, I stood in the middle of my bedroom, looking from one twin to the other, as they both screamed and cried and gasped and screamed and screamed, and screamed, and screamed, competing against each other for my attention. I didn't know which one to tend to first. The nurses had told me to go to whichever one's cry seemed more in need. Was I a bad mother because I couldn't distinguish anything in their tears apart from screams?

I was about to bawl my eyes out alongside them when Will came into the room. 'Do you need a hand, Suzie?'

I nodded and blinked tears away. He went straight to Audrey and picked her up. Audrey stiffened her legs and kicked them furiously with despair. Bellare stopped crying but whimpered as I sniffed and lifted her up, tapping at her back. Audrey stopped crying with Will, her little head jerking every now and then as she tried to look around, her mouth making sucking movements, seeking the boob. My boobs were so sore. I wanted to scream LEAVE ME ALONE but my heart hurt at the thought of turning her down.

'I'll take her, Will. I think she's hungry.'

We swapped babies. Audrey, despite being the bigger twin, seemed ravenous compared to Bellare.

'Greedy little gutso,' I murmured to her as she latched on and bolted her milk. I looked up at Will and asked, 'I hope they didn't wake you.'

'No, I met Jake in the hallway. I told him I'd help you.'

'Why?' I teared up again and was furious with myself for it.

'I'm just better with babies.' He grinned and I smiled. He had a point. He rubbed Bellare's smooth, hairless head and lowered her back into her crib, making kissy noises at her which she jerked her arms around for excitedly. I watched her and swelled with love. She was adorable. Looking down at Audrey - identical yet bigger, hungrier, fussier, and noisier - I grimaced. So, it was true…Parents *did* have favourites. Or maybe I was just a bad mother.

Will must have noticed my expression change and said, 'It gets better later. This part is the hard part when everyone is just getting to know each other. You don't love them from day one like people all say you do. It takes time.'

I nodded. 'Thanks, Will. That helps a lot.'

He kissed my cheek and whispered, 'Merry Christmas,' then left me alone with the two quiet babies.

January 2012

In the new year, 2012, Jake and I started taking the twins on outings so I got out of the house. It was very easy to stay at home and say it was too hard to juggle them, and everything hurt still from the caesarean, but Isabel insisted that it would be good for me and them.

We went to my parents' house every Sunday night and we went to the beach every Wednesday. Parking them in their massive pram in the sand and staring out at the sea was cathartic. Jake was patient. He tended to the girls while I zoned out at the land's edge.

Rinse and repeat.

Weeks went by. Before I knew it, it was my sixteenth birthday on the fourteenth of January and then January was over and the girls were officially one month old and starting to coo and make ahh noises. Jake worked on the farm with his dad and whenever he came back inside, the girls would squeal to get his attention from their tummy time positions. Michael visited sometimes and awkwardly held them for photos. Isabel watched from a distance with a disapproving sneer, but said nothing.

Our lives together were settling into an odd routine. Feeling like an outsider but being the centre of their worlds. Their little eyes followed me and tracked me and their bodies became more controlled. They stopped moving in fitful jerks and Bellare stopped crying just because her sister did, which she continued to do...a lot.

February 2012

I began toying with the idea of seeing Tamara again. I was by myself in the house most days. Isabel had got a cleaning job in the new year – she said it was out of choice but I think it was to get away from me and the babies – and Will and Jake were running the farm. I talked to my daughters but felt ridiculous for it. Just having daughters felt ridiculous, but they were cute. Each time I considered going to see Tamara, I would chicken out and sink lower and lower in mood.

The mere thought of going in and facing Tamara filled me with dread. I hated myself for what I had done to her. I never should have dropped in on her. I was young and stupid, aggressive, and irresponsible.

Gazing at my girls as I tandem-fed them, I brushed their foreheads where my surfboard had stacked into Tamara. Audrey and Bellare had perfect foreheads. Tamara would have a scar there for the rest of her life. An awfully visible reminder of the day she nearly died, at the hands of her best friend.

A tear splashed onto Bellare and went into her eye, so she winced and flinched from the burning salty water. I wiped it away and kissed her better.

'Sorry, munchkin,' I crooned, wishing I could take the burn from the salt of the wound I had given Tamara, too.

Jake

March 2012

During the night, the girls were crying. Screaming. Wailing. Sanna slept right through. I lay in my warm bed and listened for Sanna to move and quieten them through the thin walls, but there were only the cries.

I checked my watch. It was quarter to four. I was meant to get up anyway. I heaved my body out of the warm bed and went into Sanna's room to soothe the girls. A lick of irritation ran through my mind when I glanced at Sanna, facing the wall, fast asleep. I was getting up in the middle of the night to children who were not mine, but mine all the same. Their little bodies kicked and wriggled in their cribs, and they went cross-eyed as they focused on my face. Or they were trying to poop. One or the other. I couldn't tell which expression was for which intention. They were three months old now. Their little fingers wrapped around my thumb and they made sucking noises at me.

'Hungry, huh?' Grunt. Wail. Squeal. 'I guess that's a yes.'

I went and made them two bottles like my mom had taught me and fed Audrey, then Bellare. I burped and shushed them, kissing their downy little foreheads.

After I put them back down for a snooze, I went to the kitchen to make my own breakfast. Sanna got up, yawned, and said that she had to feed the babies. I chewed my toast and said, 'Don't need to. I fed them at four.'

She looked blankly at me. Dad walked into the room and chugged a glass of water at the sink before looking at us and saying good morning.

Sanna whispered to me, 'They get fed at five. Now you've fed them an hour earlier, their routine is going to be all weird. Now I'm going to have a hard day.'

'You were asleep. They were crying. What was I supposed to do?'

She shook her head at me and crossed her arms. Dad looked from me to Sanna and said, 'Ah well; time to get going.' I followed him out the door, grateful that I'd managed to escape her irritation. Sometimes it was as if she forgot that I'd chosen to do her a favour. I hadn't intended to get engaged or raise the babies. Whenever I thought about why on earth I had done that, and got myself into this situation, I'd see the way she had been running down the road with that look in her eyes, and the way she'd cried as she clung to me. I'd shudder thinking about the way her mouth drew down and twisted to the side as if in agony, her eyes glassy and her knees buckling. It became easier to remember. I'd done this for her and I'd continue to do this for her.

Sanna

April 2012

Every day the girls grew. By April, they were hitting milestones and they cried less, yet seemed to demand more of me. Audrey liked to smack people in the face when they picked her up. It was highly amusing and sent her into waves of cackles, but she wasn't a monster all the way through — she loved cuddles too. She liked to have your attention immediately, but Bellare would watch for ages before you even noticed her eyes following your every move.

I couldn't take the girls anywhere without people commenting on their stunning eyes. Their father's eyes. I shuddered when Bellare stared coldly at me. At least Audrey smiled when she saw me. Bellare looked into me and it made me cold inside.

One Sunday night at my parents' house for dinner, the twins were in a rotten mood, tugging on anything every chance they could get, then throwing it to the side with a miserable wail. One by one, each member of the family took their turn of rattling toys at either girl and copping an earful of screaming.

I hope the God damn cabinet falls on you both, I thought venomously and then my stomach sank, so I showered them with affection with tears running down my face. I wasn't a normal mother. Would a mother wish their toddlers were crushed by a cabinet? Would she?

I started crying halfway through dinner and everybody looked at me.

'Oh dear,' Mum said and got me a tissue.

Dad teased, 'You're not pregnant again, are you, Sanna?'

Jake breathed out of his nose and made a hissing sound. No, I wasn't pregnant again. I glared at him.

Later, he and Jake bathed the girls in the ensuite bathroom while Mum and I did the dishes.

'Mum?'

'*Ja?*'

'I think I hate my kids.' I avoided looking at her. I wiped the same glass with the tea towel over and over.

'You don't hate them.'

'No, maybe not,' I sighed. 'But…I don't know.'

'What's bothering you, Sanna?'

Wipe, wipe, wipe with the tea towel again. My mother grabbed the glass from me and put it down. 'Talk to me.'

I looked her square in the eye and said, 'I don't like being a mother.'

She smiled and tucked my hair behind my ear. My hair needed a cut. I hadn't taken care of it properly since I'd had the twins. Even brushing it was too hard.

'Motherhood is just hard work, Sanna.'

'I want what's best for them…and *I'm* not what is best for them.' My lip trembled. For the first time in a while, I was being honest with not only my mum, but myself, as well.

She asked, 'How can you say that about yourself? You are their mother.'

I thought of the way Bellare giggled when Jake lifted her high in the air or when Audrey reached for Jake first when we walked up to them on their playmats. I sighed. 'They like Jake better than they like me. I see the way Bellare looks at me – she judges me!' My mother looked at me as though she thought I was insane. I explained, 'Jake comes into the room and they both light up. All they do with me is cry.' I bit my lip. 'I hate them sometimes...I hate them so much.'

'You don't hate them, Sanna,' she said. She pulled me into a tight hug. 'You're just having a hard time. You need a break. Why don't you take them to visit Tamara?'

I raised an eyebrow at her. 'How would that help?'

She smiled. 'It's nice to have a friend.'

I stewed on it for the rest of the week but on Thursday night, I decided that my mum was on to something. I had said that I would go visit Tamara once I'd had the babies, and now they were four-months old and I still hadn't made it.

I called Tamara's parents to double-check if it would be okay if I took the girls to go visit her tomorrow at the hospital.

They said, 'She's not there anymore, Sanna.'

My heart lurched. Had something happened? 'Pardon?'

'She's at Gum Lodge in Cowes, now.'

I blinked. Gum Lodge was an aged-care facility. For old people – not young people recovering from an acquired brain injury and rehabbing after a coma. I stammered, 'Why is she there?'

'She's rehabbed enough to come out of the rehab facility, but not quite ready to come home.'

'So, she's...almost better?'

'Almost. She's fully conscious now. She'd love a visit from you.'

She'd love a visit. Fully-conscious. I repeated it to myself over and over after I hung up the phone. What did this mean? Would she really want to see me? Fully conscious meant she wouldn't be staring vacantly past me, right? Like…awake, awake. But if that was the case, why was she at the aged-care facility and not at home?

The next morning, Jake helped me dress the twins in their cutest outfits and he kissed the tops of their heads. I waited for him to kiss the top of my head too but he gave me an unsure smile and left with his bag hooked over one shoulder. Isabel drove me to see Tamara. I walked up the front pathway, pushing overgrown plants away from the double-pram wheels. I staggered through the door and was accosted by the stench of stifling air freshener that burnt my nostrils and the back of my throat.

It was too hot inside despite it being a temperate autumn day. It was dark and music from the '50s softly trumpeted away on a radio nearby. I rang the bell at the front desk and was greeted by a man who looked not much older than Jake.

'I'm here to visit Tamara Jenkins.'

'Sure, follow me.' He led me down the hallway, out the door and into another building. This building smelled mustier in comparison and was darker, but had pink carpet and drooping monstera plants in the hallway that lightened the room up a little. The nurse knocked on room number 17 and opened the door.

Tamara was in a bed, sitting up, with her eyes open. I gripped the pram to stop my knees buckling when she looked around at me.

'Tamara, you have a visitor today.'

Her face was blank.

The nurse whispered to me, 'She has trouble recognising faces and has dysarthria. Don't worry…She's cognitive.'

I nodded, pretending I understood what any of that even meant. I stepped towards her. 'Hi. It's me…Sanna.'

Her forehead wrinkled as she looked at me.

'Sanna. Your friend…'

'Sanna.' She heaved a big breath as if it was difficult. Her eyes went to the pram, where the girls looked back at her, eyes big and expectant. Eddie's eyes. I wondered if she'd recognise them.

'You had b-b…' Tamara rolled her eyes and clenched her fist. She looked to me with a gaping mouth and a tortured expression. She grunted.

'Babies. Yeah. I had babies.'

'D-D-D…' Her lip wobbled and she cried out in exasperation, jiggling her legs. I felt my face get hot and my heart race. I didn't know what she wanted to say this time.

The nurse placed a hand on her shoulder and said soothingly, 'It's okay. It'll come. Try again.'

Tamara slapped him away and grunted again. She looked at me and covered her face and sobbed. I swallowed hard and pulled a chair over to the bed. My heart was breaking to see her so distressed. It had kind of been better to see her unconscious and unresponsive than fighting to speak and find the words. I decided to just do the speaking for her. I got Audrey out of the pram and set her on my lap. Audrey looked curiously at Tamara.

'This is Audrey.' I gestured at Bellare who stared up at Tamara. 'That's Bellare.'

'Belle,' Tamara said clearly. Surprised at herself, she smiled.

Audrey reached up and touched Tamara's pants. Tamara slowly touched her arm. 'Au-au-au…Aury.'

I smiled. 'Yeah. Aury and Belle.'

Tamara narrowed her eyes at me but raised her eyebrows. I had to look away. She hadn't looked at me for over a year. I wanted to break down and cry, but had to be strong. So much time had passed. I was a different person to the one that had egged her on and then dropped in on her. I couldn't even call myself a surfer anymore. I was a mum.

Tamara asked, 'You...o...k?'

I laughed and wiped a tear from my eye while my nose prickled, threatening to explode with snot in an ugly cry. 'Yeah! I'm okay. How are you?'

She shrugged, and we laughed.

Tamara looked me in the eye and we both nodded together before she said, 'I...mi...ssed...you.'

'I missed you too,' I said. I heaved a huge breath of air and felt my middle go loose, finally. It had been held in tension for so many months. 'You have no idea how much I missed you.' I started to laugh but instead found myself crying. I wiped at the corner of my eye and said with a strained voice, 'I've been so lost without you, Tee.'

Tamara reached over and we hugged. She was so different but it felt like I had her back. She was alive. We were alive.

Jake

Dad was on my back. I needed to be a better father. The girls were five-months old and reaching for things from their floor mats and starting to sit up with support. They were becoming proper little babies, not just screaming newborns. Dad kept telling me to go inside and help Sanna while I could. Spend time with my children. My children. Yep. That little yet colossal lie was still common belief.

On Saturday morning, I rushed to the feed store to get everything done in record time and then spend time with "my children" like my father suggested I do in order to be a good father.

As I jogged into the shed to place my order, I crashed into Coop, who was stepping backwards out of the store dragging a thirty-kilogram bag of chaff.

'Oh, sorry, mate!' He looked up and saw me, then smiled from ear-to-ear. He was missing a top tooth. 'Jake, it's good to see you.' He reached up to shake my hand. 'I've heard you've been a busy man, eh.'

I grinned and said, 'Are you kidding? Busy isn't the word.'

Coop sat down on the gargantuan bag, crossed his arms and said, 'I heard you did really well at school. Well done, Jake, well done...' His eyes wandered to the girls' car seats in the back seat. He said, 'I didn't realize that this was the road you'd chosen.'

I ran my hands through my hair and grinned to cover up the regret. 'It is what it is, Coop.'

He asked, 'You couldn't wait for Tessa?'

'What do you mean?'

'She was heartbroken when you hooked up with your new girlfriend. She told me you were waiting here for her until you finished school.'

I almost laughed. 'Well, sorry to tell you this, Coop, but...' *your granddaughter cheated on me with her music teacher* '...Tessa made her decision and we weren't together when she decided to leave town.' What if I had gone with her? Forgiven and forgotten her selfish behavior. The thought had crossed my mind even though I knew it would drive me insane.

I added, 'And I've made my decision.' I shrugged. 'And it's okay. I'm happy.'

Coop leaned back and tilted his chin up at me. 'You ain't happy, Jake.'

I swallowed.

'What do you really want more than anything right now, eh?'

My eyes glazed as I pictured the scholarship letter I burned in the bonfire and how I could have been studying at university, eventually being a success. Eventually, settling down with a beautiful woman and having children and being able to give them the perfect middle class life. Success was providing a comfortable life for my future family…but for now, Sanna and her girls would do.

I took a deep breath. 'I want a job more than anything right now so I can look after my family…I want to be a good man.'

'Is that what you want, or is that what your girlfriend wants?'

I nodded and smirked. 'You're a wise ass, Coop.'

He smiled. 'You're already a good man, Jake. You're too young to sacrifice everything, that's all, eh.'

I sighed, a wave of misery and responsibility and old-age bowled into my gut. I closed my eyes and said, 'I just want to get a job, work through the time until my kids can go to school then Sanna can get a job and I can go to university and get somewhere in life.' Opening my eyes, I realized why I so desperately wanted to get a career and be successful: I was all my family had.

Coop seemed to realize the same thing because he asked, 'Do you still think about your brother, Jake?'

I shook my head. 'Not much these days. I've kind of…forgotten how he was, you know…he's not part of my life anymore.'

'I haven't seen your dad in here much,' said Coop.

'No, I make most of the trips in here these days.' I wondered if Coop and Dad ever spoke about anything other than me anyway.

Coop asked, 'Is he doing all right?'

I replied, 'Never better.' It was true. He hadn't touched alcohol in a long time and he was almost like how he was before Alex had died.

Coop asked curiously, 'Are you going to ask how Tessa is?'

I shifted my weight and asked carefully, 'Do I *need* to know how Tessa is?'

His tongue wet his lips and he looked around before he shrugged. 'You tell me, Jake.'

I couldn't believe it. My emotions and love life were being doubted by an old man when he knew his granddaughter broke my heart, and I was engaged with two kids. I gave in and asked with exasperation, 'How's Tessa?'

He stood up and said, 'She's staying with me for a couple of weeks but then she's off to Nashville…' He looked like he wanted to tell me something else but he just offered his hand to shake again and said, 'It's great to see you again, little mate.'

I shook his hand and nodded. 'You, too, Coop.'

I watched him go, dragging the bag of chaff behind him, until the owner of the feed store, Mick, came over to me and asked, 'I heard you say you wanted a job, Jake…'

'Eighteen dollars an hour?' repeated Sanna with a curled lip. 'That's not very much money, Jake. Almost minimum wage.'

'It's only to start off with,' I replied, bending to pull on my new pair of steel cap boots that made me feel like a little kid shuffling around in Dad's boots.

'You can't even drive a fork lift,' Sanna pointed out, the queen of negativity.

I grinned, only a little bit annoyed. 'Ergo the eighteen dollars an hour.' I put on my hat and said, 'It doesn't matter. They're going to teach me anything I need to know. I need to do this, Sanna. I need to look after you and the girls.'

'I know,' she mumbled. She hugged me and kissed my cheek, like a girlfriend would. I was so shocked that I froze, stiff with discomfort. She whispered, 'I'm so grateful that you have this opportunity, Jake. I'm so proud of you.'

Sanna

June 2012

I had expected Jake to be fired within the first week at his first ever job, but he proved to be quite the asset for the store. Word got out amongst the society of equine lovers of the female sex, or "show-humpers" as Jake's boss Mick called them, and soon the feed store was a Mecca of drooling, flirting, equestrian girls and women. Jake didn't even notice they were only there for him, but I did when I went there on Saturday mornings just to sit in the office for something to do to get out of the house.

They came in wearing their tight riding pants with their dorky long socks pulled up over their calves, wearing slippers or steel cap boots. Caps on their heads or beanies, and the same types of jackets. They cocked their hips and ran their fingers through their ponytails and flicked their heads. I'd watch them and snort. They thought they were top-shit, so far up their arses they couldn't even carry their own bags of feed.

SALT

If it got busy, I'd ring orders up on the till for Mick, just like I used to when I worked at The Surf Shack. After two weeks, Mick set me up a bank account and told me he was paying me whether I wanted to work or not. My face flushed and I held back tears of gratitude.

July 2012

Audrey started to crawl. All over the place. At work, I'd have to bolt for the door to grab her because she'd made a bee-line for it like an iguana legging it. Mick brought a playpen from his house that his own children had outgrown so he could give me a couple of extra days of work and the girls could come along. There were no more escape attempts from Audrey and she often had something to say about it – usually with a screaming fit and shaking the playpen like an inmate.

It all began to feel so…suburban and normal. I wasn't sure how to feel about it. I only felt terrible for what I'd done to Jake. If only I had the courage to admit what had happened but I could barely even acknowledge it to myself. In a way, I felt like it had happened to me because I deserved it for what I had done to Tamara. Beautiful Tamara. I ruined her life and now I was ruining Jake's.

On one of my days off, I left the girls with Isabel and took a bus to visit Tamara again.

'Where are the bab…ies?' Her voice was getting stronger but she had begun trailing off in the middle of sentences.

'I left them at home with Jake's mum.' I pulled my chair closer to her. 'Tamara…I need to know something.'

She waited.

'Do you…' I took a deep breath and swallowed. 'Do you…blame me for what happened?'

228

She was silent. I gaped at her, knowing that her silence meant what I feared. She must resent me. She hated me now. 'I'm so sorry,' I cried.

'Shut...u...p.'

I shrank into myself and crossed my legs and folded my arms. My eyes went to her fingers, that clutched at her bed sheet as if for dear life. 'You don't get...to...cr...y.' She turned away and got shakily to her feet. She stood at the window and took a deep breath. 'Yes, I blame you. You're the one...who...dr...' She began to struggle with her words and her lips massaged trying to get the shape right. She looked down and sighed. 'You're the one...'

'Who dropped in on you,' I mumbled. 'I know.'

She balled her fists. 'But I know you...are so...sorr...y.' She grunted back tears. 'I hate this.'

'I am, I am so sorry.'

We avoided looking at each other for what felt like a very long time before she said, 'All that matters...is that...you're here...n...ow.'

I nodded, unable to speak because I was afraid I would cry. 'You're still my...be...st fri...end.'

I laughed. 'Thank God.'

She smiled. 'Thank God for you...and Edd...' She sighed. 'Eddie.'

My spine shot me upright like a ramrod, and my body was ready to fire. 'Eddie?'

She nodded. 'He visits.'

I rubbed at my ear and noticed that it was boiling. I remained quiet until Tamara added, 'He's coming...to...day.'

Nausea washed over me and the room span. From a position outside of my body, I watched myself stand and put my purse onto my shoulder. 'I've got to go.'

'What? Why?'

There was a sharp trio of knocks on the door and it opened. Time slowed down. Eddie walked in, holding a milkshake from the café down the road. He handed it to Tamara and I backed away.

Eddie looked in my direction. His eyes – my daughters' eyes – met mine and he smiled as if genuinely chuffed to see me. 'Sanna!' He stepped towards my wooden body and pressed me into a hug and I tremble all over, almost falling backwards. 'Good to see you.' He pushed me away and squinted at me with a smirk and a sideways tilt of his head. 'After such a long time.' He squeezed my shoulders sharply and I gasped. The leaves were in my hair and his hand was over my mouth, filling it with dirt. His salty skin and callouses grazed my teeth.

I choked, almost vomiting. 'Sorry. I've got to go.' I pushed past him by making myself as small as possible and burst from the room. I hurried through the facility and sprinted into the street, my breath ragged and making me wheeze. The cool winter air splashed my face and the pavement was wet after a light shower had passed through while I was inside.

I jogged to the beach, ignoring the searing pain in my chest as I gasped for air. I didn't stop until I hit the sand, where I sank to my knees and let the tears come. Loud guttural sobs came out of me and wavered on the breeze and floated to the esplanade. I lost track of time until a familiar American voice called out 'Suzie?'

I looked over my shoulder to see Isabel walking through the sand, struggling to keep her balance on the soft surface.

'I'm here,' I called out, wiping my face and getting sand in my eye, sand-papering my cheeks.

Isabel came over and sat beside me on the sand. She smiled at me before she said, 'You've been gone for so long and I called the facility where your friend lives.'

I looked around and noticed that the sky had gone from gray to orange. The sun was setting. Oh no. My girls. I'd completely forgotten about them.

'I'm sorry. Something came up.'

She rubbed my back and asked, 'So, why are you sitting here?'

'I used to spend every waking minute of my free time at the beach. When anything goes wrong in my life...I just...run to the beach.' I lowered my eyes and dug aimlessly at the sand. 'Jake and I met on a beach.' I laughed for a split second and added, 'It was one of the worst days of my life...' I added in a whisper, '...but not *the* worst.'

She raised an eyebrow so I explained, 'My friend and I used to wag school so we could surf on good days. It was far enough away so our parents and teachers wouldn't catch us, but close enough that we could catch a bus. We were pretty wild kids, sometimes.'

Isabel waited for me to continue, so I did. 'The day I met Jake, everything fell apart. It's strange how our worlds collided. We saw each other but never spoke but then suddenly...it was like a total car crash.'

Isabel winced and swallowed, so I apologised. 'Sorry. I shouldn't say car crash...sorry.'

She waved her hand with a tight lip, so I went on. 'Tamara was being such a smart-arse and just annoying. She had it in for me because I was surfing better than she was. She went for a wave, and it was huge, so I thought she would chicken out because she always did.' I punched my lap with my fists. 'It's what she always did! So I went, mostly just to get up her goat, ya know.'

Isabel just nodded.

'I felt my board...hit her in the head. Right there. In the side.' I gagged as I pointed to my temple. 'The sound it made.' I gagged again.

Isabel held my hand. I shook my head.

'There were air bubbles everywhere and I was spinning around and around, and when I eventually surfaced, I saw all this...blood...in the water.' The redness of the water swirling around me in the moments after the accident blurred my vision with its awful memory, making me shiver.

I continued, 'I panicked. I just...screamed...and paddled back to shore. That's where I found Jake.'

My head throbbed as I recounted that day. 'He saved her life but I…I just ran away.'

Isabel said, 'Jake told me that he didn't know her.'

'Well…he didn't…but he still saved her.' I added, 'Will told me that Jake keeps things to himself because his brother died.'

She hesitated before she said, 'Yes, that's what doctors have said, but Jake has always kept to himself. He only ever talked freely with Alex and even then, he kept secrets.' She sighed and concluded, 'I can't help but blame myself. I couldn't help detaching myself from him after Alex died. They were so alike…it was like looking at Alex every day and being reminded by God that my boy was gone.'

I looked at the ocean and muttered, 'If it makes you feel better, Jake isn't exactly the easiest person to talk to and be close with.' I shrugged. 'I mean…we're engaged and we've never even been intimate…' I froze, noticing my error.

Isabel narrowed her eyes. I looked down.

She asked quietly, 'Why did you get so upset today visiting your friend, Suzie?'

'Because…' I took several breaths, working up the courage to come clean. 'He was there.' I looked up at her. 'I wasn't in the best place after everything that happened with Tamara. I got myself into a bad place…with a bad man. I was trying to get away from him but he…' I whispered, 'He raped me.'

Isabel recoiled but did not let go of my hand. 'When?'

'April…last year.'

Her hand slowly slid away from mine and she pushed back her hair and took a deep breath. 'The girls…' Her voice trembled. 'They're not Jake's, are they?'

'No.'

'And Jake definitely knows this?' She looked down at her hands and muttered, 'Well, of course he must know since you haven't had sex. So, this just means you've been lying all this time.'

I nodded and began to cry again Isabel pulled me towards her and I collapsed into her middle. 'He saved me. He saves me every day…and I've ruined his life.'

Jake

July 2012

It finally happened. Sanna came clean. Kind of. She came clean to Mom about everything, how I wasn't the father and I'd been a selfless hero for stepping up into the role that wasn't mine. Hadn't they raised a good man? Dad disagreed.

Mom brought Sanna home where Dad and I were entertaining one baby at a time.

'Will!' Mom barked and Dad looked up as she marched into the room; Sanna trailed behind her with her eyes puffy and her head down. 'A word?'

He handed Bellare to Sanna and they stepped out onto the patio.

I poked Sanna. 'What took you so long?'

I was thinking she had run away or something had happened with Tamara. I didn't expect her to whisper, 'The guy that raped me was there.'

My eyes widened and my throat went dry. Bellare fussed and Sanna broke down. I took Bellare off her and balanced the girls on either hip, which was getting quite difficult now they were bigger and intent to move on their own.

I led Sanna out the back door and we went out to the barn. I glanced around at the patio to ensure my parents couldn't hear us. There I gave Bellare back to Sanna and we stood under the rafters and spoke in hushed tones.

'What was he doing there?'

'Visiting Tamara. Apparently they're still close.'

'What did you say? What did he do?' I shuddered as I thought of her having to face him. 'Did he say anything?'

She shook her head. 'I can't even…remember. I just…felt sick and had to run.'

I squeezed her arm with my free hand. 'Where did you go?'

'The beach. Your mum found me.' Her eyes went wide. 'Jake, I told her.'

'You told her about the rape?'

She nodded quickly and added, 'And us. What you did. For me.'

I took a deep breath and studied Audrey's face. She looked from me to Sanna, back to me with concern, aware that something was wrong.

Sanna whispered, 'I'm worried your mum isn't going to let me stay here anymore.'

She was probably right. I chewed the inside of my cheek and thought carefully. 'It'll be okay.'

Sanna whined, about to argue but I interrupted her, 'Hey! I've said it before and I'll say it again. It will be okay.'

She took both the girls with a weak smile and walked out into the dark to go back inside the house. I got to work, trying to distract myself. I sorted the tools and oiled my truck. As I shut the hood, I jumped as I realized Dad was standing by the side of the truck.

'Dad, you scared me,' I said with a gulp, wiping my hands clean.

235

He sneered, 'You never think anything through, do yer, Jake?'

I stopped wiping and braced. Here it came.

'You have never thought of the consequences. Never.'

I waited, forcing myself to breathe.

'When you didn't replace the seatbelt in that truck, you didn't think of the consequences, either,' he murmured.

There it was. I closed my eyes, willing my soul to leave my body. I didn't want to hear it. I didn't want to hear it. I didn't want to hear it.

'He would be alive if it wasn't for you.'

He slapped the edge of my truck and shook his head. He stalked off into the dark, muttering, 'Ruined yer damn life.' It was the first time I'd ever heard him swear and it cut through me just as much as the way he blamed me for Alex dying.

I stood at the hood of my truck, holding the rag in my hands for a long moment, counting the pounding pulses that ran through my veins. I was alive, and the favorite son was dead. No matter what I did, I'd never be a good man.

I got a pay-rise, up to twenty-three dollars an hour, and I was stoked. It meant I could start to think about buying a place or at least renting. I said to Sanna, 'At this rate, we'll have a house in no time.' And we did…. kind of.

I lingered around the real estate agencies in town and around work, studying the listed ads on the front windows. A beach view caught my eye. Beach cabin. For lease. It was in a caravan park, perched on the top of the cliffs that overlooked the ocean.

I went inside and pointed at it. 'How much is this? Can I afford this?'

They told me and I nodded with a grin. 'I can do that.' The agent took me there to have a look. The park was dilapidated but the cabin was okay. It was also on the main highway so had a lot of road noise, but there was an ocean view (good for me and Sanna) and a playground (good for the girls as they got older). I stood with my hands on my hips atop the cliff and nodded.

This would be it. I could do this. I could provide for my family. I could be a good man.

Sanna

July 2012

Jake took me to a caravan park on the Bass Highway, perched on the cliff overlooking the ocean. He led me to a run-down, overused old cabin with dead pot plants on the porch, and shouted, 'Ta-da!'

I asked, 'What is this piece of crap?'

Jake's shoulders dropped. 'Sanna, this...this is our place. Our home.'

My heart soared and then plummeted. I didn't even know that it was possible to feel excitement and disappointment in the span of two point five seconds. I stuttered, 'But it's a cabin.'

'What's wrong with it?'

I shouted, 'It's in a caravan park, Jake! I don't want to be trailer trash!' It cemented in my mind what I was. I didn't want to be like those girls you see lingering outside hotels, and hospitals, 'Got a ciggie?' and pulling up my tracksuit pants to cover tattoos and living on welfare.

I started hyperventilating, sat down and stuck my head between my knees.

Jake remained calm. 'It's neither a caravan nor a trailer – it's a cabin...and it's all we can afford.'

Encroaching on Jake's parents suddenly didn't seem so bad after all. I took a deep breath. 'You should have told me about this. My parents would have given you some money for a unit at least.'

He shook his head. 'You were right though, Sanna. I can't use people. I don't want to be in anyone's debt. The rent here is cheap.' His eyes lit up and he grabbed my hands and helped me stand upright. 'We can do this.'

'But it's a cabin.' I knew I sounded childish and weak but I couldn't acquiesce to becoming trailer trash. I was from a nice house and a wealthy-ish family – now just because of one little mistake, I was going to live in squalor – probably on welfare, too.

Jake put his hand on my shoulder, seeming to read my thoughts. 'It's okay, Sanna. We all have to start somewhere. This is like our own head start in the world.'

As I dried the dishes with Isabel that night, I thought carefully through the cabin. I didn't like the idea of moving out, and I wondered if Isabel and Will had told Jake that we had to leave.

I said, 'Isabel, Jake found a cabin for us to move into.'

'I think it's a nice little cabin,' she said. 'Jake showed it to me in the real estate catalogue.'

'You think it's nice?' I said, quite disappointed. She must want us to leave after all. I had been hoping that she would be on my side and help me convince Jake that we could stay living at the farm with the babies. I never thought that I'd want to keep living with Jake's parents but I'd really come to love the little bedroom and the sounds of the cows mooing during the night that lulled me and the girls to sleep.

Isabel nodded. 'Oh, yes. But of course, you're always welcome to stay here,' she said.

'Really?' I cried.

'Yes.'

'Well…I was wanting to stay here if that's okay with you,' I admitted sheepishly. 'I don't want to live in the cabin.'

She stopped cleaning the dishes and put a soapy glove on my shoulder. 'Oh, honey. It's natural to be nervous about living away from support and help. You'll just have to give it a shot and see how you like it.'

August 2012

The days sped by. The girls were settling into a routine. Or was it me who was settling? Maybe it was the fact that I was getting more sleep as they were getting older.

Going to the feed store with them was a real highlight of my week. I loved taking orders and sending Jake out with the trolley or the forklift. It felt good to tell him what to do.

The girls sat in their playpen, clattering noisy toys, and yelling at each other with monkey-like squeals of outrage. Audrey was bossy. She was going to be a handful; I could see it. I had been so worried about the way Bellare stared as if in judgement – really worried about her having her biological father's mean spirit – but now I could see that Audrey was the one to watch. Her little chubby hands would grab at Bellare's arms and her little fingernails would dig deep, and she would scream louder than Bellare would. The number of times I'd have to lift Bellare out of the pen and work with her on my hip couldn't be counted. She was smiling at the customers and making everyone swoon over her temperament and something was swelling in my chest. Could it have been…pride?

We moved into the cabin, with its timber panel walls, lumpy linoleum and green carpet. Will and Jake carried in our new double bed. We'd be sleeping together in the same room and the same bed for the first time. We made it and tried to avoid eye contact.

My parents brought us casseroles to put in our little freezer and we stuffed them inside so the door would close after some forceful shoves. We put safety locks on every cupboard door and shoved our clothes into drawers. We assembled the futon couch and set up the television. I made everyone cups of coffee with instant coffee and boiling water from the kettle, and we all sat around in random places throughout the joined living room and kitchen. The sliding door looked out to a grassy patch and a sliver of the blue ocean horizon could be spied behind the shrubs on the clifftop.

'That deck is going to be lovely to sit out in the mornings,' my mother enthused. I didn't disagree entirely. It would be lovely. Could my ego just get over itself already?

After our parents left, Jake and I stood on the porch of the little cabin, holding the girls.

'Well,' sighed Jake. 'This is it.'

I nodded. 'This is it.'

The salt in the air hung around us and a pelican soared above us, its wings broad and its gullet deep. The beach was a hundred metres away, down the path and across some basalt. We were literally at the end of the world but at the start of a new life.

A week later, while Jake was working, I took the girls in their behemoth pram down the path to the beach. I'd been holding out on taking them down there. I was afraid if I liked it too much, I would be content. Gosh, I was crazy.

Making my way down the narrow, rocky path with the pram was difficult but the way the blue water greeted my eyes made me smile. I was finally here. I had been stupid to avoid it.

The surfers out on the horizon bobbed like mirages in the long lull between sets. I put the brake on the pram and sat down on the soft, cool sand. Wind whistled through my hair and I fell into my own mind.

I stared at the surfers and remembered all the times being at the peak of the wave and soaring down, looking high above the cliffs on the big monsters I used to ride, the board wobbling and cutting into the water under my feet. My heart racing and my eyes stinging from the salt. The cold rush of the water over my head and I got caught in the lip of the close-out. Closing my eyes and cartwheeling under the water like a starfish, waiting for the tug of my leg rope to bring me back up the surface so I could breathe again and paddle back out for the next big ride.

Audrey made noises and brought me back. I sighed and smiled weakly. I touched her foot and she stared at me as if to say 'where are you?' I dusted my hands off on my jeans and picked her up to feel the weight of her body against my heart. Her eyes went to the sea and the foaming white that rolled in and out. She wiggled and bounced as though dancing to the sound of the sea. I couldn't help laughing at her excitedness to meet the current that was no doubt in her blood like it was in mine.

'The sea. Sea. Can you say sea? Sea.'

Audrey mouthed her little lips as though she was almost ready to try, but then just touched my face, not with much grace because it was more like a slap, but it was a moment to remember. A bonding moment. I hugged her and gazed out at the water until lunchtime.

That night, when Jake came home and I served up what could be described as barely edible gluggy lasagne for dinner, I said to him, 'I can't believe I'm admitting this, but…you were right, Jake. This is it!'

AVA DUNN

He looked around the room and put his fork down. 'What happened?'

I breathed a sigh of joy that made my face warm. 'We're so close to the sea.' I laughed. 'It's actually perfect.' I gestured at the kitchen, a cluttered mess with the dishes and ugly red splash back. 'I mean, it's hideous, don't get me wrong, but it's...' I took a deep breath and nodded. 'I think it's good.'

Jake smiled with half his mouth and continued eating, 'Well, all right, then.' He snorted while chewing and had to cup his mouth. We both cracked up laughing and doubled over our plates, trying not to spit out the ghastly mush of food.

Later that night, I lay beside him thinking. I was finally feeling as if I was what I had become. A mother and a fiancée. Homely. I found my feet in the dance.

I rolled into Jake's side and held a trembling hand to his shoulder. It was the right moment to finally be lovers. He rolled over to face me.

'What is it?' he asked.

I slowly kissed him and touched his neck, pulling him closer to me but he pulled back and rolled away.

'No, Sanna.'

I deflated inside and tears came to my eyes, and I rolled over away to the other side so he couldn't tell I was crushed. We were engaged. We should be having sex. Parents to two babies, though not biological, I wanted Jake to be their dad. I stuck my thumb in my mouth and breathed slowly, biting down on my thumb before sucking on it like a baby. How was I ever meant to become the person everyone expected me to be while being turned down or judged?

Waking up the next morning was difficult. My bleary eyes and stuffy nose set the tone between Jake and me well. He got up and went to work, pecking Bellare and Audrey adoringly with baby-kiss sound, 'Muah, muah, muah,' and carrying his lunchbox under his arm.

243

I rolled my eyes and said, 'Yeah, bye.' He left with barely a glance and left me alone in the kitchen to keep feeding the girls their porridge.

I took a deep breath and looked around the cabin, and it strangled me again.

I unfastened the high chairs and grabbed both girls, putting them in their pram. I hadn't even dressed them properly but I didn't care. I had to get out of there. I hurriedly put a cardigan on and tucked a blanket over the girls' legs in the pram and battered my way through the door, strolling back down the bumpy path to the beach.

Help me, I called to the salty sea in silence. *Help me feel free and cleanse me.*

The sand was a lot cooler in the morning than it had been in the afternoon. It was early August and the mornings were cool. Sea mist would usually hang around until ten am, but it was clear that morning. There weren't any surfers out yet.

I sat listening to the hum of the water, looking at my mobile phone, scrolling through endless pictures of surfing, bikinis, tropical beaches and palm trees. I wasn't paying enough attention to what was going on around me.

'Hello.'

I jumped at the voice that was right beside the pram. My heart gave an awkward beat when I realised Eddie was standing over the pram, looking at the girls. I shot to my feet in a flurry of sand.

'Get away from them!'

He smiled sideways at me, and backed up. 'Sorry, I didn't mean to scare you.' His eyes gazed down at the girls who stared back at him with their little mouths agape.

'Tamara said you'd had babies,' he said, running a hand over his surfboard deck and picking at a bit of surf wax.

I swallowed what felt like thorns.

Eddie laughed without smiling. 'Just funny...coz I know you hadn't been with anyone else.'

I scowled at him, my mind running through what to say.

He knocked on his board. 'You surfing anymore?'

'No.'

He pursed his lips. 'Shame. You were good. Had potential, before…you know…' He glared at me. 'You nearly fucking killed your friend; you piece of shit.'

My jaw went stiff as concrete. My throat closed. My forehead grew damp with sweat that made me shiver. My hands were shaking, so I grabbed the pram and struggled to push it away from him.

He called out to me, 'See you around, Sanna.'

Halfway up the path, I had to stop. My vision blurred and I doubled over as stomach acid rose. I vomited into the bushes. The girls cried, and so did I.

Jake

October 2012

The sun set later than I expected it to. Stupid Daylight-Saving Time. I always tried to be home before the sun set, so Sanna didn't realize I wasn't coming straight home. I was skipping out on her and the girls like I used to skip school.

I just drove. Wherever I could, for however long I could. Wasting diesel, no doubt, but I couldn't go home. Sanna had been miserable for the last three months. It was an instant drag to come home and see her tight lip and rustled hair that she couldn't stop running her nails through to scratch at her scalp.

I was late. My stomach dropped when I realized the time. I walked in the door, my eyes running over the mess of clothes, unfolded, sprawled across the futon and all the baby toys over the floor, amongst unwashed dishes. The shower was running. I went to the bathroom door and knocked before Sanna yelled, 'Come in!'

She was in the shower. Audrey and Bellare were in their bouncers in the bathroom with her. They looked up at me with gummy grins.

'I didn't expect you home so soon,' Sanna mumbled.

I cocked an eyebrow and cleared my throat. 'Yeah…' I checked my watch. It was 8:00. She must not have noticed the sun setting half an hour ago. I asked, 'How long have you been in there?'

She turned the water off. 'I don't know…Does it matter?'

'Girls been bathed?'

'No, Jake,' she breathed with exasperation. 'I'll do it in a minute.'

'No, it's fine,' I murmured and started undressing them, despite their flailing chubby arms and arguments. 'I'll do it now.' I looked away as she stepped out of the shower.

There was a pause. 'Why do you hate me, Jake?'

I groaned. 'I don't hate you! Can you stop saying stuff like that?' I threw the girls' clothes in the hamper and roughly turned the tap on and water splashed up at me. 'It's just hard to come home to you when you're like this!'

'Why am I like this?'

I turned to face her. I grabbed a towel and handed it to her.

She covered herself and snapped, 'I get it. I'm damaged. I know.'

I looked down at my boots, not daring to disagree as she chewed her lip.

'What are you thinking about?' I asked in a quiet voice.

'The girls will be one soon.'

I assented and put the girls into the bathtub with their toys and knelt down beside them.

'Did I tell you that I ran into him a couple of months ago?' Sanna asked.

'Yeah, you did…that's when you told my mom about what happened.'

'No, I mean, after that. He met the girls.'

247

On my knees, I looked up at her. She scratched her head again.

'I think he knows he's the father.'

I felt sick thinking about a rapist being near Audrey and Bellare. I ran my hand down Audrey's little arm and wanted to hold it forever to keep her safe.

Sanna nodded. 'He definitely knew.'

I shook my head. 'You don't know that.'

She paced the bathroom and the girls and I watched her.

'What if he tries taking them from me?'

'Why would he?'

'Just to hurt me.'

I asked, 'Is that what you're worried about?'

She nodded. I stood up, stepped to her, and wrapped her in a hug. 'That won't happen. I won't let it.'

She sobbed, 'I just have a really bad feeling about him hanging around, Jake. It's making me crazy.'

I made sure to get home on time every night after that.

On Thursday night, a week after Sanna admitted to me what had been on her mind, I went over to my parents' while Sanna visited Michael. She'd gone to his place more and more often over the last week.

I parked my truck outside the barn and found Dad inside, repairing the ride-on mower. He came up to me, wiping his hands clean. 'Jake, what's happened?'

I tucked my chin to my chest and let out a deep whistle. 'I don't even know where to start, Dad…but I need some advice.'

After I told him about what was bothering Sanna, he shook his head. 'Well, I think you're an idiot for doing what you did in the first place.'

I rolled my eyes. 'Yeah, I know.'

'You shouldn't have done it.'

'Can we just drop it? I did it.' I couldn't help looking over my shoulder before hissing, 'I've ruined my life but don't you think I would change it if I could.'

He cleared his throat. 'Jake, why can't yer?'

My head shook as though I had shuddered. 'I can't.'

He drummed his fingers on the hood of the mower and chewed on a matchstick. 'I guess that's the cost of being a good man.'

I groaned, 'Dad, tell me you wouldn't have raised me if I wasn't yours.' He was silent so I looked closer at him. 'Dad, come on.'

He scoffed. 'I wouldn't have. No way. I would have walked away.'

My shoulders dropped and I ran my tongue over my teeth, thinking of the words to reply, but I couldn't do it. Anything I wanted to say would hurt his feelings.

I guess that was why I felt so stuck all the time. Stuck with my memories of being Alex's brother in Texas, stuck in the little Gippsland town on the coast when I didn't know anybody, stuck being a sidekick to Tessa, stuck with Sanna, stuck with not being able to go to university, stuck with these kids that weren't mine and stuck with who I was. Was I actually a good person or just an idiot? All I'd ever wanted to be was successful, so was that achieved by being good or was it by being selfish? Some of both, I guess.

The next day, I developed a squeezing sensation that branded across my entire head. I drank a few bottles of water but it didn't go away. It got so bad that I started to squint with watering eyes. Mick told me to go home. I argued that I was fine for an hour but eventually I started to feel as though my stomach was folding in on itself and I'd gag from the pain.

'Jake! I'm serious, you bloody nufty. Go home! You've got a migraine, you fool,' Mick got me my car keys and said, 'Just bloody drive safe, mate. Go sleep it off.'

At home, the bed tilted under me and my brain buzzed against my skull so much that I could hear it thumping. It was like a sledgehammer was knocking on my forehead. I gagged and clamped my eyes closed, trying to sleep. The moment black engulfed my eyes and I had the relief of "sleeping it off". Migraines were no bloody fun.

When I woke up the next morning, Sanna was gone with the girls. I texted her, asking where she was and she told me she was down at the beach.

'Michael with you?' I texted.

'No.'

I walked down to the beach; my legs heavy like lead. I found her sitting on her surfboard on top of the sand. The girls were out of the stroller and sitting up on a blanket, sucking on sand and seaweed. Sanna looked up at me with surprise. She dusted the sand off her wetsuit that was in her lap. 'Hey.'

'What're you doin'?' I asked, sitting beside her.

She gestured at the water on the other side of the rocks. 'Perfect surf conditions today.' The waves were coming in sets of two. There was a long silence as the glittering wall steepened up, up and up, followed by a ricocheting crash as it broke and a hum as the second wave, taller and bigger chased it in, before returning to the calm lull. There wasn't anybody out.

I asked, 'You gonna go in then?'

She shrugged. 'I figured that I *could* now…you know…if someone had the girls.'

'Yeah. I'm here. You can go in.'

She shrugged. 'I don't think I can.'

'Yeah. You can.'

'Yeah.'

We stared at the water for a while. It was gorgeous out there. I looked down at her board. 'Do you want me to go have a go?'

'You?' she snorted. 'You can't even swim, can you?'

'I can swim. I just don't.'

'Aren't you afraid of water?' she asked.

250

'Aren't *you*?'

She started digging holes in the sand with her fingers and keeping them submerged. She chewed on her lip. 'I dunno,' she finally admitted. 'I don't think it's the water I'm afraid of.' She feigned a smile and added, 'I can't help thinking about it.'

'That's natural.'

'You really should swim, Jake.'

I cupped the squeaking, crumbling, coarse sand in my hand. 'I don't need to; it's not in my blood like it's in yours.' I grinned. 'But I'm not afraid to if I have to,' I added.

'That's true.' She nodded. 'You went in the water to try and save Tamara.' She gave me a sincere smile. 'Thank you for that...Thanks for saving her, Jake. And me.'

'No worries,' I said and made her laugh with my imitation of the Australian slang. When she stopped laughing, I said, 'I'd do it again.'

'I know.'

'So, get out there,' I said, gesturing at the water. 'I'm here. I'll come in for you if I see you getting into trouble.'

She screwed up her nose. 'No. I don't think so...Not today.' We stood up. She squinted up at the faint moon in the sky to the right. 'I'm going to take the girls to visit Tamara...but I want you to come with me in case he's there.'

Now that Tamara was awake, it would be harder to look her in the eye. I was nervous to meet the girl that knew my fiancée better than I did and would ever really know? Though, did she? This Sanna was different to the one I had met at the beach that day. A year and a half had gone by and she was changed, in many ways.

I replied, 'I can't. Take Michael instead.'

She shoved her board and wetsuit into my hands. 'Figures,' she snapped and picked up the girls and put them in the stroller. 'I keep trying to get closer to you, Jake, and you keep shutting me down. I mean, what else can I do?' She glared at me. 'Fine. I'll take Michael. I'll go kiss Michael. I'll go have sex with Michael. Maybe I'll marry MICHAEL!'

She stomped off through the sand with the girls but got stuck and flailed momentarily before flicking her hair back and restarting. I bowed my head and followed behind her, carrying her board and wetsuit.

December 2012

The girls turned one. We had their first birthday party the day before their actual birthday. Sanna's parents hosted it at their place in Rhyll.

Michael was there right on time. He was bouncing his foot while sitting at the table. He wore long socks with burgers printed on them, shorts and a puffer jacket. I shook his hand and he bounced on his toes while nodding. 'You good, mate?' I asked.

'Yeah, yeah, yeah. Good, as.'

Sanna watched him, looked at me then looked away. Looked like he wasn't going "good as" at all. My parents arrived and Dad was wearing his best Stetson hat. Sanna was going from person to person, kitchen to living room, and back to the kitchen with blitz. Her mother made the cake and we weren't allowed to start until Tamara arrived with her disability support worker Aaron. I crossed my arms and waited. She eventually came in and everyone smiled. Tamara and Sanna hugged.

Then he walked in behind her.

Sanna's face fell and she went ghostly white. 'What are you doing here?' she snapped.

'What's wrong?' Tamara asked.

I'd never met the girls' father, but the way Sanna's hands were trembling, I figured this was him. He smiled and put his arm around Tamara's shoulder. 'What do you mean? I'm Tamara's date. We're a thing, now.'

252

I stepped towards him, balling my fists. 'A word, please, mate. Outside.'

I started walking to the door but he planted his feet and said, 'No.'

'Get out!' Sanna hissed.

Tamara raised her eyebrows and stared at Sanna with her eyes wide.

Everyone else went quiet. I felt my face prickling with heat as I said, 'Outside, man. Now.'

He shoved me away, so I grabbed his shirt at his throat and pulled him with all my strength back out the door. He swung me off him as we hit the deck outside, our boots thumping loudly on the thin wood.

'Oh, you wanna go for assault, mate. Bring it,' he snorted and raised his fists like a boxer.

I ran my shoulder into his chest to knock him backwards off the patio and as soon as he hit the ground with a wet slap in a puddle, I pulled him back up towards me and punched him as hard as I could. Michael was right there beside me, kicking him in the thighs. Sanna was screaming, 'Stop!'

'Get the fuck out of here!' Michael yelled.

We let him get up. He rubbed at his nose and pointed at Sanna. 'Don't think I can't do maths, Sanna. Those kids are one, huh. One year and eight months. Yeah. I know.'

Sanna shook her head on the patio and clutched at her chest.

'I know they're mine!' He grinned. 'See you soon, boys.'

We watched him leave, limping up the driveway back to the main road. Michael spat on the ground beside himself. 'Wish I could kill that prick.'

I turned to Sanna, in disbelief that he had come along and angry that he'd confronted Sanna like that – telling her that my girls were his. They were, obviously – but he would never be a dad like I was. Or even a dad like Michael was to the girls. I refused to let my girls be taken from Sanna by that son of a bitch.

A tear fell off Sanna's cheek. Our families and Tamara stood inside, watching with confused expressions.

Sanna murmured, 'You guys shouldn't have done that.'

I went to hug her but she walked back inside so Michael and I followed her.

'What does he…know, Sanna?' Tamara asked.

Sanna collapsed on the couch and shook her head. 'I don't want to talk about it.'

'Let's just do the cake!' My mother clapped her hands. 'Come on, y'all. Let's celebrate.'

Sanna

December 2012

I had laid that morning in our bed, softening to the touch of Jake's finger running gently along my side. Wanting to beg him *a bit higher, Jake. A bit higher.*

His hand hesitated, hovering near my breasts and stopped. He returned to tracing his finger up my side from my hip to my rib. I wanted to make love with him more than ever. I was ready.

After the party, the twins were finally asleep after their exciting day of turning one. Cupcakes, cake, toys and company. Joy drunk at the end of the party and falling asleep in their booster seats on the drive home to Kilcunda West.

Jake tried to give me his usual goodnight peck on the cheek but I grabbed his chin in my hand and laid my lips firmly on his. He and paused.

I whispered, 'Thank you for saving me today.'

He leant in and kissed me. We lay there and looked each other in the eyes.

'…and for every day.' I swallowed hard and continued, 'For what you did then…and today…and now.'

He took a deep breath and smiled. He shakily put his hands on my hips, accidentally nudging me in the ribs with his elbow. Before he could shy away, I took one of his hands with one of my own, squeezing it, and guided it over parts of my body.

Jake cried out as I placed my hand upon him and he returned the favour by touching me. His tense body slackened and he gave in to what I needed from him. He rolled on top of me and melted into me. This is what it needed to be. I closed my eyes and was finally at peace.

January 2013

Everything was finally going well. Audrey took her first steps the day after her first birthday. Bellare took half a step on Christmas morning then didn't take another until after my seventeenth birthday.

Days had a routine. I'd eat breakfast with the girls and Jake at 7:00 am before he went off to work, then I'd dress the girls and then do the dishes, letting them play with their toys in the kitchen. I'd do a workout DVD, sweating my way to get my surfer body back. The girls would laugh their little faces off watching me struggle to plank. Sadists.

At 9:00 am, I'd bundle them in their pram and make my way across the spongy strip of grass by the cliff. Dodge the rabbit holes, bounce down the steps to the beach and sit on the icy sand and let the girls play in it, crawl and waddle their way as close to the rocks at the edge of the water as my anxiety would allow. It always felt protected there in our little spot. The beach appeared to be a dead-end to the right, with its headland curving to the left. Rocks protected the sand at low-tide and even a little bit at high-tide, too.

I visualised paddling out through the channel and making my way to the left so I could ride the rights that went for what seemed like hours. I studied the horizon for the sight of a spurt of water from a dolphin or whale. I was never successful but hopeful still the same.

I'd walk back up the stairs with the girls, which was a workout on its own. I'd put them to bed for a nap. Do some washing and cleaning. Talk on the phone with Michael who was trying to find a job after finishing school last year, but he sounded groggy each time I called, as if he was still in bed.

I'd go wake up the girls and eat lunch with them. Wander outside with them again, but this time to the small playground to let the girls swing on the swing one at a time or guide them down the blue slide, laughing at their surprised faces and cheering for them when they didn't cry. Pull my hair out when they did. Collect the mail that the postie left at our doorstep and chortle at the fact that motherhood was turning me into an adult, when most girls turn into adults before becoming mothers.

February 2013

At the start of February, there was a very official-looking letter for me. I opened it as soon as I stepped inside and grew lightheaded so had to sit on the floor. Bellare flopped against me and tugged at me hair and I winced, but not because she had hurt me.

SUMMON TO ANSWER PETITION FOR SOLE CUSTODY

257

I folded the letter eight times and placed it on the floor. I swallowed hard and watched my daughters until they blurred through my tears.

I considered not telling anyone. Just going to the courthouse and telling Eddie: 'Fine...take them if you want to hurt me this much.'

I imagined them leaving and my chest hurt. I considered running away with the girls but where? I imagined doing what I should have done initially. Gone to the police and told them what he had done at the time, so he could be charged. What evidence did I have now? Why was my life one big mistake after another?

When Jake got home, I shoved the letter into his hand and said, 'Going out for a walk. Look after the girls.'

I slammed the door behind me, leaving him with the letter and the heaviness that had sat with me all day.

I did not walk like I told him I was going to; I ran. There was a cool change coming and the wind was whipping up the smell of salt from the sea.

Sweaty and out of breath, I arrived at the next beach – the beach where I had collided into Tamara's head.

A bolt of lightning flickered across the horizon, followed by the rumbles of thunder.

I made my way down the hill where the sea run-off left a creek. I powered on to the beach with heavy breaths. The wind howled between the bluff and the distant Cape. The heritage railway bridge creaked in the wind and rattled.

I kept going to the granite wall of the headland, navigating the incoming tide and the rock pools. I reached the worn rock face arch where I had scratched messages years ago with Tamara, amongst other scratched messages.

I used the light on my mobile phone to read the messages. Lovers and tourists had joined the wall, and there, fading in the centre, was "Tamara 4 Eddie". Seeing their names made me scream with rage; I picked up the sharpest rock I could find and carved into the wall so ferociously that I could feel blood trickling down my wrist. I scratched harder and harder until their names were scratched out. I stared at my artwork in the dark. I dropped the sharp little rock and wiped my bloody hand down my leg. I winced and stepped back, but lost my balance and tumbled onto the rocks.

I blinked and squinted into the moon. Why was it so bright?

'Sanna?' came a distorted voice. 'Sanna, are you okay?' I squeezed my eyes and tried to blink at the moon. I raised a hand and my head swam, making me queasy.

'Oh,' I murmured, and rolled over so I could vomit into the rock pool. I was lying on top of the rocks with the water bubbling around me. A zig-zag of purple shadowed my sight from Jake's mobile phone.

'I must have…tripped,' I mumbled, letting Jake help me up. I looked up at the trees and the inky sky. 'How long have I been gone?'

'Too long. I was worried. I thought you'd done something stupid like jumped.' Jake took his jacket off and wrapped it around me. 'Should I call the paramedics?'

'No, no, don't be silly, I just tripped…' I let him guide me to the rail trail that led back home. 'Where are the girls?'

'I left them sleeping and one of the neighbours is looking after them. They're fine. I had to find you.'

I gasped as I remembered the letter from Eddie's lawyer – he wanted to take them away – what if he was there? I went to run back home but Jake grabbed both my shoulders. 'Sanna…they're fine. They're going to be fine.'

My face screwed up and my head ached. 'I don't think they will be – not this time, Jake.'

He put both his hands on my cheeks and directed my face to meet his eyes directly. 'Trust me. Don't you trust me? After all this time? We'll work it out.'

I sobbed and he helped me limp home.

Jake

February 2013

I told Mick I wouldn't be in for work. I went to the library and pulled out every law book I could find. I thumbed through family law reports and then called a lawyer named Ben Simpson that had represented a rape victim four years ago.

We spoke about how Eddie could get a court order for a DNA test to prove he was the father. He could get custody, despite being a rapist. He had every right to see his children, even if it was rape. He could even call me into question by suggesting I was an unfit guardian for his child – even charge me with assault for punching him, and even claim Sanna was an unfit mother.

My mind swirled as he explained the processes Eddie could take to act upon his paternal rights. Everything Sanna did or did not do with the girls could affect the outcome. I went home with another migraine.

That night, I woke to the girls screaming. Slow to open my eyes after the pounding the migraine had given me, once I registered the girls were screaming, I raced out of the bedroom. It was ten past midnight and Sanna was gone from the bed. I assumed that she had gone out for a sneaky joint and got locked out. That's when I saw the man in the living room, cloaked with a hoodie, muscular upper body and flat nose. Familiar in his arrogant way of standing with one shoulder lower than the other as if to let you in on a secret. Eddie.

'You shouldn't be here!' I shouted. I lunged at him, but he bowled his shoulder into me, pinning me against the closest wall. I fired off defensive punches but only landed one. The twins screamed louder and I fought harder. I was yelling. He was yelling back.

'Get out of our house,' I shouted.

Sanna stepped forward, rocking the twins. 'Just let him talk, Jake. He said he just wants to talk.'

Eddie smirked and let me off the wall. 'Yeah. Just let me talk.'

I straightened up my tee-shirt and hissed, 'We've got nothing to talk about.' I made to go to the bedroom to get my phone. 'I'm calling the police.'

Eddie grabbed my arm and said, 'Don't.' He stretched out his hand for me to shake. 'How about we meet properly, bro? Man to man.'

I slapped his hand and he shrugged at Sanna. 'I just want to talk. See? Your beau has anger issues.'

'Jake, get him a drink. Give him whatever he wants,' Sanna said. I pulled out a bottle of bourbon and glared at her. I shoved it at Eddie. 'Take it and get out.'

His fingers wrapped around the neck of the bottle and he hesitated. I took a step back and whispered, 'What do you really want?'

'My kids.'

I shook my head. 'I don't believe that.'

He smirked. 'Fine. Money, then. Pay me for them and you can have them.'

'I don't have any money to give you.'

'Well then…I guess I'll see you in court, then, bro.'

He took the bottle and left, slamming the door behind him, causing the girls to cry again. I stormed after him, despite Sanna's calls to come back.

I shouted at his departing back, 'Oh yeah? You think the judge will give you custody of those girls when they find out what you did? What you are?'

Eddie stopped and turned. 'What am I?'

'You're a rapist!'

He narrowed his eyes at me and his mouth shortened into a scowl. 'What did you call me?'

'A rapist. You are a rapist and you are going to Hell.'

He waved his hands and twinkled his stubby fingers. 'Oooh, I'm scared.' He smirked. 'Fuckin' prove that it was rape, mate. You can't.'

'You're never getting those girls!'

Eddie got into his ute and started it, flooring it while it was still in park and gravel spat out towards me. Fury took the blood from my hands and feet and flung it at my throat. 'You call that a pick-up truck?'

He spat out the window at me and drove away.

I looked around, panting to regain the breath I hadn't realized was strained. Lights came on in the surrounding caravans and cabins, elderly faces of our neighbours and younger faces of tourists stared out at us. I shook my head at them and went back inside.

I took Audrey from Sanna and held her close to my chest. She whimpered against my racing heart. I snapped at Sanna, 'What the hell happened? How did he get in?'

'I got up to change the girls…and he was in the driveway. He said he just wanted to talk and came in.'

I locked the door. 'Never let him in again. Ever.'

Her lip trembled and she nodded. 'I didn't let him in. I told him we could talk because I thought I could talk him out of filing for custody, but he pushed through the door. I think we forgot to lock it.' Her skin was a whitish shade of blue.

I grabbed at the door and re-opened it. Despite it being locked, adding pressure to the door just allowed it to swing open. I scratched at my head. I'd have to fix that ASAP. I sighed and shook my head at Sanna, knowing she wasn't going to like what I was about to suggest. 'You have to get a DNA test done on the girls to prove that they're his children.'

'What do you mean?'

'He is a rapist, Sanna,' I said firmly. 'He raped you, but that doesn't mean he won't get custody.' I sighed. 'The only thing that is going to work is if you tell the police now, and tell them how old you were when it happened.'

She blinked at me. 'What are you saying? I can't prove that he raped me!'

'The DNA test will prove that he did.' She heaved in a deep breath. I nodded. 'Statutory.'

'Jake…you're the smartest guy I know. Thank you.'

'Don't be singing my praises just yet. It's just an idea.'

She kissed my cheek. 'But a brilliant one.'

'It'll mean you'll have to come clean about what happened to you, though.' I kissed the top of Audrey's head. 'Are you okay with that? I mean…' I took a deep breath. 'That's the only reason we're together, isn't it.'

She was lowering Bellare while I was speaking but as she squatted down and let Bellare stand, Sanna froze. She looked up at me and replied with her eyes red with tears. 'Jake…'

'It's okay,' I smiled. 'We're friends.'

I kissed the top of Audrey's head again just for something to do to hide that I was upset that we would be all over, Red Rover, once the truth came completely out and everybody knew, not just a couple of people. I said to Audrey, 'Let's get you back to bed, little one.'

Sanna

February 2013

I strolled along the gravel path and observed each caravan and cabin. Jake and I were not the only young family that occupied the park. Children no older than three wandered around, unsupervised, barefooted and in stained tee-shirts. I looked down at my girls – at their clean, bright faces and colourful clothing – and vowed I would never let them be so neglected.

I arrived back at the cabin and flinched as a window smashed. 'What the-?' I rolled the pram closer and peered around the side of the cabin. There was Billy, Michael's brother, climbing through the tiny bathroom window of our cabin. I hadn't seen him in over a year, since I went into labour.

'Billy?'

He froze, his legs dangling out and blood trickling down his arm.

'What are you doing?'

He slid out of the small window, which he had smashed with his hand, and smiled so wide and fake. 'I thought you weren't home and thought I saw a burglar.'

'So, you broke the window?' I exclaimed, applying the brake on the pram and marching over to the window to inspect the damage. Glass littered the ground – it crunched beneath my sandals. My face went hot and I put my hand on my hip and glared at him.

Billy scratched the back of his neck and smiled.

I asked, 'Why are you even here in the first place?' I moved back over to the girls but he grabbed my wrist, smearing blood over my hand and arm. 'Ew, gross!'

'I need some money.'

'Do you really think *we* have any? Hello – I'm a teen mum living in a caravan park!' I twisted my wrist free of him but he grabbed it again and pulled me closer. 'Don't; let me go! Billy!'

His grip reminded me of Eddie's and I started to hyperventilate. 'Let me go! Let me go!'

There was a strange scent on Billy's breath that resembled nail polish remover. My heart hammered in my chest. I doubled over and screamed. Billy let me go.

'Are you crazy or something? I wasn't gonna hurt ya, ya stupid moll!'

With my eyes on the blood smear and the red tinge to my arm hair, I broke into a sweat and trembled all over. I spat, 'We don't have any money.'

Billy cocked his head at me. 'So you said. I'll go ask Michael about the drugs then, eh.'

'I don't want you around here anymore.' I wobbled as I took the remaining steps to the pram. The girls looked at the scene with concern. Who was I kidding? They were one and didn't understand anything.

I sucked in a deep breath of air. 'I don't want you around here at all, ever. Do you understand, Billy?'

He flipped me off and walked off, wavering on the driveway. First Eddie, now Billy. Why were these creeps always drawn to me?

Eyes of the grotty toddlers' mothers were on me, and I shuddered. Imagine them, looking down on me. I got to work, picking up the glass when one of them came over and said, 'Ya all right, darl? Need a hand?'

I sniffled and nodded. She helped me wrap the window with cling wrap and duct tape. Her name was Hayley and she wasn't as much of a loser as I suspected she had been. She was actually a really nice person. I knew I had to stop judging people before I got to know them. I was not a great judge of character.

When Jake got home, I told him I'd found the window broken when I got home from the beach. I didn't mention that Billy had been here, looking for money for drugs. Jake thought Eddie broke the window to scare us, and I was fine with him thinking that.

Michael came over to see the damage his brother had done.

He gasped. 'Oh my God! Sorry.'

'You don't have to apologise for what your idiot brother did,' I muttered. I made him a cup of tea and asked, 'Though…why did he try getting into my cabin in the first place? He knows I don't have money and he knows that I don't have drugs.'

Michael scratched the back of his neck.

I didn't take my eyes off him and he smudged his fingers around and around the mug handle, avoiding my eyes.

'Michael, there's something up with you.'

'I'm okay,' he said slowly. 'I just took some of his ice. I'm okay now. He must have thought I hid it here.'

'You stole his drugs?' I groaned. 'You're such an idiot!'

He slurped at the tea with a shaky hand. 'It's all right, though. I'm kicking them.'

I was taken aback. I didn't realise he had actually taken the drugs, as in *used* them. I gripped the edge of the bench to steady myself. But I trusted that he was kicking them.

'You better be,' I mumbled. 'I need you clean.'

'Why?'

I leant against the sink. 'Jake and I are breaking up.'

His eyes went wide. 'You are?'

'Yeah. After the court date with Eddie.' I pulled at a hangnail. 'Everything will come out then so...Jake will be free to go.'

'He wants that?'

I shrugged. 'I think he does. I think when he signed up for it, he didn't actually think he'd be stuck with me and the babies.' I laughed. 'Kind of love him for the fact that he did, though.'

Michael paused. 'I would have, too, you know.'

I smiled. 'I know.'

He came to stand next to me and touched my hip with one hand, my ear with the other. I hugged him before he could kiss me again. I'd wait for Jake, like he'd waited for me.

The next day, I walked into the police station with Jake at my side, holding my hand with his palm facing outwards so my hand was hidden, protected.

The police officers greeted us with a 'Howzitgoin?'

The older one asked, 'What can I help you with, young lady?'

I steeled my face and took a deep breath in; Jake squeezed my hand. 'I want to report a rape.'

As I sat with Jake in the room, two police officers walked in and introduced themselves as detectives. Their names were Angel and Deetya.

'Firstly, Sanna, I just want to commend you on having the courage to come forward and report what has happened to you. It is a terrible thing, and we take it very seriously, even if it has happened months or years ago. Well done for coming forward,' Deetya said, leaning forward towards me and reaching out a hand as though she wanted to touch me.

Her colleague nodded in agreement and quietly said, 'You're doing the right thing to report this assault. We understand how frightening and devastating this experience was and we really are here to help, even if some of our questions may be intense and deeply personal. It is your decision to stop at any time, but please let us know if you need to stop for a break at any time. We need to go through the events leading up to the assault. What happened – every detail you can remember.'

The words hit me in the ribcage as though they were concrete. I slipped my hand out of Jake's and clasped both my hands together in my lap, hunching forward and I nodded. 'I think I can do that.'

Deetya cleared her throat and got out her notebook and a pen. Angel took care of the digital recorder and nodded at me to begin. I started as early as meeting Eddie through Tamara and how he used to take me surfing. He had been in a position of power over me, emotionally as well as physically. If he was taking me surfing, he was looking after me and had responsibilities like a guardian. He had known me as a younger child and taken advantage of me. Eddie was older, by four or five years at least.

The police officers listened and Deetya took notes, her blue pen scrawling faster than I could speak. When I met him, how often he took me surfing, how he'd encourage me to skip school so I could go surfing with him and Tamara – that had been more Tamara's idea but Eddie hadn't exactly discouraged us by picking us up and not telling our parents. I told them how I'd had the surfing accident and stopped surfing, but still worked at The Surf Shack. The day Eddie walked in. The day I followed him like a desperate fool and he'd kissed me in the water, given me beer (that I was too young to be drinking even now) and made me feel like I wasn't alone. The trip in the dusk, to the moment he was touching me before I vomited on him and ran, being stopped and held in the dirt at the side of the road, my mouth full of gumnuts, leaves, his hand and dirt. My shorts left behind as I ran for my life to the headlights that came around the bend – Jake's headlights. Breaking down with the memory of sitting in the car between Jake and Tessa, their silence and my brain disconnecting and refusing to understand why there was blood trickling down my bare leg.

Burying my head down into my arms on the table and I shook as the tears rolled up from my chest and out of my eyes. Jake put his arm around me and rested his chin on my shoulder, whispering, 'You did it.'

Angel stopped the recording. 'I think we better stop there. Sanna, you've done very well.'

I garbled out, 'Okay,' through my sobs and kept my head down, not wanting them to see my red, splotchy face and to see me in that moment of recalling how I had leapt into Jake's car, not even hiding my nakedness from them.

Jake said, 'I was there that night. I can give a statement, too.'

Afterwards, I was so depleted and sleepy that I could hardly walk straight out of the police station. Exhaustion took over and I felt an immense rush of relief.

Jake

February 2013

I wished I could have seen the look on that son of a bitch's face when the police showed up at his door and took him in for questioning.

I drove Sanna back home and she went straight to the bedroom, too tired to even greet Bellare and Audrey who pulled themselves up to stand by gripping onto the futon. They watched her go to the bedroom with little parted mouths then turned to me. I said hi to them both and watched them smile and sit back down, happy now that their efforts to grow up were noticed by at least one person. My mom asked how it had gone with the police.

I leaned back and spread myself, floppy. 'She did so well, Mom. She told them everything.' I rubbed my eyes with the back of my hand. 'I even made a statement about that night when I picked her up.'

'You picked her up?' she asked.

I paused. 'Yeah. I was there when it happened. I found her.'

She scratched at the corner of her mouth before slowly asking, 'Why didn't you report it to the police then, Jake?'

I leaned forward, elbows on my knees. 'She didn't want me to.'

Mom hissed, 'Jake, you could've prevented this whole debacle from ever happening!'

My eyes narrowed so hard it gave me an instant headache. 'Mom, this happened to *her*. It is *her* trauma. Not mine. It wasn't up to me. It was *her choice* to report it. Even the police told us that. Don't blame *me*.'

'I'm not blaming you!' she exclaimed. 'It just should have been reported sooner.'

I shook my head. 'Don't you think Sanna needed at least some kind of choice? Wouldn't you if that had been you…held down in the dirt by a guy? Your face shoved into the dirt and being smothered by the asshole for your first time ever having sex? Having to run along the road to God knows who and get into their car to get away?'

My mother blinked and she stepped away, visibly wincing.

'Don't you think she deserved at least some choice?' I wiped my eye, and noticed my hand was coming back wet. I sobbed and held up my hands in surrender.

'If I had to sacrifice something just to help her…' I shrugged. 'I don't care. I had to do it. She was hurt, Mom…hurt worse than we ever were when Alex died.'

I took in a deep breath but it caught and zigzagged in a few huffs before I could breathe and speak again. 'There are worse things to happen to you than someone you love dying.'

My mother began to cry silently.

I sobbed, 'Sometimes it's worse being alive.'

I stood and paced the room, until Bellare and Audrey started to cry and I sat down on the floor with them to rub their backs to calm them down again.

'You don't get it, Mom…The way her eyes looked when she got into my truck my night…I'd do anything to not see that look on someone's face ever again. It was the face of someone who thought they were about to die.'

The next morning, a glass smashed and I woke up with a jolt. I was crammed on the futon against the window. Sanna was crouching in the kitchen, picking up pieces of the glass she had dropped. 'Sorry. I was trying to be quiet,' she said.

I rubbed my head and stood up, having to pause halfway up to make sure I was fully awake by clearing my throat and yawning.

'You slept out here last night,' she said, sliding the shards into the trash bin. She put her hand on her hip. 'Everything okay?'

I nodded and went to the kitchen to make my coffee. 'Yeah, I didn't want to wake you.'

'I was awake…I heard everything you said to your mum.'

I felt the exhaustion smother me and I slumped. 'I'm sorry, Sanna.'

She chewed on her lip and her fingers tapped on the benchtop. 'I've been trying to put a finger on how I felt that night, you know. Why I forgot it for a while. I wondered if you remembered it the same way I did.'

I sighed. 'I remember every second of how you looked.' I wish I didn't, but the wide, glazed eyes flashed at me every time she looked at me.

Sanna frowned and looked out the kitchen window at the line of blue and rubbed her cracked lips. 'I remember I had to run. That's all.' She got another glass out of the cabinet and sighed. 'I can't think about what would have happened if you hadn't been there.'

'No, I agree...wouldn't be a good move.'

She smiled softly and we stood in the kitchen in the morning sunlight. She stepped closer to my body and I let her

272

hug me before I closed my eyes with a sigh and folded my arms across her back, breathing in the coconut scent of her hair.

What a strange turn my life had taken. From being kind of intrigued by this girl, to helping her escape from what could have been a murder, to agreeing to dash my dreams just to protect her, to helping her raise her children as my own...yet never loving her until I knew she was pulling away and growing up.

Audrey and Bellare called out from their room, so Sanna broke away and I followed her to get them up and out of their cribs. They were both standing in the corners where they could talk to each other in their babble and coos, and they both looked over to us in the doorway and grinned. Bellare waved and Audrey called out, 'Mum-mum-mum, da-da.'

Don't you forget it, kid, I thought. *Please, don't forget it.*

We spent the day together as a little family, playing on the caravan park playground and keeping quiet, waiting for something to come about from the statements we made. At 3:00 pm, the police car drove in and the two officers we spoke to, came to the door and we got them glasses of water.

'We have the perpetrator in custody and he's been given an Apprehended Violence Order (AVO) and has been summoned to court. He cannot come near you and if he does, you need to call 000 immediately,' said Angel. She made sure to look into Sanna's eyes and said, 'Immediately.'

Sanna nodded.

'Did he admit to what he did?' I asked.

'I can't tell you what his statement was,' Angel said, but added, 'The age difference is the thing we have to focus on and it's what will be presented to the judge in court. If you decide to go down the path of charging him with rape, we'll need DNA samples from your daughters.'

Deetya handed Sanna some papers. 'This is a copy of your own statement, some contact details for any support or assistance you may need, numbers of reputable lawyers and solicitors, the court date if you choose to attend to testify against him – it is absolutely up to you if you choose to pursue this, but please know that we are behind you and will support you in any way we can whatever your decision.'

Decisions and choices – it always came down to the choices Sanna had. I wondered what choice she would decide to take. Looking around our small cabin, with the toys strewn everywhere and the happy faces of Audrey and Bellare as they tottered around the room, flapping their arms and chatting to each other in their little special language, I wished I could make the choice for her. Fight. Fight him every step of the way. Be brave.

Sanna nodded.

I asked, 'What happens if I choose to testify on her behalf?'

Deetya's dark eyes snapped onto me as she handed me two separate pieces of paper. 'Here is your copy of your statement…and your own AVO.'

'I didn't file for one.'

'No, Mr. Adams has filed one against you.'

I screwed up my face and said, 'Why?'

'You assaulted him on December 16th, at the address of Mr. and Mrs. Smith. We already spoke with his girlfriend who witnessed it and crosschecked it with Mr. and Mrs. Smith. Have a good day, sir.'

My jaw dropped. The police women left together and Sanna and I were left alone, staring at each other with flummoxed, flushed faces.

'I wasn't expecting that to happen,' I muttered. 'Now I've got to go to court too. He's only doing this to try to get us to back off.'

'Now you can't even testify as a witness, Jake,' she whined. 'Oh my God.'

I put the slips of paper down on the bench and ran my hands through my hair, feeling that tugging sensation in my forehead returning as another migraine loomed. I hated to think how credible she would be without at least one testifying statement from someone that was there that night. Then I remembered that I wasn't the only one that was there when I found her.

I sucked in a breath and said, 'Tessa.'

Sanna slumped onto the futon and was instantly met with Audrey climbing up her leg so she lifted her into her lap and hugged her. 'Would she?'

I shook my head. 'I don't know. But we have to try.'

I hoped Tessa would agree to testify for Sanna, but I'd have to bring Sanna with me. If it was just me asking, she'd turn me down with a big fat 'I told you so'. We'd grown apart when faced with the reporting the case or not argument, so I knew I had to take Sanna to remind Tessa just what was important.

I drove the pickup truck to Coop's driveway and stopped by the drainage ditch I'd got bogged in on the day I met him.

'Jake, why are you stopping? Isn't this the place?' Sanna asked, craning her head around to check on the number that was hanging sideways off the rusty nail.

I nodded and took a deep breath in. 'It's just going to be rough explaining to old Coop that I've lied to him and I need help.'

She reached over and clasped my hand. 'Jake Ryan, you have got me through everything. It's okay if you need help too.'

I almost laughed at the thought of someone actually willing to help me and support me. I'd gotten so used to being the pillar of strength for everyone else.

My truck puttered up the winding and steep driveway and eventually pulled up in the middle of the work area between the dairy shed, the machinery shed and the silos. Coop was hosing down a rubber mat. He looked up as the reflection off my mirrors shone in his eyes.

Sanna and I got out of the car, and were greeted by barking border collies and Australian shepherds with eager noses and sharp eyes.

'Jake and Jake's missus,' Coop called. 'What brings you to my neck of the woods, eh?'

I raised my hand. 'Hey Coop. Got time for a chat?'

'Always got time for a chat, mate. Come into the shed; I'll give ya both a lemonade, eh?'

'Sounds great.'

'Where are those little toe biters of yours, eh?' he asked as he led the way into his shed where he had a picnic table and some deck chairs set up around.

'They're with my mum and dad,' Sanna answered. 'I'm Sanna, by the way.' She shook hands with Coop and he nodded with a wink.

'Poor little lady to be with Jake, eh,' he laughed.

'He's all right,' she said with a smile.

We got on with small talk. How ya been? How's ya mum and dad? How's the farm? How's things? We spoke about the weather for at least fifteen minutes and the price of milk for twenty, nursing the warm lemonade and drumming my fingers around the can before I got to business.

I put my chin to my chest and said, 'So I need to talk with Tessa, and was wondering if you could give me her new number.'

Coop looked to Sanna who stared back at him. 'Everything all right?' he asked.

'No,' replied Sanna. 'It's about something that happened to me and she was there...and I might need her to be a witness.'

Coop sighed and put his chair back. 'I was wondering when youse were going to come clean with it.'

'Excuse me?' said Sanna.

'What happened to ya.' He shook his head. 'Bad business, Sanna. Sorry to hear you went through that, love.'

'You know?' I exclaimed.

Coop sat forward with his elbows on his knees. 'Jake, it really affected Tessa…what she saw that night…and how you two didn't want to do anything about it.'

'Why didn't you say anything then?' I asked.

'I didn't know who it was. She just told me it was a girl.' Coop blinked at Sanna. 'I'm sorry…again.'

She shifted and crossed her legs, her thongs hanging off as she clacked them up and down with her jiggling foot. 'I'm not looking for apologies from other people. I just need Tessa to testify in court, Coop, because Jake has screwed up.'

I shot her a look and said, 'Cool it.'

She rolled her eyes. 'You cool it.'

I heaved a sigh and said to Coop, 'She's right, though. I lost my cool and hit the guy who raped her. Now he's landed me with assault charges – I'm summoned to court – so I can't testify because I'm not a credible witness given the…' I searched my mind for the word to describe the rage I felt when I hit Eddie. '…tension between us.'

Coop nodded, then mumbled, 'I'll let her know. She'll be in contact with ya, eh.'

Sanna leaned forward. 'But, Coop…I need to speak to her. Girl-to-girl, make her understand.'

He held up a finger to stop her and closed his eyes for a few seconds. Sanna and I waited with our breaths held.

'She was there. She understands. Say no more, love.' He shook my hand, then Sanna's. 'She'll be in touch with an answer.'

'Thank you, Coop.' I gestured to Sanna to follow me and we left.

'What if she doesn't call?' Sanna gasped as we drove down the driveway. 'Are you sure you can't just call her? She can help us out, Jake. I don't want to lose my kids.'

I gripped the steering wheel and squinted into the orange afternoon sun. 'Sanna, you'll never lose your kids. You're their mom.'

'Eddie's their father,' she squeaked and then coughed as though the word gave her allergies.

'He'll never get full custody, I mean,' I turned onto Kilcunda Ridge Road and headed home. 'He's never going to get them.' I shook my head. 'The courts aren't stupid. They've been teenagers before. They've had things go wrong for them too.'

We glanced at each other.

I sighed. 'There is no way they'll give him rights to our girls. No way.' I almost prayed in blind hope.

Sanna

February 2013

Jake and I walked into my parents' house with slumped shoulders. I'd hoped that we could have spoken to Tessa and I could have asked her myself. Surely, as a girl, she would understand.

My mum greeted us and called out to Audrey and Bellare, 'Where's Mamma? Where's Mamma?'

Audrey looked over her shoulder, met my eyes and her face erupted into a grin wide enough to swallow her entire face. Bellare followed where Audrey was looking and banged the two toys she was playing with into each other in a clapping motion. My heart swum up to meet my eyes and tears poured down. 'Hi!' I exclaimed and rushed to them, greeted by slobbery kisses and 'ma-ma-ma' sounds.

'Did it not go well?' Mum asked, standing straight and putting her hands on the backs of her hips.

SALT

'I don't know…' I breathed. I imagined the girls being taken away from me and I couldn't speak for a moment. My heart was thumping in my throat and I had to force myself to breathe.

Jake rubbed my shoulder and interrupted, 'Everything will be okay.'

He scooped Bellare up and held her high above his head. 'Mommy just needs to have a little faith, doesn't she?' Bellare chortled. 'Doesn't she? Doesn't she! Yes she does.'

I smiled weakly. 'Kind of hard to have faith in Tessa, of all people.'

Jake put Bellare on his hip and looked quizzically at me. 'Why do you say it like that?'

I shook my head. 'Nothing.' I turned to my mum. 'What did the girls eat? Did they eat anything?'

'Bellare had some avocado and Audrey had some filmjörk with blueberries.' She paused to make excited expressions to Audrey. 'Yum-yum!' Audrey grinned.

'They both had a sippee cup of milk before their nap at two.'

Filmjörk was Swedish yoghurt my mum made herself from the sheep milk. It was healthier and more nutritious than dairy yoghurt. Bellare wouldn't touch it, but Audrey ate it every time it was put in front of her. I kept trying to give it to Bellare so she'd grow. She was slightly underweight for her age and size so I was constantly putting healthy sources of fat in front of her, hoping to find something she liked. So far it was avocado and nothing else that struck her fancy.

If you'd asked me two years ago if I would be worried about a one-year-old child eating enough sources of fat, I would have laughed in your face and said you were high on something. Even with everything that had happened with Tamara, Eddie, Jake and Michael, all I wanted was for my daughters to be healthy and happy, and that was why I would have done anything to keep Eddie from having them, even for a second.

As Jake went to the bathroom, my mum leant in closer to ask me quietly, 'Why do you need this Tessa girl to help you testify that Jake didn't hit that man when we all saw it?'

I gasped. I had never told my mother. I couldn't believe that she had thought we were only trying to clear Jake's name. Of course, that's all she thought it was about.

I slid down onto the couch and wanted to go to sleep. Isabel knew, Will knew, Michael knew, the police knew, Tessa knew, Coop knew...but I had never told my parents the truth. The lie had been told for them and I'd never let the truth out.

'Sanna, you all right?' Mum asked.

'Oh, Mum...I just realised you don't know anything. At all.' She looked taken aback so I added, 'I'm so sorry.'

Mum's left eye twitched and she folded her arms. 'I think I know some things, Sanna. That was rude.'

How was I supposed to tell her what had happened to me? Jake and I had been living in the lie for so long, and I never should have accepted his offer. I just couldn't bear the thought of my mum and dad knowing what Eddie had done to me. It had hurt me, and I didn't want it to hurt them, too. Being a victim was such a personal experience, and I wanted to keep it close to me, secret, but I had let the shame fester for too long. It was corroding me.

My vision went hazy and I rubbed my eyes, not even realising that I had started to cry. I had to come clean.

'Jake isn't the father.'

The toilet flushed nearby, and the pumps kicking in drowned out the sound of my mum's confused questions in Swedish so I had no idea what she said.

'We lied,' I explained.

'So...it was Michael.'

I shook my head.

'Oh, Sanna!'

'It's not like that!' I snapped. 'See, this is why I couldn't tell you and Daddy before! It's the whole reason Jake and I lied about it. You don't understand.'

'Help me understand then, Sanna.'

The words had come out a lot easier to the police – to people who did not know me. They had been difficult, yes, but they came out, at least. Now, sitting there with my mother staring at me, waiting, I couldn't get my throat to make the sounds they needed to. My mouth went dry and I shivered with a constricted jaw.

Jake walked into the room and his eyes went to me and my mother and he asked, 'What's wrong?'

My mother turned to him, face set and teeth bared. 'You lied? You're not the father?'

Jake flinched and stepped backwards. 'No.'

'No to what?' she screeched. 'You didn't lie or you're not the father.'

'Mum!' I yelled, finally finding my voice. 'Stop it!'

'Tell me what is going on, please,' she pleaded.

I looked to Jake and opened my mouth like a fish gasping for air, still unable to work my voice to say I WAS RAPED.

Jake nodded and spoke for me. 'I said I was the father because I don't think Sanna really understood what happened to her.'

'What happened?'

'I found her. Running down the road, missing her pants, blood running down her leg.'

Say the words, Sanna, just say them. Get them over with.

Jake cleared his throat. 'She looked like she was almost dead after whatever that guy did to her.'

Mum's hand flew to her mouth and she screamed through it.

Jake took a deep breath. 'She was raped.'

Mum screamed again and grabbed me so hard I thought she was going to hit me. I yelped in shock but she clutched at me and sobbed, hugging me. I shuddered at the fact that she knew. Why? Why did it bother me so much? I didn't understand it but I let her hold me and cry.

'Why didn't you tell me?' she wailed. 'All this time…all this time.'

I closed my eyes. 'I couldn't…I just couldn't.'

Two weeks later, we had the interim custody hearing. I stepped into the room, accompanied by my mother and a lawyer that I had only recently met named Stephanie Deangelo. She had long, straight black hair that she wore out and it flanked either side of her head like justice scales, parted straight and even. I sat down between them, opposite the judge's seat. Eddie and his lawyer, a bald man whose skull reflected the blinking fluorescent light in the judge's office sat at the other end of the table. The judge, a man – I'd been hoping for a woman – sat down, and blinked his brown eyes from behind his glasses which he slid down onto his narrow nose from his grey hair.

'State your names.'

'Sanna Smith, no middle name.'

'Edwin Jordan Adams.'

We answered his short questions that he checked off on his notes to ensure we were whom we claimed to be.

'Right.' He placed his hands together in front of him at the table and Eddie and I both flinched and pretended not to notice each other. 'You're here to file for paternal rights, and custody, Mr. Adams, to two children…' He checked his notes. 'Audrey Isla Smith and Bellare Olive Smith.'

Eddie nodded. 'Yeah.'

'Yes, your Honour,' his lawyer corrected and Eddie nodded again.

'How old are these children?'

'Uh…one,' Eddie said. 'Your Honour.'

'They're fourteen months old,' I said quietly. 'Your Honour.'

'Thank you, Ms. Smith.'

'And two weeks,' I added in a hurry.

'Thank you, Ms. Smith,' the judge said pointedly. My mother smiled, looking down.

'The DNA results we've received indicate that Mr. Adams is, indeed, the father.' He looked after his glasses at Eddie for a reaction.

Eddie's lawyer said, 'My client is not disputing that claim.'

'Have you attended mediation?'

'We've spoken to the police,' I replied before Eddie could answer. 'I don't believe Eddie is a safe person to have my children around...Your Honour.'

The judge held out his hand to me and said, 'I'd like evidence of that, Ms. Smith.'

My lawyer handed him my copy of the statement I had made to the police. The judge looked over his glasses at Eddie, who clenched his jaw and crossed his arms.

'These are very serious allegations, Mr. Adams.'

He shook his head. 'Hearsay. There's no proof that it happened that way.' He tapped his lawyer on the arm. 'Here's my statement, too.' The lawyer handed over the statement and the judge read that, slowly licking his lips as he read and sighed when he was done.

'One question for you, Mr. Adams.'

'Yes, sir?'

'You were old enough to drive, old enough to buy and drink alcohol...but not old enough to make responsible decisions; that much is clear. Were you, at any time, aware of Ms. Smith's age?'

'She said she was sixteen, your Honour.'

'I did not!' I exclaimed. 'I told you how old I was and besides, you knew I was the same age as Tamara!'

Eddie glared at me and jutted his chin out at me, 'Yeah that's what you say.' His eyes were glittering at me and I shrank back into the back of the chair. My back was damp from the sweat so I sat forward again with a grimace.

'Your Honour,' my lawyer interjected. 'Mr. Adams here was fully aware of my client's age and even participated in

284

grooming activities, such as driving her places without her parents' consent, taking her surfing and, of course, as it is recorded in her statement, supplying her with alcohol when he knew she was underage. It can only be suggested that he provided her with that alcohol to influence her into behaving a particular way, and whether or not she lied about her age or not –'

'I didn't!' I cried, to which she put her palm up to shush me before continuing.

'Mr. Adams was not acting as a guardian and instead, used his power against her as an older male with influence. Even if the sexual assault had not resulted in the birth of the two children in question, his behaviour indicates that he is a predator and cannot be trusted with the care of two infants.'

My mum squeezed my hand under the table.

The judge removed his glasses and replied, 'I agree.'

'What?' Eddie spat.

The judge glared at him. 'Mr. Adams, the point of this hearing, if your lawyer has not explained it clearly enough to you,' Eddie blinked and I smirked to suppress a laugh; 'is to determine where the children are safe in the meantime until we have a final hearing to determine what kind of custody you may be given. The children, until the final hearing, will remain living with their mother and the apprehended violence order will remain in place.'

'I don't want my kids around that boyfriend of hers! He's the one who assaulted me.'

'I will take that into consideration with the final hearing, though it is recorded here that the perpetrator in your case is the sole provider and co-carer of the children. Evidence has been provided by multiple witness statements that he is a loving and kind caregiver, so that has indeed been taken into my account of the situation at hand, Mr. Adams. In the meantime,' he said, gathering his notes. 'Full custody remains in Ms. Smith's favour. See you for the final hearing on the 19th of March. Good day.'

'Thank you, Your Honour,' both lawyers said as the judge stood up and left. Relief flooded through me and I smiled so widely that my cheeks hurt. My lawyer Stephanie shook hands with the judge and then beamed at me. 'A good start.'

My mother wipes away a tear and hugged me.

Eddie and his lawyer left without a word. I walked out into the arms of Jake and Michael. They were waiting with the girls, who were both fast asleep – completely oblivious of the small hill at the base of the mountain I had got us over.

Jake

March 2013

I was on my lunch break at work when the tinny TING of the front desk bell rang. Mick was on the forklift; the beeping and humming echoed around the high stacks of feed. He was re-stocking the store with the bags of horse feed from pallets from the morning's delivery.

I'd have to go serve this customer. I put my BLT down and walked out, covering my mouth, and apologizing for the store being unattended. The young woman turned around and smiled at me and my heart rate spiked in a way that made me light-headed.

I choked down the last bite of bread and grimaced. 'Hi, Tessa.'

'Hi, Jake.' She fiddled with the blonde braid hanging at her side. 'Long time, no see.'

'Yeah, yeah,' I whispered. 'Good to see you.'

'Is it?' Her face was stony and her skin so smooth, as if she was a living filter.

'Of course.'

She stretched her arms out behind her. 'So, you raised Sanna's babies. That's nice.'

'Told everyone they're mine,' I laughed. 'Felt so bad about what happened to her that night.'

'Yeah, I know,' she whispered, looking down at her feet. 'So, I'm here because Coop told me you and Sanna wanted to see me. Told me you work here.'

'You in town long?' I asked. 'It's a long story.'

'Just today.'

I nodded and tried to hide the disappointment I knew was plastered all over my face.

'So?'

I coughed again. 'I think Sanna is the one that should ask you.'

'I don't have time, Jake,' Tessa snapped. 'Just tell me what it is.'

I took a deep breath and told her, 'She's decided to press charges against the guy that did it. I was going to be a witness, but I screwed up and I hit him.'

She licked her lips and grinned. 'You? Hit someone?'

'Yeah,' I laughed. 'Never thought I had it in me.'

'Me neither,' she sighed. 'So…Sanna needs me to be a witness?'

'Yeah.'

Tessa gazed around the store and clucked her tongue as she thought. 'I mean…I didn't actually see the guy…'

'I know.'

'I only saw Sanna.'

'I know.'

'…and that…look in her eyes…and the blood.'

I nodded and repeated, 'I know.'

Tessa shuddered. 'Fuck. That look in her eyes was the worst.' She shook her head and glared at me. 'I am still so mad at you for being so…' She glowered and spat, 'Silent.'

I swallowed. This was the main reason she left me; I knew it. A perpetrator and a bystander were both criminals in her eyes. You can have the best sex and a great chemistry, but if you didn't have that deep moral connection, you were doomed.

Tessa stared at me, waiting for me to explain or apologize for being silent, but all that I could say was: 'I know.'

'Jeez, do you say anything other than I KNOW, Cowboy?'

'Sorry.' She tilted her head at me and I nodded. 'I understand me not saying anything then was why you…left.'

She nodded. 'I always knew you wouldn't come with me when you went silent for her.'

I whispered, 'I had to give her some choice, Tessa. She was robbed of all of it.'

Tessa replied, 'I know,' then chortled softly to herself at the two words she'd just accused me of over-using.

There was a loud beeping and Mick pulled up on the fork lift and got out. 'How ya garn?' he called out and nodded in Tessa's direction, then eyed me with a cautionary expression. Probably wondered if I was cheating on Sanna with this bombshell. If he only knew.

Tessa felt his eyes on her and seemed to cower. Still so self-conscious and a turtle when it came to her body. She took a deep breath. 'Tell Sanna I'll do it. Just tell me where I need to be and I'll tell them everything.'

Relief surged through my body and I doubled over and found myself finally able to breathe without any catching or rasping that I had not even noticed most of the time. She was going to do it. Sanna had another voice. It *was* going to be okay.

The sun was setting by the time I got home. The vast orange and gold streaked through the indigo clouds and scattered the light through the green hills and over the unusually calm ocean.

The smell of the salt water and seaweed flooded my senses when I got out of my truck. I paused for a moment to watch the orb sink lower on the horizon and I breathed at last, but the realization that my time being a dad to the girls would be over soon, since everything was going to work out. It all hit me at once.

They greeted me at the sliding door with their lumbering limbs and cheery, rosy cheeks. I gave them both a big hug and Sanna passed me a can of cold cola. I cracked it open and said, 'Guess what.'

'What?'

'Tessa came to see me.' Sanna's face tightened. 'She said she'll do anything we need.'

Her face melted into a smile and she sank into the futon. I grinned and took a sip of the drink. 'What did I tell ya.'

'Everything is going to be fine and I'm going to be okay,' she breathed and laughed.

That night, lying beside each other, back-to-back, I thought about what life would be like once it returned to "normal". Sanna would have full custody, she'd get Eddie put in jail or something along those lines, and we would cease to be forced together. If Sanna had custody, I didn't.

It hadn't occurred to me before what would happen – as usual, I could never see into the future clearly beyond my own wants. I thought about being separated from the girls, and my heart hurt and made me fold into the fetal position in the bed beside Sanna.

I decided not to say anything. Losing the girls would feel like losing Alex all over again. The morning I saw his wrecked car came to mind, and the way that my dad seemed to crumple in on himself, just like the car. I kept quiet but mentally told myself to enjoy each day I had with Audrey and Bellare. Upset tummies, tears, farts and diaper changes included. Nightmares, grizzles and tantrums – I was there.

Sanna asked me one morning, 'Are you feeling okay, Jake? You seem different.'

I shook my head. 'I'm great.'

She narrowed her eyes and chopped an apple, muttering, 'I don't know why you feel the need to lie to me, but okay.'

I sighed and said, 'Got to go to work. See ya later.'

It was an odd feeling – to sense an ending looming, like the way Rio's coat gradually lost its shine; my own step lost a skip or two in it. Dad even noticed.

He leaned against the counter at the feed store and said, 'You seem down, son.'

My eyelids were heavy. The sunshine beamed in from under the roller door, my father's shadow stretching across the concrete floor, along with mine, so much shorter.

I sighed. 'Dad...we're breaking up at the end of all this and I'm...actually going to miss the kids.' I shrugged. 'They're not mine, but...they are, if that makes any sense.'

He nodded. 'I understand.'

It was the first time my father had said that to me and I let out a huff of release, my eyelids lightening.

He added, 'You know, Sanna cares a lot about you. Even if you're not together, I can't see her ever keeping you out of her life or the girls' lives. I mean...you've been a darn good father for them. She won't ever forget that.'

A tear rolled down my face and I tasted its saltiness on my lip. I nodded. 'Yeah. I have, haven't I?' I forced a smile.

I had been a good dad at least, even though it was soon becoming something I wouldn't be anymore. I could look forward to the future I had originally wanted, yet it felt empty and pointless in a way that I couldn't quite describe.

Sanna

March 2013

The week before the final hearing, my lawyer Stephanie called me into her office in Inverloch. She presented me with Eddie's plea. He would drop the assault charge on Jake if I dropped the charge of rape against him.

'Could Jake actually do time?' I asked.

'He could do two years.'

There would go all of Jake's dreams. I clenched my teeth together so hard that the clack woke Bellare from her nap in the pram with a start. Do I let a rapist go free in order to save Jake's future when he'd saved mine?

'What does that mean for the custody?' I asked slowly.

'Look,' she said, crossing her legs. 'Rapists can still get paternal rights – it's a problem in our justice system. I'll be honest with you. I think it's worth having a meeting with his lawyer, a police officer and going through mediation. See if he'll consider giving up his rights, but allowing visitation under supervision.' I put a hand to my chest without realising, noticing my heart was pounding. Stephanie murmured, 'It's a really tough choice for you, Sanna, I know, but in your heart…do you think he'll ever even visit?'

I shrugged. 'I don't know. It surprises me that he even wants them in the first place!'

She smiled gently. 'It's just a power play. I see it all the time. That's why I'm suggesting this.'

'I can't let Jake go to prison,' I croaked. 'He's done so much for me. He was only standing up for me and the girls.'

'Well, then…let's think about this.'

If it was a power play, I needed to be more powerful than he was. I needed some power in the form of alliances. Tessa was going to testify. I needed someone else that he wouldn't expect. Someone he thought was on his side and would never side with me.

I needed Tamara.

I said to Stephanie, 'No, I think…I want to try something else other than agreeing to his terms.'

'What is it?' Stephanie asked.

'My friend Tamara…is dating him.' I had distanced myself from her, but she had said I was still her friend after nearly killing her – why would she stop being my friend just because she had a boyfriend who hated me?

I explained, 'I think she can help.'

I rapped on the Jenkins' door so hard that I had to suck on my knuckles to ease the pain.

Tamara had moved back in with her parents around Christmas since she had been getting stronger each day.

Mr. Jenkins opened the door and said, 'Sanna, we thought you were the police you knocked so hard. What's the emergency?'

'Is Tamara here?'

293

Yes, she's in her room; come through.'

He opened the door and I whizzed through, breathlessly saying, 'Thanks.'

Back in the old days, I had only knocked and let myself in saying hi to everyone in passing. Now it all felt so formal and unfamiliar and it made my chest squeeze with each breath.

I made it to Tamara's bedroom and stopped in the doorway. She was on the floor, upon a purple yoga mat, stretching.

She looked around at me and said, 'About time you showed up, Sanna. I texted you after the babies' party.'

I held up my hands to show open (sweaty) palms. 'I'm sorry. It's been a bit full-on since then.' I closed the door. Tamara sat on her bed and crossed her arms.

'I'm listening,' she said with a slight slur.

'Has Eddie told you anything?' I asked.

'He told me that creep boyfriend of yours hit him because he didn't like the way Eddie looked at you. Jealous.' My head shook in disbelief. She added quietly, 'But there's more to it than that because there's no way you'd stay with a guy that controlled you like that…even if he did knock you up.'

I folded myself down to sit on the yoga mat. 'No, I wouldn't.'

She didn't blink. 'So…what is going on?'

I took a deep breath and my eyes stung with tears. I looked at the ceiling to stop tears rolling out too quickly. 'Eddie gave me beer then took me over to Summerlands. He tried getting me to have sex with him, and I said no, and he got really mad, and he…' I swallowed hard. 'I got away…after…what he did, and Jake was there. I got in his car and I didn't even have any pants on.' I sighed. 'I didn't really make sense of what happened until later, and I found out I was pregnant. Dad was so mad. He thought I'd made the bad choice.'

I looked at her and finally let the anger at my parents out. 'ME! Both of them – they didn't ask any questions – they just ASSUMED I had been doing it for fun or something.' I suppressed a gag. 'I really didn't want to admit what had happened so Jake said "tell them it was me" and he proposed. We pretended he was the father, but really...Eddie is.'

I couldn't read Tamara's facial expression. She wet her lips and blinked as if in slow-motion. She was as silent as she was the day I told her I was pregnant.

I begged, 'Tamara, please say something.'

'So that's why he wanted to go to the party,' she whispered. She put a strand of her hair behind her ear and her shoulders dropped. 'I told him it was your babies' first birthday party and he asked me out right then...Is he only with me to hurt you?'

'I don't know.'

'Does it?'

'Does it what?'

'Hurt you?' she said, narrowing her eyes at me. My skin prickled for a moment. She leant back. 'Because I'm sorry if it does.'

'It's okay,' I mumbled. 'I'm just worried about you.'

Tamara grimaced. 'I had a crush on him for years.' She looked around her room and I followed her eyes. Polaroids on her wall. Beach days. Our days. Back when just having to go to school instead of surfing was the hardest thing ever.

'I'm sorry to be like this, Tamara,' I said quietly, my eyes coming from the past and focusing on my future. 'Eddie's suing for custody and he's using Jake's assault as leverage to stop me filing the rape charge.'

Tamara reeled away from me. 'He's suing for custody? He doesn't even like kids'

'I know. He's just doing it to hurt me.' I paused. 'Can you talk him out of it?'

Tamara stood and paced her room, arms still crossed. 'This is a lot, Sanna.'

'I know.'

'Like...far out.'

She looked down at her hands and said, 'All this was happening to you and I was in the hospital. No wonder you never came to see me.'

'I did,' I murmured. 'A few times.' She looked up at me in surprise. I explained, 'A few times when you were in the coma, and then a time when you just looked at me but didn't see me or something...I don't know,' I whispered. 'Then every other time, you were doing rehab and I was too scared to wait around. I was worried you wouldn't want to see me.'

'Why wouldn't I want to see you?' she whispered. 'You're my best friend.'

'Because of what I did to you.'

Her hand went to the scar on the edge of her forehead and she clenched her fist and put it back down, away from the rough skin. She said, 'You dropped in on me...but it's not like you meant to hit me.' She looked at me with her big blue eyes. 'Right?'

'I never would have hit you on purpose.'

She nodded. 'No point dwelling on it.' She took a deep breath and said, 'Well, I'll try to talk Eddie out of it. He doesn't deserve them and they don't deserve him.'

I thanked her and we hugged.

As I was leaving, I gestured to the wetsuit hanging over her desk chair. 'You going out?'

Her eyes glittered. 'Just waiting for you to text me saying LET'S GO.'

I smiled and left.

On March 19th, I stood with Jake and my lawyer in the foyer of the court.

The final hearing was meant to be happening, but there was a delay. Eddie stood in the corner, having a heated discussion with his lawyer, and he kept pointing at me. My ears burned. Stephanie ushered us through the foyer and into the room where we would be seeing the judge. The judge eventually came into the room, but Eddie and his lawyer did not.

We waited for half an hour, my grip on Jake's hand getting tighter and tighter. Then Eddie's lawyer came into the room, sheepishly creeping to the judge to whisper in his ear. It was pointless, because we all eavesdropped intently.

His client wanted to drop the assault charges and he didn't want any custody. He was happy to sign it over to me. Happy to not have anything to do with the children.

The judge cleared his throat and I held my breath. He said, 'This custody hearing rules full custody to the mother, Sanna Smith. Court adjourned.'

I burst into tears and Jake hugged me tightly, gritting his teeth to stop himself from bursting into tears, too.

Tamara, you damn legend. You are top shit. You are it.

I was going to get him for what he did to me, and he'd never get anywhere near my girls.

I could focus on raising my girls. I wouldn't let him corrode me anymore. The good salt in my veins, the ocean salt, would heal me, cleanse me, refresh me and help me live. The bad salt, the wound, the trauma, the lies would be gone. I would survive in body and soul.

Jake

December 2013

I drove home from Melbourne, where I was studying veterinary science. I'd got in on late admissions. Sure, it wasn't medical science, but working with animals would suit me just as well.

I picked up my parents and then we drove to Phillip Island to celebrate Audrey and Bellare's second birthday. I hadn't seen them in months.

Sanna and I talked all the time on the computer and by text messages. She had moved back in with her parents with the girls. She was always sending me memes and I was continuously helping her with her homework now that she'd decided to go to TAFE to get her high school equivalent certificate. She really sucked at maths. I couldn't see her passing without my help to be honest. Some things would never change. I would always be there for her.

Audrey and Bellare greeted me with giggles and hugs.

'Hi!' Audrey exclaimed and Bellare fell on her face in her rush to get to me. I hugged each of them tightly and told them how much I missed them.

'Love you,' Audrey said.

Bellare piped in, 'Me-me.'

I laughed to hear them speak so much. They were only baby-talking the last time I had seen them. Going off to university was what I had always wanted to do, but leaving the girls had been so hard.

'They're huge now!' I laughed to Sanna as I hugged her. Her face shone so much with her smile that I couldn't look away. 'You look great.'

'You too,' she said.

I shook hands with Michael, barely recognizing him with clipped hair. The dreadlocks were gone and smooth brown hair was in its place. They'd started dating when I'd left. I'd expected they would.

Bellare toddled around, waving her wrapping paper but Audrey ran, thumping with her flat-feet on the floorboards, bouncing wall to wall, guest-to-guest, her zest for life enviable.

Michael chased her and she zoomed off with squeals. It was melancholic to watch the way he was with her as he lifted her up, roaring and blowing strawberries on her belly. My heart crushed when I heard her say, 'Stop, Daddy.'

My father met my eyes at the wrong time, and I had to turn away to hide how wet my eyes were. He followed me outside and we watched the cockatoos across the back field, pecking at the grass.

'You all right, Jake?'

I nodded and cleared my throat, wrapping my fingers around my belt buckle.

'Hurts, huh?'

I laughed through a scoff. 'Nah.'

He stepped towards me and said softly, 'Yer a good man and the best dad I have ever known.' He squeezed my shoulder. 'Best son, too.' He walked away and I cringed before I hunched my own shoulders and held back tears. Damn you, Dad, I thought.

There were footsteps behind me. I turned and realized Tamara was standing behind me, offering me a can of cola. I took it, grateful for the distraction.

'Good day,' she said, looking up at the sky.

It was blue as high as I could see, the sun hot in its summer glory. There was no breeze and it was just hot enough to bring a prickle of sweat to the surface of my skin.

I nodded. 'It's beautiful.'

Tamara brushed my arm. I froze. 'You hot?'

I shrugged and laughed awkwardly. My eyes strayed to the scar on her forehead and I looked away automatically.

'So, what's it like at uni?'

'It's great,' I answered, glad for the topic to be on something I really enjoyed and wasn't about how my father had just cured years of hurt with a few words. 'Yeah, studying large animals. Equine, bovine, caprine. Really enjoying it.'

'What made you do that?'

'What?'

'Finally go to uni.'

She leaned against the porch railing and looked up at me with her doe-like eyes.

I shrugged. 'You only get one life. You've got to do what you've always wanted to do.'

Tamara's hand flew to her forehead and she rubbed her scar for a moment, looking thoughtful. 'Yeah. I guess you do. Thanks, Jake.'

After the party, Sanna's parents agreed to stay and watch over the girls while they were passed out in their sugar crash sleep so Sanna and I could hang out, with Tamara and Michael.

First, I took my mom and dad home, then drove to the beach to meet Sanna, Michael and Tamara.

300

However, when I arrived, Sanna and Tamara were nowhere to be seen. I met Michael by shaking his hand again and asked, 'Where are the girls?'

He laughed and pointed at the water where Sanna and Tamara were paddling out on their boards, side-by-side. They hadn't surfed since the accident but there they were, out there in the shallow water, making their way out in the rip to the back of the waves.

'Oh my God,' I uttered and sat down on the sand, my knees buckling beneath me.

Michael squatted down beside me and laughed. 'I know. She's really gonna do it.'

I couldn't take my eyes off the smooth, purposeful strokes Sanna made through the blue water. Her feet even seemed to paddle. She lifted over the crests of the breaking waves and continued her mission to get out past them. She looked like she'd never stopped surfing. It had been almost three years since the accident. She had tried and failed so many times. This time I had a feeling that she would succeed.

She made her way to the back of the rolling sets and sat on her board for a while, letting the waves lift her up and gently place her back down again. 'Come on, Sanna,' I muttered and crossed my fingers. 'You can do it.'

As if she could hear me, she looked over her shoulder at a lift in the water surface, got down on her belly and started paddling, glancing at the approaching wave as she paddled. It looked exhausting.

I heard myself say, 'Please, God, let her catch this wave and be safe.' Stunned at myself for praying to God, I had to force myself to stop biting the inside of my lip.

'Come on Sanna!' I shouted.

'Come on, Sanna!' Michael joined in. 'Go baby!'

Sanna pushed up her upper body, grimaced with the effort and slid her left foot forward and rose to her feet on the board. A wide-open smile erupted onto her face and she stuck both arms out and bent her knees to cut a steady line along the white section of the wave.

The wave propelled her along and she bobbed her left foot to pick up some speed, before the wave fizzled out into white flush. She gently lowered herself back onto her belly as the wave died and she paddled back to Tamara, who caught the next one, wobbling and leaning a bit too far over but successfully riding the wave.

It was moments like that that I would choose to remember most. The bad moments sat in my mind, like the morning Alex died - the anger and chaotic desperation on my father's face was seared into my mind, just as much as the terrified expression on Sanna's face as she ran towards me. Saving people from the most awful things, like losing a child, losing your faith, losing a friend, losing yourself – it all made these kinds of moments clearer. It was the reason for living.

As Sanna and Tamara came back to the beach, Michael and I stood on the shore, cheering and clapping for them. We ran to them as they reached the sand, picking up their boards, beaming.

'Oh my God!' Tamara squealed. 'I did it! I did it!'

Michael hugged Sanna and they both laughed with excitement.

I stood aside and waited for her to make eye contact with me. She grinned. 'I did it, Jake.'

'Knew you could,' I said with a smile. 'Come here.' I wrapped her in a hug and got soaking wet.

'I couldn't have done it without you, you know,' she said quietly in my ear so Michael wouldn't hear. I gave her a good pat on the back and we broke apart.

'It was amazing, girls,' said Michael, hugging Sanna again.

'I wasn't even scared!' Tamara exclaimed with glee and pride.

'You looked scared,' teased Sanna.

She laughed. 'Okay, okay. I was shitting myself, okay!' We all laughed. Tamara looked to me and said, 'Jake, one day you have to try surfing. It is the best.'

'I'm okay on land, thanks,' I said.

She put her board gently down and said, 'I never got the chance to say thank you.'

'For what?'

'You saved my life that day.' She shrugged. 'Feels weird because I barely know you, but…thanks.'

I nodded and hid a tear that squeezed its way out of my eye. 'No worries.'

We stayed together on the beach all afternoon and turned our attentions to the bright orange sun that was reflecting all around us on the water, in the sky and even off the sea cliffs and marram grass, as well as the sand and our faces.

Sanna put both hands on the back of her head and looked out at the waves. 'Wow. I can't believe that we finally did it. We finally got back out there.'

'I know,' Tamara breathed.

'I'm so proud of you,' I said. 'I told you, didn't I?'

'You did,' she said with a smile. 'Today is that one day, Jake.' She hugged me again. 'Today is the day we'll all be okay.'

ACKNOWLEDGEMENTS

I extend my respect to the locals of the Bass Coast and South Gippsland areas. I hope to have captured its beauty as a setting.

A massive thank you needs to go out to all the mothers who shared their experience of what it was like for you to be pregnant (whether it be planned, unplanned, teen, low-risk, or high-risk) – THANK YOU. Kellie, Lauren S, Katie, Lauren K, Katie, Erin, Tara, Steph, Shawnee, Bek, Jessica, Sharlene, Vanda, Christine and Julie – sharing your experiences helped me a lot to capture what Sanna was going through.

Thank you to my dear friend Naomi for being the most encouraging friend with this novel.

Thank you to my incredibly supportive team of authors, early readers and editors. Thank you to my old class of PWE for being the first to read and critique this novel in its early days as a short story. Thank you for my teacher Nathan King for giving me confidence and teaching me how to write. Thank you also to Liam Davison. Your encouragement of this piece was touching, and I wish you were still here to read it now.

Thank you to Dr. Sue Young for your editing expertise and your insights. Thank you to Liz Rout for your editing skills and being just as excited for this novel as I was – it has meant a lot to have such a knowledgeable and supportive friend and colleague.

Thank you Dr. Sonia Talman for taking time to proofread the novel in its final days, just to ensure it was as crisp as possible. Thank you from the bottom of my heart.

Thank you to Elysia Clapin for your cover design and your continued dedication to working with me.

Thank you to the team at Faber Academy and Allen & Unwin for taking the time to consider this novel and shortlist it for the scholarship. That meant a lot to me.

Tack Britt-Marie, for teaching me Swedish many years ago and nurturing my love for all things Sweden. I will get there one day.

Thank you to my family, and my friends for their support – and putting up with me talking about my characters as though they were part of the family, too.

Also, thank you to my grandfather, Peter Rainford. Though he is no longer with us, it is him whom I must thank for giving me a love for the ocean and giving me the opportunity to grow up on the island, so I could feel that island identity I mentioned in the book. I've lost count of how many stories I came up after wandering around the Newhaven beaches with him and running around his big backyard. Thanks Granddad for putting the good salt in my veins!

Thank you to the reader for picking up this book. Thank you!

AUTHOR'S NOTE

I set out to write this book in a way as an ode to the country and for the ocean, the two landscapes which inspire me most. However, upon researching custody rights in Australia, I was horrified to learn that rapists still had paternal rights. There have even been cases when joint custody (not just visitation) has been allowed by the family court. I couldn't imagine what it would be like for a mother to have to share custody with her rapist, especially if she could not have him brough to justice for his crime. Even in some states of the United States of America, the rape must be proven and the rapist must be convicted in order to terminate custody rights. For all those women, I am sorry. I am sickened for you.

I hope by writing this book I have brought this to attention in some way and why I have dedicated this book to victims of sexual assault.

AVA DUNN

It is not fair.
It is beyond awful.
But please stay strong and know you have support.
May the good salt in your veins heal you and not corrode
you.

Also by Ava Dunn

I Lied For You
Salt
Cold Desert (coming late 2023)

You can follow Ava Dunn on Instagram @ava.dunn.author
to keep up to date with upcoming releases.

AVA DUNN

www.ingramcontent.com/pod-product-compliance
Lightning Source LLC
Chambersburg PA
CBHW010440100726
17904CB00008B/2423